SHE LOOKED DOWN, GATHERING HER COURAGE.

"Don't leave." She hadn't the nerve to add *me*. And yet, how many times had she asked that of him when they were children? Too many to count. But he had broken that promise in the end.

When she dared to glance up again, Alec still hadn't moved, but his mask had fallen away. Everything he worked so hard to keep hidden was laid bare before her: the wariness, the pain, and, most important, the desire.

Her eyes were drawn to the sensuous curves of his lips, almost indecently full for a man. How badly she wanted him to kiss her again, but not for show this time. Not for anything other than the sheer pleasure of it. The want. The *need* of it.

He stared at her for a long moment. His piercing gaze stirred something so raw within her she almost fell to her knees. "It's the shock of earlier," he finally said. "You don't know what you're—"

"Stay with me. Please."

Alec closed his eyes and muttered a curse.

A ROGUE
TO REMEMBER

A ROGUE
TO REMEMBER

A League of Scoundrels Novel

BY EMILY SULLIVAN

FOREVER
New York Boston

Copyright © 2021 by Emily Sullivan

Cover design by name Daniela Medina.
Cover illustration by Paul Stinson, cover photograph © Shirley Green Photography.
Cover copyright © 2021 by Hachette Book Group, Inc.

Forever
Hachette Book Group
1290 Avenue of the Americas, New York, NY 10104
read-forever.com
twitter.com/readforeverpub

First Edition: March 2021

Forever is an imprint of Grand Central Publishing. The Forever name and logo are trademarks of Hachette Book Group, Inc.

The publisher is not responsible for websites (or their content) that are not owned by the publisher.

The Hachette Speakers Bureau provides a wide range of authors for speaking events. To find out more, go to www.hachettespeakersbureau.com or call (866) 376-6591.

ISBNs: 978-1-5387-3730-9 (mass market), 978-1-5387-3731-6 (ebook)

Printed in the United States of America

CW

10 9 8 7 6 5 4 3 2 1

To women who dare.

ACKNOWLEDGMENTS

A hermit can write a book, sure, but it takes a village to publish one. *A Rogue to Remember* is no exception, and it is all the better for it.

Thanks to my fantastic agent, Amanda Jain, and my brilliant editor, Junessa Viloria, who both read this book almost as many times as I did and always offered up new insights. Thank you for taking a chance on Lottie and Alec and for making this debut author's dreams come true.

To my beta readers, A. Y. Chao, Colette Dixon, C. R. Grissom, Katy James, and Evi Kline. Thank you for your time and early encouragement.

To my cousin Katie for her unbridled enthusiasm for this story when I needed it most.

To the inhabitants of Rebelle Island for providing support and commiseration in equal measure.

To my family and friends for treating me like a professional writer long before I ever was one.

And to my husband, who has maintained from the earliest days of our relationship that I would publish a book one day. It only took thirteen years, but you were right.

A Rogue
to Remember

The truth is rarely pure and never simple.
~Oscar Wilde

CHAPTER ONE

❧

1897
A village near Pistoia, Italy

I have all the time in the world now.

It still felt strange to Lottie Carlisle to have every day stretch endlessly before her, especially with the season starting in a few weeks. But there was no rigid schedule to follow now. No social calls to uphold, no days at home to maintain, no balls, or picnics, or musical entertainments. No more stilted conversations with vapid young men trying their hardest to talk about anything other than her money. And, especially, no more sneering matrons and supposed friends asking why, oh *why* couldn't she make her poor old uncle happy and find a husband. The man did worry so.

Poor old Uncle Alfred indeed.

Now on the cusp of his sixth decade, Sir Alfred Lewis was considered a veritable pillar of London society, a renowned collector of antiquities whose travels as a young man had once taken him to nearly every corner of the Empire. He had even published a popular memoir on the subject. This garnered him the admiration of many and a knighthood from the queen, but very few knew that Uncle Alfred was also involved in the highest levels of government. He delighted in playing the role of a mild eccentric in public while ruthlessly protecting the Crown's interests in private.

Even Lottie barely knew the full extent of his activities—and never would.

Lottie paused to assess the canvas before her. She had been trying to capture the soft, golden light of the Tuscan hillside that surrounded her for days now, and not once had she come close to doing it justice. She managed to eke out a few more sickly clouds, then set down her paintbrush. Hopefully that was enough progress to please her painting instructor, Signore Ernesto, when he came for their lesson tomorrow. She could already hear him chiding her hurried brushstrokes. *Pazienza, signora. Pazienza.*

Patience. A word Lottie had always had little use for. But now time was all she had.

She walked over to the balustrade that separated the cottage's terrace from the steep hillside's drop and placed her palms against the sun-warmed stone. Lottie had fallen in love with the view on sight when she first came to the village more than a week ago. The owner had been reluctant to let it to a lone woman—even one who claimed to be a respectable young widow—but was not foolish enough to turn down a full year's rent in advance. Now Lottie woke up to this view each morning, while the large back terrace with its vine-covered pergola provided the ideal spot to work on her *en plein air* painting.

The air was ripe with young spring. She closed her eyes and tilted her head toward the April sky, smiling as the sun kissed her face. No doubt her fair skin was freckling even more with each passing second, but it hardly mattered now. For the first time in her twenty-four years, Lottie was free.

And all it took was complete and utter ruination.

"Signora, tu hai un visitatore," Marta, the housekeeper, said as she bustled onto the terrace. The older woman didn't know very much English, and though Lottie had engaged a tutor to help her brush up on Italian before leaving England, nothing could prepare her for the rapid cadence of natural speakers. Luckily, even Lottie could pick out *visitatore*.

Strange. Visitors never called at lunchtime, and Marta usually guarded the front door as fiercely as a hound of Hades. "What, now?"

Marta raised her eyebrow. "Un uomo bello *nobile*."

She shot the woman an exasperated look. "Really, Marta." As Lottie had explained many, *many* times already, she was not lonely and certainly hadn't any need for *affetto*. Marta had probably arranged the visit herself, and this "handsome nobleman" was actually the son of her butcher. The housekeeper gave a dismissive little shrug and then, oddly, seemed to hesitate. Lottie only understood half of what she said at any given time, but Marta never dithered over anything.

She looked over her shoulder and then gestured for Lottie to come closer. "Lui dice che è tuo . . . marito." She whispered the last word, as if relaying some terrible secret.

Marito?

Lottie frowned. It was reminiscent of *mari*, the French word for "husband," but that didn't make any sense. She most certainly didn't have a husband. Lottie didn't have anyone. She glanced at the Italian dictionary on the terrace's lone table. Hopefully the man's English was better than Marta's, or else this would be a very short visit.

"All right. You may show him out here, I suppose," Lottie said with a sweep of her hand.

Marta broke into a rare smile and nodded. "Ah, bene, bene. Una riconciliazione!" She clasped her hands against her chest, as if this was the most wonderful news. Then her eyes sparked with that all-too-familiar determination. "I bring you *tea*," she declared and hurried back into the house.

"No, Marta!" Lottie called after her. This wasn't a social

call, for heaven's sake. But it was useless. She might be the mistress, but Marta ran the house. Lottie crossed her arms and leaned against the balustrade to wait for this "handsome nobleman" to appear. The thought was mildly intriguing, given that she had barely spoken to a man under fifty since the Pension Bertolini in Florence. He had been a remarkably bland German named Hans who was traveling with his father. Hans was polite, spoke excellent English, and didn't remotely interest her. But her chaperone, Mrs. Wetherby, was undeterred: "Imagine! You could have *blond* children!"

The odious woman had viewed Lottie's light auburn tresses as an affront to common decency. A foul blemish that needed to be snuffed out before it could taint another generation. But Lottie cherished her hair. It was just like her mother's had been. She pulled her long braid over her shoulder and absently fingered the end. Her uncle's pompous secretary, Gordon Wetherby, had maintained that his aunt excelled in managing young ladies with "high spirits." Lottie could still picture the way his nose wrinkled as he said the words. Lottie wasn't proud of it, but she had taken some pleasure in imagining both his and Mrs. Wetherby's reactions to her disappearance. Though perhaps she should be thanking him instead. After all, if Mrs. Wetherby had been the least bit pleasant, Lottie might have been tempted to amend her plan.

The sound of approaching footsteps drew her attention. They were slow and heavy. One might even say portentous. This uninvited visitor was clearly in no great rush and expected her to wait. *Bello* or no, this was not the way to ensure a good first impression. Lottie fixed her most disapproving frown on the doorway, where the shadow of a rather imposing man now came into view. The doorway itself was low, and he had to stoop slightly to reach the terrace. Lottie's breath caught at the familiar movement even while her mind tried to reason otherwise.

No. He would never come here. Not for someone as trivial as you.

But before the light even touched his face, a part of her already knew. From a place deep within her bones. A place she could never erase, no matter how hard she tried.

And oh, how Lottie had *tried*.

Her arms fell by her sides as Alec Gresham, her uncle's ward turned protege, dedicated agent of the Crown, only son of the late English poet Edward Gresham, and, indeed, very *bello*, stepped out onto the terrace.

"Well hello, Lottie," he said evenly. "What a charming cottage you have here."

No wonder Marta mistook him for a nobleman. He certainly held himself like one, even though nearly every inch of him was covered in road dust. Then the man had the audacity to twist that full mouth of his into a smirk. At her.

As if he were just dropping by for tea.

As if they were still *friends*.

The word caused a faint pang somewhere in the vicinity of her heart. Lottie quickly wiped the shock from her face and glared. She wasn't naive enough to assume that Uncle Alfred, a man who staunchly refused to accept he didn't have complete control over the fates and furies of life, would simply let her be. But to send *Alec* after her?

The gall of both of them was maddening.

But if Alec was at all bothered by this frosty reception, he didn't show it. He sauntered over until he was no more than a foot away, forcing her to look up into the face that was at once both achingly familiar and surprisingly breathtaking. The trace of boyishness that had still been visible when they last met was no more, as his features had fully matured into the kind of stoic, patrician beauty the Romans had adored. His dark hair had grown so long it nearly brushed his collar, the waves as unruly as ever, and his strong jaw was lightly bearded. But beneath that easy charm the same undercurrent of antagonism crackled—just as captivating, and disquieting, as it always had been. His hazel eyes glinted, daring her to look away first. But Lottie stared right back.

Alec filled the silence by studying her with an openness that bordered on indecent. If he were any other man, she would have walked away or taken him to task. But then, if he were any other man, her skin wouldn't feel so flushed and tight, and she wouldn't have any trouble swallowing. Alec's gaze tracked the movement of her throat, then briefly flitted to her mouth. Lottie clenched her hands against the unwanted attraction swelling inside and released a breath.

"Funny. Marta told me a handsome nobleman had come to visit." She narrowed her eyes to match her icy tone. "But I see it's only *you*."

That earned her a chuckle. "I know you don't like surprises, but don't be too cross with me." He tilted his head and squinted; it was a perfect imitation of someone trying to recollect a distant memory. "How long has it been since we last saw each other, anyway?"

The act was nearly as infuriating as the question itself. There was no need to put on a show for her, of all people. Lottie loosened her jaw just enough to answer. "I haven't been keeping track."

It had been five years.

And still nothing about Alec was genuine. He only made it appear so. That was his talent—drawing people in, telling them what they wanted to hear, to see, to *feel*, until they gave him everything he wanted. Then they were discarded.

He smirked again and moved a little closer. "I'd say it's been about five years or so. Not since your—"

"Who told you I was here?" Lottie didn't have time for

this. He needed to leave. Immediately. She had not come all this way to deal with people like him and Uncle Alfred. Not anymore. "Was it Mrs. Wetherby?"

Lottie had placed the timetable for the train to Rome on her desk when she left the pension, where even her harebrained chaperone could not miss it. She also underlined the city a few times so there would be no doubt of her destination. But perhaps Lottie had slipped and mentioned the village once...

Alec shook his head. "She was sure you had gone to Rome, but I know a diversion when I see one." His eyes warmed with approval, but Lottie made sure hers remained cold.

At least someone noticed.

She had also left behind a pressed red rose and a little note—love tokens from her imaginary Italian suitor. Had he seen through those as well? That could spoil everything.

"Then I remembered how you always talked about coming here because of your parents." The smile faded along with his voice, but the words still hung heavily in the air between them.

Blast.

That was the problem with childhood friends. They knew your inner workings, your inspirations, all your closely guarded dreams, because they had been there when the seeds were first sown. But while Alec knew plenty about Lottie, it seemed like everything she thought she knew about him— or at least, everything that had truly mattered—turned out to be wrong. He was little more than a stranger. And perhaps always had been.

"After that, it was easy enough to track you here," he continued. "A young English woman traveling on her own is a bit of a novelty around these parts. Especially one with hair as pretty as yours."

She frowned at the shallow compliment even as her traitorous heart beat a little faster. "A fine story, but I can't begin to imagine your purpose in coming all this way." Lottie made sure each word practically dripped with condescension.

Alec's eyes darkened as he stepped closer, filling the air with a familiar woodsy scent that made something soft and tender curl around her heart. His formerly white shirt was unbuttoned at the throat. The sun had turned his olive skin even darker and threaded his deep brown hair with the barest hints of copper and gold. Her fingers twitched with the old urge to touch those messy waves until she folded her hands tightly against her middle.

Who knew where he had been before this: Turkey, Sardinia, Greece. Perhaps even Egypt. She had never once asked her uncle. All that mattered was that Alec had left. Living in such ignorance all these years made it slightly easier to pretend he didn't exist outside of her memories. But now he stood before her in the flesh, radiating vitality and undeniably real. Lottie caught herself staring at the tanned hollow of his throat and quickly met his eyes, but of course Alec noticed. Yet another smirk briefly hovered on those well-formed lips then vanished. Time to get on with it.

"You know exactly why I'm here, Lottie. And on behalf of whom." Then he raised a dark brow to further emphasize that she had been *very bad indeed*.

She rolled her eyes. "I did leave him a note."

"Oh yes," he scoffed with surprisingly grating sarcasm. "The one your chaperone was too terrified to send him: 'I know what I'm doing. Please don't be too cross'? Did you really think *that* was going to convince Sir Alfred?"

Lottie shrugged, unrepentant. The note had been a hastily dashed afterthought. Uncle Alfred should have been happy with two lines from her. But it was vexing to hear that

Mrs. Wetherby hadn't passed the message along. "As you very well know, trying to convince that man of anything is useless. I thought my time was better spent begging for forgiveness. And I know *why* you're here in the general sense. What I'm wondering is what you're hoping to accomplish today."

For once Alec looked puzzled. "You're to come home. With me."

Lottie couldn't stop the laugh from bursting forth. "My goodness, does Uncle Alfred always send you on his errands? I'd have thought you would be doing something far more important these days."

Apparently, agents of the Crown did not appreciate sarcasm. His jaw tightened as all traces of mirth vanished; in its place was an unfamiliar, world-weary expression that bordered on hostile. "He asked for my help. I'm here as a favor."

Lottie managed not to flinch at the trivial description. She expected to be considered as little more than an annoyance, but they both knew Uncle Alfred never *asked*. He demanded.

"And is that really all you thought it would take? You show up here unannounced and I would simply go off with you?" She laughed again. "That's even less convincing than my note."

Alec moved closer. "This isn't a game, Lottie," he began in a low, harsh voice that sent goose bumps racing up her spine. He then brushed his fingers against her elbow, and the light touch was so immediately recognizable, and so shockingly familiar, that Lottie nearly gasped. As the warmth from his fingertips sunk deeper into her skin, a heady, comforting feeling settled over her until she very nearly swayed against him. "You aren't playing house up here," he continued, unaware of her reaction. "And I don't need to provide a list of reasons because you know you cannot stay."

Lottie pulled away from the hypnotic grasp and matched his glare. "I'm afraid I can, actually. I didn't wander off and end up here by accident. I've let this house for the next *year*."

Alec's eyes went nearly black as he leaned closer. It was impossible not to notice how much larger he was now. "Then I hope your landlord will honor a refund. As it stands, you have been traveling unaccompanied in a foreign country for over a week. Did you not consider what would happen when you deserted your chaperone while staying in a pension that is extremely popular with British tourists? Did you actually think your disappearance would go unnoticed?"

His tone remained cold while only the barest hint of color stained his cheeks. It appeared that Alec had finally learned to control his temper. However, after insinuating that she was both remarkably inane and grossly incompetent, Lottie saw no need to bother with civilities.

"What kind of a fool do you take me for?" she seethed. "The whole *point* was for them to notice."

By running away in such a dramatic fashion, Lottie had hoped to create a scandal so irresistible that it would be written about before the day was out. Those letters would then reach the finest drawing rooms in London before spreading even further with the relentless drive of the most potent plague until her ruination was achieved. And if the letters didn't do the trick, Lottie had every faith that Mrs. Wetherby herself would make sure word spread. The older woman had her own reputation to maintain, but no one would blame her if a willful young lady ran off with an *Italian*.

It would be the scandal of the season, if not the year. Lottie was counting on it.

Alec stared as if she was a stranger. "You mean you...you *wanted* to be ruined?"

Lottie lifted her chin. Proud. Defiant. And entirely un-repentant. "I'd be very disappointed to learn otherwise, Mr. Gresham."

Finally he was seeing her, really *seeing* her for the first time; now he would know how strong she was, how determined, how capable.

"Oh, Lottie," Alec sighed, as if in deep pain, and pinched the bridge of his nose. "What have you done?"

CHAPTER TWO

The heart-stopping relief that came over Alec when he stepped out onto the terrace and saw Lottie standing there, the picture of health—and *alone*—was entirely too short-lived.

He had forgotten so many things, like the exact shade of her hair or the dimple on her left cheek that came out only when she laughed. He had also forgotten how damned stubborn she could be.

And how disarmingly alluring it was.

Over the years, in the rare moments when Alec dared to picture her, it was only as the girl he had first met: the sweet, seven-year-old orphan afraid of the dark who insisted she had an invisible pony named Buckles. Even earlier, while he was traipsing up this godforsaken hill, he was determined to prove that everyone else was mistaken. *Lottie* hadn't run off with anyone. No, she had merely wanted to visit the little medieval village where her late parents spent their honeymoon and hadn't even considered the havoc her little folly would cause.

Silly, lovely Lottie.

It never occurred to him that Charlotte Elizabeth Carlisle, born into one of the finest families in England, and beloved only niece of the illustrious Sir Alfred Lewis, would know-ingly do anything to destroy her sterling reputation.

But the steely-eyed young woman before him suggested otherwise.

Alec had vastly underestimated her.

A careless error. Inexcusable for an agent of his experience. It would not happen again.

Lottie watched him with hawklike concentration. Her brows, a few shades darker than her hair, pulled together, but Alec couldn't speak. It had taken him years to learn how to control his emotions, but this anger had come on so suddenly, so *fiercely*, that it nearly took his breath away. How long had it been since he let such raw feelings surface?

Oh, about five years or so.

He moved next to her and pressed his palms against the balustrade. He took a few deep breaths until the vibrant pulse of anger faded into that cool, familiar numbness. "I won't pretend to understand what possessed you to do such a thing, or *why*," he said, turning to her. "But to no one's regret but your own, your reputation is still somewhat intact."

Lottie let out a frustrated huff. "Well, that is disappointing to hear," she said dryly. "I had hoped Mrs. Wetherby would be hysterical. She threw a fit at the slightest inconvenience. I thought my leaving would at least elicit the same response as being served a lukewarm pot of tea."

Her cynicism was even more provoking. And bizarre. She had never been so cold before.

What happened *to you, Lottie?*

The question was on the tip of his tongue, yet he could never ask such a thing. He might have enjoyed her confidence once, but that had been a very long time ago.

"I assure you, she was in great distress," he growled instead. "But she has no wish for word of your little jaunt to spread, so she made up an excuse to explain your sudden disappearance from the pension."

She cut a glance at him, genuinely curious. "Did she? What was it?"

"That you went to Rome to meet some school friends, where she would shortly join you."

It was a decent enough lie, though Mrs. Wetherby had already been cracking under the pressure when Alec met her in Florence. The woman was exceptionally incompetent, but at least that toad Wetherby had guaranteed his aunt's discretion.

"Huh. I hadn't realized she was capable of such a deception. Was it accepted by the other guests? There was a trio of spinster sisters staying there who seemed to live exclusively on bits of gossip."

Alec gritted his teeth. He was unfortunately familiar with the women she spoke of. "Barely. Mrs. Wetherby had to leave the pension the day I arrived to keep up appearances. But it will all be for nothing if you don't return to England very soon."

She lifted her chin. That mulish look was another thing he had forgotten. "I won't be going anywhere. And certainly not with *you*."

"If you don't come with me now, your uncle will only send someone else later," he countered grimly. "And they might not be as considerate of your well-being as I am, especially if they learn the circumstances that preceded your visit."

No doubt there were scores of men who would be all too happy to escort her back to England. Alec was prepared to drag her kicking and screaming down the hillside for that reason alone. She swallowed hard but made no response. He glanced down and noticed that one hand was balled in a tight fist by her side. Perhaps she wasn't so composed after all...

"You should also know I didn't come here merely to save your reputation," Alec continued, taking pains to soften his tone. "Though that was the initial reason, the situation has grown more urgent. Your uncle suffered some kind of apoplexy a few days ago. Mr. Wetherby sent a telegram while I was still in Florence." Alec had never met Wetherby in person. All communication between them was strictly limited to telegrams and letters, yet that hadn't stopped him from concluding that the man was a complete ass. "He indicated that it was fairly mild, as far as these things go, but there is the danger your uncle could have another."

It was difficult to imagine Sir Alfred, who always exuded power and control, suffering from any kind of impairment, but age spared no one. Lottie's frown deepened and she looked out across the landscape. Once Alec had been able to read her so easily, but she had no reason to hide anything from him then. Now he could only guess at the conflicting emotions warring inside her at the news. As his guardian and her uncle, Sir Alfred had, for lack of a better word, raised them both. But Alec's relationship with the enigmatic man wasn't nearly as complicated as Lottie's was. And, given the circumstances, one could assume that things hadn't exactly improved over the years. "If he does, he may die."

Lottie did not respond. At this angle, without those eyes hinting at the steel underneath, she could be the very picture of fresh, English innocence. Her slight curves had grown more pronounced over the years, but her peaches-and-cream complexion was still as smooth as polished marble with a faint dusting of those freckles he had always adored. The last time he saw her, Lottie had been trussed up in yards of white taffeta for a ball held in her honor. She had looked lovely then, but he much preferred her like this. In her sensible dark blue skirt and well-loved silk blouse, with wisps of hair coming loose from her braid.

Alec fought back the urge to trail his finger down her cheek. Would she be warm and soft, or cool and hard? He leaned closer and faintly inhaled that familiar rosewater scent now mixed with the sharp tang of the oil paint that stained her fingertips. She had never looked more like herself than she did at this moment. Or maybe it was simply that he had missed her. So very much.

"Thank you for your concern," she said stiffly as she shifted away from his reach. "And for delivering the news in person, though it seems hardly worth the effort on your part. If I choose to see him, it will be on my own terms. I'm sure you have a long journey back to wherever it is you live now. On your way out, be sure to tell my housekeeper you were mistaken in coming here. You—you must have thought I was someone else."

There was a slight catch in her voice. A chink in her armor. And Alec wouldn't let it slip by.

"That might be difficult," he began, "seeing as I already told her I was your husband."

Lottie abruptly faced him, her green eyes round and wide. "You *what*?"

Alec gave her a lopsided smile. "Well, I had to get inside somehow. And I didn't think she would believe I was your brother." He gestured to the thick russet braid that snaked down her chest. Lottie's hair had always been her most prized possession, and for good reason. It was glorious. Here, with those golden Tuscan hills as a backdrop, it gave her the otherworldly glow of a Titian goddess.

"But I told Marta I was a widow!" Lottie hissed and clapped a hand to her forehead. "Oh, what must she *think* now?"

Alec's lips quirked. "She seemed rather delighted by your subterfuge, actually. I believe she imagines you came here to punish me." A corner of her mouth lifted. Apparently that was an appealing idea. "I was properly scolded for not arriving sooner," he went on. "According to her, you are much too lonely up here all by yourself."

The housekeeper had also sworn that the only man who had been inside the house was an elderly chap from the village who gave Lottie painting lessons, which blessedly spared him from the ugly task of forcing some wayward suitor's hand. Mrs. Wetherby was convinced Lottie had run away with a man, though the evidence hadn't amounted to more than a single dried rose and a pathetic note that read *amore mio*. Alec had roundly dismissed the notion that such piddling trinkets would have swayed her. But now he was questioning everything.

Though Lottie claimed she had deliberately tried to ruin her reputation, that might not have been her original plan. She could have been abandoned en route, or perhaps her suitor had failed to materialize at the agreed-upon meeting place. It was understandable why she would not admit such a thing to Alec. Less understandable, though, was why she hadn't returned to Florence immediately.

Unless she is still hoping for his return.

"Marta doesn't know anything," she snapped. "We can barely understand one another."

"Loneliness is a universal language, Lottie," he murmured. One he had mastered long ago. "And it's better for you this way. If she thinks we're married, there won't be any talk when we leave the village together."

She snorted at his caution. "That wouldn't matter."

Alec narrowed his eyes. "You aren't exactly in Timbuktu. Tourists come to this village. If people connect your actions in Florence with your stay here, it will make things worse for you. It *matters*."

"Only if I cared about my reputation."

Alec's jaw tensed. Fresh heartbreak could certainly make a person act with such recklessness. It was difficult to see anything beyond the scorching pain that burned as hotly as any fire. But what would she do weeks, months, or even years later when the pain finally faded and she was left with nothing but the charred remains of her life?

"We'll talk about that later. For now I'm more concerned with removing any doubt about our relationship. Your housekeeper's been watching us this entire time. From the window."

Lottie cast a subtle look past him. "Oh, Marta," she grumbled.

Alec caught her wrist and drew a small circle with his thumb. The impulsive gesture was something he had done when they were children and she was upset. Sometimes— *many* times—they had only each other for comfort. Lottie froze and stared down at his hand.

"I know I'm in no position to ask, but please trust me. At least with this. Whatever your issues with Sir Alfred are, whatever led you to do this, go to him now. Make your peace while you still can."

Lottie's pulse quickened under his thumb as she slowly lifted her eyes. With some effort, Alec was able to maintain his impassive expression.

"Is that why you came? So I would not have any regrets?" Her voice had taken on a husky note that ribboned through his body, leaving a trail of molten need in its wake.

Alec kept his tone carefully neutral. "I already told you why. It was a favor."

Only a state of extreme desperation would have led Sir

Alfred to involve him in the first place but calling it a "favor" was quite a stretch. The thought of anyone else being sent after Lottie had been unbearable.

"And what of your regrets?" Her hooded gaze wandered over his face, his eyes, his lips. "Or do you not have any?"

Sir Alfred's refusal suddenly came to him. He had not thought of it in years—hadn't *allowed* himself to.

Sorry, Alec. I know you're fond of her, but I can't give my consent.

Fond had not even begun to describe it.

And yet, as with all of Sir Alfred's commands, he had obeyed. Without question.

How little some things changed.

His fingers tightened around her wrist. "Everyone has regrets," Alec said more forcefully than he intended. Then he let go of her. His hand was practically throbbing.

Lottie furrowed her brow for an endless moment while she chewed her lip—a welcome sign of serious consideration. Alec nearly sighed with relief at the sight.

"The note Uncle Alfred sent you," she began. "Was...was he very angry?"

He raised an eyebrow. "Furious."

Lottie gave a resigned nod at the massive understatement.

The telegram had been only a few lines, but Sir Alfred always knew how to make his point.

Alec expected her to be more upset—she had been sensitive to her uncle's moods as a girl—but Lottie merely sighed and shook her head. "I certainly don't want him to die. I only wanted him to listen. Perhaps I should..." But she didn't finish, only stared off, lost in her thoughts.

He cleared his throat. The longer they stood like this—tense and distant—the worse it looked to Marta. The woman had let him into the house, but she was still suspicious. One contrary word from Lottie could ruin everything. She might not care about her reputation, but Alec certainly did.

"As I was explaining earlier," he said a touch too briskly, "I have an idea to help convince your housekeeper, but you'll need to follow my lead. Can you do that?" He did his best to sound skeptical. Lottie had always hated being under-estimated.

True to form, she gave him a withering look. "I'm sure I can manage, but I don't see why I should."

He stepped closer and brushed a stray curl behind her ear. She inhaled sharply at his touch but didn't object. To any observer this would look like a welcomed lover's caress. "If Marta sees me kiss you," he began, "she won't doubt a thing. She won't even remember these past weeks."

Lottie's expression didn't change, but her breathing quickened slightly. "How impressive. I didn't realize merely *witnessing* a kiss could lead to memory loss."

Alec's lips curved. "Though I've been told my talents in that realm are substantial, the point is that it makes for a better story. We need something that takes attention away from you. Imagine: Instead of a dubious young widow staying here alone and arousing suspicion, we're a young married couple on their honeymoon. The groom kept delaying their journey because of business in Florence, so the bride grew cross and came without him—very sympathetic. No one would blame her."

As he spoke, Lottie watched closely. She still hadn't learned to play the coy, bashful lady. Alec had forgotten how penetrating, and slightly unnerving, her gaze could be. It set his blood moving far more than any saucy wink or fluttering eyelash ever had.

"But when he finally arrived, and after a fine bit of grovel-ing, all was forgiven." The corner of his mouth lifted at the thought of all the ways he could beg forgiveness from her. "Who could resist that?"

Lottie's cheeks took on the most becoming shade of pink, but she let out an indignant huff. "Why is it that people always seem most titillated by stories of fallen women or romance?"

Alec's smile grew. He needed to think of a way for her to say *titillated* again. "I haven't the faintest. I've always preferred a good mystery myself. But in this case, I say we indulge the masses. And don't leave any room for doubt."

There was no need for them to actually kiss, of course; it merely needed to appear that way to Marta. But before he could clarify that little detail, Lottie spoke up.

"Fine. You may kiss me," she said flatly. Then her gaze sharpened. "But it had better be good."

Alec managed to keep his cavalier expression while internally his reaction was nothing short of pathetic. He had never been one to back away from a challenge, or turn down the chance to kiss a beautiful woman. A tiny voice inside his head suggested that perhaps it wasn't a good idea to kiss *this* beautiful woman in particular, but the half-hearted warning was easily dismissed.

"As my lady commands," he said with a dramatic sigh. Best not to look too eager.

In one swift movement, his hand laced around her nimble waist while the other cupped her nape and gave it a little squeeze. She let out a gasp as her head tilted back but didn't offer any protest as he gently set his lips to hers.

One could almost believe she was enjoying this.

As if it wasn't enough for Alec to come strolling in and upend all of Lottie's plans, now he was trying to further unnerve her with a kiss. No doubt he assumed she would be positively shocked by the mere *idea* of kissing him, but Lottie had been kissed before. Three times, actually. Ceril Belvedere had even pressed her against the wall of Lady Arlington's balcony. It had been rather exciting, at least in the moment, but this...

Once, for a very brief period, Lottie had spent untold hours imagining what it would be like to kiss Alec. And even she could not resist the chance to see if her dreams lived up to the reality.

Apparently her imagination had been *decidedly* lacking.

Yet it wasn't only the feel of his lips on hers, so firm, commanding, and confident. It was the way he held her close and cradled her in his arms. As if she really did belong to him.

As if he really did want her.

Alec squeezed her neck a bit more and her mouth opened slightly. Then he gently parted her lips further with his own. That hardly seemed necessary for Marta's sake, but then one would expect him to be fully committed to his duty. Uncle Alfred had made that plain years ago when Alec left.

He will do whatever is necessary. That is not the kind of life for a man with a family. The Crown must come first. Always.

Lottie had never once spoken to anyone about her feelings for Alec, as she hardly knew what to make of them herself. Alec's friendship had always been invaluable to her, and yet at times she had ached for something more. More than she could ever put into words. More than she ever dared act upon. But her uncle seemed to understand. There was little use trying to have secrets from a man who had spent much of his life either ferreting them out or keeping them safe. And if Uncle Alfred had known, it stood to reason that Alec did as well. Perhaps for longer than she realized. Lottie had once deluded herself into thinking that Alec had morals, a sense of common decency, and, dare she think it, a fondness for her.

But he had done a very fine job of divesting her of all those pesky illusions. Completely. Alec wouldn't think twice about exploiting anything he could in order to bend her to his will. Even something as innocent as her girlhood affection.

No, *especially* something like that.

Well, she wasn't a girl anymore, and he wasn't the only one who could be shocking. Lottie pressed her tongue to his, determined to show him *exactly* how little this meant to her—but Alec immediately froze. Her cheeks, already flushed from his attentions, burned even greater at this misstep. Rejection wasn't humiliating enough on its own; no, she must also resemble an overripe tomato. But before she could pull back and recover what little remained of her dignity, Alec hauled her against his chest so close she could feel every thudding heartbeat. With each rhythmic pulse the kiss seemed to grow only more fierce, more desperate, and more dangerous.

Lottie gathered what little remained of her frazzled nerves and raised a hand to push him away, but the appendage had other ideas. Instead, her fingers sank into his hair, mussing those thick waves, while her nails gently scraped his scalp. Alec shivered and gripped her harder, which only further weakened her already feeble resolve. Just as her knees began to tremble, Alec splayed one large palm between her shoulder blades while the other moved close to her backside and firmly anchored her against his form. Every inch radiated heat, strength, and undeniable maleness.

Unlike the other gentlemen of her acquaintance, Alec did not fritter away the daylight hours in private clubs before spending the evening enjoying more shallow entertainments. His body was a weapon, and he treated it like one. She grazed a sizable biceps, and he immediately flexed beneath her fingertips. An appreciative moan rose from her throat, and Alec only kissed her more deeply. The insidious whisper in the back of her mind suddenly grew very loud: *Perhaps this* is *real.*

Alec tore his mouth from hers, as if he had heard it. After a moment Lottie's eyes fluttered open. She was flushed. Breathless. But Alec seemed as cool and collected as before. He was staring past her with a sharp, calculating look in those fathomless hazel eyes.

"There," he murmured. "That ought to do it."

CHAPTER THREE

Once again Alec had underestimated Lottie while vastly overestimating his own self-control.

That hadn't been an issue in years—if anything, his control had been a point of pride—but Alec didn't dare look at her now. He heard her sharp, surprised inhalation as he pulled away, but if he caught just one glimpse of a pliant, kiss-drunk Lottie in his arms, he wouldn't let go. Alec kept his eyes trained on a corner of the house's stone facade as he drew his hands away from her deceptively devastating curves. She hadn't been made of marble at all but was warm and supple, with an enticing figure that could lure men to their deaths; a land-bound siren. A temptation that would most certainly drive him insane.

But far more unnerving was her reaction to *him*. Alec had felt that barely contained fire inside her. That passion simmering at the very surface, a breath away from boiling over. It might not all have been on his account—there was still the possible suitor to consider—but he sure as hell wanted to experience Lottie unbound, even if just a part of her, however small, had melted for him.

It was one thing to want a woman madly, but nothing compared to being madly wanted in return. Except to be wanted by her was an impossibility.

Thanks to your parents' shame, a match between the two of you would be a disaster for her, Sir Alfred had rightly pronounced. *You've more sense than this, Alec. And if you don't, I will take great pains to remind you.*

Now there was far too much about himself, both his past and the man he had become, that she could never know. Alec strode over to the other side of the terrace, desperate to smell something besides damned rosewater, hear something other than that soft, sultry moan, fill his hands with something other than *her.* He swung back around. She stood in the same spot, but all traces of the stubborn, frustrating she-devil had vanished. Her shoulders were slumped and her head was bowed while she nervously twisted her hands. The stark pain in her face hit him harder than any blow.

She might as well have been that cherubic girl again, appealing to every protective instinct he ever had, while he was the same surly eleven-year-old rejecting her affection in a desperate effort to maintain the impenetrable wall around himself. Until the day she finally managed to scale it. From then on he vowed to do her no harm, and to keep that damned look off her face, but now he was the cause. Alec moved to reach for her, to call her name, to soothe her, but the housekeeper chose that moment to arrive with their long-overdue tea.

Lottie immediately straightened at the sight of Marta stepping onto the terrace with a heavy tray. She ignored Alec as she walked toward the housekeeper; that cool marble facade had reappeared once again, destroying any trace of vulnerability.

"Here, Marta. Let me help you."

Together they placed the tray on a table and began arranging the tea things. Marta must have included every delicacy in the house, but Alec was in no state to eat.

Marta was prattling on in rapid Italian—she had been

delighted to learn he was fluent, and even knew a bit of the local dialect—but Alec barely heard a word. "Grazie. Puoi andare," he said and waved her away.

Marta bowed eagerly. "Prego, prego. Grazie, signore." She then scurried back into the house.

"Lord of the manor already?" Lottie quipped as she moved to pour for both of them.

Alec sat down and tried not to stare at her slender, bare hands gracefully holding the teapot. "Just trying to act the part."

A bit of tea dribbled over the spout and Lottie caught it with her finger, then promptly brought it to her lips. Alec coughed and shifted in his seat.

"About that," she said, adding a dash of milk to her cup without offering him any. "Why is Marta under the impression that you're a nobleman?"

Did she remember he took it plain, or was this merely a snub?

"I told her my surname was Petrucci. It's a very old, very well-respected family in these parts."

Lottie raised an eyebrow. "A *noble* one?"

"You could say that." Alec picked up his teacup and took a sip while Lottie turned her attention to the plate of pastries; out of all the delicacies before them, she chose an individual custard tart—a crostata con crema. Alec's favorite.

"What are you supposed to be, then? A duke? A marquis?" She passed the plate bearing the tart to him. "Oh, but do they have those here?"

Alec stared blankly at the plate.

She did *remember*.

"Yes, they do," he said and accepted the dessert. "But this branch of the Petruccis are counts." His lips curved in a smile. "Which makes you a contessa."

Lottie laughed, as if the idea was absurd. As if she couldn't marry *any* man she wanted. She had rejected Ceril Belvedere only months ago, and he was the heir to an earldom.

She chose a few amaretti biscuits for herself and sat down. "Was it difficult to speak Italian again? I've been having a terrible time of it."

Though Alec's father had been English, he had been born in Venice to an Italian mother.

"A little, at first. But it grew easier once I began spending more time here."

Lottie's mouth tightened slightly. "And when was that?"
She really didn't know, then.

Alec held her gaze. "About five years ago. The Mediterranean was deemed the most advantageous place for me. I moved around initially, but I always found my way back to Italy. Venice in particular."

His father, the superfluous third son of a viscount, came to the floating city as a young man after a family quarrel over his pursuit of poetry instead of the church. The estrangement had only deepened when he took up with Alec's mother. At the time of his death, Edward Gresham had not set foot in England in fifteen years. Though he had risen to become a well-respected member of Venetian society, it had not come without a cost. One that Alec still bore.

It didn't seem necessary to add that Sir Alfred also had a number of connections to the city and expected Alec to use his Italian heritage in order to gain closer access to the powerful Venetians who wouldn't otherwise trust an outsider, especially an English one.

"I see." Her mouth tightened again, but the grimace was more pronounced this time. "I suppose playing a reprobate Englishman must make for an excellent disguise."

"I wouldn't know. I teach at the Università Ca' Foscari now."

Lottie couldn't hide her surprise. "You're a professor?"

Alec nodded. There were already enough English repro-
bates in the Byronic mold wandering around Venice. His
middling academic career was one of the few things he was
actually proud of. "I've been putting that blasted first in
history to use."

Her eyes warmed with a hint of approval. "The Etruscans,
I take it?"

First the tarts, now Etruria. While Sir Alfred had a
well-documented passion for the Roman conquest of Britain,
Alec's interests had always verged toward the more ancient
and mysterious. "Naturally."

She smiled a little and dipped her head, but when she spoke
her tone was carefully bored. "I suppose you live alone?"

"Yes." An admirable attempt to fish for information. "I
could never ask a wife to subject herself to the demands of
my work."

Lottie glanced away. "Of course."

He ignored the stirring in his chest that came when
he uttered the word *wife* and pushed ahead. "Your uncle
explained what I was doing, then?"

It was common knowledge that Sir Alfred had the admiration of the queen and the ear of the prime minister, but few
really knew how far his influence extended. He had spent the
better part of his adult life spying for the Crown and championing the use of both foreign and domestic intelligence in
affairs of state. Though the practice had flourished during
the Napoleonic wars, since then England had fallen behind
the comparatively advanced operations of adversaries like
Russia and Germany. Those in power were slowly coming
to see the value of such information, but missions were still
underfunded and mostly undertaken by amateurs—wealthy,
well-connected gentlemen who wanted a little adventure.
Alec was one of the few men who had been specifically

recruited for such work and highly trained. At some point Sir Alfred had let his niece further into the fold, but Alec had no idea just how much she knew.

Lottie didn't meet his eyes. "He told me enough. And it was rather easy to piece the rest together after you left."

"But you didn't know I had gone to Italy," he prodded.

She was quiet for a long moment. "I never asked. For all I knew, you were in London this whole time."

Alec inhaled deeply, trying to keep his irritation in check. How could she *think* such a thing? "I haven't set foot in England since I left," he said through clenched teeth, but Lottie merely shrugged and took a sip of tea, as if it made no difference. That stung more than it should have. He hadn't come here to reopen old wounds. But then they shouldn't even be *having* this conversation. She was supposed to marry fabulously, take her rightful place at the top of society, and have a veritable litter of children by now. Yet here she was, trying to undermine her own future.

Did she truly not want those things? Or had she been led astray and then abandoned by another man? Neither possibility was appealing; the latter for the obvious reasons, as well as other, less obvious ones Alec would rather not explore. But at the thought of the first possibility, a dull pain began to bloom in his chest until he smothered it. Like all the others.

For if she did not want that glittering London life, what had all this sacrifice been for?

Lottie broke the tense silence. "I will go with you, but only on two conditions."

Alec set down his teacup, grateful to be distracted from such unnerving thoughts. "Anything."

"I want to see Venice before we leave Italy."

"Absolutely not," he barked, but Lottie was unruffled.

"I know it adds time to the return journey," she conceded.

"But this may be my only chance to see the place. I have no idea how long I will be in England. If Uncle Alfred has truly fallen ill, I'd like to help him. But if he survives, I foresee some objections should I try to leave again."

"He can't hold you prisoner, Lottie," Alec scoffed.

Her eyes narrowed. "He can do any number of things, if his faculties remain. Do you doubt it?"

Alec was silent in the face of her hard stare. In his rush to rescue her from ruin, he had given no thought to what would happen upon her return to London. Yes, Sir Alfred had been angry, but he loved his niece and only wanted what was best for her.

Of that Alec was absolutely certain.

"I assume you haven't sent word to anyone yet that you've found me. I'm willing to sacrifice a day or two, if you are."

"That isn't enough time to see Venice properly," he grumbled. But it could be more than enough time to create complications. For them both.

"Oh, I quite agree with you," she said. "But I'd rather see only a bit than nothing at all."

Alec glowered. He refused to be guilted by her. *She* had put herself in this position. If Lottie had wanted to see Venice so badly, she could have gone with her chaperone.

Then again, after only an afternoon in that woman's company Alec had been ready to head for the hills, and Lottie had endured weeks of her. Surely that deserved a stroll around Saint Mark's Square and a damned gondola ride.

"Fine. We'll go. But *only* for a day." His heartbeat quickened as he said the words, and a droll voice suggested that he was not doing this merely for her benefit.

Lottie smiled in triumph and reclined grandly in her chair. She took a leisurely sip of tea and gazed at the horizon.

"Well?" he prompted.

Her eyes cut back to his. "Oh yes. The *second* condition." She placed the cup and saucer down and folded her hands. "Once we leave here, your conduct must be as gentlemanly as possible. At all times." Alec opened his mouth, but she pressed on. "That means you are not to use my Christian name."

He kept his tone neutral. "I would never use it in public."

"You may not use it in private, either. There is no need for us to be so familiar with one another. No one calls me Lottie anymore, anyway," she added softly.

Alec gripped his thigh hard under the table. "My humblest apologies for my carelessness. I will address you formally from now on. And refrain from being too *familiar*."

Lottie gave him an irritatingly beatific smile. "In that case, I will be happy to accompany you to England, Professor."

Alec failed to suppress the little thrill that shot through him at the title. "I'm afraid you'll need to pose as *Mrs.* Gresham while we're traveling. It's a common enough name, and we certainly won't be moving in the circles you're used to, so your reputation should be safe." Then he gave her a rather caustic smile of his own.

"I told you. I don't care about my rep—"

Alec held up a hand. "I am thoroughly aware of your feelings on the subject. But I assume you still care about your *safety*. You cannot stay in a room at a damned railway inn by yourself. It's too dangerous."

Lottie seemed primed to argue but then she crossed her arms. "Fine."

"Then we are in complete agreement." Alec pushed away from the table and stalked off.

When he had received Sir Alfred's command—for Sir Alfred still never *asked* anything of him—he anticipated some awkwardness with Lottie. She had spent these last years moving among the very cream of society and would not wish to reconnect with an old, forgotten playmate like him.

But nothing could have prepared Alec for the utter contempt she now demonstrated toward her own well-being. She appeared not at all concerned by the prospect of being banished from society forever. The only world she had ever known. And even if she was personally indifferent, did she have no compassion for those who cared for her? Lottie might not have any family apart from her uncle, but she had friends, certainly. If her reputation was destroyed, she would never see any of them again. Couldn't she see how much she stood to lose? It seemed unimaginable that she would not only willingly leave but set herself on fire in the process. Even for love. Then again, not everyone shared his utter contempt for romance.

Alec had noticed the canvas on the easel when he first stepped onto the terrace. Now seemed a fine time for a closer look.

"Of course," he muttered after a quick perusal. It was remarkably similar to a small painting Lottie's mother had done when she came here on her honeymoon. The original was one of Lottie's most prized possessions and had always occupied a place of honor in her childhood bedroom. After a little while, the artist herself came beside him.

"It's good. I had no idea you painted."

"I started a few years ago."

Long after he had left, then. "I trust you haven't given up your ciphers." Lottie always had a head for puzzles and developed several when she was younger. They had often written encrypted letters to each other at their respective boarding schools.

She gave a half-hearted shrug. "I had been helping Uncle Alfred transcribe some."

"Really?"

"Mr. Wetherby gave them to me now and again. It was all very hushed up, of course. And I never tried to decipher the codes myself. He said my uncle didn't trust anyone else to do it," she explained, unable to fully mask the pleasure behind her words. "But it kept me occupied."

The back of Alec's neck tingled. Sir Alfred had always adamantly maintained that Lottie could *never* be involved in his work in any way. The risk was too great. Before he could ruminate on that further, Lottie continued: "I haven't written my own in ages, though. I didn't see the point."

For there was no one to send them to.

She stared at the view with a wistfulness that, for a moment, made her seem years younger. Alec swallowed past the lump of guilt in his throat and turned back to the canvas. "Why not paint the sunset? I'm sure it's magnificent."

"It is, but my painting instructor said I had to master daytime first. Now, though..." Her voice trailed off. He would have given anything to touch her again, even a comforting pat on the shoulder, but he doubted she would appreciate the gesture. And Alec was, if nothing else, a man of his word.

"You'll come back to finish your sunset. I promise."

Alec disappeared into the cottage soon after, leaving Lottie to stew in her thoughts. Chief among them was the wish for one more bedroom. She sat down at the terrace table and flipped through the Italian pocket dictionary until she reached the *Mar* section. Lottie dragged her finger down the page and stopped at the entry for *Marito: m. Husband. Spouse.*

She pressed a hand to her forehead as her face flushed yet again. Her measly conditions had been a desperate bid to gain some control over a situation wildly spinning away from her. She had come here to show Uncle Alfred that he could not manage her anymore, but if her actions had contributed to his illness in any way, she wasn't sure she could live with herself.

Of course, there was the chance it was all a lie, with Alec acting as an accomplice. But he had agreed to her terms. Hopefully that would be enough time to determine the truth. Then she would either return to England or slip away once again. She idly touched two fingers to her lips, remembering the sensation of his mouth upon hers. Alec kissed exactly like how she'd expected a man used to manipulating people would—with confidence, experience, and just a hint at the end of barely suppressed passion to make it seem genuine.

Lottie knew this. Knew it meant nothing to him. And yet that old, pathetic desire still coursed through every vein.

For goodness' sake, get ahold *of yourself.*

She let out a defeated sigh and buried her head in both hands. It had been a mistake to stay in Italy, born of a maudlin girlhood wish to see this village. But she would not let maudlin sentiment guide her any longer. After this she would travel farther east. Perhaps to Palmyra. Not even Alec would think to look for her there. Like painting, her interest in exploration was relatively new. She had many idle hours to fill these last years, and Sir Alfred's library was well stocked. The memoirs of Lady Hester Stanhope and Isabella Bird had been particularly inspiring. Lottie felt like she had found kindred spirits in these female explorers who had also yearned for lives beyond drawing rooms and dared to make them happen.

Sir Alfred was her mother's older brother by well over a decade, as the late Mrs. Carlisle's conception had been something of a surprise to her parents. When Lottie's parents died in a carriage accident, he was her closest living relative. But as Sir Alfred was a committed bachelor, there had been few guiding female presences in Lottie's life aside from Mrs.

Houston, his fiercely loyal Irish housekeeper. When she was younger, her uncle had been indulgent, or perhaps *negligent* was the better word. Despite the interventions of some well-meaning but weak-willed governesses, Lottie had run a bit wild—especially once she found a coconspirator in Alec. But her uncle, when he was around, seemed delighted by her impudence. When she demanded a pair of bloomers so she could ride astride a horse like Alec, Sir Alfred merely laughed and called for the tailor.

It wasn't until Lottie was sent to school at thirteen that she realized how unconventional her upbringing had been. Her classmates were not impressed by her ciphers or her horse riding. They found it shocking that she could barely thread a needle or play the piano and whispered about her being "unnatural." By then Sir Alfred was no longer quite so charmed by her willfulness. From then on, Lottie worked hard to win his approval by appearing more ladylike. The one person who hadn't ever made her feel deficient was Alec. As the son of an infamous poet and his lowborn Italian wife, he was having troubles of his own fitting in with England's elite.

We're a pair of misfits, you and I, he had written to her once. *And misfits must stick together. Always.*

But in the end, Alec had found his own way in the world. And there was no room for her on his path.

Lottie slammed the dictionary shut and headed for the cottage. The terrace had grown uncomfortably warm in the midday sun, but a nap would help to clear her addled mind. And provide fortification for the night ahead.

It promised to be a long one.

CHAPTER FOUR

❧

That evening Marta insisted on preparing a feast to celebrate the return of Lottie's wayward *husband*. She brought out course after course from the kitchen until even the strapping Alec had to admit defeat.

"Please, Marta," he groaned when the housekeeper set a tray bearing an impressive meat pie on the table. "Have mercy on a poor soul."

She clucked her tongue in disapproval and gestured to his body. To anyone else, Alec's lean, muscular frame was an ideal found in great works of art, but not Marta. "Mangia. You must eat." She then began cutting him a generous slice.

Lottie had to bury her laughter in her napkin at Alec's agonized expression. The cunning agent Gresham felled by a diminutive Italian woman. He had washed and changed before supper. Now freshly shaved and wearing a finely tailored dark jacket, he looked the very picture of a mysterious Italian count.

She should have insisted he wear a sack over his head as one of her conditions.

Alec caught her eye across the table and arched a brow. "Marta, I think my lovely wife wants some."

Her heart spiked at the word *wife*. "Oh, no. I can't—"

"Even bigger than mine." He gestured to the meat pie and then to Lottie.

Marta gave him a conspiratorial nod and whispered something. Alec flashed the woman a smile and shook his head, but a faint blush stained his cheeks. Marta laughed as she moved to cut Lottie an even bigger piece. Before today, the woman must have smiled a grand total of twice in Lottie's presence. But then Alec always had that effect on people. Lottie envied that about him, even now. Even though it was all artifice.

He smiled warmly at her over his full plate, the candlelight bathing his rich olive skin in an alluring glow.

Anyone looking in on them would think this was real. Anyone.

Don't ever forget that.

"For the bambino," Marta pronounced as she slapped a hefty slice down.

Lottie jumped and clasped her hand to her chest. "Yes, thank you," she said absently. "It smells wonderful."

Marta shot Alec a knowing look. "See? Una donna sa sempre queste cose." Then she patted Lottie's shoulder and disappeared into the kitchen.

Lottie turned back to Alec. "What did she say?"

"'A woman always knows,'" he murmured.

Lottie furrowed her brow, but Alec didn't explain further. He managed a few more bites before he threw down his napkin and pushed his chair back from the table. "If I eat any more, I will burst. And I doubt Marta will appreciate the mess."

"No, she would not." Lottie had known this moment would come all evening, and yet her hands still began to tremble. She set down her fork before Alec could notice.

"Besides," he began, "we should leave as early as possible tomorrow."

Lottie glanced up at the sound of his chair scraping back.

Alec took his time approaching her end of the table. His heavy steps echoed as ominously as they had earlier that day, until he loomed over her; it put her in mind of a big cat toying with his prey.

"Come to bed, Contessa."

Her breath caught at the honorific. Death by a thousand *Lotties* suddenly seemed merciful. "Is...is Marta still watching?"

"Not at present. But that could change any moment." His eyes remained fixed on her, his face sphinxlike, while he held out his palm. An offering. The candlelight flickered against his bare skin. How many times had she grabbed it so carelessly as a girl, never understanding the power in such a gesture?

He raised an eyebrow at her hesitation. "And a man escorts a lady from a room, especially his wife." He added, with a hint of challenge, "Surely you can endure something so trivial."

"Of course," she scoffed, sliding her palm against his. It was larger now, and the skin was rougher, but she felt that bone-deep spark of recognition again.

As she rose to her feet, Alec placed her hand in the crook of his arm. Lottie flinched at the powerful warmth rising from him; it instantly penetrated the layers of their clothing to caress the bare skin of her arm before spreading lower. Alec's dark gaze bore into hers, the candlelight still lapping at the sharp angles of his devastating face. "Do you really hate me that much?" The question was practically a whisper, almost as if he were speaking to himself.

Lottie hadn't realized she was holding her breath. "Heavens," she huffed. "I don't *hate* you. I could never..." She shook her head and glanced away. That was more than enough of an answer.

"But you do dislike me," he offered. "*Violently* so."

Her gaze snapped to his and she raised an eyebrow. "I wouldn't use the word 'violently.'"

That spoke of emotions too strong, too raw, to be controlled.

Alec smiled at that, but it didn't reach his eyes. "Fair enough." He moved toward the entryway, but Lottie hung back.

"Why did you never—"

Just then Marta swept into the room to clear the table and saved Lottie from her blunder. "A letto, tutti e due! Go! Go!" She waved her hands toward the door, practically shooing them out of the room.

Why did you never write?

There was no answer that could possibly satisfy her.

No acceptable reason that would take away the sting of his rejection. Of being cast aside so easily and forgotten by a man she had thought a friend.

Her great friend.

Once they were in the hall, Lottie didn't resume her question and Alec didn't ask. They silently ascended the staircase to her bedroom, their footsteps echoing on the worn stone. With each step, Lottie's heart beat ever faster. By the time they reached the bedroom door, it was as if she had finished a race. Alec pushed it open and gestured for her to enter first. Lottie swallowed and stepped inside. A fire was lit and the room freshly turned down. Marta had even placed a vase of cut flowers by the bedside.

A young couple on their honeymoon.

The door shut softly behind her, but Lottie couldn't move. Alec swept by and retrieved his battered satchel from the corner. He pulled out a small leather case then glanced up and noticed her still standing there. Lottie's eyes skittered toward the bed.

The corner of his mouth lifted almost in apology. "I'm going to sleep on the floor."

Was that relief or disappointment swelling within her? "I—I know."

Why not both?

She hurried toward the wardrobe and retrieved her nightgown before darting behind the changing screen. She began unbuttoning her dress, listening to the sounds of Alec rifling through his bag, no doubt preparing for tomorrow. She was pulled from her thoughts by the room's sudden silence. Now clad in only her chemise, Lottie gave herself a shake and finished changing into her nightgown. On the other side of the screen it sounded like Alec had developed a cough. "Are you all right?" she asked as she pulled on her dressing gown.

"I'm fine."

He sounded a bit hoarse. Lottie stepped out from behind the screen. Alec had removed his dinner jacket, and his braces hung limply by his sides. He seemed rather flushed.

Lottie raised an eyebrow. "You're sure?"

"Quite," he said tightly as he walked toward the hearth and leaned a forearm against the wall.

Lottie removed her dressing gown and climbed into bed. Only then did he turn around. His cheeks weren't red anymore but his gaze was wary. Disturbed. *Unsettled.* He cast her a quick glance and then continued to sort through his things.

Lottie relaxed against the pillows. "Good night."

He didn't look up. "Sleep well."

She turned on her side and furrowed her brow. Only then did she catch sight of the dressing screen. She had thrown her dinner gown haphazardly over a chair and, thanks to the angle of the fire, the shadowed outline was clearly visible on this side of the screen.

Alec must have seen her changing.

She cut a glance toward him. His back was still to her as

he looked over a map, but his entire frame radiated tension. Lottie's gaze lingered over his form until she noticed the sizable bulge at the front of his trousers. She wasn't exactly an innocent. Many of her friends had been married for years, and she hadn't spent all that time in Florence looking at statues without learning *something* about the male anatomy. Alec was clearly aroused.

He, who had so easily stopped kissing her and seemed entirely uninterested in repeating it, had been thoroughly unnerved by her mere *shadow*.

Lottie rolled her lips between her teeth. She could not smile. Not at *that*.

One big hand moved to rub the nape of his neck and he turned his head slightly toward her, but Lottie shut her eyes and pretended to be asleep.

In a few moments she drifted off to the image of Alec's rattled expression.

Alec was used to sleeping in all sorts of odd, uncomfortable places, but it wasn't the floor that kept him tossing and turning for most of the night. Every time he closed his eyes, he saw Lottie. Five years keeping thoughts of her at bay, and now he couldn't stop remembering their last encounter.

Lovely Lottie, nineteen and fresh out of finishing school, on the night of her coming out ball. Though most girls were eager to debut at seventeen or eighteen, she claimed the thought filled her with dread, so she had asked Sir Alfred to delay her own, and he had been happy to oblige her.

She and Alec had not seen one another since a brief visit at Christmas, as Sir Alfred had sent Alec to help with the excavation of a Roman ruin outside Edinburgh once he completed his master's work. It had been a thinly disguised punishment for Alec's reluctance to join the Foreign Office.

Though he secretly harbored hopes to return to Oxford and become a history lecturer, Alec had dutifully gone to Scotland as a kind of mea culpa. Yet when the opportunity arose to escape the dig for a day or two, he didn't think twice. Not even the threat of invoking his guardian's legendary ire could keep him from this.

In their letters, Lottie admitted to feeling nervous at the prospect of waltzing in public: *You know what a tomboy I always was. Now I can't help but worry I'll step on a gentleman's toe or turn the wrong way.*

Alec wrote back that he had complete faith in her abilities but promised to waltz with her himself one day: *I'll gladly sacrifice a toe for the honor.*

So of course he would take the train down from Edinburgh.

Of course he would buy a new pair of evening gloves, both expensive and impractical.

Of course he would surprise her.

She was his oldest friend. A sister, really.

Except his friends didn't seem to cherish letters from their own sisters, half of which were written in ciphers they created, or talk about them quite so much. Alec had never noticed how often he mentioned Lottie until another fellow on the dig made a crack about apron strings. Alec asked if he wanted to settle it outside. He didn't, but Alec made sure never to mention Lottie again, either.

Lottie was his secret. His safe space. His home.

And he would never do anything to jeopardize that.

When Alec arrived at Sir Alfred's grand town house in South Kensington, rather than have the hackney cab pull up alongside some of the finest carriages in the empire, Alec requested to be dropped off across the street. He had learned long ago how to navigate these upper echelons— smiling through the subtle jabs, laughing at his own expense first and loudest, showing that he knew he wasn't one of them and didn't particularly care. It was true most of the time. And much easier when he wasn't surrounded by the wealth and status he would never possess.

He watched as fashionably late guests entered the stately home just in time for the dancing to begin before looking toward the darkened landscape of Hyde Park close by. He and Lottie had mostly been together at Haverford, the Lewis family seat in Surrey. But on the rare occasions when they both weren't away at school and found themselves in London, they had spent drowsy afternoons wandering around the park with picnic baskets and one of Lottie's hawk-eyed governesses.

A kind of wistfulness came over him as he stood there in the shadows, listening to the easy laughter floating across the road. The men's freshly polished shoes glinted in the gaslight while they escorted women in glittering gowns that cost more than most people's annual salaries. Alec's own evening suit was in excellent condition, but it was also four years out of fashion, and someone was sure to remark upon it at some point this evening. As with everything else of quality he possessed, it had been given to him by Sir Alfred. Alec took a deep breath and unclenched his fist. "Remember why you're here," he muttered. Then, before he could lose his nerve entirely, he set off across the street, but instead of joining the increasingly long line of guests at the front entrance, he headed toward the back of the house.

The kitchen was a madhouse, with servants rushing back and forth as Mrs. Houston barked orders. She traveled between London and Surrey at Sir Alfred's insistence, and was considered one of the most exacting housekeepers in the city. Many had attempted to lure her to their own households over the years, but Mrs. Houston turned them all down.

As soon as she spotted Alec, her commanding expression

melted into a heart-stopping smile. She gave a few more directions to a footman, then came over. "Oh, it's such a treat to see you here, Alec," she said as she grasped his hands. She still retained a soft lilt from a childhood spent in Ireland's West Country, and her doe-brown eyes glistened with genuine warmth as she took him in. "My goodness, how handsome you look!"

Alec couldn't help blushing at the compliment and glanced down at the remarkably spotless floor. "Commanding the troops, I see. Don't go too hard on them now," he teased.

Mrs. Houston threw back her head and laughed. "Oh, they're useless. The lot of them," she said with a wave of her hand. "But it will do for tonight."

She had been a great beauty once, and was handsome still, yet she had never married, preferring instead to dedicate her life to Sir Alfred. Alec had never given it much thought when he was younger, but now he suspected something far greater than money had kept her in the Lewis household all these years.

"And Miss Lottie will be so pleased you've come," she added, watching him carefully.

Mrs. Houston had been a sort of motherly figure to both Lottie and himself. Back in Surrey they had often spent rainy afternoons in front of the hearth in her sitting room, sharing cups of milky tea and listening to stories of her wild Irish childhood. Alec could nearly taste the shortbread she always served.

He swallowed past the tightness in his throat and forced a smile. "I noticed quite the well-heeled crowd outside. No doubt she's too busy dancing with a duke to pay me any mind."

To his amazement, Mrs. Houston reached out and cupped his face right there in the kitchen. Her sharp gaze had always fascinated and repelled him. She seemed to know things, deep things, about people only by looking at them. "My boy, we both know *that* is impossible."

His cheek heated under her palm, which was rough from decades of work. She gave him another warm smile, but there was no hiding the sadness in her eyes as she pulled away. "Now, get out of the way," she said with a flick of her wrist. "Unless you plan to play footman for the night."

"I trust you don't want Sir Alfred's expensive champagne to end up on the guests," he quipped, relieved to retreat back into the safe confines of good-natured banter.

"Off with you, then."

Alec did as he was told and traveled up a back staircase that deposited him into a hallway near the receiving room. As was usually the case, Sir Alfred was surrounded by a circle of admirers of all ages looking every inch the distinguished pillar of society in his black tails and carefully styled salt-and-pepper hair. He guarded his reputation as fiercely as the Crown's secrets and had never been attached to even a whiff of scandal.

Taking in the son of the tragic poet Edward Gresham, and so soon after assuming guardianship of his niece, only increased his already esteemed character. Now in the autumn of his life, Sir Alfred was thoroughly above reproach. Virtually untouchable.

And if he weren't a man of honor, that could make him very dangerous.

"Alec! Isn't this a welcome surprise." He reached out and gave him an enthusiastic handshake. Anyone else would think Sir Alfred was speaking the truth, but Alec had spent almost as much time at the poker table fleecing his wealthy classmates as he had in the Bodleian Library. Now he was much more adept at noticing the small details that gave people away. Sir Alfred's tell was a slight tapping of his right foot. The man was profoundly annoyed, and Alec couldn't fathom why. He had been wallowing in icy mud for *months* now. Other members of the excavation team were given leave if they could be spared. And Alec certainly hadn't shirked any of his duties in coming here.

Sir Alfred pulled him closer and lowered his voice to a theatrical whisper. "Don't tell me you came from downstairs. How *egalitarian* of you." Alec ignored the remark as the crowd of sycophants chuckled along with him.

"I hope you don't mind the imposition, sir, but I couldn't miss Lottie's first ball." Alec gave him a sincere look and held on to his hand a moment longer than was polite. "I'm staying with a friend nearby, so I won't trouble you for a room."

Never mind that the massive town house had upward of eight bedrooms.

"Of course not." Sir Alfred flashed him a cool smile. "She will be delighted."

As a committed bachelor, Sir Alfred wasn't in the habit of entertaining, but he had spared no expense that night for his beloved niece. The ballroom of the lavish town house was transformed into an enchanted garden with live trees, fresh flowers, and lights covered by shades with drawings of fairies. Alec couldn't stop smiling as he moved through the crush of people. If only he could have seen the look on Lottie's face when she first entered. She must have been delighted. He searched and searched but couldn't catch sight of Lottie's cinnamon hair.

Finally he recognized Miss Abigail Thorne, Lottie's closest friend from school, though in her low-cut gown and massive crown of curls, she bore little resemblance to the awkward creature he had met only last summer. "Miss Thorne! I'm looking for the lady of the hour. Where is she?"

"Why hello, Mr. Gresham." She gave him a simpering smile and fluttered her eyelashes. "I didn't know *you* would be here." Someone moved behind her, and the young lady took the opportunity to press against Alec's side.

"It's a surprise." Alec smiled tightly as she placed her hand on his arm.

But she didn't seem to hear a word over the din of the crowd, though she did use the noise level as an excuse to lean closer to his ear. "Wherever have you been all this time? Don't tell me Lottie's been keeping you away with her upstairs."

"I've only just arrived. She's upstairs?"

"Yes." Miss Thorne scoffed. "Lord Exeter made a joke. He's very droll, you know. A renowned wit. But of course *Lottie* mistook him. She didn't say anything—Lord Exeter couldn't even tell she was offended—but went directly to her room. That was nearly thirty minutes ago. People will start to notice soon. Really, it's so unbecoming to exhibit such childish behavior during her *own* debut. If I had done such a thing at mine—"

"Thank you, Miss Thorne. I must go." Alec pried her hand off him and maneuvered through the crowd. He exited the ballroom and took the servants' staircase up to the third floor, where Lottie's room overlooked the back garden. Her bedroom door was opened a crack, and a sliver of light illuminated the hall. The rich carpet masked Alec's footfalls as he spied Lottie sitting on her bed with her back to the door. She wore an ivory satin ballgown that exposed a good bit of her slumped shoulders. Only in private would she allow her true feelings to show.

That old familiar surge of protectiveness flooded through Alec. Wit or no, Lord Exeter would not leave without hearing from him. He pushed the door open and Lottie turned around. Her cheeks were streaked with recently shed tears.

Lord Exeter might encounter his fists as well.

Lottie peered into the dark hallway as she hurriedly wiped her cheeks. "Is someone there?"

If Alec could have captured one perfect image from his entire life, it would have been the moment he stepped into Lottie's bedroom. No one had ever looked so overjoyed, so relieved to see him. Not before, and certainly not since.

"Surprise," he said with a smile as he held out his arms.

"Alec!" Lottie sprang up from the bed and ran right to him. "Oh, I'm so *glad* you're here!" She wrapped her arms around his neck and pressed her face against his chest. Alec hugged her close, not like he had in many years. Not since they were both children. But he hadn't missed the way Lottie's perfectly cut gown clung to her figure, or how her elegant coiffure, far more refined than Miss Thorne's, showcased her delicate, heart-shaped face. She had grown into a beautiful young woman.

"Did the excavation finish early? Uncle Alfred said it wouldn't end until December." She pulled back. "Or have you come to tell him about Oxford?"

Lottie was the only one who knew of his secret wish. Her face was so full of fragile hope that Alec had to press his lips together to hold back the grimace. "No, it's still going on. I could only get away for the night," he reluctantly admitted. "And I...I haven't decided about Oxford yet."

What a coward he was.

"Oh." She lowered her head, not even bothering to hide her disappointment.

He placed a finger under her chin and tilted it up. The sheen in her eyes tore at his heart. "Dear girl, I came here for *you*. Now, tell me. Why are you in your room?"

She shook her head. "It's so silly. Really."

"Tell me." He gripped her shoulders and leaned his head

closer to hers. Lord, had her eyes always been such a brilliant shade of green? However had he not noticed?

"It was only something Lord Exeter said," she demurred. "He was trying to be funny. I think."

"What did he say to you?"

Lottie's eyes widened at his dark tone, then she looked away. "He remarked on the number of guests in attendance, then said they all must have come to get a glimpse of Sir Alfred, as I certainly wasn't the draw," she explained with a wince, flushing with embarrassment at the memory. "He's right, of course. I'm hardly the most promising debutante of the season, but he said it in front of so many people. And most of them laughed..."

Alec inhaled slowly, controlling the anger that suddenly thundered through him. Her familiar rosewater scent further calmed him. "He's not a wit. He's an *ass*. Forget about him."

Lottie's lips parted in shock, but then her gaze turned adoring. Alec nearly lost his breath. She hadn't looked at him quite like that since she was a young girl. He'd forgotten how powerful her admiration made him feel. The hairs at the back of his neck prickled with a dangerous new awareness.

He patted her arm. "Come. I want a waltz." The idea of going back downstairs where any man could dance with her, touch her, whisper sweet words to her, was suddenly unbearable. But they needed to get out of this room before he was tempted to keep her there.

"Oh, no. I feel so silly now—"

Alec grabbed her hand and pressed his thumb against her wrist. Her pulse was steady, strong, and swift. "Please, Lottie. Do it for an old man like me." He moved his thumb in small circles and her heart beat even faster. As she stared at him, the very nature of the air seemed to change. They were no longer Lottie and Alec, but something more.

Something that had been building for years, steadily growing without either of them noticing. But it had been there all along, biding its time. In every letter, every charged silence, every accidental touch.

And Alec could no longer ignore it.

"All right," she said softly.

He smiled and placed her hand in the crook of his arm, as if it was the most natural thing in the world. Because it was. Because it always had been.

Alec let her enter the ballroom a few minutes ahead of him to avoid any hint of a scandal, then proceeded to dance with her not once, but three times. Sir Alfred's frown seemed to deepen a little more with every turn, but Alec was tired of living to please that man. Not if he could live to please someone else.

As the night wore on, Alec laughed harder than he had in ages, while Lottie radiated with a happiness he hadn't seen in years. And slowly, all his reservations dimmed. Though he bore no title, was not even recognized by his own family, and had no inheritance beyond the pittance his father's copyright earned, he had a world-class education and, more important, a driving hunger to succeed. Perhaps that could be enough.

By the end of their final waltz, Alec had made a decision. He drew Lottie a touch closer than propriety deemed appropriate and lowered his voice. "May I call on you tomorrow morning, before I return to Scotland?"

She beamed up at him. "Of course. Did you think to slip away without saying a proper goodbye?"

Alec grinned. "I could never *dream* of doing such a thing."

If there was even the slightest chance she would have him, he was going to marry Lottie Carlisle one day. And no one would stop him.

CHAPTER FIVE

$\mathcal{S}$

Alec awoke to purple dawn breaking across the Tuscan sky and a nasty crick in his neck. He was twenty-eight. Far too old to sleep on a cold stone floor. He sat up with a grunt and rubbed his throbbing shoulder. A bullet had gone clean through the top over two years ago during a skirmish in a Turkish market, and Alec was usually fastidious about the injury, but that simply hadn't been possible last night. Then his eyes fell on the very reason for his negligence.

Lottie slept peacefully, her hair splayed across the pillows like a lush, russet crown.

He had risked his life countless times over, fought hand-to-hand with men hell-bent on killing him, looked death straight in its black, bloodless eye, and he had always kept his head. But catching just a glimpse of Lottie behind the dressing screen last night, knowing how close he was to her barely clad figure, had strung him tighter than a bow. Hours later and he was still ready to snap. He felt like the favored target of a vengeful, ancient God. Having his heart cut out every night only to awaken and find it whole again.

Alec imagined climbing in beside her and drawing her sleeping form against his chest. He would bury his face against her neck, her hair, her soft skin, and wake his wild maiden slowly with gentle kisses until she gave him a drowsy, knowing smile. Then he would roll her body beneath his own and all her treasures would finally be his.

If only they could stay right here, forever.

Alec pressed his head against his palms and breathed deeply, ridding the fantasy from his mind. For that was all it was. He certainly hadn't imagined Lottie's full-bodied flinch when he held her hand last night, nor the look of sheer terror when she thought they might have had to share a bed. And thank God for that.

All he had to do was bring her to London. They could be there in four days. If he bungled this up in any way, Sir Alfred could end his career. Then Alec would truly be left with nothing.

Their past hadn't mattered in five bloody years. And it couldn't matter now. He had responsibilities that went far beyond his pitiful, boyish desires. Keeping Lottie safe, and safe from him, was chief among them.

"This is an assignment," Alec muttered. "An assignment. An assignment..."

He repeated the demented chant until it was seared onto his brain.

Unavoidable. Unforgettable. And unbreakable.

Come to bed, Lottie...

Alec's dark voice called to her, pulling her down into the deepest recesses of her mind.

In that shadowy space, Lottie couldn't see his face, but it was Alec all the same. His rough, wide palms slid over her skin, knowing just how to touch, how to stroke, how to tease. She twisted under his hands, trying to move out of his reach, unable to take any more of this torturous pleasure, but he only held her harder, moved faster. No one could make her body feel like this, like a fire scorching her from the inside.

Only Alec.

It had only ever been Alec.

"Lottie."

Lottie's eyes shot open. Her heart pounded nearly as hard as the pulse between her legs. Alec stood at the foot of her bed, already dressed for the day in a fresh white shirt. Sunlight streamed through the balcony, casting him in a rosy glow.

He looked concerned. "You still have nightmares?"

She blinked. "What?"

"You were tossing back and forth. I thought..." His voice trailed off as he studied her face.

Oh God. Her dream.

Lottie pressed a hand to her cheek. She was flush and damp. Their eyes met and his widened slightly. Then her heart stopped. He knew. Alec *knew* what she had been dreaming of.

Lottie turned away, wishing the bed would open up and swallow her whole. "I need to dress." Her voice trembled ever so slightly. "I'll be ready shortly."

Alec stood there for an agonizing moment. She could feel his eyes still on her, feel his hesitation, but she didn't look back. "All right," he finally said. "I'll see you downstairs."

She waited until he shut the door behind him, then let out a breath.

It took her longer than usual, as her hands stumbled over the buttons. Lottie had chosen another mostly practical ensemble for traveling: a dark skirt, a white blouse, and sturdy walking boots. But there was a decided streak of whimsy in some of her pieces. Such as the fitted scarlet jacket trimmed in velvet she now donned, which saved her from looking like a rather dowdy missionary.

Back in London Mrs. Wetherby had decried the jacket as highly unsuitable and urged Lottie to choose a different fabric in dull tan, sober black, or *perhaps* navy blue. But Lottie had absolutely no regrets about her purchase and was now doubly grateful that she had asked the tailor to nip it in closer at the waist. For much of her youth she had a thin, almost boyish figure, and even now her curves weren't anything close to voluptuous. She knew she would never be considered a great beauty. Knew she possessed too many traits deemed undesirable by the fashionable crowd. And she had made her peace with it. Lottie enjoyed dressing for herself and tried not to linger on the things she had absolutely no control over, like other people's opinions. But as she wound her braided hair into a loose knot aided by the dressing table mirror, those old insecurities suddenly gripped her. It felt as if she were entering a London ballroom for the first time all over again. Preparing to be judged and ranked by a hundred pairs of eyes—and found incredibly lacking.

That *is Sir Alfred's niece?*
She isn't as pretty as her mother, is she?
Shame about the hair.

Before she could silence the impulse or consider its origin, she dabbed a bit of rose-tinted salve on her lips and cheeks and finished packing her belongings in a small carpet bag.

Lottie then savored the view from the bedroom's window one last time. The very air seemed to call to her: *Leaving so soon?* She felt a faint pang of regret. Only days ago, the idea that she would leave so suddenly, and with *Alec*, would have been laughable. But now wasn't the time for second thoughts. If life had taught her nothing else, it was that she could endure whatever fate held in store. Lottie then picked up her bag, straightened her shoulders, and marched from the room.

*   *   *

Downstairs a plate of freshly made custard tarts was set on the worktable. Marta must have discovered they were Alec's favorite, but the woman was nowhere in sight. Lottie took a bite, savoring the buttery sweetness. She was seven the first time she ever tasted one. It was shortly after Alec had come to live at Uncle Alfred's house.

"His parents are both gone, and he has nowhere else to go," her uncle had explained beforehand, even more sober than usual. "It hasn't been an easy life for him these last years. But I know you'll be good to him, Lottie dear."

She had lost her own parents the previous summer and was intrigued by meeting another child who might be able to understand the crushing pain that had become her constant companion, to help her make sense of this strange new world. Then Alec arrived: thin, sullen, and already handsome, with the most charming accent she had ever heard. He had the self-possession of a boy much older than his eleven years— and he made no effort to hide his contempt. But upon their introduction, Lottie saw the flash of wariness in his hazel eyes. Even at her young age, she recognized that perhaps this older boy needed comfort more than she did.

Lottie spent that entire first month trying her hardest to be- friend him, but Alec thoroughly rejected her every overture.

After all, she was only a silly child, while he was prac- tically a man.

They had nothing in common.

Nothing.

Until one day she asked him questions. About his home. About his mother. His father. Then he began to talk. Slowly at first, and then all at once, like a great, rushing waterfall. How lonely he must have been. And how angry, to keep so much inside. A part of her understood, but she did not yet have the words to explain, so she listened. That was how she learned about the tarts, and how he had them on Sunday afternoons when his mother was still alive.

Lottie asked the cook to make them for tea the next day and explained in great detail *exactly* how they should be prepared. The astonishment on Alec's face when he saw them piled next to the scones and jam was well worth the weeks of barbs.

Then he turned to Lottie. "You...you did this? For me?"

Lottie nodded and gave him a shy smile. It was such a small thing. And she would do so much more, if he would only let her.

His expression transformed to something else, something her young mind couldn't quite decipher. He seemed both terribly happy and incredibly sad. Then he grabbed her hand and kissed it before her governess could intervene. "Forgive me, Lottie," he begged. "I've—I've been so *awful* to you."

"Of course," she said easily.

She could forgive him anything—*endure* anything—as long as she had his friendship.

Alec was right. Lottie had been a silly child.

She set down the half-eaten tart, no longer having a taste for it.

Just then Alec's deep voice floated through the house. He was talking to someone out front. Lottie left behind the tart and went outside. A horse and cart that both looked far past their primes sat in the drive, while a boy who couldn't be more than ten held the reins. He was speaking to Alec in rapid Italian. Alec smiled and patted the boy's arm, then began to lift Lottie's trunk onto the back of the cart. He wore the same pants and jacket from yesterday afternoon, but both had gotten a good brushing at some point, as they were now entirely free of road dust.

"What's this?"

Alec grunted as he pushed the trunk onto the bed of the cart. "Our transportation to the rail station."

Lottie lowered her voice, even though the boy likely didn't speak much English. "He's a *child*."

"Lorenzo is twelve," Alec said. "I was about the same age when I took us to the village in the dogcart for the harvest festival."

Lottie did not return his amused smile as the long cherished but *deliberately* suppressed memory surfaced. It had been the first of many outings for them. He bought her a roasted apple, and they had their fortunes told: Alec would become a great explorer, while Lottie would make a name for herself on the stage. Then she fell asleep against his shoulder on the ride back to Uncle Alfred's house. She hadn't felt so safe since her parents died. Or so cared for.

"This is hardly the same."

Alec sighed and turned serious. "Marta says he's a responsible lad, and this is a good opportunity for him. He's the man of the house and his mother is ill."

"Oh." She could hardly deny the boy the chance to earn some coin.

"It will be fine. He's only taking us to Pistoia. We'll spend the night, then take the express to Venice from Bologna."

"*Bologna?*" She had assumed they would travel through Florence, as the city was much closer.

Once again Alec seemed able to read her thoughts. "We can't go back to Florence," he said as he focused on strapping her trunk to the cart. "You spent weeks there. It's possible an acquaintance might see us together, which would only fuel the speculation I am trying to snuff out." Lottie couldn't help blushing at the idea of Alec as the dashing Italian suitor she had ruined herself over. "It's a slight chance, to be sure," he continued, "but I'd like to avoid it all the same. Bologna is closer to Venice anyway." Then he met her eyes. "Are you nearly ready?"

Though his words were brief, they belayed a wealth of experience. But then, he had been living like this for years now. The realization shouldn't have been such a surprise to her, and yet it was. Yesterday Alec said he knew a diversion when he saw one. But Lottie had completely missed the one right in front of her: a smooth, unflappable, and mildly flirtatious man. Even now, Alec's neutral expression betrayed absolutely nothing, but she began to think beyond their shared past. And what, exactly, he had been doing while they were apart.

"I—I need to pack my paints. And canvas."

"Already done." Alec gestured to the cart where the canvas was expertly wrapped, with her case of paints and brushes tucked beside it.

That he would have bothered with such a thing, while planning everything else, was an even greater surprise. "Thank you," she said. "I'll get my hat."

Alec nodded. "And I'll be here."

As she retrieved her hat, gloves, and parasol, Marta came charging out of the kitchen with a basket.

"For signore and signora," she explained, with that wide smile on her face yet again. Lottie hadn't seen her so pleased during her entire stay.

"Grazie, Marta. This is lovely." Lottie accepted the heavy basket.

"The signore is a *good man*," Marta pronounced seriously. "You will be happy now."

Lottie's smile tightened. "Grazie." Even if she had been fluent, there was nothing more she could possibly say.

They both walked outside but as they headed toward the cart, Lottie gasped. "Signore Ernesto! He should be here any minute!"

"Parlerò con lui. I will tell him," Marta waved a dismissive hand and continued to move Lottie along. "Ti stai stressando e non va bene per il bambino."

There was one word that Lottie absolutely picked up on. *Bambino.*

As she turned to gape at Marta, she tripped over a crack in the path, sending the basket and parasol flying. Marta shrieked and reached out but she was too far away. Just before Lottie hit the ground, a pair of strong arms gripped her. She looked up straight into Alec's hazel eyes.

"Careful now, or our journey will end before it can even begin," he murmured, giving her an easy smile, but his arms tightened around her.

Beside them Marta clasped her hands to her chest and let out a slew of words Lottie could only assume were testaments to Alec's superior reflexes.

"Thank you," she breathed and straightened. Alec wordlessly pulled her hand through his arm and led her the rest of the way to the cart, where Lorenzo perched patiently on the driver's seat.

Alec introduced her as his wife, then carefully handed her up into the rear seat. He watched closely as she settled herself.

Lottie raised an eyebrow. "I'm fine. Really."

Alec's brow puckered and his lips parted but then Marta hurried over with the hastily repacked basket and the parasol. She handed both to Lottie and then exchanged a few words with Alec before warmly embracing him like a long-lost son. He murmured something that made her laugh like a schoolgirl.

Lottie rolled her eyes as she placed the basket at her feet and the parasol by her side.

Marta patted his cheek then turned and waved to Lottie. "*Arrivederci*, signora! Come back with the child."

All Lottie could do was smile weakly and wave back.

Alec climbed into the seat beside her. The cart was rather narrow, and his firm thigh briefly grazed hers, but it was more than enough for the startling warmth of his skin to seep into her own, setting off a confounding mixture of relief and restlessness.

It was barely nine in the morning, and her nerves were already in tatters. Lottie scooted away until there was no more chance of them accidentally touching. Alec glanced over but said nothing. He had put on a dashing, wide-brimmed slouch hat that suited him perfectly and looked well worn. He must have gotten it in some faraway place while saving a beautiful foreign woman or stealing government secrets. Most likely both.

Lorenzo clicked his tongue and jiggled the reins. The ancient mare jerked forward, along with the cart. Alec shot his arm in front of Lottie to keep her from hitting the back of the driver's seat, but she pressed her hand against the wood panel and steadied herself.

She arched a brow. "You know I'm not really with bambino. There's no need to act as though I'm made of glass."

Alec placed his hand against his knee. "Of course." Then he turned back toward the house and waved to Marta. "You are made of steel. Always were."

CHAPTER SIX

❧

A s the cart trundled slowly down the hill, the medieval village receded and the olive trees grew dense. The mild spring air was faintly scented with their woody fragrance, and Lottie made sure to inhale as much of it as she could. The hum of insects, the chirp of birds, and the crunch of the wheels on the dirt road only emphasized the silence stretching ever tighter between her and Alec. This road didn't seem to have quite so many bone-rattling bumps as during the drive up the previous week. But then Lottie had been so elated that her plan had actually worked she might as well have been floating on air. Those feelings seemed utterly foreign now as tension practically clawed across her skin.

"So," Alec casually began. "Besides tramping around Italy and taking up painting, how have you spent these last years?"

Lottie could only blink at him. The silence-shattering question was absurd in its... banality. He might as well have asked if she had ever been to the moon.

"We've a ways to go," he explained without bothering to look at her. "Might as well make conversation to pass the time. I'm afraid I'll fall asleep otherwise." He punctuated this with a rather careless shrug, in case she had somehow missed that he was only bothering to talk to her in order to combat *extreme fatigue*.

Lottie managed to suppress a rather undignified snort. He could fall off the blasted cart, for all she cared. "I assumed Uncle Alfred would have kept you informed. Though I'm sure a man with your superior deductive reasoning can piece together the usual social schedule for a woman like me."

Lottie attended another charity ball, turned down a proposal from a useless aristocrat, had tea at Lady Ashbury's, went shopping at Harvey Nichols, etc., etc.

She was already bored.

Lottie then braced herself to hear of all the remote locales Alec had visited while she had been slowly ossifying in a London ballroom. She was obscenely jealous—and maybe just a tad curious.

"We never spoke of you."

Lottie pressed her lips together against his blunt admission. Not once in *five* years? That stung more than she would have liked. "Well. I suppose I finally did something worth mentioning, then," she said with a hint of satisfaction.

Alec jerked his head toward her. Their close proximity made the weight of his gaze even heavier than usual. "Is that what this was all about? A bid for Sir Alfred's *attention*?" His lips curled into something close to a sneer on the last word. Goodness, he really did look like a haughty Italian count.

This time Lottie couldn't hold back her snort. "Of course not."

Alec pushed up the brim of his hat and leaned closer, lowering his voice. "Would you mind explaining it to me, then? For while it may be painfully obvious to you, I'm at a loss."

Lottie matched his glare even while her heart beat furiously.

Why do you care? You were perfectly happy to go five years *without one word between us.* The retort nearly tumbled from her mouth. "I have a reason," she snapped instead. "And it has nothing to do with wanting attention."

"Then you should have taken more care instead of sneaking off like a thief in the night," he ground out as he pulled away and turned back to the road. "When I received Sir Alfred's telegram, I nearly—" He stopped himself and cleared his throat. "I went to Florence immediately."

Lottie ignored the flush of shame that burned her cheeks and crossed her arms. "Fine. I suppose I did want attention, but not...not in the way you mean."

She had wanted Uncle Alfred to *listen* to her for once. To understand that she could no longer live the shallow, stifling existence society demanded of a woman like her.

When Alec had first left, Lottie threw herself into the whirl of the season and sought to become the perfect debutante. She accepted as many invitations as she could, said yes to every man who asked to dance, and smiled until her cheeks hurt. Anything to distract from the constant ache in her heart that threatened to consume her. The more mercenary part of her had even fantasized about falling passionately in love with the mysterious heir of a dukedom. A man who had traveled the world and wore an eyepatch but decided to give up his life of intrigue to marry Lottie.

That would show Alec.

But of course nothing of the kind happened. None of the gentlemen she met were anything close to mysterious, and the only person she knew who wore an eyepatch was Abigail's ninety-year-old grandmother. By the end of her first season, her efforts had led to several proposals, but she couldn't keep the charade up any longer. Lottie rejected them all. And with no remorse.

Sir Alfred had supported her decision at the time. "I confess, I am not ready to part with you yet, my dear," he said.

Though Lottie had been surprised to hear her venerable uncle admit to such a feeling, she did not question it. The next few years passed in a similar fashion, with Lottie attending fewer and fewer entertainments each season in favor of other, more stimulating pursuits. She visited a number of salons all over the city and became involved in the movement to secure women the vote. At home Uncle Alfred helped her practice her ciphering skills, and she even assisted him in publishing a collection of Edward Gresham's poems.

But just as Lottie had come to accept—nay, *enjoy*—her burgeoning spinsterhood, Uncle Alfred became fixated on her marrying. And marrying well. He barred her from participating in anything that contributed to her growing reputation as a woman scandalously interested in intellectual pursuits, leaving her with nothing to do aside from mind-numbing society activities. Lottie did not care for balls or tea dances or interminably long musical evenings. She did not want to be another object d'art on the arm of a man who could be interchanged with any other, as long as he had the right pedigree. But her pleas had fallen on increasingly indifferent ears, until the night last spring when she publicly rejected Ceril Belvedere.

Then she had all of Uncle Alfred's attention. Much more than she had ever wanted.

"Was it a man?"

Alec's jarring question drew her from her thoughts. "What?"

His jaw was set and his brow furrowed, but his eyes flashed with an edge of something dark. Something dangerous. "I saw your trinkets. The flower and the *note*." He wrinkled his nose as if the word itself had spoiled. "Mrs. Wetherby believed you had run off with someone."

Lottie's pulse raced. It had been rather distressing how easy it was to create the illusion of her own ruin. Strange to think that something that was given such power could be destroyed by nothing more than a scrap of paper and some dried flower petals. This had only further convinced her that she was making the right decision.

But if Alec discovered it was all a sham, Uncle Alfred would know as well, and she would have no leverage. "You— you do not approve of such missives?"

The darkness grew. "I think it should take far more than that to win your heart."

The organ in question wrenched painfully in her chest. Did she dare take him into her confidence? This man who had once known everything about her? The confession trembled at the edge of her lips.

"But then you wouldn't be the first young lady to fall victim to a few sweet words," Alec said dismissively as he turned away. "And Florence is filled with conniving men who live to prey on English tourists. Especially women."

The bitterness underlying his words was surprising. Even greater was how much they hurt. She had meant to create that exact illusion, and yet a part of her hoped Alec would see through it.

Lottie focused on the horizon and fought to control her breathing. "That is the only reason you can think of for me running away?"

Enjoy your time in Florence, my dear, and prepare yourself. Because jilt or no, you will be married *by the end of next season.*

"The only one that make sense," Alec muttered.

Lottie closed her eyes and exhaled through the disappointment—the *anger*. But it was always better to be underestimated. She had been foolish to think Alec might understand. He was so like Uncle Alfred. The last thing she owed him—either of them—was her truth.

"Yes," she murmured and continued to stare at the horizon: golden hills and blue sky streaked with clouds she still hadn't mastered. "I suppose it is."

So. It had been a man after all.

Alec had been prepared for this ever since Florence, and yet the force of his disappointment was still crushing. He checked the instinct to reach for Lottie. He had forgotten how powerful that old urge was. No, that wasn't true...he hadn't forgotten. It had been deliberate. An act of self-preservation.

Though she sat mere inches from him, it might as well have been an ocean. She looked so forlorn, so utterly alone, that it rattled something deep within him. A long-neglected corner he had locked up ages ago. And for good reason.

But she wouldn't want anything he could offer, least of all his sympathies. Alec was merely a forgotten relic from girlhood. Not the man she was obviously still pining for—and had clearly been dreaming of that morning. Even a man with his *superior deductive reasoning* knew that. So Alec settled for gripping his knee instead. Hopefully the marks wouldn't be as deep as the ones he left on his thigh yesterday. When she was safely back in London, he would hunt down the bastard that broke her heart. No matter how long it took, Alec would find him and make him pay.

"And what of your life?" she began, thankfully rescuing him from those murderous thoughts. Her voice was steadier now that she wasn't speaking of her negligent suitor. "Have you spent this whole time as a Venetian professor?"

"Only for the past two years. Before that I was mostly traveling—Greece, Egypt, a long stretch in Turkey; but

Venice…" Alec paused and absently rubbed his scarred shoulder. "Venice always felt the most like home."

His permanent station in the city was also Sir Alfred's way of apologizing after nearly getting him killed in Turkey.

"That's understandable, considering you—" Lottie paused when he met her eyes. She seemed startled by her own words. "You lived there before, I mean."

It was only the second time Lottie admitted to remembering something about him. Admitted that they had once been so much more. A torturous spark flared in his chest. One that felt dangerously close to hope. Alec could think of nothing to say beyond a stilted "Yes."

His earliest years had passed quite happily in Venice, until his parents separated. Alec still didn't know what led his mother to desert them so suddenly. All he could remember was receiving a brief, teary-eyed hug from her one morning and later finding his father well into his cups.

She's left us, boy. We aren't enough for her, he'd mumbled. *Our love isn't enough.*

Alec was devastated, but his father was in no state to offer any comfort. Edward Gresham was too wrapped up in his own grief and hadn't been sober since she left. His clever, creative, funny father had been replaced with a ghostly shell of a man. One who drank day and night, and who couldn't bear the sight of his own child, for fear of seeing even a shadow of his lost love. Within the year he would go to the grave nearly penniless, and Alec was told of his mother's death a few weeks later. After that, young Alec had been carted between distant relations of his mother who wanted nothing to do with him until, strangely, Sir Alfred, an old school friend of his father's, agreed to take him in.

Even to this day, Alec had no idea what possessed the man to do it. He could no longer tell if it had been the greatest blessing of his life, or if he was paying for the many sins of his parents.

"Do you like it?"

The question pulled him from his tangled thoughts. "Like what?"

Lottie arched an auburn brow, as if he was terribly slow. "Teaching."

"Right." He gave himself a shake. "Yes, I do. It's nicc to have a bit of purpose. To feel like I'm helping people."

Her eyes lost some of their hardness. "Doesn't your work for the Crown involve helping people?"

Alec shrugged. "Sometimes." If he was lucky.

Espionage was an ugly business, and not one he ever would have chosen. But there was no need to bother her with his many regrets on that subject.

Lottie's rosebud mouth parted slightly in surprise and immediately drew his gaze. Her lips seemed to tense under his observation. Nerves, maybe.

Or maybe not. Maybe it's something else. Something more.

Alec had long prided himself on his ability to read people, women in particular, but he knew well before he set foot in Tuscany that he would never be able to read Lottie accurately anymore. There was too much history. Too much pain. His mind would see things it wanted to see, not what was truly there. Since the fateful morning when he had barged into Sir Alfred's study and declared his intension to marry Lottie, Alec had learned to be cautious. To wait for the right moment. To uncover the right information. He credited this approach to his success in the field. Other men were far too cocksure, convinced of their own brilliance. But Alec tread carefully and he was rarely wrong.

"And what of living in Venice? Do you like that as well?" Her voice had gone a bit softer.

If he didn't stop staring at her mouth, she would think him a lecher. "Yes." He forced his eyes to meet hers. "It's...it's a lovely city." And now he would get to show her. Something else sparked in his chest. "The closest thing to experiencing true magic is Venice at sunset."

"How poetic." She broke into a genuine smile he couldn't bring himself to share.

He could still picture his father in his prime—tall, hale, and happy, with his arms wrapped around his mother as they stared across the Grand Canal from the big window in their palazzo's front parlor. His eyes were filled with child-like wonder, even though he saw the image nearly every day. But then, his father had known what he had. And how precious it was. That was why he couldn't survive when it was all ripped from him. Edward Gresham knew life would never be the same. That the magic was well and truly lost. Forever.

Alec shrugged again. "Someone said that to me once years ago. I suppose there are moments when I still believe it."

Lottie continued to study him. "Only moments?"

He swallowed past the lump in his throat. "I think a moment of magic is more than enough for me these days."

Her eyes softened a little further, but they stopped short of pity before she turned back to the horizon. Alec let out a breath. If being in Lottie's presence didn't kill him, the memories she roused just might. Thankfully, Lorenzo turned around and mentioned that they would pass a brook with a shady spot perfect for a picnic lunch. "For signore and the signora," he added in heavily accented English. His tender young gaze then fell on Lottie, looking for her approval, but she didn't notice his attentions.

Alec felt a pang of sympathy for the lad. "Yes, that's fine." Then he addressed Lottie: "We'll stop for lunch soon."

"Oh, good," she said, still looking at the horizon. "I was about to start rifling through Marta's basket."

"We'll have time to rest here. Then it's another few hours to Pistoia."

Lottie nodded but her spine tensed ever so slightly. They would spend the night there before catching the early train to Bologna. Alec's shoulder was already twinging at the thought of sleeping on the floor again. No doubt they would both be more comfortable in separate rooms, but he wouldn't risk her safety. No, it would have to be one room.

One room for Mr. and Mrs. Gresham.

And there it was. That damned spark again.

After a little while, the cart trundled past a bend in the road and revealed a healthy swell of rushing water. A cluster of cypress trees on the bank would provide plenty of shade for their picnic. Lorenzo brought the cart as close to the little glen as he could manage. They were perched on a gently sloping hill that led down to the glen and the brook beyond. Alec was up and out as soon as the wheels stopped. He stretched his long arms over his head and took in the scenery. As his jacket stretched across his broad shoulders, Lottie pictured the shape of the corded muscles beneath, and how they would bunch and tighten with each movement. Like any respectable English tourist, she had spent many an afternoon filling a pad with pencil sketches of statues. He was as well built as any she had seen here, but Alec wasn't made of marble. His skin would be warm, and smooth. It would give ever so slightly when touched. Maybe even tremble.

Lottie sniffed. No. Not *Alec*.

He probably had more self-control than the statue of David. And a heart to match.

The closest thing to experiencing true magic is Venice at sunset.

Alec's stern expression hadn't faltered while he quite obviously quoted his own father. But if he felt even a touch of nostalgia, he did not share it. But then, why would she think him capable of any sentimentality? His actions, or lack thereof, said more than enough.

Alec finished his stretch then came around to the other side of the cart and held out his arms. Lottie hesitated, but then he raised his eyebrows. "Can't a man keep his wife from breaking her neck?" he asked innocently.

Lottie gave him a pointed look but relented. "I suppose."

Alec's hands encircled her waist as he helped her down. His touch was brief and entirely courteous, but Lottie's knees suddenly buckled. Alec immediately pulled her to him while his warm, woodsy scent invaded her senses. Her palms spread over his chest and her fingers tensed against the urge to stroke the musculature that lay beneath his linen shirt.

"It's—it's from sitting so long," Lottie hastened to explain. As she forced her hands to push away from him, her very cells seemed to cry out.

Alec released her. "Of course," he said smoothly, his expression as unfathomable as ever. "You go on ahead." He handed her the basket. "Find us a place to sit. I've a blanket packed away here somewhere."

Lottie gave a dazed nod as she took the basket and walked toward the river. The swift, steady sound of rushing water helped to settle her overwrought nerves. She found a spot that was an ideal combination of both view and shade, then watched the patterns of sunlight glinting off the surface of the water until she was lulled into a kind of trance. She didn't even hear Alec's approach.

"This is perfect," he said. She whirled around as he shook

out a thick brown blanket and spread it over the earth. "Here. Have a seat."

Lottie sat down on the blanket as far away from him as possible. A corner of Alec's mouth lifted, but he said nothing as he sprawled across the middle of the blanket and propped himself up on one bent elbow. "And what did the lovely Marta send us off with?" He looked perfectly at ease now, as if they did this regularly. And they had. Once upon a time.

A ghost of a smile hovered on Lottie's lips. They had picnicked often at Haverford, her uncle's estate in Surrey. Her governess, Miss Newson, had initially barred Alec from joining them despite Lottie's many fervent pleas. She didn't like foreigners and, well, the boy was just so very *Italian*. But soon enough, even the stringent Miss Newson couldn't resist Alec's formidable charm, and he was granted permission to accompany them. Those lazy summer afternoons were some of the happiest of her life. But it was useless to remember them now. They were both much changed since then.

Lottie shook the burdensome memories from her mind as she removed the cloth from the basket and began to take out portions of smoked meat, a generous wedge of cheese, a loaf of crusty bread, a bunch of grapes, and, of course, a few more custard tarts. She placed each item between them while Alec silently observed. Lottie couldn't tell for certain if he was looking at the food or at her, and she didn't wish to find out. She kept her focus firmly on the task before her. But as the seconds ticked by, something inside wound tighter and tighter until it felt as though her very skin would burst.

She swallowed and looked into the now-empty basket. "A fine feast, but it appears Marta didn't pack any utensils."

"That's no trouble." His voice, as thick as honey, nearly startled her again. "I have a pocketknife. Will that do?"

Lottie fastidiously wiped her hands on the cloth to give

her something else to do besides look at him. "It will have to." She finally dared to glance up. Alec, still lounging on the blanket like some kind of grand Ottoman, handed her an ivory-handled switchblade. Lottie reached out and gripped the handle, but Alec held fast until she was forced to meet his eyes. Then he gave her a slow, lazy smile. "Careful now. I'm terribly attached to this one."

Lottie responded with a look of mild exasperation, and Alec released the knife with a soft laugh. The handle was still warm from being nestled against his body, as if it was an extension of his person. Lottie pressed her lips together as a wave of heat rolled through her.

Honestly.

She sat up a little straighter and began to cut the cheese and meat with Alec's knife. All the while she could practically feel his watchful gaze following her every movement. This would not do. She furrowed her brow and opened her mouth to tell him to keep his eyes to himself when Alec interrupted. "I nearly forgot!" He scrambled to his feet and took off for the cart. He returned nearly as quickly as he had left, but with a bottle of corked wine in one hand. "Marta gave us this. A celebratory bottle."

Lottie's frown deepened. "It will have to wait. We've no glasses."

Alec settled back down on the blanket. "Come now. Where's your sense of adventure?" He was already pulling out the cork.

"I think my sense of adventure is perfectly fine, thank you."

"Well, I can't argue with that." He chuckled and held the bottle out to her. "But I do insist on ladies first."

Lottie huffed. "I've never in my life taken a—a—*swig* from a bottle! I'm not a pirate!"

"You most certainly are not. And thank goodness. Here."

She eyed the bottle, then let out a resigned sigh. "Very well." Lottie took the bottle from him and brought it to her lips. She took a tentative sip and somehow managed not to dribble any down her chin. The wine was rich and surprisingly smooth. Lottie took another, more substantial swallow before handing the bottle back to Alec.

"A woman of many talents," he quipped before taking a swig of his own. His eyebrows rose. "Hmm. That was better than I expected. Well done, Marta."

"I think she may have liked the signore."

He gave her a thoughtful look over the rim of the wine bottle. "Perhaps. But she was also happy. For us. For you. People like seeing a young lady safely married."

Lottie let out another huff as she assembled a rather sorry-looking sandwich with a hunk of bread. "Yes, well. Thank goodness she'll never learn the truth," she muttered.

Alec was silent for a long moment. "It did no harm," he said quietly.

She shrugged and took a bite. Of course he would say that. Thanks to Sir Alfred, Lottie was well versed in the "good" kind of lies and the "bad" ones.

But sometimes it was the good lies that did the most damage.

She met Alec's eyes. He appeared properly chastened, just like a person with any kind of conscience. "Is my uncle even sick?"

Alec's nostrils flared slightly, but otherwise his face went blank. "You think I would lie about that?"

"Yes. If it got you what you wanted."

His brow tensed. "And what is it you *think* I want, exactly?"

She remembered him pulling her scandalously close at the end of a waltz on the night of her coming out ball. How dark and warm his eyes had been. No one had ever looked at her that way before. And she had been so sure, so certain, that something irreversible had passed between them. When she had teased him about leaving without saying goodbye, he had answered so readily, so firmly.

I could never dream *of doing such a thing.*

But he must have known, even then, what he would do.

"I haven't the faintest idea," Lottie said evenly while her fingers clenched around a bit of blanket. "It's been a very long time since I had any inkling of what you could possibly want." She then took a rather defiant bite.

Alec studied her. "I see." Then he slowly raised the bottle to his lips and took another long sip while never breaking his gaze. A shiver ran down her spine, but she remained rigid. Alec set down the bottle and roughly wiped his mouth with the back of his hand. Then he raised an eyebrow, likely waiting for her to comment on his appalling lack of manners. But Lottie did not react. He could strip naked and dance a jig and she wouldn't even blink.

He bared his teeth in a hint of a smile. "So if I told you what I wanted," he began, his voice as thick as honey once again, "would you even believe me?" The question was posed like a challenge. As if he were daring her to ask him. To *beg*. His eyes flitted to her lips, briefly.

Lottie let out a slow breath. "No," she murmured while a rebellious little corner of her heart protested. His brow tensed again, stronger this time. "I don't suppose I would."

Alec took another swig of wine in response and set the bottle down hard. One scarlet drop slipped down the side. "Well. It's good to know at least *one* of us can be unfailingly honest." Then he grabbed a custard tart and stood up. "I need to speak to Lorenzo. Come when you're ready."

The brook continued to rush behind her, strong and steady, but Lottie barely heard it. She was too consumed with watching Alec march up the slope toward the cart, his strides angry and determined.

If he were any other man, she would have sworn he was hurt.

And she would have been absolutely sure of it.

CHAPTER SEVEN

❧

A lec ran through the planned route with Lorenzo once again. It was a straight shot from here to Pistoia, but staring at the well-worn map helped settle his nerves—and his temper. When he drew Lottie into his arms earlier and felt the telltale quickening of her heartbeat while her green eyes glazed over, he had to fight against the fierce urge to hold her there. No matter her wayward suitor, Lottie was attracted to him. At least a little. It shouldn't have mattered—it *didn't* matter—and yet the thrill was undeniable. Until she revealed her true feelings.

Alec assumed that Lottie didn't exactly trust him, but to hear her actually say it. To admit it seemed entirely plausible that he would lie about Sir Alfred's illness *as long as it got him what he wanted*?

It was a shock to learn how very little she thought of him.

Alec wasn't anything close to an idealist. He had spent most of his adult life toeing lines that were constantly shifting. The world wasn't black *or* white; people weren't good *or* evil. In his experience, anyone was capable of nearly anything, if given the right motivation. But there were certain things that even he swore to never do: harm a woman or child, double-cross someone who had risked their life to help him, and break the trust of those he was closest to. Abiding by those tenets mattered, for once a man started breaking his own rules, there was no telling where he would stop.

Yes, all right, he did *lie* in the course of his work when necessary. But he wouldn't lie to Lottie. Not if he could help it. And not about something important. Unless lies by omission counted.

We never spoke of you.

That was the truth, and yet it hid so much.

When he had left, Alec arranged to receive regular updates on Lottie. He needed to know how she was getting on—for her own benefit, of course. Not his. Sir Alfred had politely suggested that any communication between them would only prolong the inevitable, to which Alec agreed, but he had his own methods for securing information. It was nothing that wouldn't be printed in the gossip pages—he had no wish to invade her privacy—and at first he skimmed the reports with a decidedly clinical eye. But if she was heartbroken or disappointed by Alec's sudden disappearance, she certainly hadn't consoled herself by staying in. No, she was clearly enjoying her status as a celebrated debutante and made rather a grand splash that first season.

But as the comforting numbness that had allowed Alec to leave in the first place faded, and the reality of his Lottie-less future began to set in, he found that this approach wasn't as clinical as he thought—it was *compulsive*. He read each report looking for the slightest indication of partiality, either on her part or a gentleman's. Had she danced once or twice with Lord Crawford? Why did she go see that production of the insufferable *East Lynne*? Lottie *hated* melodramas. Mr. Wellesley had also been present at the Trenthams' musical evening. That was the *third* event they both attended that week; it couldn't be a coincidence, could it?

By the end of her first season, Alec's stomach was in knots waiting for an engagement announcement. But despite the many proposals she received, none came. He shouldn't have felt so relieved, as most of Sir Alfred's prediction had come true—she was indeed admired by the cream of society. And she was still young. It was only a matter of time.

In order to spare his sanity Alec requested to be informed only of major developments. That was how he learned of her rejection of Ceril Belvedere last spring. The public nature of Ceril's so-called jilting and his status as the Earl of Southdown's heir caused a minor scandal. Alec had been in Greece on Crown business at the time and hadn't been able to give it much thought. But now...

Sir Alfred was close to the Earl of Southdown both personally and professionally; he would have much to gain by uniting the families via marriage. Though he might have been publicly indulgent of his niece, Sir Alfred would not have borne her rejection of Ceril quite as easily as the others. He couldn't force her now, as Ceril had immediately gone on to marry an American heiress, but perhaps he had found someone else. That could certainly explain why Lottie had decided to run off with a Florentine.

Alec's stomach turned, but it was difficult to determine which was more sickening: that Lottie would have been forced into marriage or that she didn't trust him enough to admit it.

Lorenzo must have noticed his stricken expression. "All right, signore?"

Alec nodded. "I'm fine," he said briskly as he refolded the map and tucked it back into his bag.

Lorenzo gestured with his chin. "Signora comes."

Alec scrubbed a hand over his face. Now wasn't the time to ask questions. Though there was no telling if she would ever answer them. He turned as she came up behind him, and he took the basket and blanket from her without a word. When they were secured in the cart, he held out his hand and finally glanced at her. The irritation from earlier had vanished. Now she only eyed him warily, but this time she didn't hesitate as she slid her palm against his. Alec helped her into the cart, and she uttered a soft word of thanks.

"No need," he said as he climbed in beside her. "It's the very least I can do."

They passed the next several hours in an increasingly uncomfortable silence. Every time the cart went over a bump, which was rather often, Alec's knee would nudge against hers. And every time that happened, he clenched his fist. Lottie almost wished she could take back what she had said at the riverbank. His anger was surprising, but how could he possibly expect her to think anything different? And yet, that nagging pang of guilt was still there. But more than that, more than anything, she wished she didn't believe it.

Now and then Lorenzo would point at something— a crumbling monastery, a Roman ruin, a road that led to nowhere—and Lottie would nod with polite interest, but Alec barely spared her a glance until they rolled into the bustling city of Pistoia.

"The railway inn is up the road there," he grumbled.

Lottie closed her eyes and let out a little sigh of relief. She couldn't spend another minute in this cart. Then they pulled into the inn's yard. It was nothing like the quaint, tidy pensionaries she had stayed in that catered to English tourists. She caught Alec studying her reaction. He probably expected her to throw a fit, like the fussy, spoiled blueblood she was.

Any remaining guilt she had carried from luncheon

vanished. She smoothed her hands over her wrinkled traveling skirt. "How charming."

Alec raised an eyebrow but said nothing as he climbed down from the cart. He handed her down without looking at her, then said a few words to Lorenzo and pointed toward the stables.

Lottie frowned. It was getting close to sunset. The boy would likely be spending the night here. Alec turned back to her and gestured to the inn's entrance. "Lorenzo will bring the trunk in shortly."

"Where will he sleep?"

Alec stopped in his tracks, surprised by the question. "The stables. He'll want to get an early start home and leave by dawn."

Lottie glanced back toward the stables. There were a number of rough-looking fellows hanging about. "It doesn't look safe. Shouldn't he sleep here, too?"

Alec held the door of the inn open and she stepped inside. It was dark, and the ceilings were low. "Lorenzo will be fine," he said from behind her. "He'll want to stay by his horse anyway."

The innkeeper, a thin-faced man with a well-oiled mustache, took notice of them speaking English and his eyes lit up, likely already dreaming of how he could spend their money.

Lottie had seen that same expression on the faces of countless men over the years.

"Welcome to the Inn at Pistoia!" he said, opening his arms grandly. "I am Signore Garda, owner and proprietor. How can I be of service to you?"

Alec was not the least bit impressed by his simpering. "My wife and I require a room for the night," he said gruffly and handed the man some coin. "And I've a boy who needs to keep his cart and horse in your stable."

The innkeeper wasn't put off by Alec's short response. "Splendid, sir. I'm happy to inform you that the finest room in the inn is available. The views are magnificent. Some even say they are the greatest in all of Pistoia."

Alec did not return his smile. "How fortunate for us. We'll be fine as long as the bed is decent."

The innkeeper nodded eagerly. "Oh, yes, sir. In fact, the bed is one of the *largest* in the city. It used to belong to the Rospigliosi family during the Renaissance. And, since we cater to so many English visitors here, let me assure you that we offer *all* the latest amenities."

Alec arched a brow. "I've no doubt."

Lottie tugged on his elbow. Now was not the time to be sardonic. He turned toward her but kept his gaze on her hand. "Please," she whispered, then hesitated. "If it's too costly to get Lorenzo his own room, I can—"

Alec shot her a scowl as he dug deeper into his pocket and thrust some more coins at the innkeeper. "We will need *two* rooms." Then he glanced at Lottie and lowered his voice. "The boy will stay with me."

There. A room to herself. Why didn't she feel relieved?

The innkeeper shook his head with an admirable display of remorse. "I'm terribly sorry, sir, but there is only one room left. There are cots available in the stables, though," he offered with a hopeful note in his voice. He did not want to lose their business.

Alec let out a frustrated sigh and began to tap his foot. The low light of the inn cast deep shadows on his face, making him look utterly exhausted. Or perhaps he simply *was*. Her guilt returned. Who knew how long he had been on the road. And all because of her. Lottie had the sudden urge to place her hand on his cheek and stroke away the tension there.

Instead, she leaned toward him and lowered her voice. "I'm sure you're right that Lorenzo will be fine in the stables."

But her words only seemed to upset him further. Alec pinched the bridge of his nose. "No, it's not—you aren't *wrong...*" He trailed off and shook his head helplessly. "Never mind." Then he addressed the innkeeper. "We'll take the room. And the cot."

The man's grin returned. "Perfetto. Here is the key. Your room is on the top floor." He gestured toward the staircase. "I'll have your luggage brought up straightaway."

Alec took the heavy brass key. "Send a supper tray as well. And a tub with plenty of hot water. I've a mind to indulge in a few *amenities* this evening."

Lottie followed him toward the staircase. Dining alone in their room and having a bath? She lowered her voice. "The tub isn't necessary. I can wait until tomorrow."

"I didn't order it only for your sake." He clapped the arm of his jacket and a puff of road dust came off. "Come. I want to see the 'greatest view in Pistoia' before dark."

As they made their way toward the staircase, two men were descending, engrossed in a conversation that would pass as a vicious argument in England. One caught a glimpse of Lottie as they approached and shot her a wide grin. He was missing several teeth and the ones that remained were in bad shape. The other man, sporting a set of bedraggled black whiskers, did the same. "Buona sera, Signora," he said with a grand bow. The courtly gesture would have been more effective if he weren't covered head to toe in road dust.

Lottie instinctively drew back. Alec's arm came around her waist and he pulled her close to his side, but she was rather grateful for this display of possessiveness. The men didn't even try to hide their leers as they stepped closer. One gestured to her and said something that sounded complimentary to

Alec in that joking tone men always use with one another. Lottie didn't know a word, and yet she understood enough.

Men had shouted things at her nearly every day since her arrival in Italy. She didn't like it, and one particularly aggressive flower seller had almost sent Mrs. Wetherby into a fit of the vapors on the Ponte Vecchio, but ultimately it was harmless. Lottie had experienced much worse behavior in London ballrooms from men who believed themselves to be highly civilized gentlemen.

Alec's hold on her tightened. He did not respond, nor did he return the man's grin.

The silence stretched between the four of them until it became painfully obvious that he would not engage at all. The larger of the pair's face twisted in an ugly frown and he let loose a string of vicious Italian. Her shoulders tightened at the blows she expected Alec to unleash—men had dueled to the death over much less—but his only reaction was a slight tensing of his brow. The men hurled a few more words at him, which were met with the same grim silence until they gave up and walked away, already chattering on as if the confrontation had never happened.

Lottie hadn't realized she was holding her breath.

"Come along." Alec didn't even give them a backward glance as he released her and headed up the stairs. The loss of his comforting hold was immediate. That she even noticed was particularly vexing.

"You should have joked back with them," Lottie hissed when she managed to find her tongue. "They seemed very angry."

He looked amused. "I assure you, I've been in far worse situations."

By then they had reached the top floor. Alec stopped in front of the only door and fingered the edge of the key.

"Besides, I wasn't going to laugh along with those bastards," he said softly.

Now she was curious. "What did they say?"

He watched her a moment. "They mostly discussed the various animals I was born of and what I could do with them." He flashed her a smirk and Lottie let out a breath of laughter. Then Alec turned to the door and slid the key into the lock. "They managed to get one thing right, though," he added as he pushed the door open. "You *are* very beautiful."

Alec stepped into the room without waiting to see Lottie's reaction. He would have readily said the same thing to any other woman during any other mission. Acting as the charming, carefree rogue had served him very well over the years. And it would do so once again.

The bedroom was a delightful surprise: large, bright, and airy with a set of doors that opened onto a small balcony. That obnoxious innkeeper hadn't been exaggerating at all. The view really *was* magnificent. It looked out across the tiled rooftops of Pistoia, offering a glimpse of the bell tower of the Cathedral of San Zeno. And the bed was indeed one of the largest he had ever seen, with an elaborately carved headboard that would put Catholic church pews to shame. There wasn't much else in terms of decoration, but the room didn't need it.

Alec turned to share it with Lottie, but she still stood in the doorway, staring at him in disbelief, as if he had pulled a rabbit from his hat. Then she gave a little laugh and shook her head dismissively. Annoyance spiked through him. Why couldn't she just accept the compliment with a simper or blush, like every other woman?

"You doubt that you are?" The words came out more harshly than he intended.

Lottie shrugged as she crossed the room's threshold. "I've always tried not to place too much importance on what some people think of my appearance."

Alec cocked a brow. "It isn't only 'some people.' I seem to recall you were once a celebrated debutante."

"That was five years ago. And mostly on account of my mother's pedigree and my father's wealth," she demurred. "Last I checked, the fashion plates were full of buxom blond ladies."

The corner of his mouth lifted. "More's the pity then," he murmured, taking pains not to cast a sweeping glance down her form. "Most gentlemen can appreciate a wide variety of feminine attributes."

She narrowed her eyes. "And most women would like to be valued for more than their looks."

"Of course." Alec grinned. "I would never *dare* suggest otherwise." A dull note of warning began to buzz at the back of his mind. He was taking far too much pleasure in their exchange.

Then the indignant expression returned; he loved when she looked at him like that, as it usually precluded a delightfully sardonic comment. "That may be true in your case, but I'm sure I don't need to explain that most men do not appreciate intelligence, or even the very illusion of it, in a woman."

Alec then leaned forward conspiratorially. "And as a woman of intellect, I'm sure you already know that most men are idiots."

Lottie's color heightened and she pressed her lips together. "I've a third condition," she began. "No more compliments. Of *any* kind."

"I'm not sure I can agree to that," he chuckled. "But I'll try." At those last words her eyes warmed and Alec had a sudden, vicious craving to know her thoughts.

Damn. That wasn't supposed to happen, either.

"Come." He turned abruptly and moved toward the balcony. "You must see the view."

Alec immediately regretted this decision, as the pair of them barely fit on the tiny balcony. The sky above had begun to flush pink from the setting sun, while the cathedral's bell tower gently pealed the hour. It was as if the heavens and earth had conspired to design the perfect romantic moment. He longed to pull her to him once again and feel her side melt against his. She might not think she compared to the so-called buxom ladies in fashion plates, but to Alec her gentle curves had been the perfect fit. He settled for gripping the railing in front of him instead.

"My goodness," Lottie breathed as she took it all in, entirely unaware of the direction of his thoughts. "Who would have guessed?"

"It's one of the things I love about this country. You can be in a crumbling alleyway one moment, then turn a corner and you're in the most beautiful, glowing square filled with life." Out of the corner of his eye, he saw Lottie turn to him.

"Didn't . . . didn't your father write a poem about that?"

Alec gave a reluctant nod even though he knew he should be grateful for the subject change. Nothing dampened the mood quite like his father. Edward Gresham had found both fame—and infamy—writing about his beloved adopted country. "'And as I stood in Saint Mark's Square, with the pantomime of life all 'round, I saw how little I had lived before and how much was left unbound.'"

Lottie smiled. "That's it."

"I thought Edward Gresham was considered much too vulgar for proper young ladies."

Lottie clucked her tongue. "Perhaps that was true a decade ago, but he's considered something of a romantic hero now."

Alec couldn't stifle his derisive snort. He had seen first-hand the devastation that had come from such love. There was nothing remotely romantic about it.

"Besides," she went on, "I refuse to limit my reading to what is considered 'proper.' That would be incredibly boring."

"I can't argue with that."

Lottie tilted her head, considering him. "Did you *really* not know of his reputation?"

He shrugged and turned back to the view. "I left all that business to your uncle. What do I know about poetry?" It had been a relief to have someone else manage the copyright. Sir Alfred had always talked of putting together a collection of his father's work, and Alec happily gave his blessing to keep Edward Gresham's short, tragic life from being stripped of all meaning. As long as he had nothing to do with it.

"I'd say you know quite a lot. More than most people," she added.

Alec's hands tightened on the railing, but he didn't respond.

Lottie cleared her throat. "The edition Uncle Alfred released of the collected poems sold out its entire first printing. The second went even faster."

Alec vaguely remembered that his payments had increased for a time, but his focus had been on how the money would be spent.

"And I helped put it together."

At that he faced her. "I didn't realize you were such an acolyte."

A faint blush stained her cheekbones. "I wasn't. It was merely something to do at first. Something more interesting than making calls, anyway. But the way your father wrote about Italy with such passion, such love, as if he were writing about a person..." She paused and shook her head. "I had always wanted to visit the village, you know, because of my parents. But after I read his poems, I wanted to come here for the rest of the country as well."

Spurred by her words, a memory suddenly surfaced: Alec traipsing over a bridge on a warm spring afternoon, his father's large hand clutching his own. They were swinging their arms back and forth while Alec repeated lines of poetry back to him. *It won't stand up on the page if it cannot stand up to life*, his father had explained. The conviction in his voice still rang out across the decades. They had spent so many days just like that: wandering around the city while his father worked out rhythms.

"And has Italy lived up to your expectations?" His voice had gone a bit thick.

Lottie gave him a soft, sad smile. "In a way." Then she sighed. "But I hadn't realized that he wasn't writing about a country so much as the nature of love."

Alec's fingers gripped the railing even tighter. "Yes. My mother was quite a woman."

She was immortalized in his father's poems as a dazzlingly beautiful but humble laundress whose hazel eyes and silky, gold-spun curls had arrested him from across a canal. The pair had fallen deeply in love before they even spoke, and she was rescued from a life of hard labor.

A devastatingly romantic story. Not a word was true.

Lottie gave Alec a puzzled frown. "That was part of it, certainly," she began slowly, as if she was choosing her words with the utmost care. "But I wasn't speaking only of romance. He loved the both of you; the life you all had together. I found that most affecting." She paused to take a breath. Or to gather her courage. Alec braced himself for what was coming. "And it helped me to understand later why he ... he—"

"—drank himself to death."

Lottie closed her eyes against the words. Only then did Alec realize he had practically shouted them. He heard Sir Alfred's chiding voice, as he always did in moments like this:

A gentleman never breaks.

"I'm sorry," she whispered. "I didn't mean to upset you." When she opened her eyes, they glistened like two emerald pools.

Alec wanted nothing more than to sink into them, to be swallowed whole by their fathomless depths until he was enveloped in suffocating, comforting numbness. An impossibility. "I'm not upset. It was ages ago. I barely remember either of them." He didn't bother trying to mask the flat, hollow tone in his voice. For Lottie wouldn't dare challenge him.

It was widely accepted that his father had died from "heartbreak" after his wife's passing. This fitting, understandable, and, most important, sympathetic explanation likely contributed to his posthumous reputation as a romantic hero. Alec would always be grateful to Sir Alfred for covering up the truth—that his mother had actually been married to another man, had *chosen* to leave, and had died years after Edward Gresham, a rather important revelation Alec had not known until it was far too late.

"He did love you, Alec," she offered. "You mustn't ever think he didn't."

Now he understood the wisdom of Lottie's second condition. Hearing her say his name in such a sweet, gentle tone sent a thundering shiver of longing down his spine that would have brought a weaker man to his knees. Her eyes filled with tender sympathy as she slowly reached for his hand, on the verge of breaking her second condition. But Alec would not let her soothe him as if he were a little boy crying over a scraped knee. He simply couldn't. If she touched him now, he would never let her go. He would pull her down into the murky depths with him, and she deserved so much more. Even a Florentine con man was preferable to what little he could offer.

Alec whipped his arm away with such force that Lottie jerked back. "Dammit. I'm sorry," he burst out and pulled a hand roughly through his hair. It seemed he couldn't talk about his parents without going a little bit mad himself. He began to say more but was interrupted by a sharp rap at the door.

Lottie immediately moved to answer it. "That must be your amenities," she said lightly, as if his outburst had never happened.

Alec could only stare after her, frustrated and helpless. Her cool mask had descended once again. And he must bear it.

CHAPTER EIGHT

Lottie's hand trembled as she gripped the doorknob. She shouldn't have pushed Alec to talk about his father. He would never touch her in anger—that was the only thing she could say for certain—but the force of his outburst had still been a surprise. Alec wasn't made of stone, after all, and she hadn't seen him lose his temper like that in years. Not since he was much younger. But for a very brief moment, she caught a glimpse of the passionate creature he had once been, of the boy who had simply *blazed* with life.

Even he couldn't have put on that kind of devastation. Blistering anguish like that came only from within. Built upon a foundation forged from extreme loss. Lottie had the same scaffolds inside, but her walls were erected to protect what few memories she had of her beloved parents.

Alec's, though...Alec's held back pain. And rage.

I'm not upset. It was ages ago. I barely remember either of them.

They were lies. Every one.

He had spoken of his mother a little when they first met, but never his father. Lottie had always assumed he hated the man. That he had been a brute. And so she hated him, too. It wasn't until she worked with Uncle Alfred on the collected poems that she learned anything about the mysterious Edward Gresham and came to understand that Alec's silence wasn't born out of hate at all, but agony.

I don't believe I ever knew a more dedicated father, Uncle Alfred had explained. *There was always a darkness to Edward, even when we were schoolboys, but Alec brought him such joy. He had been well for so long that no one expected him to fall as far as he did after the loss of his wife. I was in Venice at the time, but Edward refused to see anyone. Even Alec couldn't pull him out of it. No matter how hard he tried. I never saw anything so heartbreaking as the image of that boy pounding helplessly on the door of his father's study. Sometimes he spent all day at it. But Edward never let him in. Not once.*

This revelation had stunned Lottie. *What must it have been like to fight so desperately for his father's life,* she had wondered, *and still lose?*

Alec had been gone for three years at that point, and so her newfound sympathy eventually faded away; but now, in the face of his obvious grief, her heart broke all over again for him. He certainly wouldn't want her pity, though. And it seemed that he didn't want her help, either. She pulled open the door to reveal two maids holding a sizable tin tub, while two more carried a large cistern of steaming water between them. All four were dark-haired beauties, likely sisters, who looked incredibly perturbed to be there. Until they caught sight of Alec.

"Buona sera." Lottie waved them in and stepped aside.

The maids marched into the room and began setting up the bath with swift, competent movements. Two poured the water into the bath, while another added a generous helping of sweet-smelling oil and flower petals from a small basket. The fourth retrieved a screen from a corner of the room and neatly arranged it by a chair laden with fresh towels. All the while, each one took every opportunity to throw brazen looks at Alec. If they had actually been married, Lottie would have been rather piqued—not that she could blame them.

Alec leaned against the balcony's doorway with his hands in his pockets and his eyes cast down, oblivious to their attentions; his mouth was set in a hard line and his brow was furrowed in deep concentration. The setting sun bathed him in that perfect pinkish glow artists only dream of. He resembled a powerful Roman general mulling over strategy on the eve of battle.

Lottie's heart beat even faster than before, when she stood frozen in the doorway taking far too much pleasure in his declaration.

You are *very beautiful.*

She had thought herself long immune to the shallow flatteries of men, so it was unsettling how badly she had wanted to believe him. But to what end? Finding her attractive certainly hadn't stopped him from leaving five years ago. No, there was little to be gained by catching the eye of a man. Better to be treated with respect, considered an equal. Though that seemed even more elusive. Lottie began riffling through her carpet bag, if only to have something to do besides stare at him.

After the maids finished preparing the bath, Alec gave each of them a coin. They all finally deigned to speak and made a great show of profusely thanking him. The prettiest one even went so far as to place a palm on his chest, cooing, "Sei un uomo così gentile, generoso." Alec's only response was to pluck her hand off his person. She gave a haughty sniff at his rejection and swept grandly out of the room while the other three followed. Not one spared Lottie even a glance.

She rolled her lips between her teeth, trying to contain her laughter, but it was no use. Alec shot her an irritated look but he, too, was fighting back a smile.

"You might want to apologize to the young lady. I see a great future for you here, working alongside Signore Garda."

Alec raised an eyebrow, amused. "Is that so?" He rubbed his jaw in mock consideration. "I suppose there are some similarities between espionage and innkeeping."

"You must admit, it would be an excellent cover."

"That is true. You'd be surprised by how useful inn-keepers are."

Her smile faded at the unintended implication of his words. "Yes. I can imagine." Alec must have questioned the inn-keeper in Florence, a sharp-eyed British emigre. Lottie had taken pains to avoid the older man when she slipped away from the pension, but perhaps she had not been so careful.

He seemed to guess at her thoughts. "You take your time here," he said, gesturing to the bath. "I'll go see about our dinner. Make sure that door stays locked."

Then he was gone before Lottie could manage another word.

By the time Alec returned, Lottie had washed, dried, and changed. After a bit of dithering she had donned a pale blue tea gown, as her sensible skirt and blouse were dusty from the road. If she had still been in her cottage, she wouldn't have given it a thought, but the lacy gown was designed for more intimate company and meant to be worn without a corset. Lottie then chided herself for even *worrying* about such a thing. It seemed unlikely that Alec would be scandalized, if he even noticed.

Lottie sat in a chair by the window plaiting her damp hair and watching the sky turn ever deeper shades of pink when she heard the key in the lock. The door swung open, and Alec bent down to retrieve the tray he had brought up with him.

As he entered, a heavenly smell filled the room, and Lottie's stomach quietly rumbled. It had been hours since their respite by the river, though it felt far longer.

"I've brought provisions," Alec announced as he moved to set the tray down on the table bearing two plates of food, a small pitcher of water, and two glasses. "Roasted chicken. Signore Garda assured me they still use their nonna's recipe. I—" He glanced up as she stood and paused.

His eyes moved steadily down her form with such deliberateness that it nearly felt like a caress. Lottie stood a little straighter and tried to ignore the growing appreciation in them. It did *not* matter. And she did *not* care. When she took a step forward, Alec's eyes leapt back to her face before he immediately looked away.

"I—here," he mumbled as he set the tray down on the table. "Here it is."

Lottie took a seat. "It smells delicious," she said briskly, hoping to cut the tension that suddenly filled the air. "Won't you sit down?"

Alec shook his head emphatically, as if she had offered him poison. He took a large step back from both the table and her. "I'll wash up. Before the water goes cold." Lottie gave an artfully careless shrug and picked up a fork. But Alec remained in place watching her. She cast him an inquisitive glance and he snapped to attention and moved toward the tub behind her.

As she cut into the tender chicken, the screen scraped along the floor. She smiled to herself. Who knew Alec was so modest? But then came the telltale rustling of clothing being removed. Lottie's throat suddenly went bone dry, and she poured herself a glass of water from the pitcher. Just as she brought it to her lips, there was a light splash as Alec stepped into the tub. She immediately pictured one long, well-muscled leg joining the other as he slowly eased himself into the tepid water. Alec let out a faint sigh and the water sloshed around the tub, making room for his tall frame. Lottie took a generous sip from her cup and attempted to focus on her food. It was excellent. If Signore Garda's *nonna* were here, Lottie would compliment her profusely. Then again, the woman would likely be far too preoccupied by the large, naked man in the tub behind her...

Lottie gave herself a shake and cut off another piece of chicken, but as she began to chew, Alec started humming the "Major-General's Song" from *The Pirates of Penzance.*

Lottie began to mutter the lyrics while she ate, all in a losing battle to distract herself.

I am the very model of a modern Major-General,
I've information vegetable, animal, and mineral...

The light splashing was now accompanied by the steady sound of scrubbing as Alec soaped his body. An image of tanned, soap-lathered skin flashed through her mind. Lottie shook her head and continued to focus on the lyrics.

I know the kings of England, and I quote the fights
    historical
From Marathon to Waterloo, in order categorical—

Lottie had nearly gotten through the entire song while Alec hummed and scrubbed and rinsed until she thought she might go mad. Finally, blessed silence returned and Lottie let out a little sigh of relief. But it was only for a moment.

Then the sloshing grew to a furious crescendo as Alec rose. Before she even knew what she was doing, Lottie turned around. Like the screen in her room the night before,

Alec's shadow was clearly visible; Lottie was spared the most intimate details, but there was still plenty to see. Alec's usually wavy hair now hung in wet ringlets around his head, and the curved lines of his arms were exposed as he reached back to scratch his neck. Water cascaded down his body as he bent over to grab a towel off the chair and wrapped it around his trim waist. As Alec stepped out from behind the screen, the sight of his bare chest was so riveting that Lottie failed to turn around in time. Alec glanced over and immediately froze. He caught her full on gawking. With her mouth hanging open.

Alec had always appreciated the female gaze. Watching a woman admire his appearance was, in his opinion, an underrated pleasure. Vastly more erotic than having someone submit to his own desires. But when he stepped out from behind the screen and found Lottie staring at him with such obvious lust, it felt like a torture designed by a particularly vengeful god: being wanted by the one woman he could never have.

Alec had gone days without sleeping or eating. Had marched for miles through oppressive, unbearable heat with only the hope of water. Had played (and won) an eight-hour game of poker against two men with separate orders to kill him afterward.

But he was not strong enough for this.

Her pale blue confection, with its well-placed bows and lacy undergown, was a far cry from the sensible skirts and blouses she had worn the previous two days. It was just the right combination of sweet and sensual; the overrobe gave the appearance of demure innocence while the open front still called attention to those delicate curves that lay beneath only a few flimsy layers. For once, Alec had been grateful for a tepid bath.

Now his scalp tingled with the kind of predatory awareness big cats must feel when they spot a tasty gazelle. A fleeting look, a suggestive remark, or an accidental touch was one thing, but Alec had not prepared to be outright *ogled* by her.

Lottie's cheeks turned an impressive shade of crimson while they stared at each other, and after the longest moment of his life, she finally turned away. "Oh, goodness. I'm sorry!" She buried her face in her hands.

Alec took a step toward her before remembering he wore absolutely nothing besides a towel. "Hold on." He let out an irritated huff and quickly retrieved a clean shirt from his bag. Alec moved back behind the screen, though it was doubtful even Lottie would be bold enough to turn around for another eyeful now, and dressed with a speed usually reserved for life or death situations. He had absolutely no idea what to say.

Your conduct must be as gentlemanly as possible. At all *times.*

He had assured Lottie it would not be a problem, but apparently it was not his own conduct he needed to worry about. His skin was still damp from the bath, but the very thought of those plump lips parting for him once again, of her velvety tongue boldly tangling with his own, made him hot everywhere. Alec pressed a hard hand against the front of his trousers. At the moment the only thing stopping him from throwing her over his shoulder and taking her to bed was that second condition. But one word of encouragement from her and he would tear that bloody dress off with his teeth.

Even if she is attracted to you, it won't last.

He might as well have leapt back into the tub. Lottie might have been openly admiring his figure, but that didn't change anything between them. Though he could concede that she might have had feelings for him that went beyond friendship before he left, she had made it abundantly clear over the previous day that she didn't trust him and hadn't denied that a man was involved in her flight from Florence. She might have even purchased that very dress with *him* in mind. Even as Alec acknowledged the fellow had excellent taste, his stomach twisted with a strange mixture of jealousy and sympathy. He was quite familiar with using pleasure as a distraction from heartache.

And how poorly it worked.

He didn't want that for Lottie. No doubt her interest was merely due to the novelty of their situation, and it would fade with a little more time. So time was what he would give her. Alec took a deep breath and gave himself a shake before he emerged from behind the screen, now fully dressed. Lottie hadn't moved an inch. Her face was still buried in her hands. Alec took the seat opposite her. Better not to talk about it. To act like it was nothing. Because it *was* nothing. And, in the meantime, dinner still needed to be eaten.

After a few moments, she looked up. "Wh-what are you doing?" Her complexion had begun to return to its normal color, as bewilderment replaced embarrassment.

Alec shrugged and took another bite, praying this strategy would work. "I'm starving. Are you going to eat that?" He pointed to her remaining piece of chicken with his knife.

Lottie stared at her plate and then back to him. "Oh. No, you can have it."

Alec reached over and speared it with his fork. As she continued to watch him eat, the tension slowly eased from her shoulders. He finished and sat back in his chair, taking care to meet her eyes with an open, friendly expression. Perhaps that was all it would take. It had to.

But then Lottie began to frown. "Al—"

"It's fine," he said quickly. Dear God, he couldn't listen to his name on her lips yet *again*. "You don't need to explain. Everyone is curious now and again."

Her frown deepened. "Curious?"

Alec tried to ignore the incredulous note in her voice with an encouraging nod even while he wondered what, exactly, she had done with this mysterious suitor of hers. He could practically see the questions hovering on her lips, and the longing in her eyes that betrayed a deep ache that could only be soothed by intense, physical pleasure. At some point during her silence, Alec's hands had found their way to the edge of the chair and he dug in hard, waiting for her answer. If she pushed him right now, even a little, he wasn't sure he had the will to deny her. And then there would be hell to pay for them both.

Then, finally, thankfully, Lottie blinked and nodded. "Yes. Right." She rose to clear their dishes.

Alec released a long breath and relaxed his grip, but it would be another few seconds before he could stand. After Lottie had stacked their plates on the tray, she glanced toward him. "I think I'll retire now. It's been a long day."

"Very good." He remained seated and ran through the plans for tomorrow in his head, but all the while he listened to the sounds of her washing up and changing. It was soothing to hear someone go about their evening routine, and his heartbeat slowly returned to normal.

After a few minutes, she appeared from behind the screen, now wearing her nightgown and an ice-blue silk wrapper. It was a good deal plainer than her tea gown, but the lack of accoutrements meant there was little to distract the eye from her figure. He resumed his iron grip on the chair, but Lottie paid him no mind while she rummaged through her carpet bag and pulled out a book.

"What have you got there?" he asked in a strangled voice.

Lottie showed him the cover. "*Hints to Lady Travellers: At Home and Abroad.*"

He let out a snort. "I suppose they'll print anything these days."

"This book hasn't gone out of print in nearly ten years. Women *do* travel, you know. And often alone." Then Lottie raised an eyebrow. "I had no idea you had become so conservative."

"I'm nothing of the sort," Alec protested. "I didn't realize there was a demand for such information."

"Well, it may interest you to know that I'm hardly an outlier. Haven't you heard of Gertrude Bell, or Isabella Bird?"

Alec shot her a sour look. "*Yes.*" Isabella Bird's extensive world travels had made her a household name, not to mention the first woman allowed to join the Royal Geographical Society. Why, Sir Alfred knew the woman personally. And Alec had quite enjoyed Bell's *Persian Pictures*. "I've no objection to adventuresses."

"Just as long as I'm not one of them?"

Alec narrowed his eyes. Those women were different. They had built their whole *lives* around discovery—and it hadn't come without a personal price. "I certainly hope you aren't intending to travel farther east. It's dangerous."

Lottie pointedly ignored his gaze as she moved to the bed. "Whatever I do after this is not any of your concern."

Alec opened his mouth and then quickly shut it. He longed to challenge her, but with what? She was absolutely right. He pulled a hand through his hair, strode over to his own battered bag, and spent the next several minutes taking his frustrations out on his toiletries. After a few satisfying bangs, he cut a sidelong glance at Lottie. She had removed her wrapper and was tucked under the covers reading by the light of the little bedside oil lamp.

He imagined her cuddled up on a narrow camp bed in a canvas tent while a sandstorm raged outside, perfectly content. Was that really the kind of life she wanted?

"You aren't going to sleep on the floor again, are you?" Lottie didn't bother looking up as she flicked a page.

"What?" He was distracted by a trail of freckles that ran down the side of her neck before disappearing beneath the nightgown's neckline, like the world's most erotic treasure map.

She met his eyes and shrugged as if she had suggested something utterly harmless, like opening a window. "The bed is massive, and you do look tired."

Alec shook his head slowly. "I don't think so."

Lottie gave him a pitying smile. "You're being rather silly about this. We won't be anywhere *near* each other."

Alec cleared his throat by way of answer. It was a fair point. The bed could easily sleep four, but it wasn't the size that worried him.

"Besides," she added slyly, "it's not as if we've never slept next to each other before."

Of all the times to call upon their shared past…

"That was *different*!" he sputtered.

Lottie canted her head and studied him, as if he was a coded message to crack. "How so?"

Alec gritted his teeth so the words wouldn't slip out: *You didn't have* breasts *yet*.

The summer he was twelve and she was eight, they had spent the night in a little playhouse in the woods that Lottie called her "fairy cottage." They ate tinned food and slept side by side in two camp beds pretending they were American pioneers. It was entirely innocent, but when the gamekeeper discovered them the following morning, Alec was sent to Sir Alfred's study, where he was promptly caned without any preamble. Alec made no protest and shed no tears, but he did not forget his guardian's parting words: *I'm a patient man, Alec. But you need to learn your place. And it is* not *with her.*

He was then sent back to school even though term wouldn't start for another month.

When he returned for Christmas, Lottie nearly made herself sick from crying so hard. She didn't stop until Alec hid them behind a curtain in the library and pulled her onto his lap.

After a time, she calmed down enough to speak: "Promise me you won't go away ever again," she sniffled into his shirt. "Promise you won't leave me."

"Not if I can help it," he vowed, full of the kind of righteous anger only the very young can muster.

But there was nothing he could do then. Neither of them was in control of their lives. And Alec could not afford to anger his guardian any further. He knew very well there was nowhere else for him to go. After that, Alec always made sure to keep a proper distance between himself and Lottie, especially in Sir Alfred's presence. When she grew a little older, she understood and reciprocated. They were still friends, of course, but an invisible wall grew between them. It wasn't until the night of her ball that he dared to hold her so close once again.

Lottie still stared at him, awaiting his answer. "We were children," he growled.

And that was all he intended to say on the subject.

Before she could make one of her snippy replies, Alec turned away and pretended to look for his coat. "There are a few more things I need to do this evening. Get some rest. I'll be fine."

"But—"

"And I want to check on Lorenzo. Make sure he's settled."

There. She wouldn't argue with that.

The rest of his plan involved staying the hell out of this room until she was fast asleep. Alec pulled on his coat and headed for the door. Her expression had softened into something resembling acceptance. "All right." But just before she turned back to her book, disappointment flickered in her eyes. Alec's fingers slipped against the doorknob before he resumed his iron grip. So be it. Let her be disappointed by him. She should be used to it by now.

"Don't wait up for me," he said as he flung open the door and stamped out of the room.

CHAPTER NINE

〜

After Alec's rather loud exit, Lottie made several valiant attempts to concentrate on her book, but it was useless. Even when he wasn't in the room, the air still seemed to hum with tension. As if the very atoms themselves restlessly awaited his return. Lottie finally tossed her book aside and turned down the lamp. Perhaps it hadn't been very sporting of her to tease Alec about sharing the bed, but when she caught his heavy-lidded stare, a wave of heat had seared her from the inside out; his steady gaze pinned her even from across the room, until he blinked and turned positively *missish*.

She hadn't really meant anything untoward by the suggestion—the bed *was* massive, and he had been covertly rubbing his shoulder all day. His scandalized reaction was all the more surprising, given how easily he had brushed off her ogling of his naked person only minutes before. Then when she alluded to their childhood sleep-out, Alec had blushed so furiously she thought steam would shoot from his ears. His clipped response was little more than a growl, but it sounded as if he was fighting against something.

And losing.

Lottie thought she'd buried her ridiculous romantic streak

years ago back in London, but for a glimmering moment it had taken hold of her heart and whispered its seductive delusions once again:

He does *want you. All this must have happened so you could finally be together.*

Until Alec had practically catapulted from the room, leaving her alone with only her pitiful desires for company.

Lottie closed her eyes and tried to will herself to sleep, but instead her mind summoned the image of Alec's bare chest dusted with dark hair still damp from the bathwater. She had never given much thought to something as ordinary as collarbones before, but now she longed to have another look at his.

No, that wasn't right.

She didn't want anything as innocent as a simple *look*. Lottie craved something deeper. Something darker. To drag her tongue along the length of each one with studied care, so she could savor the taste, the smell, the texture of his skin. She hadn't ever wanted to do something so purely carnal before. Now she positively ached for it.

Lottie opened her eyes and let out a frustrated sigh. This lingering uneasiness between them, as if something had been left unsolved, would drive her mad. That was why she loved puzzles. There was always an answer. But her and Alec... their jagged edges no longer seemed to match. And no matter how hard she mashed them together, they would never fit. At least, not in the way she had once wanted.

That is not the kind of life for a man with a family.

Uncle Alfred had been quite right at the time, but Lottie wasn't a naive nineteen-year-old anymore. Perhaps it wasn't that the problem was unsolvable, but that she needed to change her answer. Alec might not want a family, or a wife, but he must want *something*. And she hadn't imagined the heat in his eyes, just like she hadn't imagined the evidence of his desire the previous day.

Lottie twisted the warm sheets in her hands. She had spent the last five years waiting for someone else to spark even a hint of what she had once felt for Alec—and it had all come to nothing. *Worse* than nothing. For no matter what Alec or Uncle Alfred tried to say, her reputation had already been irrevocably damaged the night she publicly rejected Ceril Belvedere.

Lottie had been blindsided by the priggish young man's ardent kiss on Lady Arlington's balcony, as well as the clumsy proposal that followed, but she had refused him in the gentlest terms she could think of: "I'm afraid we don't suit."

At first Ceril appeared to be equally blindsided by her answer, but then his rather pallid complexion turned bright crimson and his slender frame began to quake.

"You—you're rejecting me?" he sputtered, staring down at his freshly polished shoes. She had never seen him speak with such emotion before. About anything.

Lottie couldn't help feeling sorry for him. She, too, was familiar with the pain of rejection and moved to pat his shoulder. "I apologize for any disappointment this may have caused you; it was never my intention."

But before she could make contact, Ceril suddenly looked up; his dark eyes were filled with hatred and Lottie immediately drew back her hand. Her suggestion seemed only to anger him further. "*Disappointment?*" he snarled. "Your father was nobody. *I* will be an earl. You should be grateful I ever paid an old maid like you any mind."

Lottie knew she should walk away then. Knew she should keep her mouth shut, and not cause a scene. Let him throw his little tantrum and be done with it. After all, he was hardly the first man to spout such drivel, but the trouble was Lottie hadn't ever felt this *tired* before.

She was angry. Affronted. And she refused to listen to this horrid little man cast aspersions on her beloved father, whose life had been worth ten of his.

"Yes," she seethed. "How could I not be grateful for the attention given to my fortune." She stepped forward until it was Ceril's back against the wall. "And my father may not have been born into a title, but he certainly possessed enough sense to balance his accounts."

Ceril looked positively shocked to have his less-than-honorable intentions, as well as his family's reckless spending, called out so plainly. Then the frown returned, darker than ever. "The rumors about you are true. You're nothing but a jilt. *And* a tease."

If she had been a man, Lottie would have called him out. She had only ever been polite, as etiquette dictated she be to every man who asked her to dance or made conversation. There was no point wasting anything more on him. Without another word, she spun on her heels and returned to the ball-room, but instead of letting her go quietly, Ceril had been right behind her and took no pains to hide his extreme displeasure. It was clear to everyone what had happened between them. But all sympathies fell to the desirable young bachelor, not the lady on her fifth season.

Such was the way of things.

Even Uncle Alfred would not defend her: "I've tried to reason with the chap, but he won't have you now. He's planning to offer for that damned American glue heiress instead. You could have been a *countess*, Lottie. I won't indulge in your silly notions any longer."

Those "silly notions" had been waiting for a love match. For what was the use of having her own fortune if she couldn't even do that? "Uncle, you can't have expected me to marry Ceril—"

"Ceril Belvedere is *exactly* the kind of man you should marry." Before she could illuminate him on the finer details of what *exactly* that meant, he plowed ahead. "I made a terrible mistake in allowing your mother to marry whomever she wanted, and look what happened to *her*."

This accusation had rendered her speechless.

Lottie's father was the only son of a wildly successful Scottish tool manufacturer. Not a blue blood by any means, but John Carlisle was well educated and ambitious. He had met Lottie's mother, Ada, while she was admiring the June roses in Regent's Park and later described it as "love at first bloom." Though tongues had wagged over the parvenu groom, the Carlisles enjoyed an unusually happy marriage, until they died in an all-too-ordinary carriage crash in Richmond.

Lottie's eyes prickled. "That was an *accident*," she said thickly.

"And it will not happen to you," he vowed. Uncle Alfred was always absolute in his opinions, but she had never seen this nonsensical side of him before. "I can only assume that a case of nerves has led you to behave so irrationally," he continued. "You need rest. Take a trip somewhere and prepare yourself. Because jilt or no, you *will* be married by the end of next season. Even if it's not anyone of quality."

Lottie could only imagine the type of man who would offer for her now: a moldering aristocrat desperate for funds or some politician Uncle Alfred needed to manipulate. Or worse. It was then she understood that she could never bargain with him again. And it was then that she first began to form her plan. But though it had been fairly easy to create the illusion she was ruined, making it true was another matter entirely.

There were benefits she had not considered. At least, not until Alec turned up on her doorstep...

At some point in the night, hours after he left, Alec returned. Lottie heard him stumble around the darkened room before he came to the edge of the bed and watched her in the shadowy darkness to make sure she was asleep.

"Lottie," he murmured, loud enough to get her attention but soft enough not to wake.

She bit down on her lip. This was a trap. She wanted so badly to answer him, to pull him down on top of her, to have one rough palm spread her wide and take what she gave, but not now. Eventually, he sat down on the other side of the bed. Then came the sound of boots dropping on the floor. Alec let out a weary sigh as he laid down on top of the covers. A man in control would have been able to share her bed without reservations, while a man determined not to lose control would have slept in the chair.

But Alec seemed torn. And when he finally let his guard down, there would be Lottie waiting to be ruined.

It had taken hours before Alec rebuilt his will to the point where he could enter their room. And yet, as soon as he stepped inside, it promptly crumbled to bits. The very air was filled with her scent of rosewater and warm skin. But after days of too little sleep, that bed was enticing as hell even without the presence of Lottie. He only needed a few uninterrupted hours of rest. Then he would fully regain his control. *And* his reason.

That night his sleep was mercifully dark and dreamless.

Until it wasn't.

In the waking hours the rules governing polite society and his remaining shreds of self-control separated them. But here, in the deepest recesses of his subconscious, Alec was free to do as he wished, as he *desired*. Here Lottie wanted him.

And only him.

Alec approached her from behind and slipped his arms around her waist. He buried his nose in her loose hair and inhaled deeply as he pulled her body against his own. On the terrace their layers of clothing had kept them apart, but now only a slip of gauzy silk came between them. He smoothed a palm slowly down to her hip, then drew her round, ripe bottom against his aroused flesh.

He could feel everything—her soft gasp, the warmth of her skin, every beat of her thudding heart.

"Are you frightened?" he whispered, letting his lips graze the soft shell of her ear.

She let out a short laugh. "A little."

Alec's mouth curved. "I'll be so gentle, my love."

Lottie raised an arm and stroked his hair, just as she had done yesterday. "I know. I trust you."

The words tore at his heart, as painful as they were pleasurable. He had done nothing to earn her trust, but he would take it all the same. Then she pressed back against him and Alec nearly lost his mind as the shock of pleasure radiated through his starved body. He rolled his hips, reveling in the feel of her soft flesh cupping his swelling erection. It had been so long. *Too* long. But he had been waiting this whole time. Waiting for her without even realizing it.

He moved his hand away from her waist and skimmed his fingers along the curve of her small but shapely breast. Then he began to gently pluck her nipple with his thumb and forefinger. She drew in a long, ragged breath.

"Do you like that?" he murmured.

She laughed again, but it was shorter and more breathless this time. "I suspect I'll like anything you do."

His response was little more than a desperate grunt. Alec slid his hand down her side. The silky gown slipped between his fingers as he drew up the hem. Then he brushed ever so lightly against her sex. Lottie moaned her encouragement and her fingers curled tighter in his hair, tugging at his scalp. He pressed harder, working that most sensitive spot. Of course, because this was a dream she was already shuddering toward her release. But his dreams had never been so detailed before. He could feel her slickness, could practically taste the salt of her skin.

And yet, he needed more. He needed everything.

"Alec."

The sound of his name on her lips spoken in such raw desperation pierced the veil of sleep. Alec's mind tried furtively to cling to the fantasy as it slipped through his fingers like grains of sand, but then he woke to the sound of rustling and the feel of a warm body pressed against his own.

One that could only belong to Lottie.

Alec's eyes shot open. His arm was flung possessively around her waist and his *hips*—Christ, he was practically grinding them against her backside.

He immediately pushed away from her and fell directly onto the floor, landing on his back in a room-shaking thud. Alec stared up at the ceiling in a daze as his heart still pounded from the turns of his wicked mind.

After a moment, Lottie poked her head over the side of the bed and blinked sleepily. "Are you all right?"

He let out a relieved sigh. Thank God she had slept through his attempted ravishing. "Fine. I...I must have had a nightmare."

Lottie stared at him. "You were asleep?"

Alec shot up off the floor. "You *weren't*?"

Her brows rose in shock and she sat back on her knees.

He took in the deep flush on her cheeks and lips, and in the early-morning light the rosy tips of her nipples were just barely visible beneath her sheer cotton chemise. Alec's fingers twitched and he turned around as his cock began to stir again, as if he was nothing more than a randy schoolboy. But wasn't this the very stuff of a schoolboy's dreams? Alec pressed a hand roughly against the front of his trousers and took a calming breath as an unsettling thought came to him: Had *any* of it been a dream?

He whirled back around. Lottie hadn't moved from her place on the bed—and still looked freshly tumbled.

"Alec," she murmured. Her voice, husky from sleep, sounded exactly as it had in his dream; like the very devil herself was calling to him. But if Alec took so much as a step toward her now, it would be all over. He would not stop until he wrenched everything from her, from them both. Lottie had no idea how deep the rot inside him went. Not a clue. And he needed to keep it from her.

I imagine I will like anything you do.

Alec ignored the throbbing between his thighs and raked a hand through his hair.

"I'm sorry if I—I violated you in any way," he said. "This is entirely my fault. I should have slept on the chair."

She reared back in confusion. *"Violated?"*

Alec let out a desperate huff and placed his hands on his hips. Her reaction was not helping matters. She should be mortified. Outraged. Disgusted. Not—not *hurt*. "Well, what else would you call it?"

"You didn't force yourself on me," Lottie insisted. "I thought you meant—" she began, then seemed to think better of it and shut her mouth.

"What?" he demanded, his voice tight with anxiety. "Did I say something?"

God damn it, if he had spoken *any* of it aloud, and if she questioned him on it now, he would fall apart.

Lottie's eyes widened. She hesitated, wetting her lips, their fate on the tip of her tongue, but then she shook her head. "No. You didn't."

Alec let out a sigh, but the relief was cold comfort. Barely a taste of her, and it was already miles better than anything he had experienced.

He turned his head away. "Then for God's sake I wish *you* had."

Lottie winced at the anguish in his voice. She didn't know which felt worse: his worry over her reaction, or his very palpable regret for having *touched* her in the first place, however briefly.

Though Lottie's heart had begun to pump with furious anticipation when Alec's arm had slowly wrapped around her waist drawing her firmly against him and offering a tantalizing tease of what lay beneath his clothing, it was nothing compared to the pure joy that had burned through her when he murmured *my love*. But the utter horror that crossed Alec's face shortly afterward made it clear that he certainly hadn't been dreaming of her.

"It was nothing. Really. You were obviously asleep and it was a momentary indiscretion. There's no need to make this into more than it was," she said stiffly. If he had so easily brushed her off last night, she could do the same now. "*I* certainly won't."

Alec blinked slowly. "Forgive me," he began. "I didn't realize it was of such little consequence to you."

Lottie clenched her hands against his bone-dry tone. "Well, I'm certainly not going to give in to a *swoon* because your penis pressed against me for twenty blasted seconds."

Lottie had never said the word *penis* aloud before. To anyone. Not even herself. She was rather proud not to have stumbled over it. "Yes, I *do* happen to have a basic knowledge of biology," she railed on in the face of his obvious shock, masking her hurt with impudence. "And in case you weren't aware, women are just as prone to desires of the flesh as men are."

Alec collected himself enough to shoot her a murderous look. "I am quite familiar, I assure you."

Lottie ignored the jealous flare in her chest and lifted her chin. "Then we understand each other," she said with a calmness she most certainly did not feel. "You've also answered a few lingering questions I had about the male anatomy, so thank you for that."

He let out a sputtering cough. "*What?*"

"You needn't worry. I'll be sure to put the knowledge to good use with a willing partner next time."

Alec's mouth dropped open, but she did not wait for his response. Lottie rose from the bed with all the regality of a queen and moved to the washstand. Her hands barely even trembled as she performed her ablutions. Alec remained in place but she could feel his gaze burning a hole in her back.

"You go too far, Lottie," he finally muttered.

Her eyes began to prickle against the hurt swelling inside her, but she squeezed them shut until those tears dried up. She would rather die than cry in front of him now. When she turned around, Alec was bent over his bag, packing with swift, agitated movements.

"I had no idea you were such a hypocrite." She barely spoke louder than a whisper, but Alec immediately stopped and glared at her.

"I beg your pardon?"

"You expect me to feel shame for my desires. For my

experience." Lottie made sure to sound as authoritative as possible. The last thing she wanted was to reveal exactly how *limited* her experience was.

"That's not—"

"But you have no right to judge *me*. I know what men in your position are like," she continued.

Alec's glare remained, but he swallowed. Hard. "Is that so?" He took a step toward her.

Lottie managed a nod and focused on steadying her breathing. She would not show him *any* weakness.

"Enlighten me, then." He took another step, his eyes burning into hers.

She gripped the side of the washstand. "You are willing to do anything, use anyone, if that gets you what you need."

No desire.

"So don't you dare try to act like someone noble. Someone with morals."

Nothing but anger.

At that, he came to a halt. Alec's jaw worked as he considered her. "And you're suggesting that activities of a carnal nature are among the many *things* I do?"

She gave him a hard look. "I know they are."

But Alec moved again, and this time he didn't stop until they were mere inches apart. Lottie was forced to tilt her chin up to meet his eyes. Then he leaned over and murmured by her ear. "Now where did you get an idea like that?" His warm breath tickled her neck, like it had only minutes ago. "Don't you know those spy novels are fiction?"

Lottie dug her nails into her palms against the shiver of pleasure that stole over her and remained in place. "Don't *mock* me. And it's not an idea. Uncle Alfred said as much when you left. That you were looking forward to it."

Alec pulled back. "He told you that I planned to use

seduction to get information?" He spoke as if the idea was absurd, but his jaw tightened yet again.

More or less.

Lottie didn't even blink. "He said you were the best man he had ever recruited. That he expected great things from you. And that you would use *any means necessary*. The implication was very clear." Her voice began to break on the last word, but as she moved to push past him, Alec caught her by the shoulders. She gasped as the warmth from his hands shot through her. She hadn't realized how cold she was.

"And you just *believed* him?"

Her stomach twinged with guilt at the desperate note in his voice. Of course she had. It never crossed her mind to think otherwise. Until now.

"What alternative was there?" she demanded. "You certainly weren't there to offer one."

Alec didn't answer. Instead, he immediately released her, as if her very skin scalded him, before letting out a frustrated, foul curse. "He shouldn't have told you that."

"Why? Is it not true?" As she said the words, something lifted inside her chest. It was a moment before she recognized it as hope.

Alec hesitated, but then the wild look faded. "No," he admitted. His voice had gone soft. "It's true...I'm sorry."

Lottie bristled. "You needn't apologize to me for doing your duty," she mumbled through her disappointment. What a fool she was.

Alec watched her closely. "Perhaps, but I want to anyway. And for just now," he added. "I shouldn't have spoken to you that way. I wasn't trying to shame you. I only meant..." He paused and furrowed his brow, searching for the right words. "I only meant that such things are better when they truly mean something."

The implication being that with her it meant nothing. She certainly wasn't the woman he had been dreaming of. Lottie lifted her chin. "Then perhaps you should take your own advice," she tossed off.

Alec let out a surprised laugh. "You know, I quite agree with you on that," he said bashfully. Then he turned around and moved toward his bag. "Shall I send for a maid to help you dress? The train is supposed to leave at nine."

"Yes. Please do," Lottie answered despite the wretchedness churning inside her.

CHAPTER TEN

❧

When they arrived at the station in Bologna, Alec dashed off a quick cable to Mr. Wetherby in London explaining that they were traveling through Venice to avoid meeting anyone in Florence. Wetherby had been adamant in his instructions, but hopefully Sir Alfred would be so overjoyed Alec had found Lottie that he wouldn't care about their little detour. What Alec really should have done was scrap the plan entirely and send Lottie home on her own, but he simply couldn't.

Or wouldn't.

The express train to Venice was, remarkably, on time for once. As they took their seats in first class, Alec sent up a silent prayer to every saint and god in charge of travel to spare his tattered nerves. Lottie slid into the seat across from his own and turned to the window, a vision in a demure pink-and-black plaid traveling gown and matching wide-brimmed hat. It was trimmed with a few blooming pink roses that bordered on obscene. He should have made her change. She would *never* blend in wearing that, but since their argument at the inn, they hadn't spoken beyond what was necessary. Everything was perfectly polite. Eminently civilized. And yet, Alec couldn't stop thinking of her body eagerly pressing into his, of her fingers curling into his hair, and of his hand moving between her thighs. Whether it had been real or part of his fevered dream mattered little; he wanted it all.

Alec had been with his share of confident women over the years, but the sight of Lottie standing in nothing but her chemise boldly declaring her intention to find a *willing partner* had still managed to shock him. Somehow the girl he had once known so well had grown into one of the most surprising women he had ever met.

It was incredibly arousing.

Alec shifted in place, though it offered little relief. What he truly needed was a moment alone. But even more irksome than his unsated desire was Lottie's revelation about Sir Alfred. It extended far beyond the bounds of common decency regarding what an uncle should discuss with his niece, but it was the timing that set Alec particularly on edge.

For five bloody years Lottie had been under the impression that not only did Alec enthusiastically use sex as a weapon but that he was damned *good* at it. He gritted his teeth once again against the outrage that had threatened to consume him all morning. Plenty of men considered bedding unsuspecting targets a perk of the job, but Alec did have some morals.

There were times, especially when he was younger, where he slept with women during missions, but they were either agents like him or seasoned informants used to the game. The distraction had usually been more trouble than it was worth.

And Alec hadn't done that in a very long time.

However, it seemed rather self-serving to point out this discrepancy to Lottie merely to make himself feel better. Besides, he still used his charm to manipulate people when necessary. And he had not once felt anything like remorse.

She was right. He *was* a hypocrite.

But that still didn't explain Sir Alfred's actions. Alec had done exactly what the man demanded—he left immediately and never contacted Lottie again. Why bother maligning him further?

As the train pulled away from the station, Alec cleared his throat. Neither his body nor his mind could sit across from her for the next four hours. "Would you like anything from the dining car?"

Lottie shook her head and continued to stare out the window. "I'm fine, thank you."

Alec rose. "Remember. If anyone asks, we're married."

"Mr. and Mrs. Gresham," she responded automatically. "I know."

Alec hesitated. He should say something comforting. Something to reassure her. So she would know she *could* trust him, at least in this.

Not likely now, chap.

At his silence, Lottie finally tore her gaze away from the window and raised her eyebrow. "Are you doubting my ability to remember a simple *name*?"

The corner of his mouth lifted at her sardonic tone. "Not at all. I was just thinking how nice it is to work with such a competent partner for once," he added, savoring the look of pleasant surprise that crossed her face. It was doubtful he would ever see it again.

Alec made his way to the dining car and slumped into a booth, but his mind was still fixed on the past, and how he had come to be the man she thought so little of.

He had always assumed his deeper feelings for Lottie began on the night of her coming out ball, but the first spark had been a year earlier when he attended a small dinner party at Sir Alfred's London town house. His guardian had been talking of his future for months, but Alec was reluctant to make any firm commitments. He assumed the invitation was

Sir Alfred's version of a peace offering, but during predinner drinks, Alec was introduced to several men—two from the Home Office and one from Naval Intelligence. Then he understood the true purpose of the evening.

Alec excused himself shortly before dinner was announced—under Sir Alfred's disapproving glare, but he needed to be alone. Blessed relief had flooded through him as soon as he stepped into the silent library. Alec let out a heavy sigh and walked toward the hearth. A fire had been lit and he was immediately drawn to the comforting glow.

"Tell him you won't do it," Alec muttered as he stared at the flames. "Tell him you don't owe him anything more. For God's sake, how *long* are you supposed to be indebted to him?" He curled his fingers into a fist and was about to pound it against the mantel when someone loudly cleared their throat behind him.

Alec spun around and found Lottie tucked up on the window seat with a book on her lap. She gave him an amused smile. "Are the guests really so boring you'd rather converse with the fireplace?"

How would he *ever* be a spy if he couldn't even deduce when he was alone? "I didn't know you were back," he blurted out once he recovered from his shock.

Lottie had spent the summer traveling the continent with the family of a school friend. They had not seen each other since Easter. She set aside the book and placed her feet on the floor. As she crossed them, Alec caught a flash of slim ankle. She must have slipped off her shoes. "After the French Riviera Abigail's father decided he had seen enough of the continent, so we came home early." Her mouth briefly tightened with disappointment. Then she brightened. "Now, tell me why you're skulking about the library instead of talking with my uncle's boring friends."

Boring indeed. Lottie hadn't any clue just how powerful her uncle was. Alec himself hadn't realized it until a few months ago. And he couldn't say a word to her about it. Guilt settled deep in his belly.

"You won't ever make new friends if you don't try," she continued as her lips curved in an impish smile. She was only teasing him. Possibly even mildly flirting with him. Attention from women was hardly anything new, but Alec's ears still grew hot. They hadn't been alone in a room together for many years. He scratched his fingers against the smooth surface of the mantel as he tried to brush the thought aside, but it stubbornly remained.

"I don't need any more. Apart from you."

This wasn't entirely true. Alec had friends, but they kept a polite distance, both of their own accord and his. At school everyone knew about his father, the tragic dead poet, that he had married a servant—a *foreign* one—and how his uncle, the current Viscount Gresham, still refused to acknowledge Alec's very existence.

Lottie was the only person who had ever seemed interested in him. Not where he had come from or what had happened. Just him. What else could one call that but friendship?

Her teasing smile faded but her steady gaze seemed to bolt him to the ground.

"I enjoyed your letter from Cannes," he pushed on while the air thickened between them. "Are you disappointed not to have gone on to Italy?"

Lottie openly stared at him for another excruciating moment, until Alec's ears grew hot once again, but then she shrugged and glanced away. "No, not really. I'd rather not have my first experience tainted by Mr. Thorne's complaints. Besides, Italy isn't going anywhere. I'll journey there some day."

"Yes, you will."

How innocent they both had been. Alec's chest ached with a useless desire for the impossible. To travel back to that exact moment and make the opposite of every decision that had followed. A vicious longing now flooded through him to storm back into the compartment, to tell Lottie the truth about everything, to fall at her feet and selfishly beg forgiveness for all his sins. It was sheer madness, and yet he shifted a foot, braced his hands on the table, and began to rise from his seat, determined to do just that, when someone called out his name. Alec looked up as a fashionably dressed older man sauntered down the aisle toward him, and his heart plummeted.

"I thought that was you, Professor! Enjoying your school holiday, I see."

It was none other than Signore Cardinelli, one of Italy's more unscrupulous businessmen and a major player in the country's constantly shifting political scene. He counted several of the more corrupt cabinet ministers among his closest friends—though less clear was whether these friendships stemmed from camaraderie or coercion.

Alec gripped the edge of the table and plastered a smile on his face. He had met Cardinelli under innocent enough circumstances—he liked buying ancient artifacts and sought Alec's opinion on a piece of Etruscan Bucchero earthenware he was considering—but the signore had gone on to become his most valuable source, and the greatest gain of his intelligence career. No matter what Alec thought of him personally, it was vital that he keep things amicable between them. His association with men like Cardinelli was exactly why he needed to stay away from Lottie. Why he could never truly be forgiven. Alec had made his choices. And now he had to live with them.

"Hello, signore. This is quite the surprise."

"I should say so! I was thinking of inviting you to dinner

this evening." Cardinelli grinned but his sharp gaze closely watched Alec. He possessed a rare kind of animal magnetism Alec had only seen in one other man: Sir Alfred. "I've a guest coming who has an interest in Etruscan art. You two should meet."

"It's kismet, then."

"And where are you traveling from?"

"Pistoia. I was visiting some friends over from England. Yourself?"

"Roma. Business. You know how it is," he said with a wink.

Where Cardenelli was concerned, that could mean anything. Alec would need to send word to Rafe Davies, his point of contact. The signore's activities were always of great interest to the Crown. "Would you care to join me for a drink?"

The man glanced toward the doorway. "Tempting, but I saw the most alluring creature boarding earlier. I think she came this way. She looked English. Did you happen to see her? She wore a pink gown and was in possession of a divine backside."

Alec bit the inside of his cheek. What a poet. "Sorry. Haven't seen anyone matching that description."

"Oh, *you* wouldn't have missed her," Cardinelli laughed.

"Come, signore," Alec cajoled. "One drink." His mouth was beginning to strain from smiling so tightly.

The man let out a wistful sigh and, thankfully, took the seat across from Alec. "Ah, well. She's probably too expensive for me these days." In addition to a long-suffering wife who mostly lived abroad, Signore Cardinelli had a rotating group of mistresses, each one younger than the last. Alec didn't know where he found the time, let alone the stamina.

The man then gave him a wily look as the waiter handed them menus. "And as you know, I am a man of *exquisite* taste."

Alec flicked his eyes to the menu. "I would expect nothing less, signore," he said lightly, while hoping for all the world that Lottie wouldn't have a change of heart and come looking for him.

Once she was alone in the train cabin, Lottie let out a sigh and settled into her seat. She pulled out the hat pin and gently lifted the hat off her head and placed it beside her. She might as well be comfortable for the long ride. As Lottie nestled deeper into the seat, the very sight of the fussy piece of millinery made her smile. Lord knew she needed something to lift her spirits. She had the hat and matching walking gown commissioned before she left for Italy but didn't dare wear it while in the presence of Mrs. Wetherby, as the woman thought pink clashed with her coloring. It wasn't exactly appropriate for train travel, but Lottie was tired of waiting for the right time to wear it. She frowned as she ran a finger along the hat's brim. A person could spend their whole life waiting, only to be left with nothing. That seemed like a rather obvious lesson she should have learned a long time ago.

Lottie rubbed her temples; they hadn't stopped throbbing since her argument with Alec. His outrage had been surprising, but it was the deep hurt that flickered briefly in his eyes that haunted her still. What *exactly* had Uncle Alfred said all those years ago? She pinched the bridge of her nose as she tried to recall that awful morning after her coming out ball.

Lottie had awoken feeling lighter than air. Invincible. The fear, the sadness, the loneliness that had been slowly creeping in the last few years were gone, all thanks to Alec's surprise appearance. She had always cared for him, of course, and wouldn't deny she found him as handsome as ever. But more important, he was her dearest friend. Her champion. And yet something had changed between them on the dance floor. He looked at her differently, held her closer, spoke softer. Or maybe it had been earlier, when he appeared at her bedroom door, as if she had conjured him out of her misery. Lottie hadn't realized how very much she needed him until he was there hugging her, assuring her everything would be all right.

And Lottie believed him. Completely.

He had promised to call as soon as he could that morning, and Lottie was so excited she could barely eat. Uncle Alfred already knew of her intention to marry for love, and who better than Alec? The more she thought about it, the more right it felt until no one else would do. Only Alec. She could wait until he finished the excavation in Scotland. She could even wait until he secured his future at Oxford. She could wait as long as it took if it meant spending the rest of her life with him. Lottie dressed quickly and then hurried downstairs to the parlor where she waited, and waited, and waited.

But he never came.

Around noontime, Uncle Alfred entered the room. "Well, hello Lottie." But she couldn't return his easy smile and he noticed her stricken expression. "What's wrong? Are you ill?"

Lottie shook her head. "No, I—have you heard from Alec?"

Uncle Alfred gave her a confused look. "Why, yes. We were in my study talking just now."

Lottie stood so abruptly that the book she hadn't been reading fell to the floor with a heavy thud. "Oh! I was so worried I—"

Uncle Alfred held up a hand. "My dear, he's already left. He almost missed his train back to Edinburgh."

She sat back down. Her head felt fuzzy all of a sudden.

Lottie couldn't make herself understand what he was saying, and yet the words seemed to steal the very air from her. "*Left?* Did he say anything?"

Uncle Alfred raised an eyebrow. "About you? No. We only talked about him, I'm afraid. Alec's decided to do his duty to the Crown."

Uncle Alfred continued talking, but Lottie's ears began to ring. She knew a little about her uncle's activities on behalf of Her Majesty's government, but not once had she ever thought *Alec* wished to be involved. The work could be dangerous, and he could be gone for months traveling to the farthest corners of the empire. How...how would they be together?

"I don't understand. Alec doesn't want to work for the Crown," she insisted. "He's interested in the Etruscans."

Uncle Alfred gave her a long look. "We've been discussing it for nearly a year."

Lottie tried to inhale, but it was as if the wind had been knocked from her lungs. This whole time, all those letters, he had kept this from her?

"There are some loose ends to tie up in Edinburgh, but he should be going abroad in a few weeks," Uncle Alfred continued. "Egypt. Possibly Turkey. The more adventurous, the better, I gather." He smiled proudly. "It was nice, wasn't it? Seeing your old chum once again?"

It was such a trivial description of who Alec was and what he had come to mean to her that Lottie didn't know where to begin to correct him. All she could focus on was the most immediate hurt.

"But...he didn't want to say goodbye?" Her voice broke on the last word. She hated how pathetic she sounded. Uncle Alfred's eyes softened, like they used to when she was a little girl. He walked over to the sofa and sat down beside her. "I was afraid of this, you know..." His voice trailed off and he shook his head. "I thought it would be better if he left. And Alec agreed."

"You told him not to—to *speak* with me?"

Uncle Alfred tsked. "You make me sound like an overbearing brute. I didn't want you to get hurt." She opened her mouth to protest, but he held up his hand. "There's no use denying it. I saw how you looked at him last night. But you mustn't believe everything you see. Haven't I taught you that?"

Lottie bristled. This was absurd. "You've taught me to be wary of people I didn't know. But this is *Alec*." She had never once spoken to her uncle in such an obstinate tone.

"And he has changed very much," he immediately countered. "You've always given Alec the benefit of the doubt, Lottie. It's in your nature to see the best in everyone, just like your poor mother."

Lottie stiffened. Uncle Alfred rarely mentioned his beloved sister, but he had never said such a thing before. Did he not approve of Lottie's father? How could that be?

"He came here specifically to make arrangements with me," Uncle Alfred continued. "It was merely a coincidence that he happened to be in town the night of your ball."

Lottie shook her head. "No, he said he wanted it to be a surprise—"

"Then why did he arrive so late?" her uncle pressed. "And why has he already left? Whatever he told you, whatever he may have *wanted* you to think, you weren't a part of his plans, Lottie. You were only an afterthought."

Her cheeks stung, as if he had slapped her. The words pressed on a raw spot so deep, she had forgotten to guard it.

But Uncle Alfred still watched her closely, with those sharp, all-seeing eyes of his. "What did he say to you, exactly?"

Lottie hesitated. Uncle Alfred had always protected her, and yet a voice inside whispered, *Don't*. "Nothing," she answered. "Only that he didn't want to miss the ball. I suppose I thought..." She hung her head, too embarrassed to finish the sentence.

I thought he came for me.

Uncle Alfred squeezed her hand. "He wanted you to feel special. Especially after that horrible Lord Exeter was so rude." Lottie looked up in surprise, but of course Sir Alfred knew. Nothing escaped his notice. Ever. "And you did, didn't you?" He waited for her reluctant nod. "It certainly wasn't malicious, Lottie, but it was still inconsiderate in the end. That's why he's right for this kind of work, you see. Men like Alec need to act quickly. Decisively. Without regrets. They can't waste time worrying about anyone else because it could expose them to danger. He saw the chance to do some good, to brighten your day, and he took action."

Lottie frowned at this explanation. It didn't match up at *all* with the Alec she knew.

"You'll see that now," Uncle Alfred added as if he'd heard her protest. "You're still thinking of him as that young boy you first met, or the charming fellow who comes round for holidays. But it will be different now that he has a life of his own. I'm afraid we're much too stodgy for him. While we're stuck in London, he'll be off having great adventures, escaping danger, and meeting many glamorous people."

Lottie flinched at the knowing look he shot her.

"He has a long and illustrious career ahead of him," Uncle Alfred continued. "Of that I've no doubt. He has the best instincts I've ever seen. But that requires a great deal of sacrifice, you know. A willingness and an ability to do whatever it takes to win using *any means necessary*."

He paused, waiting for his words to sink in. Lottie had to bite her lip to keep it from trembling.

"And he'll do it, Lottie. Actually, I think he finds that

part the most appealing," he said with a chuckle. "You're an intelligent young woman. I don't need to tell you what that will mean for a handsome man like him."

Deception. Intrigues. *Seduction.*

Her uncle sighed. "In any case, that is not the kind of life for a man with a family. With responsibilities. Obligations."

It went against everything Alec had ever spoken of wanting. Everything he had ever claimed to hold dear. Was all of that a lie as well? But it must have been. Otherwise, he would have stayed. He would have bothered to talk to her.

Still, Lottie made herself ask: "You're sure that is what he wants?"

"Alec?" Uncle Alfred laughed, as if the very question was absurd. "Oh yes, my dear. *Quite* sure. In fact, I think he may be the best man I've ever recruited."

CHAPTER ELEVEN

The door to the compartment swung open, and Lottie sat up with a start. She had only meant to rest her eyes for a moment but the gentle motion of the train must have lulled her to sleep. She turned expectantly toward the doorway, but instead of Alec an older woman dressed in deep purple appeared.

"Oh! I'm so sorry. Did I wake you?" The woman's graying temples indicated she was likely on the other side of fifty, but her full cheeks gave her a distinctly cherubic appearance.

Lottie offered her a sleepy smile. "It's all right. I hadn't meant to doze off." She glanced out the window. The train had stopped at a station. "Would you mind telling me where we are?"

"Padua. Only an hour or so to go before we reach Venice." The woman returned her smile and settled into the seat across from her. "I am Mrs. Huntington."

"Mrs. Gresham."

"And are you traveling all alone, Mrs. Gresham?" There was the slightest note of censure in her voice.

Lottie shook her head and gave what she hoped was a bashful smile. "My husband is in the dining car." How easily the lie slipped from her lips.

The woman's eyes lit up. "Is this your honeymoon?"

Lottie paused. She and Alec hadn't discussed their back-story, which now seemed like a rather large oversight on both their parts. "Yes," she answered before the moment could turn awkward.

"How terribly romantic!" The woman punctuated her statement with a dramatic sigh. "I wanted to go to Italy on my honeymoon, but my dear late husband couldn't bear the thought of Italian food, so we never went abroad."

"I'm sorry for your loss."

Mrs. Huntington waved a hand. "Oh, it's been over a decade since poor Godfrey left me. But here I am, finally making the journey. Not alone, of course. I've a girl in second class. The daughter of my neighbor back in Milton Keynes. A Miss Abbott. She is about your age. I'd have paid for her to travel with me in first class, but the girl is such a chatterbox that I need the break."

Lottie gave her an understanding nod, though she rather suspected Mrs. Huntington was a bit of a chatterbox her-self.

The woman settled her hands onto her lap. "Now, you must tell me of your itinerary so far. I'm always curious to hear of other peoples' travels. And please, spare no detail!"

Though it had been easy enough to lie about her marital status, Lottie found inventing an entire honeymoon far more difficult. Yet Mrs. Huntington truly did wish to know every little detail, and asked questions if they weren't provided, so Lottie spent nearly half an hour recalling her time in Italy, substituting Alec as her travel companion instead of Mrs. Wetherby—though she opted not to give him Mrs. Wetherby's chronic indigestion.

Just as Lottie began to talk about the village, the door opened and Alec entered the compartment. But his usual aloofness instantly dissolved as he caught sight of their companion. He put on an affable smile and his entire countenance seemed immediately lighter, as if he really was nothing more than a humble history professor. The change was so swift and complete Mrs. Huntington didn't appear to notice.

"*This* must be your husband. I've heard all about you, Mr. Gresham. But your wife neglected to mention how very handsome you are." Her eyes lingered over his frame in a manner Lottie didn't much care for.

Having a handsome husband must be a rather tiresome business.

Alec continued smiling politely even in the face of the woman's ill-mannered stare. "Yes, I'm afraid my wife only married me for my inner beauty," he quipped. "But I confess that sometimes a man likes to be appreciated for his looks." His eyes caught Lottie's and he flashed her a little smirk she couldn't help returning.

Mrs. Huntington tittered. "And he's *funny!*"

Lottie gave her a tight smile, then addressed Alec: "This is Mrs. Huntington. She wanted a detailed account of our honeymoon itinerary."

"Of course," he said smoothly and gave a short bow to the woman. The corner of his mouth lifted again as he took the seat next to Lottie. "How far have you gotten?"

"To the village."

His gaze warmed. It was just the sort of indulgent look a new husband would give his bride. "Ah. My favorite part."

And just the sort of thing he would say.

Lottie couldn't help blushing at the lie.

"It sounds lovely," Mrs. Huntington interrupted.

Alec was obliged to address the woman. "Yes. It was."

"Wherever did you hear of it?"

He turned to Lottie. "May I?"

"Please," she said with a grateful nod. "You tell it so much better than I do."

He smiled again before turning back to Mrs. Huntington. "My wife's late parents traveled there on their own honeymoon. I'm not sure if she's mentioned this yet, but we grew up together." Then he paused and gave Mrs. Huntington a remorseful look. "I'm sorry, I should have asked this before. Where are you from, madame?"

"Milton Keynes," she declared, having no idea that he was fishing for information.

"Ah, well, we are from Surrey. Our families' properties bordered each other, so for many years we spent every holiday together." Then he looked back at Lottie. "She was my first friend."

Her throat tightened at the words, and she turned toward the window.

"It was idyllic, really," he continued before his rapturous audience. "The kind of childhood one dreams of. Our days were filled with all sorts of endless adventures..."

As the fabled Veneto region sped by outside, Lottie listened while Alec wove a story from both truth and lies. Strangely, her heart ached nearly as much from the falsehoods. For how different things might have been for them both if all of it were true.

Mrs. Huntington clasped her hands to her chest. "And then when she came of age, you married!"

"No," he said swiftly. Lottie turned back to Alec. His expression had darkened. "Not then. My family's fortunes changed suddenly, for reasons I'd rather not discuss. We were forced to sell our home and move far away."

Mrs. Huntington sucked in a breath. "But you never forgot her."

Alec shook his head. "Of course I didn't."

Lottie's eyes began to sting. She didn't like this game anymore.

Mrs. Huntington leaned forward. "How long was it before you found each other again?"

Alec, the devil, paused before answering. "Five years."

The woman fell back against her seat. "*Five* years! Oh, the separation must have been so difficult for you, my dear."

Lottie glanced at him from under her lashes. His expression had taken on that unfathomable quality once again. "Yes," she answered, pushing past the burn in her throat. "But it was the silence that was hardest to bear." He turned the full weight of his gaze on her then and Lottie's cheeks flushed under his heavy scrutiny, but she continued. "I came to believe he had forgotten me. Long ago."

Mrs. Huntington was scandalized. "Sir, did you not *write*?"

But his eyes never left Lottie. "I had nothing to offer her back then. No fortune, no future."

Her heart turned over. He couldn't truly believe his lack of fortune stood between them. With her inheritance, she had no need to marry a wealthy man. They could have built their own future. Together.

"And her parents did not approve."

Lottie's breath caught. No. It was only for the story. It *had* to be. Uncle Alfred had no reason to stop them from marrying. Alec had left of his own volition. Because he had been determined to serve. Because he wanted to live a life beyond anything she could offer. She searched for the answer in his eyes, in his face, but he only stared back as solemn as ever.

Across from them Mrs. Huntington clucked her tongue. "Still. Not one word in *five years*?"

Alec finally gave the woman his full attention. "I did not want to give either of us false hope. It seemed cruel to do so."

"But you were *torturing* the poor girl!"

"I know that now, Mrs. Huntington," he said with a rueful smile. "But I was an ignorant youth at the time. Blinded by pride. When I had finally made something of myself, I returned to the house she had grown up in, but she was long gone. No one would tell me where she was, so I searched far and wide, crossing countries and then continents looking for the girl with the russet hair and emerald eyes. But she was not anywhere a fashionable young lady of means might travel to—not in Paris, nor Rome, or Zurich. Then, it finally came to me. I hurried back to England. To the secret place only we knew about, an old fairy cottage not one mile from our childhood homes. And there she was. There she had been the whole time."

Lottie couldn't speak. Couldn't *breathe*.

Every limb vibrated as she wavered between wanting to slap Alec and kiss him senseless.

"If I hadn't been so blinded by my ambition," he continued. "By being the man I thought she wanted, I would have found her that much sooner. All I had to do was look inside my own heart." Then he turned to Lottie. "Luckily she forgave my ineptitude in the end. Didn't you, my darling?"

She hated how easily he manipulated her, and how very much she ached for all of it to be true. If only she could forgive him. If only he would ever ask her to.

Alec reached out and gently brushed his thumb across her cheek, catching the lone tear that had escaped.

"Yes," she whispered, closing her watery eyes against the rest. "Yes, I did."

And in that moment, it was indeed the truth.

The wine Alec had shared with Signore Cardinelli in the dining car must have gone straight to his head. He was used to spinning tales at the drop of a hat and had a reservoir of stories to draw from, but most of what he had told Mrs. Huntington was true. As was the pain in Lottie's voice when she spoke of his long silence. And her forgiveness.

How easy he made their reconciliation sound. If only that was all it took. If only uttering a few words could be enough. But they weren't those people.

Lottie's eyes fluttered open, and she looked down. He had taken her hand in his, where her single tear had stained his glove. His very soul burned with the need to kiss away the rest still brimming there, but he merely gave her hand a gentle squeeze before he turned to Mrs. Huntington.

The woman was looking between them with something akin to awe. "My, that is quite a story." Then she glanced out the window. The train had begun to slow down as they approached the station. "Oh! I must go find Miss Abbott. I told her we would depart together. Her mother will never forgive me if I lose her to a *Venetian*." She gave them a genuine smile as she rose. "It has been a most sincere pleasure to meet you both. I hope you enjoy Venice and wish you every happiness on your marriage. I daresay you've earned it."

"Thank you," Alec said, while Lottie gave her a weak smile.

Alec had uttered a thousand lies and pretended to be a dozen different men over the last few years, but never had he wanted something so much to be true.

As soon as the door shut behind Mrs. Huntington, Lottie tore her hand from his hold and moved to the now-empty seat. Alec tried to catch her eye as she busied herself with smoothing her hat brim.

It wasn't a lie. I meant every word.

"Lottie."

Did my silence really torture you so?

Her fingers curled ever so slightly, but she didn't look up.

Forgive me.

"I think it's best if we adhere to my conditions from now on."

"Of course. My apologies. I got carried away." But this time she offered no forgiveness, only continued to smooth phantom wrinkles from her hat brim.

Alec gritted his teeth against her clipped tone as he scrubbed a hand over his face. "We need to leave as soon as the train stops. I met someone in the dining car earlier, and he can't see us together. I would have mentioned it sooner if we had been alone."

She gave him a curious look, but only nodded. There was no sign of tears now. The tension that had originally driven him from the compartment filled the small space once again and brought Alec to his feet.

Lottie paused in her fiddling. "Are you all right?"

"I'm perfectly fine," he snapped. "Just hurry up, will you?"

She let out an irritated breath as she began to pin the hat onto her head. "The train hasn't even *stopped* yet. What do you intend us to do, leap onto the platform?"

Alec pulled aside the compartment's curtains ever so slightly and glanced into the hallway. "Something like that." Hopefully the signore was still in the dining car finishing the rest of the bottle Alec had left behind.

Lottie rolled her eyes and stood. Alec followed the movement of her white-gloved hands as she smoothed the front and sides of her skirt. Cardinelli was right about the way she looked in that gown. She glanced up and caught him staring. Her eyes darkened, but her mouth remained hard. "Well, then. Lead the way, Professor."

Alec tucked her arm into the curve of his elbow against her disapproving frown and drew her out into the hallway. "My pleasure, Mrs. Gresham."

Lord, that felt far too good.

They waited by the exit so they could be first to depart. Alec focused on the growing crowd. Luckily there was no sign of Signore Cardinelli. As soon as the exit door was opened and the stairs brought over, Alec stepped out and handed her down. The exodus from the second- and third-class trains nipped at their heels, but Alec knew this station like the back of his hand. He pulled Lottie along through the pulsing crowd of vendors and visitors.

"Wait! What about our bags?" She shortened her steps to keep up with his long strides.

"I already took care of it. They'll be delivered to my flat." Alec couldn't slow down. He wouldn't feel better until they were safely in his home and she had changed out of that damned dress. Preferably into something as alluring as a nun's habit.

As if that would matter.

"Oh, could we take a gondola?" she asked as they exited the station, her voice laced with excitement. He glanced down at her; their arms were still entwined, and her face turned up to his, so beautiful, so full of hope. To any casual observer they probably did look like a newly married couple. His chest ached even more than it had in the train cabin. How easy it was to pretend with her.

Their pace slowed to nearly a crawl as the crowds swelled around them. Alec drew a little closer to her, and Lottie didn't protest. Her lips parted, but she simply gazed into his face, so he continued until the curve of her hip pressed against his side. Her soft, feminine form warmed his own, while her light rosewater scent slowly sank into his skin. Something even deeper in his chest twisted and wrenched like a sapling branch in a rough spring storm, but it did not break. The heart could survive unimaginable loss. It was designed to do so. But could Alec's survive losing her again?

Lottie shivered against the light breeze and leaned toward him. "Not even a quick trip to Saint Mark's?"

A lock of hair fell across her eyes. Alec had to fight against the urge to brush it away.

The square would be mobbed with tourists now. Perhaps...perhaps it would be all right. He hated to disappoint her more than he already had. Alec forced himself to turn away from her, lest they stand on the street until sundown. "Fine, but we must—"

"Well, isn't *this* a pleasant surprise!"

An all-too-familiar voice boomed from behind them. Alec squeezed his eyes shut and silently let out a string of curses that would make the Virgin Mary weep. His damned distraction had cost him. He turned around with a scowl, but Signore Cardinelli was too busy eyeing Lottie to spare him a glance. "Alec, you devil! Of course you would keep this alluring creature all to yourself," he said with a laugh and placed a kiss on Lottie's hand. Only then did he meet Alec's eyes. They narrowed slightly. "Not that I blame you."

Lottie gave him a polite smile and glanced back at Alec. He caught the flash of unease in her expression, though she hid it well. She had worn the very same look when he found her with Mrs. Huntington, but he would again take care of this. They were in his world now. He rubbed a small circle against her inner arm with his thumb.

Trust me.

She still didn't look at him but relaxed slightly against his grip. It was a start.

"Signore Cardinelli, allow me to introduce my cousin," he said. "Miss Gresham is visiting from England." The signore knew full well that Alec was a bachelor, but Lottie would catch on quickly. "The signore has an interest in antiques. I have provided him with appraisals on several occasions."

That, at least, was true. "All of which caused the prices to increase," he said with a teasing laugh. Then he gave Lottie an oily smile. "*Cousin*, eh? I had no idea a rascal like this one came from such enchanting stock."

Lottie dipped her head. "Yes. I'm afraid Alec is the black sheep of the family." Then she leaned in toward him conspiratorially. "I'm sure I don't need to tell *you* why."

Signore Cardinelli was struck dumb, then he threw his head back and laughed. The knot between Alec's shoulder blades untwisted ever so slightly and he laughed along with the man. She had adapted even better than expected. It was a bit unnerving.

"Alec, you must bring her this evening. I told your cousin I'm having a little dinner party later," he explained to Lottie before flicking him a sharp glance. "And I'm afraid I won't take no for an answer. Is this your first time in Venice, Miss Gresham?" he asked with impeccable politeness as he held out his arm.

Lottie's smile was more genuine this time. "Yes. We were on our way to Saint Mark's." She tugged out of Alec's grip and graciously accepted Signore Cardinelli's arm.

"Oh, how convenient! I'll walk with you. It's on my way." Alec muffled a snort at the obvious lie, but neither paid him any mind. "Now, tell me where you were before this..."

Signore Cardinelli's voice faded into the street noise as they strolled in the direction of Saint Mark's. Alec stood in place, watching the pair of them. After a few steps, Lottie turned back. "Aren't you coming, *cousin*?" Her green eyes were bright with mischief, and likely more. Alec gave her a subtle frown but followed. No doubt Lottie thought she was punishing him by cozying up to the signore.

If she knew only the half of it.

As they made their way through the crowded streets,

Alec kept a sharp eye and ear out, waiting to jump in and rescue Lottie from the signore's prying questions, but there was no need. She easily deflected each one by asking plenty of her own, having quickly realized that Signore Cardinelli's favorite subject was himself.

Lottie learned more about him in ten minutes than Alec had in ten months.

The base of his skull tingled. She *liked* this game. And was rather good at it.

But then, why wouldn't she? Simply living with Sir Alfred provided them both with an intuition his colleagues would kill for. The man's lessons had sunk deep into their blood, whether they were aware of it or not. Lottie was incredibly perceptive, highly intelligent, and perhaps in possession of more secrets than she let on...

It was all very hushed up, of course.

And I never tried to decipher the codes myself.

Alec flexed his fingers. His instincts had never led him astray before. There was a game afoot here. One far more complicated than a runaway niece.

And he would ferret out the truth. Whatever it may be.

CHAPTER TWELVE

As the unlikely trio slowly wended their way through the labyrinthine streets, Lottie made sure to keep Signore Cardinelli talking about himself—a decidedly easy task. She had spent the last five years stroking the egos of men back in London, as a lady did not dare venture to talk about herself unless asked to do so. And in her experience, few men ever bothered beyond the barest preliminaries. While he prattled on, she took in the salt-crusted palazzos slowly crumbling into murky canals, the slices of pale blue sky overhead, and caught snippets of dialect from Venetians as well as the many foreigners who called the floating city home. But more than the sights and sounds—and smells—of Venice, it was Alec who commanded most of her attention. Even though he remained a few steps behind them, Lottie was never not intimately aware of his looming presence, listening to everything that passed between her and the signore and watching with hawklike focus.

She was still stinging from Alec's duplicitous speech to Mrs. Huntington and hadn't missed the chance to needle him a little by flirting with Signore Cardinelli. But the longer she talked with the enigmatic Venetian, the stronger her suspicion grew that the man was far more than what he seemed, and that Alec's connection to him likely went much deeper than a shared interest in antiquity.

When they were just a few minutes away from Saint Mark's Square, the signore bid them adieu. He made a great show of kissing Lottie's hand once more.

"Thank you for a charming walk, Miss Gresham. Your cousin is a most fortunate man. I trust that this will not be our last meeting." He raised an eyebrow and glanced in Alec's direction.

Lottie gave him her most winsome smile. "As do I, Signore Cardinelli."

The man tipped his hat to Alec, who returned the gesture, and then went off in the direction of his nearby palazzo. Without a word Alec led her in the opposite direction with a thorny expression on his face that was likely meant to warn her off. Lottie pointedly ignored it.

"He was rather nice," she offered.

Alec's only reply was another derisive snort.

He still hadn't learned that she did not give up so easily. "Do you not like him?" she asked innocently. "You seem to know each other quite well."

Alec kept his gaze ahead. "It's work. That's all. We have been helpful to one another upon occasion." He gestured in the direction of the square up ahead and quickened their pace.

"In regards to his collection of Roman and Etruscan artifacts?"

Signore Cardinelli had gone on for some minutes about his treasures, boasting that his was one of the largest private collections in Europe.

Alec flicked her a cool glance. "Among other things."

"Are we not going to dinner, then?"

"Absolutely not," he barked and walked even faster, moving a few steps ahead.

"Why?" she pressed, determined to fracture his marble facade. "You can't possibly be worried about a man twice my age with a penchant for ancient crockery."

Alec suddenly stopped short and whirled around. Lottie bumped right into the solid wall of his chest. For an instant she was sorely tempted to press against the warm musculature and inhale his woodsy scent, but Alec stepped back and put his hands on his hips. She suspected he took the same stance with students who tried to submit late work.

"Don't be fooled by him," he scolded, likely using the same tone as well. "Sir Alfred taught you better than that."

She shot him a glare. "I can *manage* the signore."

Alec held her gaze, his expression now more thunderous than thorny. But Lottie refused to be cowed by him. "Luckily you won't have to," he snapped and turned on his heel.

Lottie grudgingly followed. In another minute they entered Saint Mark's Square, where they were drawn into the bustling crowd and promptly separated by a large group of German tourists. Her sharp cries of "Pardon" and "Excuse me" went unheeded. Lottie had endured her share of ballroom crushes, but panic began to claw up her throat as she was carried along in a veritable sea of strangers. An older man with an impressive gray mustache began speaking to her in a jovial tone. Lottie smiled politely and exchanged a few basic pleasantries that covered nearly all of her German, but when she turned away the man caught her elbow. He murmured something else, and based on the direction of his leer Lottie suspected it was nothing she wished to translate. She tugged on his arm, but the man's grip tightened. Lottie opened her mouth to chastise him, but Alec was suddenly beside them. If his expression had been merely thunderous before, it now bordered on apocalyptic.

He shouldered his way between them and uttered a string of guttural words to the man, who swiftly held up his hands. His eyes had gone wide with fear. Alec then grabbed her wrist and pulled her across the square.

"There was no need for such dramatics," she insisted, even as her heart still raced in her chest. "I had the situation in hand."

Alec kept his gaze fixed ahead. "Of course you did. But then I wouldn't get to practice my German."

Lottie glanced back. The man had gone deathly pale and immediately turned away when their eyes met. "What did you say to him?"

A chilling smile tugged at Alec's lips. "Nothing appropriate for a lady."

"I think the circumstances suggest otherwise," she said dryly. "I'm afraid I must insist."

Alec let out an aggrieved sigh as they came to a stop under one of the archways of the Doge's Palace. "It won't translate to English exactly," he began with all the authority of a seasoned professor, "but I explained to the gentleman that if he didn't let go of you, I would take great pleasure sending him back home with his bollocks in a box. More or less." He then scanned the square. "Now, what do you wish to see first? The basilica or the bell tower?" When she didn't directly respond, he cut a glance to her. "You do know your mouth is hanging open."

Lottie schooled her expression into something slightly more composed. "The basilica, please."

"Excellent choice," Alec said as he offered his arm.

Lottie hesitated. It was so much easier to be angry with him.

"Come now," he prompted. "I don't want any more Germans snatching you up this afternoon, or I'll run out of threats."

Lottie reluctantly slid her arm through his, and they joined the line of visitors waiting to enter the famous Basilica San Marco. Her eyelids fluttered at the sensation of his tall frame so close to hers while her mind groused that she didn't *need* his protection. She was perfectly capable of waiting in line without a guard, but it was hard to remain quite so indignant while standing beside him in the April sun. As they slowly edged toward the entrance, his intoxicating presence was akin to a rather potent narcotic, and Lottie gradually found herself leaning closer and closer to him, like a trembling vine stretching toward sunlight. At first, Alec's arm muscles tensed and flexed against her approach. But then slowly, so slowly, he began to respond in kind, subtly adjusting his hold without uttering a word.

By the time they entered the basilica his arm had slipped down around her waist and his hand gripped her from the bottom of her rib cage to the top of her hip. The warmth of his wide palm melted through her gown and spread across her skin. As if pulled by unseen strings, Lottie turned her head toward him until her chin was scant inches from the lapel of his coat. A puff of his warm breath caressed her temple. He must be looking down at her. If she tilted her head upward, Lottie was certain her lips would meet his. She could almost feel his full mouth settling over her own, coaxing a deep, demanding kiss.

That morning, while he was still half asleep Alec had promised to be gentle, but Lottie was more intrigued by the rather commanding aspects of his nature. She liked needling him because even though he could have easily dismissed her, Alec always found a way to engage. To push back. But so far he had retained much of that stony facade. What, then, would it take to make him crack completely?

Just as her knees began to quiver at the thought, a pinch-mouthed docent loudly cleared her throat and threw an icy glare in their direction. Lottie inhaled and straightened, breaking from Alec's hold. Their stance was decidedly inappropriate for a house of worship.

"Sorry," Alec mumbled thickly, as if he had been roused from a dream.

Lottie stepped away and turned her attention to the architectural wonder around them. She had come here to see the many treasures of Venice. Not to engage in acts of public indecency. As they slowly made their way through the grand cathedral, Lottie silently marveled at the Byzantine mosaics, the great golden altar, and the relics of Saint Mark. All the while Alec kept a safe distance, just out of touch but never quite out of mind. Thank goodness Lottie wasn't particularly religious, as the direction of her thoughts would surely damn her for all eternity.

She was still flushed when they stepped back into the square. Without a word Alec took her arm once again and led her around the basilica's bell tower. She kept her eyes on the redbrick building, a world-famous symbol of the city, while Alec pointed out various features, like the golden weather vane crafted to resemble the Archangel Gabriel and the lion faces that topped each of the five bells. It was a pleasure to listen to him. Alec had a lovely speaking voice, low and smooth, and clearly knew much about the subject.

"Do you fancy going to the top?"

Lottie shook her head as she took in the lofty spire. "Not really. I don't care for heights."

"Hmm. And yet I seem to remember you had a habit of climbing out of your bedroom window."

She did her best to school her smile and continued to take in the structure's details. "I hadn't developed the fear then. Besides, I wouldn't exactly call it a habit. I only did it a few times."

And always in order to meet him.

"Come," Alec urged. "This is your one chance. Don't let fear win."

Overhead, the bells of San Marco pealed, as if beckoning her. A sharp pain twisted inside her, born of both forgotten memories and impossible futures. She could not bear to go with him and make even more. Lottie shook her head. Alec let out a soft sigh, but he pressed her no further.

He continued to play tour guide as they wandered the halls of the Doge's Palace but only gave the history of each site, saying nothing about his own experiences. His father had written several poems that featured a young boy much like Alec reveling in the floating city's treasures. Lottie pictured him here in the square chasing pigeons, making friends with street performers, and gorging on sweets from charmed vendors until he was carried home fast asleep in his father's arms. Did Alec know of the poems that described such scenes, or was it all too painful for him to even contemplate? Lottie had always found refuge in her memories of her parents, but it wasn't the same for him. And perhaps never had been.

"Shall we take a gondola to my flat?" he asked. "We'll have a lovely view of the Grand Canal along the way."

She met his gaze for the first time since they had entered the square. Alec's hazel eyes took on an amber glow in the setting sunlight as he stared back at her with his usual intensity. But there was an edge of vulnerability about him now that made him seem years younger. It was as if she was seeing Alec, the Alec she had known, once again. And, unlike his caresses this morning, this was intentional.

Lottie suddenly had trouble swallowing. In the space of a moment her throat had gone bone dry.

"Yes," she said in a thin voice she barely recognized. "That sounds perfect."

* * *

Alec helped Lottie into a gondola and took the seat across from her. She was avoiding his gaze again, just as she had for the last hour or so. She might have possessed a hearty streak of cynicism, but Alec acknowledged that Lottie was still too unguarded to be working for a man like her uncle. Learning to conceal one's soft underbelly was of paramount importance in this line of work, though even Alec was finding it increasingly difficult to do so the longer he was in her presence. Showing her around the square, holding her so closely outside the basilica while she blushed under his touch, watching that look of curiosity melt into awe as she took in the sights—it was just the sort of thing a honeymooning couple would do. Just the sort of thing he had dared dream of once...

As the gondolier launched them into the bustling canal, Lottie's eyes widened first with surprise and then delight. She shot him an excited grin as they sliced through the water. Alec's lips curved as her head swiveled back and forth, eagerly taking in the busy waterway with her painter's eye. Their gondolier began warbling a tune. Something about thwarted love. Normally Alec hated this bit. It was drivel for tourists. But being with Lottie made it tolerable.

No. Far better than that.

Her gaze came to rest on him then and he wanted to believe with every fiber of his being that her eyes softened, just a little, because of him.

"You look rather content," she said.

Alec raised an eyebrow. "And you sound rather surprised."

Lottie gave a little shrug. "Only because I haven't seen you like this since..."

Since he had come barging back into her life.

Alec shifted in his seat. "Yes, well. I suppose it's due to my surroundings."

She nodded but kept focusing on the Venetian gothic structures that lined the canal. "It is beautiful here. I can see why you made this your home."

I wasn't speaking of the city.

But Alec kept the words to himself. There was no point. She was leaving. And if he couldn't get a handle on himself, she would need to make the journey without him. Neither spoke for the rest of their ride, though the canal provided plenty of distractions. Once they docked, Alec helped Lottie onto shore, paid their gondolier, and led her toward the battered palazzo he called home.

As they turned onto his narrow street, Alec caught sight of a small dark-haired boy with large brown eyes sitting on the front steps of his house. A smile touched his lips as the boy clambered to his feet and waved enthusiastically.

"Who is that?" Lottie asked.

"Nico. He lives in the flat below mine."

The boy rushed over to them, explaining in Italian that he had been waiting for Alec's return ever since their luggage was delivered earlier. Then he began detailing *everything* that had happened during Alec's brief absence. But his excited rambling about a particularly enterprising pigeon was cut short when he finally took notice of Lottie and sketched a grand bow. "Buon pomeriggio, signora."

Lottie returned the greeting and seemed utterly charmed by the little scamp.

Alec pressed his lips together, trying not to smile too much. "Nico, this is my friend, Miss Carlisle," he explained. Alec had been teaching the boy English for the past few months, and he was a remarkably quick study.

Nico's face lit up. "I am honored to meet a friend of the professor."

"And I am honored to meet you as well, Nico. Have you lived here long?"

Alec flicked her a warning glance that she ignored. Of course she would not miss a chance to do a little digging...

"Two years," Nico said proudly. "We are very lucky to have found the professor. He is the most generous—"

"All right, Nico," Alec cut in. He could feel Lottie's speculative stare as he slipped the boy a few coins. "Go down to the trattoria and bring back some risi e bisi for dinner. It will be too much for the two of us, you know how big those portions are, so take some for yourself as well."

He nodded enthusiastically. "Yes, Professor!" Then he darted down the street.

Lottie followed the boy's departure then turned back to him. "That was clever of you."

Alec stepped away to open the palazzo's heavy front door. "He won't take anything otherwise. He already knows I charge a pittance for rent." But even Nico wouldn't pass up the chance to sample the Venetian rice and peas dish that was popular this time of year. He gestured for Lottie to enter first, but she stood on the front step, head tilted back to take in the palazzo's faded beauty. "You *own* this place?"

"Yes," he said, with a hint of pride. "Every last crumbling bit."

"Who does Nico live with?"

"His mother and aunt. They are seamstresses."

Lottie met his eyes and her brow tensed with worry. "No father?"

"Not one that makes himself useful," he muttered. Then they stared at one another in silence until he motioned for her to enter again. They couldn't stand in the damned doorway forever. Lottie gave herself a little shake and moved past him into the entrance hall.

The palazzo was once a grand place but had fallen into disrepair over the years. Alec was slowly trying to bring it back to its former glory, but that required a great deal of money he didn't have. He had spent nearly all his savings cleaning the place and seeing to the most pressing repairs, like the rather large holes in the floor. Now it was reasonably tidy, and safe for a curious boy like Nico.

Lottie craned her neck as she took in the entrance hall's high ceilings. Her lips parted as she noticed the massive Venetian glass chandelier hanging above their heads. "How beautiful."

Alec and Nico had spent the better part of a week polishing each individual crystal droplet. The boy was always eager to help, and his mother was grateful to have her energetic son occupied.

"My flat is on the top floor." The words came out gruffly, but Lottie only nodded and headed toward the sweeping staircase. They ascended in silence, but as soon as they reached the landing outside his door, she abruptly turned around.

"Please, let me help you. It's the least I can do," she pressed. "You did agree to bring me here."

Alec stuck out his chest just as Nico used to do before he learned to mask his charitable efforts. "No."

"If you won't do it for your own sake, then do it for the boy's. And his mother."

That was far harder to dismiss, but he still had a scrap of pride left. "I can take care of them. Keep your money."

Lottie flinched ever so slightly before changing course: "Then we should go to the signore's dinner tonight. He said there would be a collector there."

Alec's jaw tightened at the very thought of that bastard

conversing with Lottie once again. "I don't want you involved with him," he said through gritted teeth.

Lottie folded her arms across her chest. "You're being absurd. This collector would pay for your expertise. And Signore Cardinelli likes me. If we go, you'll stay in his good graces."

Alec leaned forward. "That you would even make such a suggestion demonstrates how very little you know," he snapped. "He is a dangerous man."

She snorted. "He can't harm me by flirting. Or is this about my reputation again? Are you still determined to save me from *ruin*?"

His breath quickened at her mocking tone. If the signore had any clue who Lottie really was, and how desperate Sir Alfred was to see her safe, he would manipulate the situation to get what he wanted. And Alec simply wouldn't let that happen.

"I'm not some helpless little girl anymore," Lottie continued with a stamp of her foot. "I'm capable of taking care of myself. And I don't need your protection."

She said the words so dismissively. As if his concern meant nothing to her.

"Oh, I see," Alec said with deadly calm as he slipped his hands in his pockets and took a step toward her. "I didn't realize you knew how to defend yourself."

She hesitated and backed away. "Well, not exactly—"

"Ah. Then you must be able to wield a dagger."

"No—"

"Shoot a gun?"

Lottie shook her head. A faint blush stained her cheeks, but Alec would not stop. He stepped forward until Lottie's back was against the wall and there was nowhere for them to go. Until he was close enough to count the freckles on her nose.

"So, you'll just *talk* your way out of any trouble. Is that it?" he demanded. "Make a few quips and hope that tongue of yours is sharp enough to save you?"

Her eyes fell. "I...I hadn't thought—"

"No, you most certainly have not. But *I* have." Alec slammed his palm against the doorjamb and Lottie straightened. His eyes burned into hers with all the intensity of his anger. His fear. "I know you're proud for eluding your ancient chaperone, but this isn't flouncing around Tuscany. This isn't bloody *ball*room gossip. That man has half of Italy's blood on his hands. It's already bad enough he thinks you're my cousin, but if he had any idea who you really were. If he knew about your uncle, he would—"

Fuck.

Alec couldn't even think the words. He pulled away from her and pressed his forehead to the wall. He took a deep breath, then another, and another, until his heart rate was close to normal. "My protection may mean nothing to you." Lottie began to protest, but he plowed on: "But if anything ever happened to you because of me, I would...I would..." He could not will himself to say the rest.

In all the years he had been doing this, he had never had to consider anyone else's safety besides his own before. Now her very life could be in danger because of choices *he* had made.

It was simply too much.

Lottie placed her hand on his wrist. He was trembling. "You would what?" she said softly, pressing her thumb against his flesh.

Alec turned his head toward her but kept his other hand fixed firmly to the doorjamb. She watched him closely, those green eyes were searching for something. Desperately. A very large part of him wanted her to find it. To find him once again. Alec dug his nails into the worn wood frame. It began to splinter under the weight of his worry. And his want.

"I don't know." His mind buzzed with a hundred different thoughts and fears, each one worse than the last. "Christ, Lottie," he whispered, harsh and urgent. "I don't even know."

She leaned in a little closer until her scent mingled with the charged air between them. But just as her lips parted, the door of his flat swung open.

Rafe Davies, fellow intelligence agent, occasional flatmate, and the closest thing Alec had to a friend these days filled the doorway with a delighted grin on his face. "Terribly sorry to interrupt, but I got tired of waiting for you to come inside."

Alec recovered from his surprise and immediately tucked Lottie behind him. "You're supposed to be in Egypt."

Rafe ignored his sharp tone. "Change of plans. You know how it is." He shrugged and peered over Alec's shoulder. An easy enough task, considering he was several inches taller. "Hello, there," he said to Lottie, flashing her a dazzling smile. "I'm Rafe. And who might you be?"

"Don't answer that," Alec growled, then he grabbed Lottie's hand and pulled her into the flat.

Unease rippled through his body as Alec stalked across the flat's receiving area and through the large, light-filled parlor. He didn't stop until he reached his bedroom door and flung it open. Anyone with half a brain could guess what they had been on the verge of doing.

A mistake.

"Go inside and wait for me," he murmured.

For once Lottie didn't protest. She merely nodded and slipped into the bedroom, but not before she glanced behind him. When the door was safely shut, he spun around. Rafe watched from across the room, looking like the cat that got the cream. He would be expecting the full rundown, as usual. But this was different. This was *Lottie*.

As Alec walked toward his friend, he tried to return that smile, but it felt more like a grimace.

Rafe pointed his chin toward the bedroom. "I see you picked up something on your trip down south. I thought you didn't like English women."

"What makes you think she's English?"

Rafe let out a hearty laugh at his caginess. "I heard you talking in the entry hall, you oaf. *And* the landing."

"Were you listening by the bloody door?" Alec scoffed.

"Well, you weren't exactly quiet," Rafe pointed out, still amused. "Why, I don't think I've *ever* heard a woman speak to you that way." Then he tilted his head, considering. "Come to think of it, I could say the same for you. And here I thought you were a gentleman."

Rafe was a few years older and had served the Crown far longer, first as a naval officer before his recruitment as an intelligence agent. His father, the late earl of Fairfield, had been working in the diplomatic service after the death of his first wife when he met Rafe's mother, an eccentric young actress on the cusp of stardom after one of her performances. Rafe spent most of his childhood abroad, due to both the nature of his parents' careers and the scandal their marriage created. His four half siblings still refused to acknowledge his very existence. Yet Rafe rarely seemed bothered by this and instead embraced life with a breezy joie de vivre that was at turns irritating and infectious. Now he eyed the door with a level of interest Alec couldn't stand.

"She's a redhead, isn't she? Bit hard to tell under that absurd hat. Is she as feisty as she sounded?"

Alec's hands fisted. "Fuck. You."

That caught Rafe by surprise. Not an easy feat. "Why don't

we sit down. I've brought a bottle of that beastly local wine I know you like."

Alec shook his head. "I'm busy. And you can't stay here. State your business and then leave."

Rafe gave him a pitying look, as if he were an obstinate child crying over nothing. "Alec, you know I can't do that."

They stared at one another for a solid minute, but they both knew it was only so Alec could maintain some shred of dignity. Rafe was a damned good friend. Alec would have to find a way to thank him later when he didn't hate him quite so much.

"Fine," he grumbled and sat down hard on the flat's thread-bare sofa.

Rafe broke into another easy smile. Always calm and collected. Someone could be trying to tear his limbs off and Rafe still wouldn't lose his head. "Jolly good. I'll get us some glasses. Would your friend like to join?" Alec cast him a warning look, and Rafe shrugged again. "Suit yourself." He came back with the uncorked bottle and two dusty glasses.

Rafe held one up to the light and frowned in disapproval. "I thought you had a woman come round to clean?"

Alec snatched the glass and began to pour the wine. "I do, but I doubt anyone's used these since—" The words caught in his throat.

Since my father.

Rafe studied him. "You know, you might give a thought to moving somewhere else," he said lightly. "Somewhere without quite so many memories."

Alec let his icy glare speak for him as he passed Rafe the glass, then poured his own. His living arrangements were another subject *not* up for discussion. "So what happened to Egypt?" he prompted.

Rafe took a sip of the sweet red wine and made a face. "You know, for a half Italian you have a terrible palate."

Alec finally managed a laugh. "Blame the English half then."

Rafe nodded in agreement and set down his glass. "Egypt is off for now." He lowered his voice. "It appears we have a leak. And from rather high up. I'm meeting with someone from the Foreign Office later. But that's not why I'm here. When did you last speak with Signore Cardinelli?"

Alec's neck prickled. "Today, actually. He invited me to a dinner party he's giving later."

"That's perfect," Rafe said. "There's a woman who should be in attendance. Madame Noir. You'll need to make contact with her."

"Who is she?"

"Another French aristocrat of dubious origin with a line of dead husbands behind her, each one more important, and wealthier, than the last. She's currently the mistress of one of Germany's most profitable military contractors." Rafe leaned forward in his chair. "It is believed she will be there tonight to secure a deal." He then paused for effect. "It appears the good Signore Cardinelli may be moving into arms dealing."

And with one of England's greatest adversaries, no less.

"That's absurd," Alec scoffed. "Why would he invite me then?"

Rafe's eyes narrowed. "My guess is he'll double-cross her, for the right price."

It was Cardinelli's usual move: dangle someone or something out on a line and wait to see who bit the hardest. For months now Alec had been warning his superiors that if he was this willing to turn on others, he would do the very same to them. But they didn't seem to care. So far the information had been worth the risk. But they would have to pay the piper at some point, and Alec damned well didn't want to be there when it happened.

"Fine. Let him. Why am *I* supposed to snuggle up to a Frenchwoman?"

"Because you will need to warn her that loyalty is not one of the signore's stronger traits. And make an alliance."

Alec muttered a curse. Apparently his superiors had decided to finally listen. And expected him to be the one to turn the tables on the signore.

"She could be a valuable informant. Imagine: a direct line to a German military contractor." Rafe's eyes practically sparkled.

Every now and then Alec was reminded that Rafe had actually *chosen* this line of work. He wasn't a true believer, exactly, but he enjoyed it in a way Alec had never quite managed. But then, for him, this hadn't been a choice.

A bone-deep weariness settled over him and he suddenly felt ten years older. "Can't you go?" It was a useless question. Signore Cardinelli tolerated Alec only because of their shared interests. He had no use for a so-called philistine like Rafe.

Rafe shook his head. "My presence won't be welcome. Which is unfortunate, given what I've heard can happen at these parties." He then added a suggestive eyebrow waggle.

Alec had only ever been to Cardinelli's palazzo on business, but he, too, had heard the whispers.

"It has to be you. And it has to be tonight. Madame Noir is leaving for Paris in the morning."

Alec didn't bother replying. "If you're thinking of your friend, I'd be happy to keep her company," Rafe said a little too eagerly.

"No, that won't be necessary," Alec managed to growl through his iron jaw. "As it so happens, the signore invited her as well." If he dared to show up without her, the door would be slammed in his face. But the moment he saw anything vaguely salacious, they were leaving. Mission be damned.

Rafe cut a glance to his bedroom door. "She won't be sore if you pay another woman attention right in front of her?"

I know you will do anything *to get what you need.*

Not this time. He would find another way to make the damned alliance.

"No," Alec said firmly. "That won't be an issue at all."

"We need this, Alec. No distractions tonight."

"Of course." Rafe moved to leave, but Alec held up his hand. "I've a favor to ask before you go. I'm looking for information on Sir Alfred. Whatever you can find. Anything he may have been involved in lately."

Rafe raised a dark brow. "That's rather vague."

Alec rubbed his temples. "Yes, well. I'm not yet certain of what I'm looking for. But I know something's not right."

Rafe sat back in his chair. "So, the golden boy has finally seen the light."

"What the *hell* is that supposed to mean?"

"As long as I've known you, you've been Sir Alfred's acolyte, and there have been whisperings about your beloved mentor for twice as long as that. Though it would take a hell of a lot to topple him. I've tried to talk about your unquestioning loyalty before, but you wouldn't hear of it."

Alec blanched. The conversation Rafe referred to had been over two years ago. After Turkey, when Alec was almost killed pursuing a lead at Sir Alfred's personal request. It was the only time he had taken a life. It had been entirely in self-defense, but Alec still saw the man's face sometimes in the dead of night.

"So, tell me: What's changed?" Rafe prompted.

Alec kept his face blank. "It's only a hunch."

Rafe gave him a skeptical look but didn't press him. That

would come later. "I'll do some digging. Perhaps this London contact can help." This time they both stood. Alec walked him to the door and they shook hands.

"Good luck tonight," Rafe said. "And do let me know if you have any more of these *hunches*."

CHAPTER THIRTEEN

❧

After Alec closed the bedroom door behind him, Lottie paced back and forth, waiting for her heart to stop skittering. She should have insisted on staying with him, or at least *asked* who that handsome, dark-haired man was, but she was still reeling from their exchange outside his door. Alec had been holding himself back, straining against some unseen force, but for one brief moment his carefully controlled facade had fallen away again.

Lottie let out a sigh as she stripped off her gloves and removed her hat. She tossed them onto the bed and sat down on the edge. It didn't appear that Alec spent much time here, as the room was mostly empty. Aside from the bed, there was a small, battered wardrobe, and tucked away in a corner was a piece of furniture shrouded in a dust cover. Based on the dimensions, it was probably a desk. Like the rest of the flat, the room had high ceilings and tall windows. The afternoon sunlight saved the room from looking too dreary. It must have been lovely once, but now the walls were sun bleached, the plaster was chipped, and the tiled floor was scuffed and worn. Why on earth would Alec wish to *own* this place? She had caught a glimpse of the Grand Canal through the parlor window, but the view didn't seem a fair trade for living in a run-down old palazzo.

When her heartbeat had returned to normal, she rose from the bed and pressed her ear against the door. All she could hear was muffled voices. The man must be another agent. And yet Alec had looked terribly put out by his appearance. She gave up on listening and walked over to the covered piece of furniture. A swipe of her finger revealed an impressive layer of dust. Whatever was under there hadn't seen light in ages. Lottie lifted up a corner and peeked underneath. Her suspicions had been correct. It was a desk. A rather beautiful one.

She glanced cautiously at the door again, then gave herself a shake. It was only a piece of furniture, for heaven's sake. Not Pandora's box. Lottie carefully pulled the cover off so as not to release a cloud of dust and revealed a beautiful, black, lacquered writing desk with an elegant gold chinoiserie design painted over the surface. She ran her fingers over the smooth, cool edge. The fine heirloom seemed entirely out of place compared to the rest of the unremarkable furniture. The desk's surface was empty, but the lone drawer held two small picture frames of a man and a woman.

One was a pencil sketch of Edward Gresham similar to the image that had been used in his collected works; Lottie picked it up to have a closer look. This must have been a sketch the artist composed during one of the sessions for the formal portrait. Edward Gresham had been a handsome devil, and Alec shared his father's dark hair, strong nose, and powerful jaw.

She replaced the frame and picked up the other, much smaller portrait. A miniature, really. The woman must be Alec's mother. Lottie had never seen her likeness before. The late Mrs. Gresham had been a simple laundress here in

Venice when she met Alec's father and, at least according to the startling number of poems he had written on the subject, it was love at first sight. Edward Gresham must have had this portrait commissioned after they married. The corner of Lottie's mouth turned up. How very like him to eschew the convenience of photography for the romance of the painted image.

Mrs. Gresham was, unsurprisingly, strikingly beautiful, with fair hair and hazel eyes. It was easy to see how she could kindle true love in the heart of any man. Lottie squinted and drew the frame closer. There was some kind of inscription along the bottom: Contessa Maria Petrucci.

That name...

It's a very old, very well-respected family in these parts.

The blood rushed to her face as she stared at the inscription. Perhaps this wasn't Alec's mother after all. Lottie scrutinized the woman's face again. No. The likeness wasn't as strong as his father's, but it was there all the same in the color of her eyes and the sensual shape of her mouth. And she certainly matched Edward Gresham's descriptions of his great love. But if that were true, then she hadn't been a common laundress at all. She was a noblewoman.

Lottie slowly returned the miniature to its place. There could be any number of perfectly valid, perfectly boring reasons why Edward Gresham hid his wife's identity, and why Uncle Alfred hadn't corrected the information even after their deaths. But the simplest—and most salacious—rose to the surface:

Maria Petrucci was never Edward's wife.

And if that were true, then Alec was illegitimate.

Shuffling came from the other side of the door. Someone was approaching. Lottie quickly replaced the dust cover and returned to the edge of the bed, doing her best to hide her shock. Questions burned in her brain, but she couldn't ask them. At least not now. If Alec wanted her to know the truth, he would tell her. Wouldn't he?

The door swung open and Alec entered. He looked tense and agitated, but his eyes immediately softened once they fell on her. How badly she wanted him to share the truth with her. To *trust* her.

"Are you all right?" he asked.

She nodded. "Is your... friend still here?"

"He just left." Alec sat down beside her and stared at the floor. "But he'll be back."

Goodness, how tired he looked. Lottie had the urge to stroke away the tension from his brow, but that insurmountable wall seemed to separate them once again, now built of more secrets than she could count. "He's an agent, isn't he?"

"Yes. We often work together." Alec turned to her. "And it appears that my presence is required at Signore Cardinelli's this evening after all," he said with marked displeasure.

"Oh, is that so?" Lottie said, feigning wide-eyed innocence.

Alec frowned, not at all fooled. "Don't think this gives you the chance to play detective. You're only coming because I doubt I'll be admitted without you." Lottie smiled but Alec's frown only deepened. "You'll stay away from Cardinelli. Give me your word."

"I will," she reluctantly agreed. "And what will you be doing while I'm busy *not* talking to the signore?"

He slanted his gaze to the window. "It's better the less you know," he said coolly. "But I... I won't be myself tonight. Do you understand?"

Lottie pressed her lips together. That could mean all sorts of things.

For once, Alec didn't try to hide his feelings. But she

couldn't tell which troubled him: fearing for her safety, or what she might think of him after this evening.

All the more important that she show him her mettle. And that she could accept him, no matter his past.

"Yes. Perhaps I'll finally be able to see this *charm* I've heard so much about." She then placed her hand on top of his and gave it a reassuring pat. "Don't you worry about me."

Alec let out a soft breath. "I do, though," he murmured, while staring at their hands. "How can I not?" Then he glanced up. All she could hear now was the crushing vulnerability that laced through every word, the uncertainty behind every gesture.

Lottie's smile faded as his eyes were drawn to her mouth. They darkened just as they did in the hall, right before she had nearly kissed him. Her stomach tightened with anticipation, emphasizing the hollow ache inside her, but as she began to lean toward him, Alec tore his hand away from hers and stood. "Your trunk is still downstairs. I'll bring it up," he said briskly. "And I'll see about having someone come to help you dress. Nico's aunt has aspirations to become a lady's maid. She might enjoy the chance to practice on you." Lottie shook her head to protest, but he held up a hand and forced a smile. "I insist. If we must descend upon Venetian society tonight, we can at least do so in a grand fashion." Then he turned on his heel and left the room.

A little while later, Alec returned with Lottie's trunk and a pretty, dark-haired young woman.

"This is Valentina. She will help you."

The young woman grinned and clasped Lottie's hand in both of hers. "I am so happy to meet you, signora."

"Please, call me Lottie. My, your English is excellent."

Then she turned to Alec. "I see you've kept yourself busy, Professor."

Color suffused his cheeks as he turned away. "You can use this room," he said as he led them into the bedroom next to his own. Most of the furniture was also covered in dust sheets, but Alec pulled a few off, revealing a gilt dressing table and a matching full-length mirror even finer than the desk in his room. Valentina pulled over a chair and immediately began to unpack her beauty instruments, but Alec seemed riveted by a silver-plated brush, comb, and hand mirror that rested on the tabletop.

Lottie's heart twisted as another realization hit her: Alec hadn't bought this dilapidated palazzo; he had inherited it. From his parents.

And this must have been his mother's room.

Alec reached out and grazed the handle of the brush with his little finger. "Use whatever you need." Then he glanced over and Lottie nearly lost her breath. He looked just as lonely, just as lost, as he had on the first day they met all those years ago.

"Thank you."

He gave her a short nod. "I have to see to a few things before this evening. But I leave you in Valentina's most excellent care. You can trust her. With anything," he stressed.

"I'm sure," Lottie murmured, confused by his sudden gravity.

Alec then cast another longing glance at the dressing table before he left. Lottie stared after him, wishing for all the world she could ease his pain. But it would take far more than a plate of custard tarts this time.

"Come sit," Valentina said with an engaging smile.

Indeed, the young woman was thrilled to have the chance to practice her skills and must have thanked Lottie a dozen times over. After two days of travel, Lottie's hair was a wretched mess. She tried to apologize to Valentina, but the girl waved her hand. "Not to worry. I will help." She then loosened Lottie's pathetic excuse for a Psyche knot and began to gently comb through her hair. At Lottie's urging, she chattered happily about her desire to become a lady's maid abroad.

"You don't want to stay here in Venice?"

Valentina frowned. "No. There is nothing for me in this city. Not anymore," she added softly. Her mouth then twisted with the familiar expression of regret.

"But what about your sister, and little Nico?"

"They have the professor now. He will watch over them," she said with a certainty that made Lottie tense.

I can take care of them.

Alec's earlier assertion now echoed in her mind. It had been unexpectedly devastating. For years Lottie had wanted her independence, to belong to no one but herself. But in that moment she craved to know what it felt like to be under his care not at the behest of her uncle, but because he truly wished it. Lottie chewed her lip. Surely Valentina's sister was as comely as she was, and Alec obviously doted on Nico. A fellow countrywoman—a fellow *Venetian*—could provide him with a kind of understanding that Lottie would never be able to match.

Valentina's sharp gaze met hers in the mirror. Her eyebrows rose. "No, signorita. I did not mean—" She paused and shook her head. "My sister has the misfortune to only love Nico's father."

"And the professor?" Lottie heard herself ask.

Valentina shrugged and turned her attention back to her work. "I have never seen him with a woman. Until you."

Lottie looked down at her hands. She had no wish to see the ridiculous blush that was spreading across her face. Still, it meant nothing. Why, she all but *forced* Alec to bring her here in the first place.

And yet...

Any more talk of Alec ended as Stella, Nico's mother, arrived to press Lottie's gown. She was, indeed, a pretty woman but far more serious than Valentina. There was a hardness about her that likely came from shouldering a great deal of responsibility at a young age. Stella didn't appear to know much English, or perhaps she was not as loquacious as her younger sister. She greeted Lottie and gave her sister a fond kiss on the cheek, then immediately set to work.

After Valentina had finished brushing out Lottie's hair, she artfully pinned her mass of curls in a heavy knot at the back of her head. Then she teased a few long tendrils to spill gracefully over her shoulders. Once Valentina finished, the sisters helped Lottie dress. She had found the gown in a little shop in Florence run by a rather forward-thinking seamstress. A fine lady had it commissioned, but then she disappeared without paying. The gown was cleverly designed with a corset built into the bodice, but that didn't stop Stella from fastening it within an inch of her life. Lottie pressed a hand against her waist and let out a breath. "Perhaps it could be loosened a bit?"

Despite the language barrier, Stella knew exactly what Lottie meant. She soundly shook her head and guided Lottie over to a floor-length gilt mirror. "See?"

"Oh my goodness," Lottie murmured. She both looked, and felt, like an ethereal creature. A Botticelli goddess come to life. The Florentine gown was made of diaphanous ivory-colored silk and tulle with a daringly low bodice that fit like a second skin, enhancing her figure in all the right places before giving way to a fuller skirt tastefully embroidered with flowers that seemed to spring from the very dress itself. More gauzy fabric was generously draped along her shoulders, like fairy wings.

Even Stella nodded with approval. "Si, questa è una bellissima creazione."

Lottie turned to Valentina. "I've no doubt you will make a wonderful lady's maid," she said, pressing several coins into the girl's palm.

Valentina's eyes widened at the amount and she gave Lottie a broad smile. "Grazie, signorita."

"Do let me know if you need a reference."

"But, the professor said I was to go to England with you."

Lottie tilted her head. "What do you mean?"

"When you return tomorrow. He said you could not go by yourself." Valentina gave her a worried frown. "Is—is that not right?"

I have to see to a few things.

You can trust her. With anything.

Alec had already planned their separation without one word to her. Again.

"Oh," Lottie said softly as understanding washed over her. "Yes. Yes, of course. I—I wasn't thinking." She managed a tight smile and the girl relaxed.

The sisters spent a few more minutes cooing over her before they led Lottie into the parlor. Alec leaned against the doorframe of the balcony that looked out onto the Grand Canal; he cut a striking figure against the breathtaking view. The sun had just begun to set, and Lottie inhaled at the purple sky and deep gold clouds tinged with red. The dome of Basilica San Marco was visible in the distance. Alec turned at the sound of her entrance, but his face was cast in shadow against the brilliant light framing him. He had changed into a black evening suit with a white shirt and bow tie. Severe and elegant. The sight was nearly as breathtaking as the sunset. Lottie hadn't seen him dressed so formally since...

...since the evening of her coming out ball.

When you fell in love with him. And then he broke your heart.

Without so much as a backward glance.

Lottie struggled to swallow past the lump in her throat while her scarred heart thundered in her chest. What was she *doing* here? She had been happy in her little Tuscan cottage. Perhaps a bit lonely at times, but one could be lonely anywhere. Even in a house full of people. And yet, after months of meticulous planning, after she had finally started making a new life for herself, she had given it all up as soon as Alec came calling. Because he was always unavoidable. Forever inescapable.

And she still loved him. Even now. Even after everything.

The moment seemed to stretch endlessly between them until she became that pitiful, friendless orphan once again, clambering after Alec, begging for his friendship, desperate for the warmth, the care, her duty-bound uncle could never provide, to feel wanted, needed, by another person.

Promise you won't ever leave me again.

Her cheeks now burned at the memory. Back then she had no shame in revealing such raw emotions to him. In admitting how much she needed him, how small and weak she was without him. What had he said in return? She couldn't remember now. But it didn't matter. She had her answer. She'd had it a thousand times over already.

The ladies faded into the background as Alec wavered before her eyes. She knew he was speaking, and yet the words couldn't penetrate her woolly mind. Just as her vision began to blur, his warm hand clasped her upper arm—the only part that wasn't covered by her evening gloves. She trembled under his touch as he anchored her to the ground. To this moment. With him.

"Look at me." The commanding tone washed over her, cool and calming. His voice was even deeper than usual, and the very sound felt like a long, lingering caress.

It would take a lifetime to forget him now, if she was lucky. One could not outrun their own memories, and she had amassed so many more over the past few days. Lottie blinked, and her eyes flickered to his face. Alec was so close she could see the flecks of gold in his irises. His intense gaze pierced straight through to her chest, but she would never know what it felt like to belong to him. She was just another obligation. Just another part of his duty.

"Sit." Alec guided her down to the sofa. Then he called to one of the women behind her and asked for food and drink. Lottie frowned as he kneeled before her. He would wrinkle his trousers before they even left, but Alec didn't seem to care. He took a tray from one of the ladies and handed her a plate of the rice Nico had brought earlier. "Here. You must eat. I thought you were going to faint right in front of me."

Lottie gave no response. She did as she was told, barely registering the taste of the food. After a few bites, Lottie moved on to the glass of wine. It was cool and sweet. She drank deeply, greedily, until Alec clucked his tongue and stilled her hand. "Careful. I can't have you foxed before supper," he said with a small smile, then he took the glass, stood up, and walked over to the sisters.

While they spoke, Lottie stared blankly out the window waiting for the wine to swirl through every vein, deaden every nerve, strangle every sense. She was tired of feeling so much. And for a man who didn't appear to feel as much for her in return.

Tonight she needed numbness. Blessed emptiness.

Behind her Alec thanked the sisters for their work, and some more coin was exchanged. They left on a swish of skirts before the front door shut softly. Alec stood in place for what felt like hours, then she heard the slow, heavy tread of his footsteps. Lottie's pulse quickened a little more with every step, and the sweetness from the wine turned metallic on her tongue. Dread and desire warred within her. She dragged her eyes away from the window and onto the floor until the toes of his freshly polished shoes came into view.

Alec stopped a foot from her. "As I was saying before you nearly toppled over, Valentina has outdone herself."

Lottie drew her gaze slowly, steadily, up Alec's form until she reached the eyes she had once known so well. "Yes. Luckily, I seem to have acquired her services when I leave. Tomorrow."

Alec had the decency not to look away. "It was what we agreed upon. One day in Venice. And then you leave."

But not without you.

"It will be all right," he continued. "As long as Valentina accompanies you home. She's been wanting to go to England anyway, and this seemed like the perfect opportunity. I've paid for her ticket and given her funds for lodging. You aren't obligated to hire her, but I'm sure a reference would help."

"Of course," she murmured.

Home. It had been ages since any place had felt like that. Lottie turned away. She couldn't bear his stony expression. "You're sending me away," she whispered, hating the weakness in her voice. He was still only thinking of her blasted reputation. Of fulfilling his duty.

"It's for your own protection."

Lottie met his dark gaze. *Mine, or yours?* But she kept the accusation to herself. Some unspoken emotion briefly flashed across his face, but she could not make him speak, no matter how badly she wished for it.

"You don't have to do this," he finally murmured. "You can stay here tonight."

That was certainly the more sensible choice. But Lottie hadn't come to Italy in the first place to make safe choices. She came here to be bold. To put everything at stake—her reputation, her future, and, it seemed, her heart. None of that should change because of Alec's presence. She would still have a life to live once he had gone. That she knew very well. If he wanted her gone, so be it. Let him stay in this crumbling palazzo. Let him run his little missions. She did not need to subject herself to his manipulations after tonight. Until then, she would enjoy herself.

Lottie held out her gloved hand. It no longer trembled. "Thank you, but I believe I'll be going out."

Alec studied her for a tense moment. His brows pulled together in a slight frown, but he took her hand and pulled her to her feet. "You will let me know the minute you feel unwell."

"Yes, but duty comes first, Professor Gresham. Always."

Alec drew her arm into the crook of his elbow and stared straight ahead as he led her toward the door. "As if I could ever forget."

CHAPTER FOURTEEN

I must confess, I was expecting this evening to be a bore. So I begged the signore to invite at least one terribly handsome man." The enigmatic Madame Noir leaned in a little closer, enveloping Alec in a thick cloud of expensive amber perfume. "I'll have to thank him later," she murmured while holding his gaze.

Alec forced a smile. "I didn't realize I was filling an order, Madame."

"And I didn't realize history professors could look like *you*. Thank goodness I was educated by nuns, or I never would have learned a thing!"

The Frenchwoman let out a full, throaty laugh and briefly touched his wrist. She must have been beautiful once, and the years had still been kind. She could be mistaken for much younger, in the right light. But she carried herself with an innate confidence that came only from age—and experience.

Under different circumstances Alec would have enjoyed her company. Tonight, however, it was torturous.

All he wanted was to be back in his flat with Lottie. They didn't have to touch, or even speak. It was enough to sit in companionable silence and watch as she took in her first Venetian sunset.

And far more than a coward like him deserved.

It was unnerving how well she still knew him after all these years. Alec had forgotten what it meant to be truly understood by another person, as well as the heart-stopping pain that came from disappointing them. Lottie was clearly hurt by his managing behavior, but she would see the wisdom in their separation soon enough and be grateful he had taken such measures. Tomorrow afternoon she would board a train bound for London with her reputation still intact and a limitless future to look forward to. His only regret was that he hadn't been the one to tell her his intentions, and so he accepted her punishing silence.

As soon as they arrived at Signore Cardinelli's palatial home they had been whisked out onto the terrace for drinks. Lottie ignored his offer to fetch her something and walked away. The Etruscan collector, if there had ever been one, never appeared, but Madame Noir had sidled up to him once he was alone. Apparently she had a preference when it came to gentlemen, and he fit the bill perfectly. No doubt she would be open to any suggestion he made; they could slip upstairs where he could draw a promise from her any number of ways. It would be the work of only a few minutes. And yet he couldn't make himself do it.

The dinner gong sounded, and guests began to move toward the dining room. There must have been thirty or so people in attendance. Far more than Alec had assumed. It made monopolizing Madame Noir much easier, but he kept losing track of Lottie. Alec cast a subtle glance over the well-dressed crowd—a mixture of lesser European nobility, distinguished locals, and wealthy foreigners from around the world—but there was no sign of her cinnamon tresses.

"I believe your *wife* is with Mr. Drakos." There was a distinct edge to Madame Noir's voice.

So much for subtlety.

Alec turned to her with a rueful smile. "She's not my wife." He couldn't lose Lottie *and* botch this assignment.

"Oh?" Madame Noir maintained her bored tone, but Alec hadn't missed the slight rise of her dark brows.

He placed a hand over his heart. "Dear Miss Gresham is my cousin. The youngest daughter of my late mother's favorite sister. This is her first time in Venice and her chaperone has fallen ill, so I offered to act as her escort this evening."

Madame Noir's brown eyes slowly warmed as he spoke. Not even she was immune to a man so *devoted* to family.

She flashed her enigmatic smile once again. "Oh, how very sweet of you to watch over her. I wish I had such a thoughtful cousin protecting me when I was her age. He might have saved me from my first husband," she added with another laugh and fluttered her fan. Then Madame Noir quickly scanned the terrace. "There she is." She nodded toward the far end of the crowd. "See? She is talking with Mr. Drakos. I'm told he owns a very successful olive oil company. He even has his own *island*."

Alec squinted. He had met the Grecian businessman earlier—late fifties or early sixties, a head shorter than Lottie, and a downright bore. He had wrangled Lottie into what appeared to be a deep conversation. Her head was bent slightly and her delicate brows were pulled together in concentration, but in that exquisite gown she seemed other-worldly. A celestial being brought down to earth. It was as if the goddess Flora was listening politely to an undergardener's petty lament. Relief swelled inside him, and he turned back to Madame Noir.

She gave him a knowing smile. Her eyes then lingered on Lottie. "A lovely girl, your cousin. Even with that hair."

Alec bit the inside of his cheek to keep from lashing out.

He offered his arm, and Madame Noir eagerly took it while pressing her sizable décolletage against him. He glanced down and managed to flash her a smirk.

Bold lady.

As they shuffled toward the dining room, he kept the conversation light, and she laughed at all his terrible jokes.

Good. She liked him already.

For nearly two centuries the palazzo had belonged to a powerful Venetian banking family, and the dining room was the house's showpiece—a cavernous space painted a rich, sensuous red that gave way to a brilliant frescoed ceiling that rivaled the Sistine Chapel, while the walls were adorned with priceless art and antiques. It seemed that everywhere one looked, there was something even more magnificent. Alec still lost his breath just a little whenever he entered the room.

Even Madame Noir seemed impressed. "My goodness," she whispered.

As they paused to take in the room's many treasures, his gaze tangled with Lottie's. Mr. Drakos was still talking beside her, but she didn't appear to be listening this time. She was worryingly pale once again, like she had been in his flat. Alec was a moment away from casting Madame Noir aside and gathering Lottie in his arms when her gaze fell to where the Frenchwoman pressed against his side, her arm wrapped snuggly around his own. Lottie's mouth tensed, as if she had tasted something bitter.

Something like disgust.

Alec's neck burned under her inspection. Lottie, who had been born with everything and seemed determined to throw it away, had no right to judge *him*.

Her eyes snapped back to his, as if she had heard his thoughts, and her stare bore into his from across the room.

Mr. Drakos began pointing to a suit of armor against the far wall, and she reluctantly let him lead her to the other side of the room. Alec inhaled slowly and pushed her from his mind. He had done it exceedingly well for years. Surely he could manage the next few hours.

Alec turned to Madame Noir, who was still taking in their surroundings. "Shall we sit, Madame? I'd love to hear more about your life in Berlin."

She squeezed his arm with her free hand. "And I would be happy to oblige, Professor."

His plan to sit as far away from Lottie as possible was derailed at the very last minute, no thanks to a bickering couple from Brussels who cut in front of him without so much as a glance.

Madame Noir leaned closer to him. "One can expect nothing less than utter rudeness from the Flemish," she whispered then clucked her tongue in disapproval.

The only two remaining seats were directly across from Lottie and Mr. Drakos.

Alec held back his grimace and led Madame Noir to their seats. As they approached, she inhaled sharply and held up her fan. "Do you see the man seated on the other side of your cousin?"

Alec glanced over and gave a subtle nod. A late arrival. Alec would have noticed him on the terrace, as he was the only other man under fifty besides himself, but his attire made sure to loudly announce his presence. He was dressed in a purple velvet evening jacket with a matching striped waistcoat. It was the very height of continental fashion—and made him look ridiculous.

"The Honorable Mr. Morley," Madame Noir explained. "*Highly* eligible. I think he is in line for one of your dukedoms," she added in an awed whisper.

Annoyance prickled through Alec. "Is that so?" The man

seemed unbearably obnoxious. Of course he would end up a duke.

She playfully tapped his arm with the tip of her fan. "Don't try to hide your delight, monsieur. I can see those wheels already turning in your head. There are mamas who would give their right arms to have their own daughters seated next to him at dinner. The poor man spends most of his time abroad to escape them."

Poor indeed.

Just then, Lottie let out a laugh. Mr. Morley was much too close—why, his lips were practically *brushing* her ear.

"Oh, it has already begun!" Madame Noir said in delight.

He cut another glance across the table as he pulled out Madame Noir's chair. Mr. Morley was doing the same for Lottie, and she seemed all too delighted by his chivalry. Despite the man's highly questionable sartorial choices, Alec had to admit he was handsome. Most women seemed to prefer blond-haired and blue-eyed men. His jaw tensed against the flare of jealousy blistering his insides. But he brushed the ugly feeling aside. If this led to a match, Sir Alfred would nominate him for a medal. And this was exactly what he wanted for her. A duke's heir could give her everything.

Everything you never could.

Alec turned away and took his seat beside Madame Noir, giving her the most charming smile he could muster. Let Lottie enjoy the man's company. He had work to do.

At first Lottie had been worried by the prospect of sitting next to an Englishman all evening. What if Mr. Morley recognized her or questioned her false identity? But as it turned out, Mr. Morley lived largely abroad—and had few interests beyond himself. Lottie made sure to smile and nod at all the right places, and by the time dessert was served she had said nothing beyond a few generic platitudes.

"How very interesting," she responded automatically, as the man prattled on between generous mouthfuls of molded ice cream. She blinked slowly. That waistcoat of his was starting to give her a headache.

When she opened her eyes, Mr. Morley was giving her his full attention. And a rather too interested smile. "I say, I can't remember the last time I had such a charming dinner companion."

Lottie held back a snort. Out of the corner of her eye, she noticed Alec look their way after having easily ignored her for the past hour. She swallowed her irritation and smiled at Mr. Morley. "Why thank you, sir."

She could never manage this degree of pretense in London. Then again, she had never been motivated by petty jealousy before. Luckily, Mr. Morley didn't notice her act. The gentleman seemed to miss quite a lot.

"So then, where are you off to next, Miss Gresham? Venice is all well and good if you like swamp water, but you really *must* go to Florence."

It was the third time he had asked her that question and the second time he had told her to go to Florence, but she managed to keep smiling. "I'm afraid I'm due back in England. But do tell me what *you* love about the city." She turned back to her dessert as the man began to prattle on again.

Was this all it took to do Alec's job? Tell people what they wanted to hear? Give them what they wanted to see? A smile here, a laugh there. Stroke their egos until they were soft and pliant. Until they let their guards down.

It was rather easy. Disturbingly so.

And yet, in a way it was exciting to be a different version of herself. She might have even enjoyed the exercise if it didn't include watching Alec flirt with a beautiful, sophisticated Frenchwoman.

Who is old enough to be his mother.

Lottie chastised herself for the uncharitable thought. She would be lucky to look half as alluring as Madame Noir, even now. As if on cue, the woman let out another sultry laugh, and Lottie couldn't stop from glancing over at them. She had thrown her dark head back and clasped a hand against her enviable décolletage. Alec grinned down at her, as if she was the most charming woman he had ever met.

Lottie's chest pinched. Was he *really* that good? Or was it not an act at all?

She couldn't decide which would be worse.

"Miss Gresham, are you well?" asked a soft voice beside her.

Lottie turned to Mr. Drakos, who gestured to her spoon. It had begun to tremble in her tight grip. "Thank you. Yes, I'm fine," she murmured and set down her spoon. Lottie gave him a gracious smile as guilt swept through her. She had mostly ignored the kind man all through dinner because he hadn't suited her purposes, and because one could listen to the finer details of olive harvesting for only so long. An unsettling shiver moved through her. Perhaps this wasn't so easy.

Lottie glanced up and met Alec's piercing hazel stare. Madame Noir was busy talking to the man to her right, so it seemed he had found a moment to acknowledge her presence. Lottie cast him a subtle frown. He needed to concentrate on his so-called business, not her. Goodness. What if he took the woman to bed? Surely he would spare her *that* indignity. Before she could ponder this further, Signore Cardinelli announced that they would all retire to the drawing room for light refreshment and music.

Beside her, Mr. Morley clucked his tongue. "I can't *stand*

this continental habit of keeping the sexes together. It's the only time I long for England. Men need a good smoke after a meal. A chance to talk properly."

Lottie raised an eyebrow but spoke in her sweetest tone. "Why, Mr. Morley, have you not had your fill of proper conversation this evening?"

The odious man had the decency to redden. "There are some topics much too delicate to discuss in front of ladies. Business. Politics. That sort of thing."

"Well, I can't speak for every lady, but I'd be happy to discuss politics with you. In fact, I have a number of opinions I've wanted to share with someone who possesses the ability to vote in our government." She then fluttered her eyelashes.

"Hear, hear." Madame Noir raised her glass from across the table and gave her a wink.

Mr. Morley eyed Lottie warily, as if she had suddenly turned into a live python instead of a woman with opinions. Then he appealed to Mr. Drakos. "I'm sure *you* agree with me."

"I believe the ladies should be heard," the older man said with surprising disapproval. "Otherwise, it makes you Englishmen seem terrified of your own women. Though I suppose you must be. Why else deny them the vote?"

Mr. Morley's eyes nearly bulged out of their sockets, and Lottie had to smother a laugh into her napkin. Apparently his dilettante ways stopped at the idea of women's suffrage. She caught Alec's eye from across the table, but he seemed even less amused than before. Couldn't he at least give her a *smirk*? Surely that was allowed between cousins...

Beside her, Mr. Drakos stood and held out his hand. "I would be happy to escort you into the drawing room, Miss Gresham. And we may discuss anything you wish," he added pointedly.

Lottie smiled and accepted his hand. She had done nothing to deserve such kindness from him. "Thank you, sir."

As they all stood from the table, Alec once again took Madame Noir's arm in his. They exchanged a warm smile and the woman had the audacity to reach out and brush the back of a gloved finger to his cheek.

The pinch in Lottie's chest suddenly burned so sharply, so deeply, that she nearly lost her breath.

"I think you may need some air, Miss Gresham." Mr. Drakos made the gentle suggestion as they entered the drawing room. "Let us go out onto the balcony."

"Yes," she rasped, twisting away from the happy pair. "That sounds perfect."

He placed a warm hand on the small of her back and guided her toward the open balcony doors just as Madame Noir's enchanting laugh floated into the room.

CHAPTER FIFTEEN

❧

A lec spirited Madame Noir away to a secluded corner of the sumptuous drawing room so they could talk more "privately." They had entered in time to see Mr. Drakos escort Lottie outside, and this spot offered the best view of the balcony doors.

"Really, Professor," the woman cooed as they sat down on a rich velvet couch. "She will be fine. Let her enjoy a little freedom while she is away from home." She then placed her palm on Alec's knee. He raised an eyebrow, but she took his silence as encouragement and slid her hand up a little higher, a familiar glint in her eye.

Alec had learned much about Madame Noir over the last several hours, but nothing that confirmed any of Rafe's claims. She did briefly mention her attachment to the military contractor, but it seemed that neither one was anything close to a practicing monogamist. It seemed highly unlikely that she was here to secure an *arms* deal on his behalf. Just another one of Signore Cardinelli's teases. And Alec certainly wasn't going to bed her over it. If that part was so damned important to Rafe, he could bloody well do it himself. Alec had another idea.

He plucked Madame Noir's wandering hand from his knee

and clasped it between his. Then he leaned toward her and lowered his voice. "You know I'd like nothing more than to spend time with you this evening, but I have my cousin to consider. How long are you in Venice?"

A meaningless question. He already knew her plans.

The great lady pouted. "This is my last night. Then I return to Paris." She began to stroke his palm with her index finger. Well, she was certainly persistent.

"I see," Alec said slowly, as if he were considering a rendezvous. "My cousin will return to England shortly. But perhaps once she is gone . . ." He deliberately left the sentence unfinished. Let her think whatever she wanted.

The pout disappeared and she leaned in even closer. "That is a delicious idea, Professor," she purred. "Have you been to Paris?"

"Yes. I confess, I did not care for it."

Her smile deepened. "Then give me the chance to change your mind. I do so *love* a challenge."

Movement on the balcony caught Alec's eye, distracting him for only a moment, but it was more than enough time for Madame Noir to wrap her hand around his neck and press her pillowy mouth to his own. Before he had a chance to react, she pulled his bottom lip between her teeth and gave it a saucy bite. Alec let out a startled grunt and gripped her by the shoulders in order to push her away, but she misinterpreted his reaction and pressed even closer.

It was then, of course, that Lottie returned from the balcony.

And, thanks to Alec's prime position, she had a perfect view of the two of them. He managed to wrench his mouth away from Madame Noir's in time to see the expression on Lottie's face before she darted from the room. Any lingering doubt about her feelings for him vanished in the face of such crushing disappointment.

"Lottie!" Alec stood up so quickly that Madame Noir slipped from her chair and fell right on her bottom. He blew out a frustrated breath and began to help her up, but she batted his hand away.

"Enough. I am not interested in a man who so is preoccupied with his own *cousin*," she hissed as she resumed her seat.

"Madame, let me explain—"

With a smooth flick of her wrist, she opened her fan. "I don't *care*. Good night, Professor." Then she turned pointedly away from him. Their conversation, and any hope of securing an alliance, was over.

Alec sighed and headed for the door Lottie had passed through. He crossed the hallway and then entered another room as grand as the last, but after two steps, he stopped in his tracks. Several couples in various stages of undress huddled in every available corner. He glanced back through the doorway of the room he had just exited. Madame Noir appeared to have already recovered from his rejection with Mr. Drakos. Alec turned away before he could see any more.

So the rumors were true, then. Anger gripped him as he stalked down the marble hallway. What had he been thinking, bringing Lottie here? He had to find her. *Immediately.* He passed by another room as the good signore himself emerged with two giggling courtesans.

"Where are you off to, Professor?"

"I'm leaving," Alec growled.

The man's face screwed up in a frown. He shooed the young women away and blocked Alec's path. "But the festivities are only beginning. And we still have much to discuss. I noticed you seem to be enjoying Madame Noir's company. I have some information about her that might interest you . . ."

Alec knew he was supposed to take whatever crumbs this man offered, especially now that he had failed to win over

Madame Noir herself, but all that mattered at the moment was finding Lottie.

"I don't give a damn, Cardinelli. I'm looking for my cousin."

Signore Cardinelli managed to give him a pitying look. "Come now, Professor. Are we not friends? We both know that only a certain kind of lady travels alone with an unmarried man." He even gave him a wink. "It isn't very gentlemanly of you not to share her."

Before he could think twice, Alec had grabbed Cardinelli by the lapels and hauled him against the wall. "If you so much as touch a hair on her head, I will kill you myself." He then unceremoniously dropped the signore, who stumbled inelegantly against the wall, and continued down the hallway.

"You will regret that, Professor!" Cardinelli called after him, his tone full of rage. "I won't stand for such treatment in my own home!"

As Alec hurried through the stately home, various sounds of a decidedly amorous bent wafted through the air, but there was no sign of Lottie. Alec grew increasingly more irritated, until he turned a corner and saw a figure peering into a partially opened doorway.

"Lottie!" he hissed.

She straightened and turned toward him, looking very much like a mischievous child caught in the act. God only knew what she had been watching. Alec strode over and grabbed her arm. He then tugged her down the hall, not even stopping to see what had arrested her attention so.

"Oh, is there somewhere else we're needed? Admittedly, those two seemed to have things well in hand."

Was she really making *puns* now?

"We are leaving," Alec said through gritted teeth. "*Obviously.*"

They rounded another corner. Down another hallway and they would reach the back entrance.

"I hope you aren't leaving early on my account. That hardly seems necessary."

Alec gave her a black look. "I assure you, it isn't."

"I had no idea you were such a degenerate," she continued lightly. "Most surprising. And to think of all the fuss you made over sharing a bed."

"Shut up, Lottie." Alec stopped and pulled her toward him until they were mere inches apart. "This is work. I *told* you I—" he broke off. Lottie shot him a confused look and he brought a finger to his lips.

Just then he heard a voice demand, "Over here! Quickly!"

The sound of footsteps echoed down the hallway they had just come from. Without another word he pulled Lottie deep into a shadowed alcove and shielded her with his body. If anyone walked past, his black-clad figure would hide them far better than her iridescent gown. Her skirts swirled around his legs, but otherwise they did not touch. Alec pressed his forearms on either side of her, and the marble wall was blessedly cool against his warm palms. He closed his eyes so he could focus on the footsteps, but he couldn't ignore Lottie's quick breaths. She was so close they tickled his neck.

The footsteps grew louder. At least two people, possibly three. Alec could identify the strident gait of Signore Cardinelli, who was joined by someone much larger, likely one of his powerful guards. His entire body tensed. They stopped perilously close to the alcove, and Alec instinctively moved closer to Lottie. She inhaled sharply as the lapels of his dinner jacket brushed against her décolletage, but he canted his head toward the hallway.

Cardinelli was talking to another man. Their voices were pitched low, but Alec heard enough: "I want them found immediately. And bring the professor directly to me. He and I have unfinished business. Use the girl as you wish."

Alec swallowed hard. Thank God Lottie barely spoke Italian.

They exchanged a few more words, then Signore Cardinelli retreated back down the hallway while the guard stalked off in the other direction.

Alec let out a sigh and pressed his forehead to the wall just above her shoulder. A strand of her hair brushed his ear, and he nearly succumbed to the urge to lean his cheek against her mass of curls. At some point Lottie had taken hold of his shirtfront with trembling fingers. All her earlier bravado was gone now.

"It's all right." He placed his hands over hers and eased her iron grip.

"I heard the word 'professore,'" she said, her voice uncommonly strained. "Are they looking for you?"

Now that danger wasn't quite so imminent, Alec was very aware of how close they were, and how Lottie's curves brushed his frame. He couldn't stop himself from sneaking a glance down at her décolletage, which strained and swelled against the fabric of her dress with each rapid inhalation.

"It's nothing. Don't worry."

Something flickered in her eyes. Then her concerned frown deepened to a glare as she pulled her hands out of his. "I don't know why you were following me anyway. You seemed pleasantly occupied when I left," she added under her breath.

Alec's jaw tightened. Now was hardly the time to discuss his kiss with the madame. He turned around and moved toward the hallway. No one was about. He beckoned to Lottie and she grudgingly pushed away from the wall. "There is a boat waiting for us," he explained in a low murmur.

"You expected we would have to sneak out like a pair of thieves?"

"I try to prepare for every possibility. Stay close to me." Alec held out his hand. Lottie stared at it with a sour look. "Please," he prompted. She let out a sigh and took it. Alec gripped her hand and gave her a reassuring squeeze. It was the best he could do for now. As they stepped lightly down the hallway, Alec listened for the slightest sound of footsteps. He was prepared to do whatever it took to keep her safe, but he loathed the idea of committing an act of violence in front of her.

It does not matter. Let her see you for the animal you are.

Lottie tugged his hand. "You're hurting me," she whispered.

Alec immediately gentled his grip and gave her an apologetic smile that she did not return. At the end of the hallway was a heavy door that opened onto the back. From there it would be a short walk to their meeting point. Alec tested the knob and cursed. Then he knelt down and pulled out his lock picks. It took only a few moments before the ancient mechanism released and the door slowly opened. Then he glanced back. Lottie was looking at him with something close to awe but quickly schooled her expression.

He smiled again as he stood. "I wouldn't be much of a spy if I couldn't pick a lock."

"No," she said dryly. "I suppose not."

He held out his hand again, and she readily took it this time. They crept outside and Alec guided them along the palazzo's back wall, taking care to stay in the shadows until they reached a little slope that gave way to a dock.

"Our boat will meet us there," he murmured. Lottie followed his gaze and nodded. He did not add that they would be dangerously exposed until then. If they were spotted, they would have only a few precious minutes to escape. Alec looked around one last time, but there was no one else about. He took a deep breath and hurried them toward the dock. He did not dare look back until they reached the end.

"Where is it?" Lottie asked tightly. "Where is the boat?"

"See there?" he gestured to a light out on the lagoon. "That's for us. The driver has been keeping watch."

As if on cue, the light began to move toward them. They stood side by side waiting as the nimble little vessel came into view. It would be here in less than a minute. He had kept her safe. Alec closed his eyes as the tension slowly ebbed from him.

Then came the telltale creak of someone stepping onto the dock. It was the same imposing guard from the hallway stalking toward them. He was a head taller than Alec and outweighed him by at least thirty pounds. All of it muscle.

Beside him Lottie whimpered.

"Watch the boat," Alec told her, his voice deadly calm.

"What are you going to do?"

He shot her a glare. "*Charlotte.*"

Lottie's eyes widened and she immediately turned around.

Alec pulled out the switchblade he always kept nestled in his breast pocket and waited until he could see the whites of the brute's eyes. Then in one swift motion he released the blade, striking the man below his left shoulder. He let out a grunt and fell to his knees just as the boat pulled alongside the dock. The driver was a man called Marco, who also ferried tourists around the city.

"Go," Alec said, pushing Lottie toward the boat.

But she clung to his arm with surprising strength and dug in her heels. "Not without you."

Alec glanced back. Despite the knife buried in him, the guard was attempting to stand up. There was no *time* for this. Alec lifted Lottie off her feet and practically tossed her into

Marco's arms. She wrenched around and looked back at him with a wild desperation that cut him to the quick. "*Wait.*"

Alec forced himself to ignore her and caught Marco's eye. "Go at my signal," he said in Italian. "No matter what."

Marco gave a single nod as he held fast to Lottie, who was still crying out and trying to wriggle from his grasp. Without another word Alec turned around. Then he pulled out the stiletto knife he kept strapped to his ankle and marched toward the guard. "Leave now and I won't kill you."

The brute clutched weakly at the handle protruding from his shoulder. His sleeve had already turned crimson. "If I let you go, I'm good as dead anyway, Professor. The signore doesn't take kindly to failure," he panted.

Alec brandished the stiletto. "Your odds are still better with him."

The guard let out a low chuckle and went back down to both knees, raising his palms in surrender. "Fine," he said wearily. "Everyone knows I faint at the sight of my own blood anyway."

Alec stepped closer and thrust the tip of the stiletto against his opponent's sizable chest. "Then I suggest you make it so," he said viciously. It would take a determined push to pierce the skin and could leave Alec vulnerable to attack, but he would stop at nothing to keep this man away from that boat.

The man cast a dazed glance past Alec. "Is she worth it?" They both knew the signore would not soon forget this.

"She is worth *everything*."

A knowing smile played on the man's lips and he let out a faint laugh. Then, all it took was a mere glance at his sleeve before he fell heavily on his side.

Alec kept his eyes on the silent figure as he backed toward the boat and climbed in. As he entered the tiny cabin, he felt Lottie's arms come around him, felt her tears wet his collar, heard her desperate cries of relief, but only one thought echoed in his mind as the craft pulled away from the dock.

She is safe.

As the boat sped across the lagoon, Lottie clung to Alec, not caring a whit how desperate she appeared now. She *was* desperate. Besides, even if she had wanted to move, Alec's powerful arm held her fast by his side. How close they had come. And how very stupid she had been. Lottie did not know if the man they left on the dock was still alive, but she was certain that Alec would not have hesitated to kill him if needed.

And that he would have sacrificed himself to save her life.

She buried her face against his chest as a shudder came over her. Alec's hand dropped from her shoulder to her waist and he pulled her closer, but he had yet to utter a word or even look at her. Not since that terrible moment when he pushed her into the boat, and she realized that he'd intended to stay behind. In the instant before he turned away, his face had been like nothing she had ever seen—as pale and hard as a plaster mask—while his eyes gleamed with bone-chilling menace. And single-minded purpose.

Before another shudder could overtake her, Alec let out a little sigh: "That was my favorite switchblade."

Lottie jerked her head up. "What?"

"I found it in Turkey," he said evenly, as if their very *lives* hadn't been in danger just minutes ago. "It was nearly fifty years old. I'll never be able to replace it." He shook his head.

"I—I'm sorry."

Alec finally looked down at her. His face was half in shadows in the darkened cabin, but there was only heart-stopping tenderness there. Alec skimmed a hand over her hair, barely touched her curls—as if he feared she would shatter. It was nearly impossible to reconcile this man with the one on the dock, but they were both Alec. And Lottie wanted all of him—to know every facet, every mask he wore, every emotion he tried so desperately to hide from the world. And from her.

"It wasn't your fault. I never should have brought you here. Not to this house. Not to Venice. I knew the danger, and I did it anyway," he murmured the last words, as if he was speaking to himself, then turned away once again. "She caught me by surprise, you know," he added. "It meant nothing."

It took Lottie a moment to realize he was speaking of the Frenchwoman. "I believe you," she rasped. Her voice had gone hoarse from crying. "You don't need to explain anything to me."

Alec faced her then. His eyes now gleamed with something else. "I want to," he insisted. "Regardless of what your uncle once told you, the things I do are never for pleasure. They serve another purpose entirely."

"But how can you stand it? Watching you with her, I thought—"

"It isn't always like that," Alec interrupted, then he paused. "In my experience it is far easier to be with someone I don't care for than to be with someone I do."

Lottie had the feeling they were now treading on quicksand. She hesitated. "How do you know?"

Alec turned away again. A sliver of moonlight touched his cheek, making his olive skin look almost porcelain. "Because. I kissed someone. Only once. And that told me everything I needed to know."

The admission would have suffused her with joy, if not for the grim certainty in his voice. He thought such feelings were a hindrance.

She kept her words brief, so her voice wouldn't crack. "I see."

He glanced at her and raised a dark brow. "*Do* you?"

Lottie thought of her pathetic conditions, how even the lightest of his touches set off a storm within her. "Yes." She moved to bury her head against his chest once again, but he gripped her by the shoulders and forced her to meet his gaze.

"Then you see that I cannot put you at risk again. I *cannot*." He abruptly released her. "Tonight you saw what I am capable of," he began again. "And there are things I have done that can never be forgotten. That is why you must go."

Lottie bit her lip against the anguish in his words. Yes, she indeed saw what Alec was capable of. But nothing would ever be as frightening as those endless seconds after he pushed her onto the boat and stayed behind on the dock. Lottie could face anything now. Because she knew with maddening clarity what it felt like to almost lose him.

"No," she said gently. "That is why I must stay."

Alec let out an incredulous laugh. "You're in shock. You have no idea what you're saying."

Lottie gritted her teeth against the irritation that suddenly flared inside her. "I absolutely do—"

"*No*," he cut in harshly. "You know absolutely *nothing*. And that ridiculous plan of yours proves it." Alec turned fully toward her in challenge. "You think ruination will gain you freedom, but you have not thought of the consequences. And how this will *always* follow you."

"I know what to expect," she insisted.

"How?" he demanded. "You've never been an outcast before. You don't know what it will be like, what people will say about you if—"

She could not keep her own incredulous laugh from

bursting out. "Goodness, is that really what you've been trying to save me from all this time? Gossip?" she sneered. "In that case I'm afraid you're much too late. They already *do* talk about me."

This caught him by surprise. "What do you mean?"

Lottie exhaled. Was he really so blind? "I am an unmarried woman of large fortune who has rejected nearly a dozen proposals of marriage," she said slowly. "If I were a man people would toast me, but because I dare to have standards I am met with ridicule. And contempt."

"But, your friends—"

"My *friends*?" Lottie bit off. Now it was her turn to rage. "My friends have been the very *worst* of it. What others may whisper behind my back they have said to my face. To them I am an object of pity. Of derision. All while they readily submit to men who care nothing for them beyond the money or status they bring to the marriage." Lottie shook her head. "I cannot fault them for seeking out the comfort of a gilded cage, especially when they are afforded few, if any, alternatives. But since I am fortunate enough to have money of my own, I refuse to endure the same fate."

"I...I had no idea you felt this way."

"Of course not," Lottie snapped. "Why would you? Men like *you* expect ladies to be fulfilled by afternoon calls and embroidery. To freely relinquish our autonomy to our husbands and fathers who claim to know better. But I am not interested in *any* of that."

A heated silence passed between them.

"I assume you haven't kept these thoughts to yourself." Alec's face was barely visible in the dark cabin, but she swore he almost sounded amused.

"I tried. At least at first. Until I started attending suffragist meetings last year." She paused as an unexpected smile came over her. "I've never been so inspired than while watching those fiercely intelligent ladies demanding to be treated as the equal of any man. I learned so much from them. Of a life beyond what I had ever dreamed was possible." She pressed her lips together and swallowed. "I invited my friend Abigail to come with me once, but she told Uncle Alfred instead. He was horrified and put a stop to all of it, claiming the meetings weren't safe. That some of the women were radicals—which they were—but *I* wasn't in any danger. Later he admitted he was worried about how it would affect my reputation, as no man in his right mind would want to marry such an 'unnatural' woman."

In the darkness Alec let out a low curse.

"After that it was back to the same routine of tea dances and afternoon calls. Of trying to entertain men who couldn't be bothered to hide their desire for my money." Beside her Alec moved to grip his knee. "But then there was some awful business with Ceril Belvedere last spring." She shuddered at the memory of his forceful kiss and absently touched her lips. "He did not take my rejection of his proposal well. And yet, *I'm* called a jilt. A tease." She couldn't keep the indignation out of her voice.

"I am sorry for that," Alec said. "It was badly done on his part, and certainly not your fault. Any fool could see that."

His words swirled around her heart. No one had ever said anything against Ceril's behavior, not even her uncle. All his ire had been directed squarely at her for rejecting such a "worthy" suitor. Then Lottie frowned. "You know about Ceril? I thought you hadn't spoken about me with my uncle."

"I didn't learn of it from him, but yes," he admitted after a breath. "I did know."

There was something hidden in that pause. Something he was hesitant to reveal. And if she pushed too hard now, she might never learn the truth. Luckily, Lottie had grown quite adept at waiting these last five years.

"But believe me," he continued, his voice sterner now. "Things can be so much worse for you."

He was right. The trouble was, Lottie simply didn't care anymore. Her voice rose with each word, rough and urgent. "I can't end up in some loveless society marriage pretending that everything is fine when it so *obviously* isn't. I won't do it. There is too much to lose."

"Then don't," he urged. "Wait for someone you truly care about." His voice turned thin and reedy as he spoke those last words, and he paused to clear his throat. "But don't give up on the possibility. If you throw your whole future away now, you will regret it."

"I can't," she cried. "Uncle Alfred insisted that I marry a man of his choosing by the end of the season while he still has some control over my inheritance."

"*What?*" Alec's voice rang out in the darkened cabin. "And you didn't think to mention this?"

"I—I assumed you knew," Lottie said weakly as guilt flooded through her.

Alec huffed. "I've sins aplenty, but *forcing women into marriage* isn't among them." Then he muttered a curse. "I knew you thought poorly of me. Knew you didn't trust me. But dammit, I didn't realize..."

Dear Lord. She had *hurt* him. Lottie didn't think she had the ability to do so. It now seemed superbly childish not to have told him earlier.

"I'm sorry. I don't know if he would have gone through with it," she added. "But I couldn't take the chance."

"So you decided to ruin yourself as insurance," he said flatly. "With that man in Florence."

Lottie was tempted to correct him, but he was already sore

enough. "I *hate* that term, you know," she muttered instead. "Why does my entire worth depend upon my sexual experience, or lack thereof, while men can bed as many women as they like and are congratulated for it? How is *that* fair?"

"Lottie," Alec murmured gently.

But she wasn't in the mood to be coddled. "It's insulting. It's the height of hypocrisy. You must see that."

"Of course I do," he huffed. "And you're right. It isn't fair. But I don't make the rules—"

"You don't have to enforce them, either," she countered.

"For God's sake," Alec grumbled as he scrubbed a hand over his face. "I'm not trying to *enforce* them, but I'm not exactly in a position to ignore them, either, am I?"

Lottie turned away. He had a point. And she knew it even better than he realized. But she couldn't be the one to bring up his parentage.

Outside Venice floated by, a mixture of moonlit stone and glowing torchlight. "All I ever wanted was what my parents had: a partnership built on love." Her voice cracked. "It seemed such a simple thing when I was a girl. I actually thought I was being prudent. Reasonable. But I might as well have been wishing for a fairy tale."

"Don't say that," he pleaded even while he stubbornly held himself away from her.

"Why?" she demanded, facing him once more. "Why should I live with such illusions? Isn't it better to accept the reality of the choices before me? As far as I can see, I have two options: submitting to a loveless marriage or remaining a free woman of means at the expense of my reputation. I won't bother asking what choice *you* would make if you were in the same position." Lottie stopped and inhaled slowly, wrestling to maintain some control over her sharp tongue. "I know it won't be the life I have known, but I welcome the challenge.

Even the fear. All of it. And I would destroy my reputation a thousand times over again if it meant feeling the way I have these last few days..."

It would have been so easy to say *weeks* instead, but she let the words hang there in the darkness between them. Alec slowly leaned toward her until she could feel wisps of warm breath on her neck. Until his heat wrapped around her as tightly as his embrace. Lottie fought back against the urge to press against him. To feel his strength and weight surrounding her once again. But not now. Not yet.

She turned toward him until their faces were mere inches apart. His features were still hidden in the shadows, but she could feel his heavy gaze upon her. "Because it has been my choice," she continued. "Can you understand that?"

Alec let out a long sigh, but before he could answer, the boat came to a rocking halt and the driver announced their arrival. "Quickly now," he said, immediately moving toward the exit. As the boatman handed Lottie onto the dock, he gave Lottie a friendly wink. Alec then exchanged a few secretive words with him before joining her. She did not regret speaking so plainly to him, but there was still so much that remained unsaid, and she sensed that Alec would reveal the full truth only if necessary. Only if it was a matter of life or death.

CHAPTER SIXTEEN

❧

It was well after midnight, and the streets were eerily quiet as Alec led her back to his home. They walked side by side, but at no point during the short walk did he move to touch her. What little intimacy they had uncovered minutes ago had vanished now that they weren't inside the cabin's comforting darkness. Instead, his sharp eyes were consumed with scanning their surroundings, while his countenance projected a formidable prowess that would ward off all but the most determined of troublemakers.

"We weren't followed," he said, answering a question that hadn't even occurred to her. They rounded a corner and came to a stop in front of the once-grand palazzo. All the windows were dark. Nico, his mother, and aunt had no doubt been asleep for hours. "No one knows where I live. Not even the signore. And no one would ever assume I was daft enough to live *here*."

Lottie's heart twisted in her chest. "It's your parents' house, isn't it?"

Alec nodded, but he still did not look at her. She would have given anything to know what he was thinking of: His mother's death? His father's unstoppable descent into madness? But then, such thoughts must never be far from him. Alec had chosen to live among those ghosts.

"Come," he said. Lottie followed in silence as he entered the house. In the entryway he lit a single candle and led them up the winding staircase toward his flat. In the daytime, the palazzo's faded grandeur could still be seen. But now the single flickering candle threw strange shadows against the high walls that only seemed to emphasize the many years of neglect and decay.

Alec came home to this every night, Lottie thought with a shiver as she followed him into the flat. The window shutters had been left open, and the main room was illuminated by the silvery moonlight. Alec paused to light a small candelabra. "It's rather medieval now, but someday I hope to have electricity," he said with an apologetic smile. Then he led her toward the bedroom with the desk. The one that contained so many secrets.

Alec entered the room and placed the candelabra on a bedside table. Then he turned to face her. "Get some rest. If you need anything, I'll be right outside." He gestured toward the threadbare sofa in the main room.

Lottie's heart twisted again. Alec wouldn't even sleep in the other bedroom that still housed his mother's things. She sat down on the bed and grazed a finger against the worn coverlet. "You must have so many memories here," she murmured and glanced up shyly. Alec's face was hard, but his eyes burned witch black in the candlelight.

"Too many," he said in a low voice. "Sleep well. You have a long journey ahead of you tomorrow." He turned to leave but Lottie came to her feet. She pressed a trembling hand tightly against her abdomen.

"Alec. Wait."

She had spoken his name so rarely these last days that it felt like casting a spell, an invocation for a power far greater than any she possessed. Alec immediately stopped before the doorway. His entire frame tensed. He turned halfway toward her. Just enough for a shard of moonlight to illuminate his strong profile. "You're scared?"

"Yes." It wasn't exactly the truth, but Lottie would say close to anything if it drew him back to her. He turned all the way around and stepped closer. Though his face was as hard as before, his gaze seemed to penetrate straight to the hot, pulsing desire building within her. A weaker woman would have crumpled under what could easily pass as a glare. But not Lottie. She knew what that glare was hiding, and she would not leave Venice without uncovering it.

"You have nothing to fear now," he said gruffly. "I promise."

She looked down, gathering her courage. "Don't leave." She hadn't the nerve to add *me*. And yet, how many times had she asked that of him when they were children? Too many to count. But he had broken that promise in the end.

When she dared to glance up again, Alec still hadn't moved, but his mask had fallen away. Everything he worked so hard to keep hidden was laid bare before her: the wariness, the pain, and, most important, the desire.

Her eyes were drawn to the sensuous curves of his lips, almost indecently full for a man. How badly she wanted him to kiss her again, but not for show this time. Not for anything other than the sheer pleasure of it. The want. The *need* of it.

He stared at her for a long moment. His piercing gaze stirred something so raw within her she almost fell to her knees. "It's the shock of earlier," he finally said. "You don't know what you're—"

"Stay with me. Please."

Alec closed his eyes and muttered a curse.

It was the *please* that finally broke through Alec's last remaining barricade, though it had been steadily crumbling for the past hour. The overwhelming desire to protect Lottie from every possible danger was nearly as consuming as his desire to have her—but only nearly.

When Alec had left all those years ago, he had been certain that doing so would ensure her future. Sir Alfred made it clear that with him gone, Lottie would marry a respectable man of good standing and become a pillar of the community, as was her destiny. But if he stayed, Sir Alfred promised to do everything in his power to ruin Alec. With his scandalous heritage and lack of fortune, who was he to tear her away from the only world she had ever known merely in exchange for his pitiful little heart?

She may be happy at first, Sir Alfred had allowed, *but in time she will come to resent you. Will you sentence her to that fate?*

If he had loved her any less, perhaps he would have.

But instead Lottie had surprised them both and found her way in the world, on her own terms. Alec could not help but admire her for it—even if his worry had nearly driven him mad. She might want him for comfort this evening, but she had already proven she did not need him. Not the way he needed her. Since he had first stepped out onto that hillside terrace in Tuscany, somewhere, in the deepest part of his heart, Alec had wished for something like this. Prayed for it.

When he opened his eyes, Lottie was slowly stripping off her evening gloves. He had yet to respond to her declaration beyond a muttered curse, and the sight of her bare arms was not helping. The open shutters let in the bright moonlight, casting her in an otherworldly glow. Standing there proud and tall in her gown, she looked like a fairy queen—one who came to visit every five years for only a few precious hours. Alec's mouth filled with both the familiar tang of regret and of longing so visceral, so all consuming, that it suffused every cell of his body. She met his gaze, those green eyes as sharp and determined as ever, and Alec had to swallow past the lump in his throat. He was wrong. She was no fairy queen, but a warrior goddess.

"Tell me what you want." He tried to inject the words with a cold, clinical authoritativeness to mask the pathetic need currently coursing through him.

"I…I want you to touch me," she breathed. As her eyes heated, a kind of desperation stirred within him, a brutal greed he had never before experienced. And he craved more.

Her hands then went behind her back and the gown puddled to the floor. She wore only a paper-thin chemise. "The corset is built into the bodice," she explained with an impish smile.

"A modern marvel," Alec managed to quip, while his gaze roved all over her body, taking in every newly exposed inch: the slope of her slender shoulders, the length of her arms, the delicate collarbones framing her décolletage, the soft swell of each breast. A shard of moonlight illuminated her pale skin dotted with freckles. If they'd had all the time in the world, he would kiss every one.

Lottie canted her head. "Are you going to stand by the door all night?"

Alec's eyes lifted to hers. He had been staring. Coveting, really. Yes, he would always covet what he could never truly possess. Lottie held out her hand and Alec willed his legs to move. As their palms slid against each other, the shock of familiarity was as strong as ever, even through his gloves. Alec tore them off. Then, in another instant, he crushed her against his chest and thrust a bare hand into her silky hair, sending those thick russet waves tumbling out of her coiffure. Lottie stared up at him in wide-eyed surprise at his sudden movements. Alec forced himself to take a steadying breath and focus on the moment, before he gently set his mouth to hers.

The very air seemed to crackle as their lips touched, just like their last kiss, but Alec had been an entirely different man then. One whose walls were still intact. One who had no idea what he was getting into. And one who had grossly overestimated himself.

How could this be only the *second* time they had kissed? The thought of kissing her again had become a steady, insistent murmur these last few days. But now it was as if a whole orchestra had reached a violent crescendo. Something burst forth inside him, like a bird escaping its cage. As if kissing her freed him. Made him anew.

And he could not let her go so easily this time.

Lottie pressed her lips harder against his, kissing him like her life depended on it. Like he was her only source of air. And Alec was no better. He kissed her back with equal hunger until the taste of her lips was no longer enough. He brushed his tongue along her bottom lip. It was only a cursory, cautious lick to gauge her interest, to see if she would grant him entrance, but she let out a squeak of delight as her fingers tightened and twisted in his hair. Then she boldly pushed her soft, velvet tongue into his waiting, eager mouth.

Damn.

"Lottie, wait," he said raggedly, breaking the kiss. Alec tried to pull back but the lapels of his jacket were fisted in her hands.

She shook her head stubbornly as she tugged on his shirt. "I'm tired of waiting."

Alec chuckled. Try waiting *years*.

Before he could do something incredibly foolish, like voicing such a thought, Lottie rose on her toes and found his lips again. His arms automatically went around her and he pulled her close once again, until her entire body, every bloody, lovely inch of her, was pressed against his. But it still wasn't close enough. He needed nothing between them—no skin, muscle, sinew—nothing until their very hearts could beat as one.

The thought gave him a start and she pulled back, concerned. "What is it?"

Alec shook his head and tried to speak, but it was far too much to put into mere words.

She began to move them toward the bed and Alec followed, helpless to resist. He, who never gave an inch during such intimacies, was suddenly at her mercy. Utterly. Completely. At some point he had lost his control—no. He knew exactly when. It had been slipping away since he'd beheld her once again. Only it was so gradual he hadn't realized until it was all gone from him. Until it was far too late.

Alec laid her down gently on the bed and smoothed his palms over the feather-soft skin of her shoulders and arms. He dragged one fingertip slowly along the curve of her collarbone, and she let out a light laugh. "That tickles."

"Does it?" He gave her a devilish smile even while his heart ached. How badly he wanted to know everything that made her laugh. One hand cradled the nape of her neck, his thumb drawing back and forth across the sensitive skin below her ear, while his other hand slowly journeyed lower. All the while he watched her face for any sign of reticence, of regret. She could still change her mind, and if she did he would halt. But as his fingertip moved from tracing her collarbone to the lacy edge of her chemise, she arched up. His hand automatically opened as she pressed her breast into his waiting palm.

It had been over a decade since Alec first lay with a woman and yet, based on the whimper that escaped his lips, he might as well have been a virgin once again. His fingers closed greedily around her small but shapely breast. As he gently cupped and caressed the firm flesh, a glazed look came over Lottie, and she pulled him down for another succulent, plundering kiss—all lips and teeth and tongue. He wanted to move slowly. To spend hours simply kissing her, but his overwrought body would not heel. Alec jerked down the front of her chemise and plucked the tip of her nipple between his thumb and forefinger. Lottie began to writhe beneath him, and a series of increasingly urgent cries vibrated against his mouth. As they continued to devour each other, he pulled up the hem of her chemise in rough handfuls and nearly ripped off her drawers. His hand then skimmed over the supple flesh of her thighs and along the lacy edges of her stockings to the tuft of feminine hair. He wrenched away from her lush mouth to brush a featherlight touch over her most intimate place. Lottie canted her hips forward in response and he rewarded her eagerness with a long, lingering caress that slowly turned deeper. More insistent.

She let out a heart-stopping gasp, and her eyes flew open with a mixture of surprise and pleasure that Alec planned to never forget. After a few moments of trial and error, he found the motion and pressure that seemed to affect her the most. Then he dipped his head and drew her rosy nipple between his teeth. The mere taste of her rosewater-scented skin sated him more than any banquet ever had.

She breathed his name and arched even higher, her fingers digging into his scalp, holding him to her breast, as if there was a chance he might pull away. While he continued to suck, his free hand began to gently pinch her other nipple, and the evidence of her desire grew heavier and warmer under his fingertips. He coaxed her steadily toward her release, feeling every shudder of pleasure, every muffled sigh, every twist of her hips, until every muscle seemed to tighten at once.

He pulled away to watch as Lottie's lips parted, gasping in wordless cries at the sensation rioting within her. Then her brow tensed before it all slowly faded into an expression of pure bliss.

His erection had grown so stiff and hot it was nearly painful, but it didn't matter. This was enough—more than enough. More than he had ever dreamed. To simply touch her, to watch those emerald eyes grow heavy with pleasure, to hear her cry out with desire built by him, by the two of them together. She could get on with her life, and he could have just a little bit of her. A memory to keep. He pressed a soft kiss against her lips and she brought her arms around his shoulders. Her hands slid under the collar of his jacket and he shivered at her smooth touch, but it was another moment before he realized she was easing it off.

"Lottie," he murmured, but she only tugged harder, until he was obliged to remove the garment himself, lest he become trapped in his own dinner jacket. He stood from the bed and pulled the jacket off, while Lottie watched him with a dark, ravenous look that threatened to undo him all over again. Her eyes followed the jacket as he let it drop to the floor, then returned to his face.

She uttered just one word: "More."

A thrill shot through him at the idea of disrobing before such a rapt audience. He sank one knee on top of the bed, looming over her partially clad figure, and began to unbutton his waistcoat, though his fingers slipped more than once, until it, too, joined the jacket. Her hand traveled between her thighs, and she pressed it against the still-sensitive flesh. Alec inhaled sharply at the sight. Lottie gestured to his suspenders with her chin. "Those too," she murmured.

He pulled each one off slowly, deliberately, riveted by watching her watch him, of pleasuring herself to his image.

"You're so lovely," he breathed. "You can't imagine."

She gave him a dazed smile while her heavy gaze tracked every movement. As he began to unknot his bow tie, she sat up and placed her palms on his thighs. Alec's breath caught as she slid her hands upward, and his mind darkened. She brushed lightly against the fall of his trousers at first, then pressed harder. Alec hissed and moved to stop, but he was much too slow. By the time he grazed her wrist, his pants were already unbuttoned and those elegant tapered fingers took hold of his length. Pleasure blazed through him, hot, reckless, and unstoppable. He was at her mercy now, no longer showing her how to be touched but craving her touch for his own sake.

She adjusted her grip, experimenting with different holds until he showed her what he liked best. After a few strokes she swiped her thumb over the moistened tip, and Alec let out a hoarse groan. Lottie glanced up, and the corner of her mouth lifted in a slow, seductive smile. Christ. He could expire at this moment and die fairly happy from seeing that expression. But then she spoke.

"As I was leaving the palazzo, I paused by an open door," she began, her voice low and husky. "The one you pulled me from. Did you look to see?" Alec managed to shake his head. Lottie lowered her eyelids in a rather ironic display of modesty, considering what she was presently doing. "A man was seated in a chair and a woman knelt before him. I saw her take this in her mouth."

He squeezed his eyes shut and immediately saw her in the same position. "Lottie." He meant to say her name as a warning, but instead it came out sounding anguished. The plea of a desperate man.

"I've heard of such things," she continued, "but the practice never sounded very appealing. Now, though ... with you ..."

Fuck.

The thought of her even *considering* such a thing was more than he could bear. More than he could allow.

"I—"

The rest of his noble protest died in his throat. Died at the sight of those luscious pink lips parting for him.

The heat of her mouth alone forced Alec to the very edge as a pleasure greater than he had ever known rocked through him. Her movements were tentative and inexperienced, but it did not matter. Alec had never been this hard in his life. A sound ripped out of him, high-pitched and unrecognizable, almost like the wild keen of an animal. He was speaking, too, though he could barely make sense of his own words beyond *Yes. More. Dear God. Lottie.*

But before he could lose control completely, he gathered his wits enough to pull her eager, gasping lips away. Her eyes were heavy lidded, as if she had felt as much pleasure in performing the act as he had in receiving it. Then she pulled her chemise over her head and fully revealed the most perfect pair of breasts the Almighty had ever created. Somehow Alec managed to look back to her face, and then he understood.

Lottie wanted far more than his touch.

She would not stop until he had all of her.

And he would do it.

It was if all the air had been drawn out of his lungs. "Lottie," he protested again, but he was terribly weak and she knew it. "You can't want—"

She brought her palm to the side of his face and rubbed her thumb against his cheek. "But I *do* want, Alec," she whispered thickly. His heart nearly beat out of his chest, but before he could fully absorb this, she laid back down on the bed, offering her body to him. "Please."

If her first *please* had decimated his self-control, the second severed whatever remained of his reason. The idea that she would need to ask this of him, as if he were doing *her* a favor, was incomprehensible to his lust-addled mind. Of course he would do this. Of course he would make love to her. There was no other course of action available. He would have done anything, *anything*, for her in that moment.

He stepped out of his trousers and ripped his shirt off so hard that several buttons scattered across the floor. Lottie let out a short laugh that turned into a gasp as his body moved over hers. He, too, was startled by the sensation of her soft skin against his own; at once both tantalizingly novel and yet so achingly familiar. So damn right. He smoothed a palm up one of her stockinged thighs and slowly rolled it off. Their eyes met as he tossed it aside and moved to the other one. She said nothing, only stared at him in silence. Watching. She was nearly naked beneath him, but so much more seemed to be bared in that gaze. Alec had to look away. As he removed her other stocking, Lottie opened her thighs, and he gladly sank between them. Then he pressed greedy, succulent kisses all along her shoulders, the ridges of her collarbones, and the hollow of her throat, while her fingers dug deeper into his hair.

"I need more," she begged again. "I need you."

I need you.

She rubbed her nest of curls against his arousal, still hard as granite. Some primal part of him took over then, and he began slowly pushing into her voluptuous, silken heat. Lottie positively quivered beneath him, and her impatience only seemed to increase, which in turn further stoked the already scorching fire within him ever higher. She pressed her mouth by his ear and let out a string of desperate, lust-fueled words—*yes, more, please*—while she cradled his backside in her hands, urging him deeper until she suddenly let out a sharp cry and tensed.

Alec immediately froze as alarm flooded through him.

Lottie's eyes flew open. "No, don't stop," she pleaded, but her voice was tight with pain. A sound that brought him back to his senses.

There had never been a Florentine lover.

No cad who had used and deserted her.

And no matter what Lottie felt about being "ruined," this created complications for them both. Alec gritted his teeth, trying to ignore the intense pleasure still blooming inside him. He cupped her jaw and urged her face toward his. "Why didn't you *tell* me?"

She met his gaze, as clear-eyed as ever. "Because. I wanted it to be you," she said. "So badly."

His rusty old heart creaked a little. "But I've hurt you." He knew that could be interpreted in a hundred different ways.

He had heard the desperation in her voice earlier. The willingness to do whatever it took to secure her future.

I won't bother asking what choice you *would make if you were in the same position.*

"No," she breathed, applying it to this particular moment. "It's not nearly as painful as I expected."

The rigid set of her features said otherwise. Even if she *was* only using him, he found he didn't much care at the moment. "If we're going to continue—"

"Do . . . do you not want to?"

He huffed a laugh at the uncertainty in her voice. "I want you to enjoy it."

"I am," she insisted with her usual stubbornness.

Alec couldn't hold back his smile. "Well, then I want you to enjoy it even more."

He drew his other hand between them and found the bud of

her sex. He began to rub it gently, watching as the tension in her brow slowly faded and her eyes warmed. They could talk later. When they were both clothed. And his brain was fully functional. For now, he only wanted that look to grow.

"Oh. That *is* better," she murmured.

Alec swallowed the urge to gloat as she pulled him closer until every one of his senses was filled with Lottie. Only Lottie. He dragged openmouthed kisses across her brow and down her neck, stopping to nip her earlobe and whisper the sweetest words he could think of. He grazed the sensitive bud once again, listening closely for any lingering sounds of pain. The thought that he had hurt her at all was unbearable, but all he heard now were those delicate little breaths quickening with every feathered touch. Slowly, so slowly, Alec pushed until he was fully sheathed in her velvet heat. Then he began to gently pump his hips.

She suddenly moaned his name and tightened her thighs around his waist. Alec let out a ragged gasp at the mind-melting sensation and could no longer hold back. The sound of his name on her lips, uttered in the throes of pleasure, propelled him toward a sharp, aching release that verged on painful—but not painful enough to distract from the words thundering in his mind: *God, I love you.* He remembered to withdraw only at the last possible moment, the force of his release so strong he saw stars. How easy it would have been to spill his seed inside her and bind them together forever, but he would not force her hand nor bring another bastard into the world.

He pushed back the damp curls that had fallen across her face and pressed his forehead to hers. They stared into one another's eyes. His must have been as wide and wild as hers. Neither said a word, for there were none that could properly explain what had passed between them. Every little shred of him seemed to have shifted, turned inside out, been born anew. He hadn't even felt like this when he lost his virginity. Why, he couldn't remember the woman's *name* now. It was as if every previous experience had been wiped from his memory, rendered meaningless when compared to this. But underneath the euphoria that still surged through every vein, a sinking, sickly dread gained hold. All this time, he had lived in utter ignorance. Confined to his fantasies. Alec hadn't realized what bliss it was.

But *this*.

Of all the missteps of the past few days, this was by far the worst. The last five years had been somewhat bearable, but now his heart would never be whole again. Not without her. Alec nestled his head against the crook of her neck and silenced his mind with the sound of her pulse returning to normal. He had dreamed of falling asleep wrapped in Lottie's arms thousands of times, but for this one night it would come true.

CHAPTER SEVENTEEN

An eternity appeared to pass while Lottie caught her breath. It seemed impossible to imagine that her limbs would ever be untangled from Alec's, that her racing heart would ever not pump with such vicious joy. Nothing she had imagined could have prepared her for his tenderness, for the way his own heart seemed to shatter at their joining, as if it had been his innocence that was taken. He nuzzled her neck with a kind of boyish pleasure and she hugged him tighter, loving the feel of his body, no longer as coiled as a spring, pressing down against her own.

Eventually, Alec pulled out of her embrace and walked over to a small washstand in the corner. Lottie was pleased he didn't attempt to hide his naked form—and that his backside was as impressively muscular as his front. She gripped the sheet tightly between her fingers, already aching to touch his skin again. He had been hot everywhere. Hard, yet soft. Such an apt description for both the body and mind of this man. She made sure to avert her gaze once Alec returned with a pitcher of water and soft pieces of damp linen. He sat down beside her and began to gently wipe her stomach and thighs with such care that her heart began to race once more, but when he pressed between her legs she inhaled sharply. Alec immediately stilled.

"Sorry," she mumbled sheepishly. "I—I didn't expect the soreness."

He stared at her with that unfathomable expression once again. "No," he finally said as he looked away. "I'm the one who should be sorry."

Before Lottie could object, he stood and returned the pitcher to its resting place. Then he came to the foot of the bed, hands clenched in fists by his side while his hazel eyes burned hotly in the moonlit room. For one agonizing moment Lottie thought he would announce his intention to sleep elsewhere, but then he laid down behind her and pulled her against his chest. Lottie let out a breath as he enveloped her in his powerful arms and sleep began to overtake her. For so long she had ached to be held like this—held by *him*.

I wanted it to be you.

It had been a relief to speak the truth, even if she hadn't been quite bold enough to say the rest: *It's only* ever *been you.*

But she would. Soon.

Lottie fell asleep almost instantly and woke hours later in the exact same position as dawn began to break. She could not remember the last time she had slept so soundly.

She smiled and leaned back, loving the heat of his embrace and the feel of her skin against his. His arms tightened around her automatically, as if even in sleep he couldn't bear to let her go. She could have happily wiled away several more hours just like that, but after a few minutes an urge of a different sort called to her. One that could not be ignored. Lottie gently extricated herself from Alec's hold and picked up her crumpled chemise. She pulled it over her head and crept from the room, closing the door quietly behind her.

After making use of the washroom, Lottie stepped out onto the small balcony off the parlor with the intention of watching the sun rise. The air was already rich with the mossy smell of the lagoon, but even the pungent aroma couldn't wipe the smile from her face. She would savor every second of this day. This new beginning. She hadn't even felt like this after arriving in the village. But then, that had been an escape. This was a start.

Lottie spent the next few minutes happily imagining their idyllic future, until the distinct sound of a key scraping into the lock of the flat's door cut through her reverie. She turned around just as the door eased open to reveal Rafe Davies. Their eyes met across the room, and for a very brief moment Lottie swore his brow tensed. She stepped back into the parlor as he sauntered over, dressed in an evening suit and looking as crisp as he had the previous day.

"Well, good morning." Rafe gave her a sly smile, as if he knew some delicious secret about her. Lottie nearly strained her neck looking up at him. The man had to be over six feet tall. He was more broad shouldered than Alec but leaner limbed, with straight brown hair perfectly combed.

"It's a bit early for visitors."

He let out a soft laugh and his dark gaze roamed over her figure.

Goodness, she was standing there in nothing but her chemise. Lottie blushed and folded her arms across the gauzy fabric at her décolletage, though it didn't do much.

Rafe's smile grew. "How was your evening?" His voice was deeper than Alec's, and goose bumps broke out across her arms at the silky tone. "Did you enjoy the signore's party?"

The teasing note on the last word made it clear he knew very well what sort of things happened at the villa.

"We left early." Lottie lifted her chin a little higher. "I take it your evening is just ending?"

Rafe's smile vanished. "Aren't you observant." He stepped closer until the toes of his polished shoes nearly touched her slippers. Then he leaned over and murmured by her ear. "I heard that our mutual friend did not complete his task, as he was distracted all evening by his *cousin*." Lottie's head pulled back. Rafe was spying on Alec? "You will leave. Today."

She met his thunderous glare head-on. "That isn't your decision."

"It isn't yours, either," he growled, and his lip curved in a sneer. "Alec can have his fun. We all do. But it will not affect the work."

"And what *is* the work, exactly?"

He let out a sharp laugh and looked at her with renewed interest. "I like your spirit. No wonder Alec was compelled to give up his monkish habits." Rafe leaned down until his warm breath tickled her throat. "However, my means are far greater than his. You are a woman of business, no? Whatever he is paying you, I'll double it."

Lottie was so mortified by his offer that she couldn't speak. But Rafe seemed to take her silence as consideration and moved even closer. She instinctively jerked away and slapped him soundly across the face. They both froze, and her eyes went wide with shock. She had *never* slapped anyone before. As Rafe slowly turned back to her, Lottie steeled herself to meet his outrage. But he merely cocked his head. "Who *are* you?"

She tried to push past him, but Rafe blocked her way and crowded her against the wall. "Answer me, dammit. Who do you work for? What do you want with him?" All traces of irreverence had vanished. This was a man not to be trifled with. He pressed his palms on either side of her body. They did not touch, but he effectively caged her in.

Rather than give him an answer, Lottie turned her head.

Rafe let out a growl of irritation. "I've a strict policy

of not harming women," he said through gritted teeth. "But if you've put Alec in danger, I may be forced to make an exception."

Lottie met his dark brown eyes. He was deadly serious. "He's not in danger," she choked out as her heart pounded. "And I don't *work* for anyone."

Rafe's glare deepened. "Then I'll ask again: Who are you?" Somehow his calm tone was even more unsettling than his anger; the promise in his words spoke of things she had no wish to experience. But she couldn't. Alec had told her not to tell anyone, and this man already admitted to *spying* on him—

"I should warn you that I'm not known for my patience," he growled. "*Out with it.*"

"I'm a friend," she gasped. "I've known him for years."

Rafe pulled back a little and eyed her. "Prove it."

Lottie blinked. "How?"

"If that's true, then you'll know."

Uncle Alfred.

Her stomach twisted as she spoke, as if she was revealing some closely guarded secret. "His guardian was Sir Alfred Lewis. He was eleven when he came to England. After his parents died."

But Rafe's face remained hard. "Who told you this information? I can have you brought up on charges of treason for interfering in Crown business."

"No one! No one told me!"

"Then how do you know?" His voice was unbearably smooth, controlled, but there was a harsh, frightening look in his eyes.

Lottie merely shook her head, unsure of how to answer.

"Trust me. You won't like the jail cells here."

"Because," she choked out. "Because *I was there.*"

Something like fear flickered across Rafe's face, and he immediately stepped away. Lottie sank to the floor. All she could hear was the pounding of blood in her ears. Rafe loomed over her, but she wouldn't look at him. He was the very last thing she *ever* wanted to see, but after what felt like hours he uttered a single, short curse.

"You're Lottie Carlisle."

She didn't bother to respond. Rafe bent down, but Lottie shied away. He whispered another curse. "I'm—I'm so sorry. Please, let me help you."

Lottie shook her head, but he swept her into his arms anyway. Before she could protest, he had already placed her on the ancient sofa. Lottie steadied herself as he moved to the flat's tiny kitchen. Eventually, he returned with a cup of tea. When he knelt beside her, she flinched.

His eyes filled with remorse. "Here." He handed her the steaming brew. "It's chamomile. It will help calm your nerves." Lottie cut him a skeptical look as a light, flowery scent rose from the cup. "It's a traditional remedy," he offered.

Lottie cleared her throat. "Aren't you a fount of knowledge."

He gave her a weak smile. "It comes with the job, I'm afraid."

Lottie took a tentative sip as Rafe watched. She couldn't stand the guilty look on his face, as if she was a figurine he had carelessly knocked off the shelf. "You know who I am, then?" The silence was becoming excruciating.

"Of course I do," he said softly.

Lottie frowned. What was *that* supposed to mean? She glanced at him. Perhaps she could use his remorse to her advantage. "What did Alec tell you?"

Rafe's gaze turned sympathetic. "I'm afraid you'll need to take that up with him."

Lottie let out a little huff. "*Now* you're loyal?"

His eyes narrowed. "I beg your pardon?" The dangerous growl returned, but Lottie wasn't scared anymore. She was too furious on Alec's behalf.

"You had someone *watching* him last night."

"That was for his own protection," Rafe insisted. "He wasn't himself yesterday. I could see that he was distracted. And if I had known *why*—" He stopped before finishing the thought and shook his head. "You of all people should understand why I was concerned. And why you need to *leave*."

Lottie held her tongue. She had no intention of taking orders from this man. He didn't appear to be any kind of friend to Alec, no matter his reasons.

Rafe seemed to read her very thoughts. "If he is at all distracted, that will put him in danger," he insisted.

"He has business with me at the moment," Lottie sniffed. "Your mission, or whatever it is, will have to wait."

Rafe lifted an eyebrow. "Is that so? My apologies, then. I'm sure another opportunity to gather time-sensitive information about one of our greatest adversaries will arise whenever is most convenient for *him*."

How on earth could flirting with a Frenchwoman lead to that?

But that was just the sort of thing she could never know and would have to accept.

No questions asked, and no answers given.

Ever.

Rafe sighed. "Forgive me. This has been a trying morning for you, I'm sure. And I don't mean to belittle whatever this…this *business* you have with him is, but Alec's work for the Crown is vital. He can't walk away. Not now."

Doubt suddenly gripped her in the face of Rafe's certitude. She had thought—had *hoped*—that last night would change everything. But people didn't change their minds after one evening, especially someone like Alec.

If he were interested in any kind of future with you, then you could have stayed in Tuscany.

Or he would have written over the years. Or said goodbye.

Or never have left in the first place.

But he had done all those things. And hadn't once expressed anything close to remorse these last few days.

Lottie looked back at Rafe. His eyes had never left her. "How long have you known him?"

"We met during his training." His lips curved at the memory. "Our backgrounds are both…irregular, so Alec was assigned to me. I've never met anyone with such a loathing for the work along with a preternatural talent for it. But I suppose that's unavoidable when one grows up with a man like your uncle."

A cold pit began to form in her stomach. "I thought he wanted to serve."

Rafe let out a bark of laughter. "Alec? God, no. That was Sir Alfred's doing, though I can't imagine how he convinced him. But then Alec's always tried to please that man, even when it nearly got him killed."

"Killed?"

Rafe ignored her shock. "I can give you a few more hours together, but when he wakes, tell him to meet me at ten. He'll know where. By then I should have the information he requested."

Lottie gave a dazed nod, but she was still reeling from his revelation. Why on earth had Alec never *said* anything?

"Perhaps you could convince him to give up this place before you go. I swear it's slowly sucking the life from him. He's altogether too much stuck in the past," he added, his double meaning clear.

Lottie swallowed past the lump in her throat and met his eyes. "But I am here. *Now.*" Her voice trembled with urgency.

"So you are." Rafe stood and straightened his collar. Then he paused and gave her a decidedly pointed look. "But don't make this harder for him than it needs to be. Or yourself, for that matter."

When she was alone once again, Lottie rose on unsteady legs and walked toward the other bedroom. Her mind was blank as she retrieved her dressing gown from her trunk. She then performed her ablutions as if in a trance, barely registering the splash of water against her face or the taste of her tooth powder. It wasn't until she passed by the dressing table's mirror and caught a glimpse of her haunted reflection that she came to her senses.

She halted before the elegant table and ran a finger along the smooth edge. Then she sat down heavily on the chair and buried her face in her hands as the weight of so many uncovered secrets bore down on her. Both pain and anger warred within her. Uncle Alfred's meddling went far deeper than she had ever suspected. It wasn't exactly a shock to learn that he had lied to her about Alec, but to know that he had continued to maintain the illusion for all these years, even when faced with her deep pain and loneliness, was chilling. But it was the threat to Alec's very life, as well as his own deceptive behavior, that she was still grappling with when she felt a soft touch on her shoulder.

She sat up with a start and met Alec's gaze in the mirror. He let out a sigh of relief. "When I woke and you weren't beside me, I grew worried."

The tight ball of anger in her chest loosened at his obvious distress. "I couldn't sleep." Her eyes then fell on the sight of his hand still resting on her shoulder. Alec took notice and quickly pulled it away, giving his head a shake.

"Right. Well." He cleared his throat.

She turned around to face him. In his haste to find her, he had put on a pair of rumpled trousers but hadn't managed a shirt. Lottie's eyes roamed over his bare chest, taking in the finer details that had been hidden in the shadows the night before. Though his muscular chest was reminiscent of a Roman statue, it was dusted with coarse, dark hair. A little shiver went through her as she recalled the delicious feel of it against her skin. Then she noticed a scar about an inch long near his collarbone. It was the same place he rubbed whenever he thought no one was looking.

The things I do are never for pleasure. They serve another purpose entirely.

"We need to talk. About last night," Alec said, commanding her full attention. "And why you let me take your virginity."

Lottie blushed at his frank words. "I thought the answer would be obvious."

Alec narrowed his eyes. "Was it merely insurance in case Sir Alfred forces you to marry?"

Lottie couldn't even muster her anger at the insinuation. Of course he would think her motivations were so duplicitous. He had spent so long surrounded by lies. Living to deceive. But there was another way to be. Another path they could take. And she would show him what acceptance felt like. She stood. "No. That was the last thing on my mind. I thought only of you."

Alec's frown turned wary as she placed a hand on his shoulder. "What are you doing?" Lottie traced the small scar with the pad of her thumb. The skin was a few shades darker and rougher.

She heard the fear underlying his words, but Alec made no

move to stop her as she leaned in and pressed her lips to the wound on his shoulder. He let out a small sigh and her mouth curved against his warm skin as the tension slowly eased from his muscles. Then she pressed her cheek against his shoulder. "How did you get it?"

"I was following someone. They noticed."

Lottie pulled back. After last night she could now picture how such a scene might unfold. "Were you frightened?"

Alec looked past her. "I should say I wasn't. But when I heard the first shot scream past my ear, a fear different from any kind I have ever experienced came over me. I haven't felt it again." He then met her eyes with what seemed like great reluctance. "Until last night."

Lottie smoothed her palm over the scar. "It must be hard to always have this as a reminder."

"He paid the greater price in the end."

His stony expression first broke her heart before filling it with anger. She might be able to forgive her uncle for his overprotective behavior toward her, but it seemed impossible to imagine that she could ever forgive him for the part he had played in Alec's life these last few years. Why had Alec ever agreed to Sir Alfred's demand in the first place? The idea that any of it might have had to do with her was too maddening to bear. She lifted on her toes and moved to kiss him, as if she could will his sadness away with the force of her regard. His expression remained unchanged as she drew closer, but just when her mouth was a breath away, he pressed a finger to her lips. "Wait." His hands then came around her waist, and he lifted her on top of the dressing table.

As he pushed up the hem of her nightgown and wrapper, she grew breathless. The urgency of his motions sent a shuddering pulse through her. She eagerly spread her legs and moved to pull him closer. But Alec shook his head.

"I've a debt to settle with you." As he spoke, he lightly stroked up her inner thigh with the back of his fingers. "And, if nothing else, I always pay."

Lottie frowned in confusion, but before she could voice her question he sank down, dragging his warm palms along her bare thighs. She sucked in a trembling breath as she realized his intent. Alec's mouth curved in a small smile before he gripped her bottom and hauled her to the edge of the dressing table.

"*Alec*," she gasped as he set his lips to that most private of places. She tried to pull back from the intense sensation, but he held her fast. The dressing table had a massive three-paned mirror, and Lottie sank back against the center pane, which only opened her to him more. Alec let out a low moan of approval. Her eyelids fluttered open and she glanced to the left. The smaller pane offered a perfect view of Alec pleasuring her. As active as her imagination was, even Lottie could not have conjured the scene before her—Alec on his knees, his dark head buried between her legs, while one wide palm gripped the flesh of her pale thigh, as if he was as hungry to perform the act as she was to receive it. The very idea seemed to turn her insides to liquid, and she pressed forward. Alec let out another moan of approval, and Lottie gasped at the feel of his lips rumbling against her oversensitive flesh. She sat up and pulled her hands through his thick waves. He slipped a finger inside her, much as he had done the previous night, but when combined with his demanding mouth it made a release far more intense begin to kindle.

"Oh God," she sobbed. It was too much too fast. She twisted her fingers in his hair in a half-hearted attempt to stop him, but Alec's only response was to add a second finger. He then gently pressed up while increasing the pressure from his lips and teeth, creating an aching need so intense, so relentless, that her eyes began to water. Alec held her fast as he dealt out the twin pleasures of his fingers and lips until her release broke. Wave upon wave rioted through her until she thought she would perish. Until her very bones seemed to dissolve into nothingness. No wonder the French called it "the little death."

Before she had even begun to recover, he rose to his feet and began to gently bite and kiss her neck, working his way up. "There," he spoke roughly by her ear. "Now we're even."

Even. It seemed impossible to imagine ever matching the pleasure he had just given her.

She slumped against him and pressed her damp cheek to his chest, still catching her breath. "Tell me it isn't always like this."

CHAPTER EIGHTEEN

❧

Alec squeezed his eyes shut, as if that could somehow stop her words from shredding him. How could they have both been so stupid, letting things come to this? He longed, with every cell in his miserable, broken body, to deny it. But nothing had ever compared to being with her.

Nothing.

When he had first awoken and found himself alone, his foggy mind was convinced it had been a dream. All of it. The crushing disappointment had driven him from the bed. And to her. Last night she had taken his breath away, dressed in her fine gown and perfectly coiled hair, but she was even more beautiful here in the early-morning light, sleep mussed and bleary-eyed, dressed in a simple nightgown and wrapper. He couldn't abide the pathetic tenderness she inspired in him. This dangerous desire not merely to have her, but to make her happy.

Lottie curled her fingers against his scalp, mindless of his internal castigation. "Please," she whispered, tightening her thighs around his waist. "Please, Alec."

He knew he should push her away. End it all. Tell her to pack her things and leave, but he had absolutely no defense against her begging for it. Begging for *him*. His cock started throbbing as soon as she set her lips to his wounded flesh. Alec wound her hair tightly around his fist and exposed that elegant white neck scattered with freckles. His breath caught at the faded love bite below her ear. Last night he had left that mark upon her. Only his lips had ever touched that flesh.

"What, Lottie?" He whispered darkly before dragging his teeth along her neck. "Is this what you want?"

"Yes," she panted, already mindlessly canting her hips toward him.

An unfamiliar kind of possessiveness suffused through him, and his frce hand practically tore the buttons off his trousers. But as he began to enter her, he forced himself to move slowly—as slowly as he could stand. Until he was torturing the both of them.

Her trembling palms scrabbled over his back seeking purchase, pulling him even closer. But it wasn't enough. He needed to possess her as she possessed him. If only for a moment.

Alec slipped his hand under the back of her knee and pressed it toward her chest, opening her even more. To him. Only him.

I wanted it to be you.

So badly.

Her words from the previous night echoed through his addled mind. She wanted this. Wanted *him*. The thought would never lose its novelty. Even long after they had parted. Years from now, when this piercing need had once again dulled to an endurable ache, he would remember these few hours as the brief time when he had possessed everything he ever wanted.

He pushed deeper, and deeper still.

"*Alec.*" At the thread of surrender in her gasp, Alec pressed a heavy palm against the mirror, already breathless. There would be a very obvious handprint to clean later, but he couldn't think on that now. God, he really hadn't exaggerated how good she felt. He could have never even imagined experiencing such perfection. Lottie let out a low, dazed laugh and hugged him closer because apparently he said that bit aloud. Alec gave a shake then slowly began to roll his hips in controlled upward thrusts, as gently as he could manage. Despite her enthusiasm, she was still new to the act, and he didn't want to hurt her more than he already had. But then the little minx started to push back *against* him, and the sensation was shattering.

"Oh fuck, Lottie," he babbled. "You can't do that. I won't last." But he was already thrusting harder, unable to control his desire for her.

"I don't care," she gasped and continued to writhe against him, using his body for her own pleasure. He moved his hand between their rolling hips to swirl her slickness against the hot bud of her sex, and she instantly clenched around him.

"Oh, God," she whimpered.

Alec leaned over by her ear. "Look," he growled as he took her chin and turned her toward the mirror. "See what you do to me?" He pressed his cheek against hers, barely recognizing the man reflected back at him. He shouldn't reveal such hungry lust, such blatant need. And yet he lacked the will to stop. Their eyes met in the reflection for a few heated moments before Lottie gazed up at him in bewilderment. As if she couldn't believe the erotic tableau before her. Alec then took that lovely mouth in a hard kiss and wrenched himself from her, no longer able to hold off his own release.

He pumped for what felt like an eternity. As if every desire he ever had for her was bursting from him now.

But that was impossible. Alec would never stop wanting her.

When he had finally finished, he sank against her welcoming body and pressed kisses into the curve of her neck, along her collarbone, and against the hollow below her throat. He couldn't stop touching her, reveling in her, tasting her. He needed to take whatever he could now.

She let out a squeak of laughter and shifted in his arms. "Your beard tickles. Does it always grow so quickly?"

Alec smiled against her skin. "I'm afraid so." He wanted his life to be filled with moments like this—her taste on his lips, his seed on her thighs, and her laughter in his ears.

She was giving him a dreamy smile while her fingers played in his hair. But her eyes were edged with sadness. He ignored the uneasiness prickling inside him and moved to place more kisses along her bare shoulder where her wrapper and nightgown had slipped a little. Soon he was sucking at the sensitive place where her neck met her shoulder. Lottie let out a delicious little moan, then pulled back. "Not *again*," she said with a short laugh. "Rafe said you're to meet him at ten."

Alec froze. "How do you know that?"

"He came here early this morning asking about last night," she said absently, still moving her fingers through his hair. "Actually, he was under the impression that I was your mistress."

Something deep and dark rumbled inside him. Alec stilled her hand. "*What?*"

This time she noticed his displeasure. "Only for a bit!" she added. "But he was still very angry. He thought I was working for someone and trying to sabotage you. He even threatened to have me imprisoned. So I had to tell him who I was. Then he understood. But that was all right, wasn't it?"

The way she made it sound, as if it was only a little mix-up, made him even angrier. But this time he was mad only at himself.

Alec stared at her and tried to control his breathing. "Tell me he didn't touch you," he growled.

Lottie's eyes widened at his tone. "No. He didn't. But he..." Her fingers twisted in her lap.

"*Tell me*, Lottie," he urged.

"I was frightened, is all."

"You should have woken me immediately. I could have dealt with him."

Rafe's interrogation skills were legendary. Alec had seen grown men weep after only a few minutes with him. Being frightened was the bare minimum of what Rafe was capable of.

"No, it was all fine. He apologized, and we talked for a little while. Then he left."

An ugly suspicion suddenly came over Alec. He hated it. Hated himself. But he couldn't seem to control it. "What did you talk about?"

"Nothing," she answered too quickly, then caught her mistake. "Venice. My plans."

He raised an eyebrow. "Rafe must have been riveted."

"I—I don't know what you mean."

Alec shrugged. "He doesn't usually bother with idle conversation where work is concerned. Though I suppose he makes exceptions for beautiful women." He grazed his fingertips along her hip. "Not that I blame him."

Lottie shivered at the touch. Alec then dragged his hand upward to lazily stroke the valley between her breasts. Her nipples hardened, and those rosy tips were just visible beneath the gauzy nightgown.

"Especially if he saw you wearing only this."

Lottie glanced away. "It wasn't like that."

Alec grasped her chin and forced her to look at him. "It never is, darling," he said with a cruel smile. "Not at first, anyway. It must have been exciting, being caught unawares by a strange man. Do you find him handsome? Plenty of women do."

She pulled out of his grip. "Are you actually jealous? We talked about *you*."

Alec immediately went rigid. "What the hell does that mean," he growled.

That was *far* worse. If Rafe had said one bloody word—

"All this time you let me think you wanted this life. But it wasn't your choice, was it?" There was no judgment in her gaze. Only sympathy.

It was infuriating.

Alec clenched his hand in a fist and gave no answer. "I can't imagine what you mean. Of course it was my choice."

Lottie worried her lip with her teeth. There was still more to come. He clenched his other hand until she finally spoke. "Alec, I know about your mother."

His uneasiness transformed into a sickening dread. He swallowed down the bile rising in his throat. "Know what?"

"I—I found her portrait," she explained, confused by his caginess. "She wasn't a laundress at all. And that name, Petrucci—"

"Her husband's," Alec finished.

Then she still didn't know the very worst of it. Alec hid his relief behind a glare. It was short-lived.

"Why did you never tell me about her? All those years..." Her voice trailed off but she had the audacity to look hurt.

As if it were that simple.

As if it hadn't ruined *every bloody hope* he had ever harbored for her.

Never tell her? He was supposed to share his greatest shame with the girl who had been utterly adored by her parents? Who had been separated from them only by a horrible accident?

Who had never once been given any reason to doubt that she was loved, completely?

Even now, his neck burned with shame. With rage. He suddenly felt like doing something purely destructive, like smashing the mirror behind her or shoving his father's writing desk into the canal. No. It would have killed him to stand there and tell her the truth. To reveal that his own mother had *chosen* to leave him, that his father had rather die than live for Alec, and that their choices had taken away his own. Ensured that he would never, ever, be good enough for her.

So he had left instead.

"I don't owe you anything." He turned away from her and hauled up his trousers.

"You're wrong," she said softly.

Alec whipped his head around. Lottie still sat on top of the dressing table, hands demurely on her lap, despite having just been thoroughly ravished. To think, only days ago he had lost his breath over the sight of her gloveless. "What?" he barked.

"You owe me some honesty."

Alec glared as he fastened the buttons. Her eyes dipped down to his hands and she swallowed. Christ. The pair of them were like dogs in heat.

"About what?" he prompted.

"I'm right, aren't I? You came to the house the morning after my ball to see me. But it was Uncle Alfred who made you leave. And told you not to write."

How pathetic that made him sound. How powerless. It was stomach turning. And every word was true. It had taken Sir Alfred less than a minute to expose Alec's every weakness, unearth every last doubt.

You can't marry my niece because you are illegitimate. And even if the world doesn't know the truth, I do.

"I didn't write because there was nothing for me to say," he snapped.

But Lottie just shook her head. "It's more than that."

Are you so certain of her love for you? Of what she can withstand? She won't fully inherit for five more years. Until then you will have nothing.

"Fine. I didn't write because I didn't think you cared." It was somewhat closer to the truth. "And you were entertaining suitors as soon as I left."

She could be married by the end of the season. If you have any affection for her at all, you won't deny her this chance to find happiness.

Lottie sucked in a sharp breath. "How can you say that? I was heartbroken when I found out what happened. How you just *left* without a word."

The remains of his wretched little heart lifted at the revelation, but it was too late now. He had made his bed long ago.

"And even if you didn't know how I—I felt about you," she continued as her voice began to break, "we were *friends*, Alec. You didn't even say goodbye."

If you leave now, I will do everything in my power to help your career. But if you try to contact her in any way, at any time, so help me God, I will ruin *you.*

It had been an impossible choice, but one he had made all the same. But as Alec stared at Lottie's anguished face he wondered, and not for the first time, if he had chosen poorly. Guilt ripped through him, tearing open the long-scarred wounds where his love for her had once blossomed. Giving up the chance to court her properly had been agonizing, but it was losing her friendship that had left him a shell of a man. He pushed it all down as far as it would go—all the sorrow, all the regret, all the desire—just as he had been doing for the past five years. What remained of him wasn't worth her attentions.

Alec gave her a bland look. "Then I suggest you let my actions speak for me in this case."

"I did," she growled as she slid off the dressing table. "For *years* I did." Then she flashed him the same defiant look she had that first day on the terrace, when she proudly revealed her plan for ruination. "But you should have continued to keep your distance then, if you wanted to keep up the pretense."

She was right, of course.

Alec's tenuous control slipped even further. "You think too much of yourself. Do you know what our friendship was born of, Lottie? Convenience. Proximity," he spat the words, repeating the same ones Sir Alfred had said to him five years ago.

Do you think you would ever *have been allowed to consort with someone like her otherwise?*

"You were so lonely, so desperate, you would have been friends with *anyone* who paid you the least bit of attention. What we had was not a true friendship. It was an obligation. And I was glad when I could finally be rid of it."

Of all the things he had said and done in his wicked life, that was the cruelest.

"You're *lying*," she whispered angrily as tears filled her eyes.

"I have always been a liar, Lottie," he said. "You just didn't want to see it."

She shook her head. "No, no. He already stole five *years* from us. Don't give him our past, too. You don't owe him that."

"I owe him *everything*!" Alec roared. "The clothes on my back, the food in my belly, the very thoughts in my head. He paid for it. All of it. For *years*. And don't think he ever let me forget it. That is the very *least* of what I owe him."

"But—this house," she stammered. "Your parents didn't leave this to you?"

He uttered a dark laugh. Unlike her, Alec's parents were unable to leave him a vast fortune. "They were renters. My mother had no money of her own, and my father spent most of his life deeply in debt. He died a pauper. This house was my reward for Turkey. For having a bullet driven through my flesh. For taking a life. All in service to *your* uncle."

"I don't understand—"

"Yes," he snapped. "How could you possibly understand what it's like to be disowned by your own flesh and blood. Beholden to someone else. Someone who didn't even *want* you?"

"*I* wanted you!" She pressed her palm against her chest. "Do you think I never felt lonely, or unwanted? Like a burden to Sir Alfred?"

"It wasn't the same," he insisted. "You are his *niece*. He loves you."

"But you *were* loved," she cried. "By me." Then she flung herself into his arms. His traitorous hands immediately gripped her. "And I love you still. We love *each other*."

Every word felt as if someone was plunging a butcher's knife deep into his heart. Over and over and over. She wouldn't stop. She would never stop. Not until he burned everything between them to ash.

Yes, he wanted to say. *Yes, but love isn't enough.*

His love wasn't enough.

"You're hysterical."

She pulled back to face him, her eyes wild and desperate. "See? You don't deny it. For why would you come to the village? And make love to me? Why any of it? You do love me. You *always* did."

He shook his head and braced his heart. "Sir Alfred

threatened to end my career if I didn't bring you in." The threat was true, but Lottie wasn't the only one who was sentimental. Far from it. Alec would have gone searching for her the minute he learned what had happened, whether Sir Alfred asked him to or not. But it would do her no good to know that. "And even I'm not strong enough to resist a beautiful woman begging me to have her."

"He could have sent someone else, though. It didn't need to be you. Don't you see what this means? He approves now. We can be together."

The hope in her face was agonizing. It meant nothing of the sort. Sir Alfred had taken a gamble, to be sure, but he knew how deep Alec's self-loathing went.

The trick to successfully telling a lie is to choose something that is either close to the truth, or something the other person might already be disposed to believe is true. One wrong move, and this house of cards would tumble.

Alec took a deep breath. He would not come back from this.

"No." He spoke slowly. Calmly. As one might do with a small child. "All it means is that now he will need to find you a husband who won't care that you've been ruined. I could have chosen you five years ago. But I didn't then, and I won't now. Nothing's changed."

She stared at him in shock for several excruciatingly silent moments while Alec's heartbeat thundered in his ears. Then something flickered behind those wide green eyes, as if a light was being extinguished. Her Lottie light. Her body stiffened as she slid out of his arms.

When she finally spoke, her tone was even. Free of any emotion. "Yes. Of course." Her face was as blank as her voice. The mask had returned.

Alec tried to ignore the icy regret currently clawing up his spine along with the clammy sheen of sweat that had broken out over his body and headed toward the door. "Your train will leave soon. I'll send Valentina to help. Take her with you. If not for your own sake, then for hers." He hesitated in the doorway and looked over his shoulder. Last time he had just left. But now...

"Goodbye, Lottie," he murmured.

She winced, as if the very words themselves caused her injury, and he immediately strode from the room.

They would not meet again.

CHAPTER NINETEEN

$\backsim$

Alec entered the bar he and Rafe used as a meeting place. It was mostly empty given the early hour. Rafe was already standing in his usual spot at the end of the counter calmly sipping his coffee and joking with Gianni, the bartender. Beside him was a small glass of grappa.

"I thought you might need this," Rafe explained unprompted as Alec approached. "Christ. You look like hell."

Without a word, Alec picked up the glass and swallowed the contents. The warm burn cut through the numbness that had enveloped him for the past hour. Then he set the glass down, turned to Rafe, and immediately punched him.

"God damn it, man!" Rafe cried out, clutching the side of his face.

Alec turned to Gianni and pointed to his glass. "Another."

The man simply nodded, not at all fazed by Rafe's yowling, and went to retrieve the bottle.

"I suppose I deserved that," Rafe said as he felt along his jaw. Alec had only clipped him. They both knew he could have hit him much harder. "But you could have told me who she was. I might not have—"

"—*threatened* her?"

"I thought—"

"I know what you thought," Alec bit off and turned away. In all the years they had known one another, Alec had never seen Rafe express anything close to the regret clearly etched on his face now. But it wasn't enough to quell the anger churning inside him. Gianni refilled the glass, and he drank it as quickly as the first. "I appreciate your complete lack of confidence in my abilities, by the way. So tell me, who was the plant last night?"

Rafe hesitated. "Drakos."

Alec let out a harsh laugh. "Is he even an olive oil magnate?"

"Yes," Rafe said testily. "Mr. Drakos is an international businessman and a valuable Crown asset. You were acting strangely yesterday, so I called in a favor. Thanks to him last night wasn't a complete loss."

Alec shot him an expectant look. "Well? What of Madame Noir?"

Rafe wouldn't meet his eyes. "Nothing useful. Yet," he couldn't help adding.

"A bloody waste," Alec grumbled. "All of it."

"I'm going to ignore that remark because you have every right to be angry with me. But be that as it may, I still have a few questions of my own. Starting with how the hell *Lottie Carlisle* ended up in Venice. With *you*."

Alec let out a breath. "She was taking a tour of Florence and disappeared. Made it look as though she had run off with someone."

"Naughty girl," Rafe said with a smirk, then immediately winced. "Dammit," he hissed, then gestured to Gianni. "Something cold, pronto."

Alec gave him a rather satisfied smile before he continued. "Sir Alfred telegraphed me asking for help."

Rafe pressed a cool glass of ice against his bruised skin

and groaned with relief. "I'm sure that must have cost him a great deal of pride to ask such a thing of you."

"Hardly. He knew exactly what he was doing. That I would immediately set out to find her," he murmured.

"How did you manage to track her down?"

"A hunch. Her parents had spent their honeymoon touring Tuscany. Lottie always talked about someday visiting a particular village where they stayed. I asked around and someone remembered selling a train ticket to a woman matching her description. And it fit."

Rafe raised a skeptical eyebrow. "It seems you've been having a number of fruitful hunches lately."

Alec stilled, remembering his words from yesterday. In the tumult of this morning he had entirely forgotten *why* they had arranged this meeting in the first place.

"So you arrived in this village and there she was. I take it there was no man about?"

Alec shook his head. "She was alone."

"Well, then she must have been happy to see you."

Alec recalled the thunderous look on her face. He should have turned around and left right then. He could have told Sir Alfred where she was and been done with it. "What makes you think that?"

"She went with you, didn't she?" Rafe shrugged. "Or maybe she had tired of her little adventure and wanted another." The sly grin returned, slightly diminished. "She did look freshly tumbled this morning. I thought you didn't sleep with virgins."

Alec gripped the empty grappa glass so hard the stem cracked.

Rafe let out a surprised laugh. "My God, I was only teasing. But thank you for answering *that* question. She's game for anything, though, isn't she?" Rafe's eyes glinted with a kind of admiration. "Slapped me clean across the face when I got too fresh. She's not at all how you described her."

Alec didn't like his knowing tone one bit. "What do you mean?"

"You always made her sound so angelic. Like she needed protection from the big bad world."

Alec bristled. "Well, that was more the case when we were children." But up until a few days ago he had still believed that about Lottie, hadn't he?

Rafe looked thoughtful as he set down the glass. "You know, it's rather surprising that she never entered the field herself," he mused. "Many women can be an asset. And she certainly has the character."

"Sir Alfred never would have put her at risk. She's his only family. It's one of the few things he values."

"But there are plenty of things she could do that wouldn't be dangerous. She could gather information." Then Rafe's gaze narrowed. "Say, during a trip to Italy."

Alec's neck heated. Remembering his earlier suspicions, he chose his next words with extreme care. "What are you suggesting?"

"Only that it sounds rather convenient to me," Rafe said a little too casually. "She goes through all the trouble of leaving Florence, cooking up a delicious story, and settling in a place *you* just happen to know about—then drops everything as soon as you appear."

"You've got it all wrong—"

"Do I?" Rafe asked sharply. "Because what *I* see is a woman loyal to Sir Alfred Lewis accompanying you on a mission. And then distracting you at the *worst possible moment*. Sir Alfred doesn't have the influence he once did. And he isn't content to fade into obscurity, like his contemporaries."

Alec's voice grew deadly quiet. "Lottie hates this business, and she came to Italy in part to escape him."

"Then why did she leave with you?" Rafe pressed.

He would have to say it. In order to quell Rafe's suspicions, he would have to say it. "She loves me." Uttering the words was even more painful than hearing them. Because it meant a part of him, however small, believed them.

"You sound quite certain."

But you were loved. By me.

And I love you still.

Alec swallowed hard. "I am."

Rafe held his gaze. "And yet you never told her the truth. How her uncle essentially blackmailed you into service."

Alec's eyes widened. It was all a trick, but before he could speak Rafe held up a hand.

"Please don't hit me again. I'm only trying to make a point."

"Yes, I can *see* that," Alec groused and turned away. "I told her what she needed to know. To ensure she left."

"I can't imagine she went willingly."

You were so lonely, so desperate, you would have been friends with anyone *who paid you the least bit of attention.*

"After the things I said to her, she had no desire to stay."

Then he had stormed out of the flat and skulked in the shadows across the street, telling himself it was only to make sure she and Valentina left in time to catch the train. Not because he was so pathetic that he craved to see her just once more.

"She will be safe now," he insisted. "If it means she must hate me, so be it."

"I'm not certain she's safer in England." The slight note of foreboding in Rafe's voice sent a chill through Alec.

"The leak."

Rafe's eyes held the answer: *Sir Alfred.*

Alec let out a foul curse. "Whatever he has done, Lottie isn't involved. I will swear on my life—"

"I know," Rafe nodded. "I thought it could be a possibility, but not after this morning."

"And yet, you let me think the worst."

"Only so you would see that you have the chance for something more. Don't let your pride get in the way."

"You think this is pride?" Alec let out a bitter laugh. "I've no pride to speak of. I'm the boy whose own *parents* didn't even want him."

Rafe tilted his head. "Is that all that's stopping you? You can't let your parents' mistakes rule your entire life. Even I know that."

Alec bristled again. Rafe was making far too much sense far too early. "A mistake would indicate they felt some kind of regret."

"I was going to tell you this right away until you *hit* me, but I learned something rather interesting last night about Sir Alfred. In addition to the possible treason, of course. What do you know of his time in Venice?"

"When he was here decades ago?" Alec tried to recall what he knew. "Only a little. He frequently wrote about his travels, and Venice was among them. I believe he stayed with my parents for a time."

Rafe's grave expression was unsettling enough, but then he spoke. "Sir Alfred was already a spymaster by then. And, according to my London contact, your mother was working for him. I'm not sure your father even knew."

It was as if Alec's very blood had frozen in his veins. He couldn't make his mouth move.

"Last night I was introduced to a man who worked in the same ring," Rafe continued. "This fellow was shocked to learn that you would have anything to do with Sir Alfred after, as he put it—" Rafe paused to clear his throat "—after what he did to your mother."

"Did *what*, exactly?"

"This man didn't know all the particulars, but he claimed that Sir Alfred used your mother to get information about her husband, the count, in exchange for money."

His parents and their damned debts. He furrowed his brow. "There were times during my childhood when she would leave abruptly. Sometimes for weeks. My father claimed she was visiting family. When I was a boy I believed him, but later, after I learned the truth about their relationship, I assumed she had been with her husband. And that those visits led to their eventual reconciliation." He shook his head, still trying to make sense of it all. "Could she really have been *spying* on him then?"

"It's very likely, yes." Rafe then hesitated.

"What?" Alec could barely get the word out. He would not like whatever came next.

"Well, according to this source, eventually the count discovered her. And he was furious. I'm not exactly sure how it all came about, but in the end she was forced to return to him. For good. He called it a sacrifice."

A sacrifice?

It felt as if someone had punched a hole in Alec's chest. "But why did she never tell my father any of this? He died thinking the very *worst*."

"There's only one person alive who can answer that."

Sir Alfred.

Rafe had more to say, but Alec heard none of it. He didn't realize what he was doing until he was already on the bustling street. Already racing toward the train station. Already too late.

Alec braced a hand against a wall, struggling to breathe

as his entire world crashed all around him. This massive deception had shaped everything he ever believed. Tainted every relationship he ever had. He silently raged for the years Sir Alfred had stolen from him, for his family torn apart, for his parents' doomed love—all to sate the infinite ambitions of powerful men.

But the very darkest thoughts were saved only for himself.

For no matter what had happened decades before or what choices his parents had made, he alone had driven away the woman he loved that morning. He alone had uttered the words designed to break her heart. And he alone had turned his back on the one person who had been there, always, when he had bothered to let her.

Lottie didn't want a place in society, a circle of blue-blooded friends, or a man of impeccable pedigree. She wanted only *him*. And Alec hadn't bothered to listen. Had never once dared to consider that he could be enough for her, that his illegitimacy didn't matter, or that he could be wrong about what she truly needed.

Just like his mother before him, he had thought of his leaving as a sacrifice that would only benefit Lottie.

But Alec and his father had suffered unimaginably when Maria Petrucci left.

What if they both had been wrong?

Alec felt achingly empty, as if someone had carved out his insides. He walked around for hours trying to make the hollowness go away. But no matter how many steps he took, it remained. By the time he found his way back to his flat, the daylight had begun to fade.

The feeling only intensified as he trudged up the stairs, entered his front door, and made his way to his bedroom. Without thinking he hauled off the sheet covering his father's desk and nearly wrenched the drawer out entirely. His trembling hand closed over the miniature. Over the face that had haunted him as a boy.

He had seen his father's image a few times over the years—always unexpectedly while perusing newspaper articles or magazines. But never his mother's. He took a breath and turned it over in his palm. The hollowness grew and grew inside him until he crumpled to the floor under its great weight. He had forgotten everything about her, and nothing at all. As if time itself was immaterial. Meaningless.

He stared until his eyes watered, devouring every tiny brushstroke. Every curved line. Every gradient of faded color. Until he could take no more. Then he gently set it down beside him and pressed the heels of his hands against his damp face. And there on his knees in a room bathed in twilight, Alec finally wept.

CHAPTER TWENTY

❧

"D oes London always smell like this?" Valentina asked, wrinkling her nose as they exited the first-class carriage and stepped onto Euston Station's busy platform.

"Oh no," Lottie replied. "It's usually quite worse."

Valentina's horrified expression inspired Lottie's first genuine laugh in days and reconfirmed that hiring her had been an excellent decision. Her previous maid had left service to marry last year, and Lottie hadn't been in a hurry to find a replacement. But the vibrant young woman had proved to be a more than capable lady's maid—and an even better traveling companion. Without her, Lottie doubted she would have ever made it to England, let alone remembered to change her undergarments. Valentina had appeared in Alec's flat shortly after he left and found Lottie in a heap of tears. After letting loose a string of insults directed at the absent Alec, Valentina took charge and had her changed and packed in less than an hour. The journey home had passed by in a blur of European landscapes while her battered heart and mind replayed her last moments with Alec.

What we had was not a true friendship. It was an obligation. And I was glad when I could finally be rid of it.

Just as Lottie began to sink into that familiar pit of despair, a tall, slender man appeared before them, having shoved his way through the crowded platform. It was Mr. Wetherby, her uncle's secretary. The man had the ear of Sir Alfred and far too many opinions about her life. He was also the nephew of her erstwhile chaperone, Mrs. Wetherby. He shared his aunt's pallid complexion, light blue eyes, and sharp nose, along with her penchant for criticism and Lottie as a favored target.

"Miss Carlisle," he said, bowing from the neck. "I trust you had a pleasant journey." He looked past her. "Where is Mr. Gresham?"

"He stayed in Venice. My maid accompanied me."

Mr. Wetherby barely acknowledged Valentina and didn't bother to hide his relief. "Might I ask *why* Mr. Gresham did not accompany you?" he asked after a moment.

She lifted her chin. "No, you may not. Where is the coach? I'd like to see my uncle as soon as possible."

Mr. Wetherby gave her a wide-eyed stare, then quickly recovered. "This way."

He escorted her and Valentina to a hackney carriage. "Your uncle did not want anyone to see the family crest," he explained once they were inside. "So far we have been able to suppress all news of your little diversion." His lips curved ever so slightly on the last word.

Blast.

Yet another failure. At least she had been properly ruined. Uncle Alfred would learn the truth soon enough. Or most of it.

Lottie looked out the window. Nothing but swarms of people, polluted air, and a dull, gray sky. She hadn't missed this one bit. "I hope your aunt enjoyed the rest of her trip."

Mr. Wetherby clicked his tongue. "She is happy to know that you are *safe*, Miss Carlisle. She is an old woman and you gave her quite a scare."

Lottie bit her lip. Now that there was some distance between them, she was feeling a little more charitable toward
her chaperone. "I am sorry for that. I would like to write to
her and apologize, if you think she will welcome it."

She cast a cautious glance at Mr. Wetherby. His usual
expression of contempt had softened to something that looked
an awful lot like interest. "Yes. I think she would appreciate
the gesture," he murmured. Lottie was the first to break
their gaze.

The silence stretched as they inched toward her uncle's
South Kensington town house. She let out an impatient sigh.
London traffic. Another thing she hadn't missed.

"I trust Mr. Gresham was a gentleman?" Mr. Wetherby
asked as he leaned toward her. "I know of his reputation," he
added in a low tone so Valentina wouldn't overhear.

Lottie's eyes snapped to his. The man was serious. "If you
harbored such doubts about his character, I wonder why he
was even sent to fetch me in the first place."

Mr. Wetherby sat back against the seat. "I wanted to go
myself, but your uncle thought Mr. Gresham would find you
faster. That took precedence." His mouth set in a grimace. "I
suppose he was right."

"You wanted to assist your aunt?" It was the only reason
she could think of. As far as she knew, Mr. Wetherby had
never left England.

He stared at her with those unsettling blue eyes. "If that
is easier for you to accept at the moment, then yes. I wanted
to travel a thousand miles in order to escort my *aunt* home."
Then he turned away.

Could Mr. Wetherby really be insinuating that he had feelings? For her? It wasn't anything she wished to confirm.

The carriage then mercifully arrived at the imposing town
house. It was merely one of several Uncle Alfred owned.

The Lewis family coffers were quite sizable, but it was the business of secrets that kept him in such luxury. A shiver rippled through Lottie as she crossed over the threshold. She had never liked this house and vastly preferred Haverford, with its lush grounds and warm furnishings. It was there that she had first met Alec, where they spent holidays, and it had been the setting for so many of her happiest memories.

The town house was made to cater to the London social set. Remarkable objects from Uncle Alfred's priceless collection amassed over his lifetime could be found in every room announcing to all who entered that its master was powerful. Important. Irreproachable. But the house had always felt cold to Lottie. Even at the height of summer.

Dalton, the ancient butler, offered them a characteristically stoic greeting. "Miss Carlisle. I trust you had a pleasant trip to the continent. Lovely to have you home."

"Thank you, Dalton," Lottie smiled. "I've acquired a maid along the way. Can you send Valentina to Mrs. Houston?"

Before the butler could answer, Mr. Wetherby pulled her aside. "Mrs. Houston remains at the house in Surrey. Only a skeleton staff has been kept on. Your uncle did not want his illness to become known."

Lottie could not hide her shock. Her uncle was normally so exacting that he insisted Mrs. Houston keep house wherever he was in residence. That he would send her away now, when he was in such a state, was unimaginable.

"I will gladly show the young lady to your room, Miss Carlisle," Dalton intoned behind them.

"Thank you," she called over her shoulder. Mr. Wetherby was already herding her toward the stairs. She briefly exchanged a glance with Valentina, whose worried brow only unsettled her further.

"Mrs. Houston should be here. Forgive me, but this makes no sense."

Mr. Wetherby didn't even look at her. "That isn't your concern."

Lottie gritted her teeth. This cloak-and-dagger business was becoming ridiculous. Over the last few years, Uncle Alfred had constantly worried about his influence. If it were anyone else, they would have been called *paranoid*. But not Uncle Alfred. He merely claimed to be cautious. It was exhausting.

They made their way down the darkened hallway toward her uncle's suite of rooms. Mr. Wetherby paused by the door. "You should prepare yourself, Miss Carlisle," he warned. "By all accounts your uncle has made a remarkable recovery, but he is still much changed. He has lost the use of his right arm and his speech is slurred at times, particularly in the evening hours."

Guilt swelled in her chest. Over the last few days she had barely thought of her uncle with anything other than anger. "I see."

Mr. Wetherby began to soften ever so slightly, but then he caught himself and stood even straighter. "I'm afraid I can allow only a short visit today. The best time to speak to him is in the mornings, as that is when he is most alert."

Lottie bristled at his high-handedness. Mr. Wetherby was her uncle's secretary, a trusted employee, certainly, but here he was acting like the head of the family. Like Uncle Alfred's *heir*. "I have no desire to exhaust him, sir. I myself have had a tiring journey."

Mr. Wetherby's face remained hard, but his words were oddly gentle. "Of course you have. I'll see to it that your maid has everything you require."

Lottie nodded. "Thank you."

Mr. Wetherby gave a soft warning knock and entered the suite's sitting room. All the curtains were drawn and a fire was lit in the hearth, while a gas lamp provided a warm glow. The air was stifling and filled with a familiar medicinal aroma. Lottie instinctively held her breath. Once as a child she had spent weeks in the sickroom while ill with a fever. The smell of astringent still turned her stomach. An older nurse sat in a rocking chair leafing through a magazine. The door to Uncle Alfred's bedchamber was open, and Lottie caught a glimpse of his massive four-poster bed.

"Mrs. Ragmoore, I've brought Sir Alfred's niece."

The nurse smiled at Lottie and rose from her chair. "Oh, the famous Lottie!" she said in a thick northern accent. "I've heard plenty about you. Your uncle will be so happy to see you."

Lottie returned the woman's infectious smile. "It's very nice to meet you. Thank you for taking care of him."

Mrs. Ragmoore glanced back at the doorway. "He's just woken from a nap. He might be a little spotty, but he'll be wanting to see you. Make sure to talk loud and slow. And don't worry if he doesn't respond right away. Give him time and he'll get the words out."

Lottie pressed her hands against her stomach to settle her nerves. "I understand."

Mrs. Ragmoore turned and led the way into the bedroom. Uncle Alfred was propped up in his bed resting against a mountain of pillows. The nurse approached his bedside. "Your niece is here, sir," she practically bellowed. The old man turned toward her, but Lottie stood frozen in place, trapped in the doorway.

Mr. Wetherby had to guide her toward the bedside. As she drew closer, she inhaled sharply. Uncle Alfred, usually the most commanding presence in any room, was now a shadow of his former self. He had lost a great deal of weight and looked so frail in his buttoned-up nightshirt that Lottie found herself blinking back tears.

"It's all right," Mr. Wetherby murmured. "He wasn't eating very much at first, but now his appetite has begun to return."

She was suddenly very grateful for his presence. Without thinking, she gripped his arm. "Thank you," she whispered. As Mr. Wetherby's gaze took on an unfamiliar intensity, Lottie turned away and moved beside Mrs. Ragmoore. "Hello, Uncle Alfred," she said with a watery smile. "I've heard you've fallen ill."

The old man stared at her with crushing relief. "Lottie." His voice was low and hoarse. He reached out his trembling left hand while the other lay motionless on his chest.

Lottie immediately gripped it in both her palms. "I'm here."

Uncle Alfred then slowly glanced behind her. "Alec?" he asked as he turned back to her. The hopeful note in his voice was devastating.

Lottie had to swallow hard past the lump in her throat. She shook her head. "He stayed behind. In Venice."

Uncle Alfred looked disappointed but gave a little nod. "I see."

Though she had every reason to hate Alec, all she felt was remorse for his absence.

Whatever your issues with Sir Alfred are, whatever led you to do this, go to him now. Make your peace while you still can.

But Alec needed to make his peace with Uncle Alfred just as much as she did. If not more.

Lottie glanced at Mr. Wetherby. The earlier heat was now gone, replaced by an all-too-familiar frown of disapproval. Any talk about the past or Alec would have to wait for morning. "Alec kept me safe, Uncle. He did his duty. You should be very proud."

But Uncle Alfred didn't seem to be listening. He simply stared at her, as if she was some kind of angel. Then he squeezed her hand and pulled her closer. Lottie leaned down, so that he didn't have to speak any louder. "I *knew* he would find you. The only one," he said in his faint, trembling whisper. He then gave Lottie a broad smile. The kind she hadn't seen in years. The tears she had been holding back spilled over her cheeks and she let out a sharp sob.

"Yes," she managed to say. "You were certainly right about that."

His gaze flitted behind her shoulder. "You will be safe now. Always." He then exchanged a look with Mr. Wetherby, who stood a few feet away.

Lottie glanced back at the man, but her uncle said no more. His eyelids drooped heavily.

"Get some rest, Uncle," she murmured and placed his hand on top of his chest. "I'll see you in the morning. First thing." But the elderly man was already dozing off.

"Come, Miss Carlisle." Mr. Wetherby cupped her elbow and guided her out of the room and into the hall. "I'm sorry. That must have been terribly upsetting for you."

Lottie allowed him to lead her to her room. Uncle Alfred's last words were unsettling, but then he must be confused by so many things at the moment.

"Yes," she said softly. "Al—Mr. Gresham seemed unaware of how ill he truly was. If I had known..." Her voice trailed off. She could not say for certain what she would have done differently.

Mr. Wetherby's mouth tensed. "Mr. Gresham was not fully informed of the situation as a precaution. In case he decided to tell anyone of Sir Alfred's condition."

Lottie stopped in her tracks. "He would never betray my uncle."

"I don't mean to disparage him. As I said, it was merely a precaution."

Lottie narrowed her eyes. "What aren't you telling me?"

Mr. Wetherby's flat stare betrayed nothing. "You're tired, Miss Carlisle." He then gestured toward her bedroom at the far end of the hall. "You need rest."

When they reached her bedroom door, Lottie faced him. "I assume that once I enter this room, I will be able to leave freely?" She kept her tone light, but the question was serious.

He reared back. "I am no *jailer*, Miss Carlisle. Like you, I only want what is best for your uncle."

"In that case, you wouldn't object to me speaking to him in private tomorrow morning."

Mr. Wetherby's jaw tightened ever so slightly. "Of course not."

Lottie gave him a beatific smile. "Wonderful. Have a good night, Mr. Wetherby." Before he could say another word, Lottie stepped into her bedroom and shut the door right in his face.

Lottie slept fitfully, as she had every night since leaving Venice, with Alec's dark voice echoing in her mind. But instead of his cruel dismissal of their friendship, she now recalled his words about Uncle Alfred.

I owe him everything... and don't think he ever let me forget it.

How could you possibly understand what it's like to be beholden to someone else? Someone who didn't even want you?

Eventually she woke up with a start, tangled in the bedsheets with a faint sheen of sweat on her brow. Lottie pressed a hand over her eyes and sighed. She still could hear the raw pain, the shame in his voice. How she had longed to be enough for him this time. To believe that love could mend all those old wounds. But perhaps he was incapable of such attachments now, given all he had endured. Lottie took in a deep breath. She had lost him once before and could recover again.

But it would be so much harder this time.

Lottie's eye caught on the small painting on the nightstand. She picked up the frame and brought her mother's Tuscan landscape close. Lottie had imprinted this image in her mind long, long ago, but it was as if she was seeing it anew. Now she had been to that special spot herself and saw it with her own eyes. Lottie smiled and traced the edge with her finger. Her mother had done an excellent job capturing the clouds. Lottie always felt a dull ache for her lost parents, but it sharpened to a pinprick and threaded through her heart as she imagined them, so young and in love, spending long, hazy days in that sun-drenched little village.

She wanted to talk to her mother now—about the village, and Alec, and the mess she had made of everything—so badly it nearly made her sick.

Lottie placed the frame back on the nightstand and climbed out of bed. She couldn't stand being in this house much longer. There were too many memories, too much pain lurking in every shadow. She would set things right with Uncle Alfred, wait until he recovered, and then go off somewhere else until her heart mended itself, or at least until the ache was slightly less devastating. It didn't matter where, as long as it wasn't here.

CHAPTER TWENTY-ONE

❧

After Lottie washed and took a few bites of a cold bun, Valentina helped her change into a cream blouse and sober black skirt. The sartorial frivolity she indulged in while in Italy had no place in this house. As she headed for Uncle Alfred's suite, she couldn't shake the feeling that she was heading into a gauntlet armed only with questions.

It was still early enough to hope that Mr. Wetherby hadn't arrived yet, but as soon as she entered the suite's sitting room, her heart sank. The man stood as dour and rigid as ever, talking with the nurse. He glanced at Lottie and immediately lowered his voice.

He murmured a few more words then turned to her. "Miss Carlisle." He flashed her a tight smile. "How did you sleep?"

"Very well, thank you. Good morning, Mrs. Ragmoore."

"Morning, Miss Carlisle," she said warmly. "Your uncle's been asking for you already."

Lottie's chest loosened with relief. "I'll go in." Mr. Wetherby stood firmly in place, watching her with his usual severity. She felt his heavy gaze on her as she opened the bedroom door. Unlike yesterday, the room was filled with soft sunlight. And there was Uncle Alfred, sitting up in bed, already waiting for her.

He smiled. "Good morning, my dear." His voice was stronger, but he spoke slowly and the words sounded muffled. As if they had first been doused in honey.

"Good morning, Uncle Alfred." Lottie shut the door quietly behind her and leaned against the knob, taking him in. "You're looking more hale today."

He chuckled and nodded at his shrunken frame. "I'm skin and bones."

Lottie couldn't disagree with that, but there was more color on his cheeks and as she drew closer, he watched her with that familiar sharpness. He may be a shadow of his former self in many ways, but his mind was still there. At least for the moment.

Lottie drew a chair close to his bedside and sat down. "I know you must be very angry with me about Italy. And I am so sorry for what's happened to you." She paused and glanced back at the door, then leaned in closer and lowered her voice. "But I won't apologize for leaving Mrs. Wetherby behind in Florence."

Uncle Alfred still had that fond smile on his face. "She is rather awful," he acknowledged. "Alec's cable said he found you in a village near Pistoia. The one your parents visited."

His congenial tone rendered her momentarily speechless. Was he not going to reprimand her at all? "Yes. I went there directly from Florence."

"I should have known."

Lottie bowed her head. "Why did you send him, Uncle?" she asked softly. "It could have been anyone else."

Uncle Alfred was quiet for so long, Lottie didn't think he would answer. "I didn't think you would agree to go with anyone else," he finally said. "And I'm not sure I trusted anyone else with you, either." The words, and what they truly meant, stung. "No, it had to be him."

Lottie's eyes began to prickle, but she met his gaze anyway. "I wish it hadn't," she whispered.

He gave her a sympathetic look she couldn't bear. Uncle Alfred, still able to see straight into her very soul. Even now. "He stayed behind in Venice?"

Lottie nodded. "We—we did not part on good terms."

"That is probably for the best," he sighed. Another long moment passed as a shadow clouded Uncle Alfred's face. Lottie knew he wasn't supposed to exert himself, but she was determined to have answers.

"I know about his parents," she began. "That his mother was married to another man. A count."

He immediately turned to her with a wariness she had never seen before. "Oh?"

She leveled her gaze. Of course he would not make this easy. "Did she really give up Alec?"

"She had no choice," he muttered.

Lottie furrowed her brow, but before she could prod further, Uncle Alfred continued: "Her husband was the worst sort of scoundrel. Nearly twenty years older. Involved in all sorts of political intrigues. Had more mistresses than anyone could count. But he was a charming old devil, and their marriage forged an alliance between two very old families. They fought often, though. Maria was always leaving and coming back. Until she met Edward. The count was actually glad at the time, as he had a new mistress of his own." His voice grew stronger as he spoke, and his words came out faster, but he still kept his eyes fixed elsewhere, as if channeling the spirit of decades past. "Edward kept her occupied. Happy. He didn't even mind about the child, as long as they didn't parade him about too much."

"How—how do you know all this?"

He faced her. "Because I was there. In Venice."

There was no need to explain why.

Lottie's stomach turned. "But, if the count didn't care..."

"She began to inform on her husband."

Lottie swallowed against the bile rising in her throat. Uncle Alfred and his wretched business once again. A family hideously torn apart, the parents dead, and their son wrecked for life, all for what?

"We almost had him, too," he groused, as if *that* were the real tragedy. "So many damned times." Uncle Alfred's left hand clenched the bedsheet. "But the bastard always managed to slip away. Then, somehow, he found out about his wife and threatened to have Edward thrown in jail unless she came back to him permanently. So she made a bargain. Her life for his. Not that it mattered in the end," he added bitterly. "When Edward was with her, he could keep the darkness at bay, but once she was gone he succumbed to it completely."

"Did you not tell him the truth?"

He looked scandalized. "That would have put *everything* at risk. No," he insisted, shaking his head. "I couldn't do that. Edward should have been stronger. Like his wife."

Lottie took a few deep breaths until she could speak without shouting. "What happened to Alec after his death?"

"The count drew the line at allowing his wife's bastard son to live under his roof. None of Edward's family knew who she really was. They thought the idea of Edward marrying a common Italian was a disgrace; they *never* would have taken him in if they'd known the truth. So he was shuttled around to some of Maria's distant relatives for a while. Then the contessa finally wrote, begging that I watch over him." He paused, lost in his memories. "She must have been quite desperate to send him to me. But I suppose I owed her that." He trailed off.

Lottie managed to hold back her vitriol, for there was still more she needed to know. "But why—why did you never tell him the truth?"

"She thought it would be harder if he knew, especially while she was still alive. And I agreed. Neither of us expected the count to outlive her."

A pit formed in her stomach. "You forget, Uncle, that when you finally told Alec the truth, you didn't tell him everything. He thinks she did not *love* him. That she chose to leave. It's been torturing him all these years."

Uncle Alfred shook his head. His expression turned foggy. "No. I—I told him it wasn't her choice." But he didn't sound at all sure.

"No, you didn't," she protested. "You only told him enough to make him *leave*. To make him think that he could never have me."

Uncle Alfred turned to her then. She was furious with him, but the shock in his face still pained her. "I did. You're right." Then he looked away again. An old man now paying for his sins.

"What really happened that morning after my ball?"

"I knew," he began, still not meeting her eyes. "I knew as soon as he showed his face. I thought I had more time. That you would forget all about him during the season. How could you not? He had no money. No family. No real prospects."

"That's not true," Lottie cut in.

That old familiar fire blazed in his eyes. "Was I supposed to stand aside and let you become a *professor's* wife?"

"Yes," she whispered, but he had already turned away again.

"He came to see you the next morning, and he was so determined. So certain. Just like his father had been, the fool.

But this was different. Even if I hadn't needed his service, you weren't the contessa. You still had everything to lose. How could I live with myself if I let you marry him, when I alone knew the truth of what he was? So I used what I had. He asked for my consent, and I refused. When he asked why, I told him."

"Was that all?" Her voice wobbled.

He gave her a look. Of course it wasn't. "I may also have intimated that if my wishes were not observed, word would get out about his parents, about *him*. The scandal would ruin you both and you would come to resent him for it."

Lottie's throat tightened. "Oh, Uncle Alfred..."

"He could have fought me on it, Lottie. If he had truly wanted you, he would have found a way."

Lottie blinked in disbelief. "*How?* You threatened to expose him. To ruin his father's legacy. Don't you see? You had all the power and Alec had none."

Uncle Alfred stubbornly shook his head. "Love means stopping at nothing. But his mother gave up. So did his father. And so did Alec."

Lottie stood. "You don't know anything about *love*. All you've ever known is war. But love...love is sacrifice. Love is putting someone else above your own *wants*. Alec's mother understood that."

Uncle Alfred made no response, lost in his memories once again.

"I must tell him. He must know the truth." A panicked feeling suddenly came over her. "Then he might—he might—"

Come here. For me.

Uncle Alfred swung his head toward her. He seemed to read her thoughts. "No." He reached over and rang a small bell. "The vicar is coming this afternoon."

"What?"

"I need to know you are taken care of. And after Italy, I can't trust your judgment." Uncle Alfred's tone was flat and cold. "I had hoped for someone with a better pedigree, but I've run out of time. And Mr. Wetherby has assured me he will do right by you. I'll make sure you have a small allowance for the duration of your life, but I intend to leave everything else to him."

At that moment, the would-be groom entered the room accompanied by a large, imposing man Lottie had never seen before. There were laws designed to protect the rights of married women, but Lottie was more interested in avoiding the institution entirely. If it came at the expense of her fortune, so be it.

She looked between them and backed away. "You cannot make me marry him. And especially not when I love someone else!"

Uncle Alfred let out a sigh. "Have you no self-respect, girl? Alec has made his choice. If he wanted you, you wouldn't be here."

"But he didn't *know*. He never would have agreed to this."

Mr. Wetherby decided to cut in. "He was informed of these plans," he said dryly. "He knew what would happen upon your return."

Lottie turned to him with wild eyes. "You're *lying*."

Mr. Wetherby raised his brows, startled by her outburst, but did not answer. Instead, he looked helplessly at Uncle Alfred.

"Now, Lottie. No need for such dramatics." It was the smooth tone he had used all through her childhood. *You are being a silly, willful girl.* "Think of it as a sacrifice, if it helps. I know it helped his mother."

The large man advanced on her and dragged her from the room. A cry rose in her throat. There was no way out of this. And, whether he knew or not, Alec had led her here. Her panic increased to a fever pitch, and she didn't notice the cloth in his hand until it was placed over her nose as she gasped for breath. Mr. Wetherby caught her shoulders as she began to crumple to the floor.

Lottie came round on her bed as Mr. Wetherby waved a vial under her nose. The feel of his arm around her shoulders made the bile again rise in her throat. She shoved him away.

"What did he give me?"

Mr. Wetherby tried to mask his graceless stumble by straightening his jacket. "A mild anesthetic to calm you. How do you feel?"

Lottie shot him a glare. "Like I was drugged."

"I'm sorry you found out like this," he said with a decent amount of guilt. "I wanted to tell you last night."

"As if that would have been any better." She turned away from him. "Leave me alone."

"If that is what you want," he said and moved toward the door.

The words filled her with anger. *Nothing* about this was what she wanted. Lottie bolted from the bed. "Have you no shame, sir?"

He faced her fully. "I certainly don't wish to force you, Miss Carlisle. But it is a well-known fact that women are not capable of making logically sound decisions, especially when it comes to marriage."

"That is hardly a fact based on *science*."

He looked quite put upon. "I don't mean to insult you. Or your intelligence, of which I have the utmost respect." Lottie let out a sizable snort, which he ignored. "But your actions have been thoroughly reckless as of late. If nothing else, think of your fortune—"

"Yes, I'm sure that is of *great* concern to you," she snapped.

A flush crested his cheeks, but his eyes remained hard. "My father was bankrupt when I was a boy, you know. Being poor is a tedious business. I intend to avoid it at all costs. And I've three younger sisters who, unlike you, pray for the safety of marriage."

Lottie's chest pinched with guilt. All her life she had enjoyed a certain amount of freedom others would die for. Yet she saw only barriers, not the walls that shielded her from the worst consequences of her own behavior. And all thanks to a fortune she had done nothing to earn. "Let me sponsor them, then. If you give up this plan now, I will finance a season for each one."

He uttered a dark laugh. "What good would that do from a ruined woman? If you are so moved to help them, you would do much better as their sister-in-law."

Lottie crossed her arms. "It won't matter anyway. No clergyman in the world would agree to this!"

"You're right," he said coolly. "That means you have a choice to make."

The certainty in his voice set her even more on edge. "What *choice*?"

"You can marry me, or you can be institutionalized."

Lottie's mouth dropped open. "You wouldn't."

"There are many women who have done far less than you—and paid for it for the rest of their lives."

Lottie couldn't hold back her shudder. He was only trying to scare her. "Uncle Alfred would never agree to that." Maybe in his most desperate moment he would have considered such a threat, but certainly not now. She would rather take that chance than willingly submit to this man for the rest of her life.

Mr. Wetherby took a step closer. His blue eyes practically glowed with malice. "I can persuade him. Believe me. And I know my aunt would be happy to testify to your reprehensible behavior."

"Not if I ended up in an *asylum*!"

His eyes narrowed. "Are you willing to test that theory?"

Lottie was silent as her heart pounded in her ears.

Mr. Wetherby shook his head. "You are not seeing things clearly right now. But I will promise to be a good, honorable husband. And that is more than most men would do for you."

Lottie swallowed. "What of my love?"

Mr. Wetherby scowled at the word. "I have never been a sentimental man, Miss Carlisle. I understand that you have an . . . attachment to Mr. Gresham because of your shared past. But it will fade in time. Especially given that he hasn't returned the sentiment."

Lottie flinched. "You may be right about that." When he appeared to relax a little, she continued, "But you must also recognize that the human heart is not ruled by logic alone. Even if my feelings for him are based on the past more than the present, even if they are not *mutual*, they are feelings all the same. And, I must tell you, I acted on them. We both did."

Mr. Wetherby watched her. "I see."

Lottie let out a little sigh of relief. Finally, this madness would be stopped.

"Thank you for your honesty," he said tersely, then stepped toward her. "But you should call me Gordon. At least when we're in private."

Lottie tried to back away but came up against the bed. "You—you can't still wish to marry *now*," she sputtered.

He stopped mere inches from her person and his mouth curved into something close to a smile. "You do realize I agreed to marry you even when we thought you had run off with an *Italian*."

Lottie couldn't manage more than a dazed shake of her head.

He then leaned in so close that his pungent aftershave tickled her nose. "It's a bit of a relief, actually," he drawled. "Now I won't have to be gentle with you tonight." He reached out and cupped the back of her neck. Though his grasp was firm, he stroked her hair with surprising softness.

"You horrible man," she whispered.

"I will be whatever kind of man you wish, Lottie. If you want a brute, so be it." Then he pressed his mouth to hers in a hard kiss. Gordon Wetherby was no mere toady. He was as calculating as Uncle Alfred, and in less than an hour he would have control over her fortune, her person, her entire *life*. She pressed her hands against his chest, prepared to push him away, but then an idea sprung forth. And she had just one chance to enact it.

She fought down her revulsion and began to move her trembling hands in slow strokes. Gordon had a rather muscular chest—not that she ever planned to see him shirtless. He immediately pulled back, surprised and panting hard. Lottie could now recognize the signs of desire in a man. He wanted her. Badly. And she would use that to her advantage.

Lottie took a deep breath and silently prayed that she could pull this off. "I...I had no idea you were so passionate," she said in a breathy voice.

He inhaled slowly and stared deeply into her eyes. "I've long had a passion for you, Lottie. And unlike that bastard, I will not walk away from this. Ever."

Lottie managed to flash him a coy smile at the unsettling words and continued to stroke his chest. "And yet you claim to not be sentimental."

He actually blushed.

"But if we are to do this," Lottie began in her most simpering tone, "may I make a request?"

Gordon gave a dazed nod as if he were truly enchanted by her.

"This is my only chance to have a wedding. A week wouldn't make much of a difference. And it would give us more time to get to know one another." She pressed her cheek against his, and he shivered. "Don't you want your family there? Your dear aunt?" Thank God he couldn't see her grimace at the words.

Gordon sighed and wrapped an arm around her waist. "No, my darling. Given your uncle's state, we shouldn't delay." He actually sounded remorseful as he pulled back. "I am sorry you can't have a proper wedding." His gaze then fell on her lips and grew hot once more. "But I don't think I can wait a week to have you. Not now." He bent to take her mouth in another hungry kiss, but this time Lottie pushed him away and stalked to the other side of the room.

"Leave me, then."

He began to walk toward her but stopped at her sharp look. "If you won't give me a week, at least give me an hour."

His eyes hardened once again. "You always did want more than you deserved. Very well. But you will pay for it later." Then he spun on his heel and left.

The click of the lock echoed through the room.

CHAPTER TWENTY-TWO

S o, this is where you grew up?" Rafe raised an eyebrow as
he scanned the quiet streets of Sir Alfred's tony neighbor-
hood. "No wonder you never pick up the check."

Rafe was here in an official capacity to deal with the leak
and unofficially to help Alec. Though Alec had initially
balked, he was glad not to be alone now. They departed
Venice on the next available train, then had to wait a day
in Calais due to the weather, which put them two days
behind Lottie.

"That's rich, coming from an earl's son." Alec cast him a
glance before continuing to look out the hackney's window.
"We were in Surrey most of the time, anyway. That is, when I
wasn't at school." He pressed his lips together as Sir Alfred's
properly imposing town house came into view. Alec banged
on the roof of the carriage and it stopped across the street.
He pressed a hand against his knee to still his jittering leg.
The closer they had come, the more restless his nerves grew.
They watched the town house for another few minutes, but
not a soul came in or out, and the curtains were drawn over
every window.

The hairs at the back of his neck prickled. "I don't like this."

"Perhaps they went to Surrey."

Alec's heart sank at the idea. He needed to see Lottie. *Now.* "Let's find out."

As they alighted from the carriage, another pulled up in front of the town house and a spritely man in dark clothes wearing a vicar's collar emerged.

As they walked across the street, the vicar took notice of them. "Good afternoon. Are you here for the wedding?" he asked with a cheery smile.

Wedding?

Alec stopped dead in his tracks and his hands immediately tightened into fists.

"Steady now," Rafe murmured as he stepped forward to greet the vicar. "Yes. We are cousins of the bride."

"Oh, how wonderful! I must admit, the summons I received yesterday made this all seem *very* mysterious. I felt a bit like the priest in *Romeo and Juliet*. Hopefully this wedding has a happier ending!" He laughed at his own terrible joke. "It's always preferable to have at least *some* family in attendance."

"Our dear cousin doesn't know," Rafe explained. "It's meant to be a surprise, you see."

"Ah! Even better! Well, you should come round the back with me, then. Those were my instructions."

Rafe and Alec exchanged a subtle look. "That sounds perfect," Rafe said, then flashed that easy smile that always got him exactly what he wanted. As the vicar led the way to the back entrance, Rafe gave Alec a spirited wink.

But as they stepped onto the grounds, Alec's heart leapt to his throat. Whatever happened next wouldn't be so easy.

"I suppose our uncle gave the staff the day off," Rafe offered as they made their way to the servants' entrance. There was still no sign of anyone about.

The vicar nodded. "I was told that discretion was of the

utmost importance." Then he turned to Alec. "Sir Alfred is quite an important man, I take it?"

Alec gave a noncommittal grunt in reply. He was busy studying the third floor. Lottie's bedroom window was slightly open. An image of her standing before a mirror in a wedding gown flashed across his mind, and he dug his nails into the skin of his palm.

"My cousin is a man of few words." Rafe gave the vicar an apologetic smile. "But yes, our uncle *is* important."

"I see." The vicar's lips pursed and he turned back to Rafe. "Do you like the chap your cousin is marrying? A Mister...Wertherby? Have I got that right?"

"*Wetherby?*" Alec roared.

Rafe clapped a hand on the vicar's shoulder to shield him from Alec's furious glare. "Terribly sorry. He has very strong feelings about pronunciation. English teachers," he added, rolling his eyes in commiseration. "You know how fastidious they can be."

The vicar cast Alec a disapproving frown. "Yes, I do."

A minute later they reached the back entrance. "I was told to go right in and up the stairs," the vicar explained as he pushed open the back door that led to the kitchens.

Alec tugged on Rafe's arm. "Wetherby is Sir Alfred's bloody *secretary*," he hissed.

"Well then. I'd say he no longer has any qualms about mixing work and family. Come along." They followed the vicar into the kitchen, which was just as deserted as the outside.

"What time is the ceremony supposed to start?" Alec practically growled. Being in this house again set him even more on edge.

"Three o'clock. You won't come upstairs?" The vicar gestured up ahead.

"We don't want to spoil the surprise." Rafe again gave him

that friendly smile. "And you won't say a word, right, Vicar?" He added a wink and the vicar melted a little, now putty in Rafe's capable hands.

"No, of course not. I won't want to ruin anything."

"I can't thank you enough. We'll come right after the ceremony begins. So there isn't a commotion."

The vicar nodded along, as if this all made perfect sense, and disappeared up the stairs.

Rafe wiped the smile from his face and turned to Alec. "We only have fifteen minutes. How well do you know this house?"

"Well enough to know where the servant's staircase is." Alec pointed to a small doorway in a corner of the kitchen. "And what floor her bedroom is on."

"Good man. Let's go."

He headed toward the staircase, but Alec hesitated. What if she *wanted* this? What if he had driven her right into Wetherby's arms? The man had come across as a pompous ass in their exchanges but could be a veritable prince in the flesh.

Alec wasn't sure he could face that.

Rafe glanced back. "Come on, then. Before the vicar returns and I have to flirt with him some more. I'm running out of ways to explain your ridiculous behavior."

The hallway outside Lottie's bedroom was deserted, but voices could be heard in the downstairs parlor. Alec crept over to Lottie's bedroom while Rafe kept watch at the main staircase. He tested the knob. Locked. One point for Lottie *not* wanting to marry the dashing secretary. Alec signaled to Rafe then pressed his ear to the door. "Lottie," he whispered while knocking softly. "Are you in there?" There was the faint sound of mattress springs creaking as she rose from the bed and shuffled closer.

"Who's there?" she asked in a muffled voice.

Alec's stomach tipped from the weight of his regret. How many miles he had traveled these last few days, yet it was this slight distance that now felt insurmountable. He had to clear his throat before he could answer. For all he knew she would still prefer being locked up. "It's—it's Alec."

She nearly shrieked and pulled on the doorknob. "Oh, Professor Gresham! Please help. I'm trapped!"

His heart plummeted to the richly carpeted floor. "Valentina? Where is Lottie? Is she well?"

There was an ominous pause on the other side of the door. "Someone's coming," Rafe interrupted.

Alec glanced down the hall and back to the door. "*Valentina*," he hissed, but before he could say more, their presence was discovered.

"Who the devil are you?" A man about Alec's age, tall and thin with light blond hair and blue eyes, was prowling down the hallway. "The *both* of you?"

Alec faced him. "Alec Gresham. Mr. Wetherby, I presume?"

His glare turned malevolent. "You've got a *hell* of a nerve, showing your face here." Apparently he had an inkling of what his bride had gotten up to in Venice.

Alec raised an eyebrow. "I won't take etiquette lessons from a man who locks up women."

The man narrowed his already beady eyes. "That is none of your concern. Get out of this house."

Alec adjusted his gloves. "No. I think *you* will be opening this door."

Rafe moved uncomfortably close to Mr. Wetherby. "I'm happy to assist you," he added cheerily.

Mr. Wetherby cast him a wary glance, then quickly frowned. He grumbled something under his breath and pulled a key out of his pocket. Alec stepped away from the door while the blood pounded in his ears, first from outrage and now from nerves. Why, Lottie might very well shut the door in his face, and he deserved nothing less.

Once the key turned in the lock, Valentina pulled open the door, her face tight with anxiety. Alec shoved Mr. Wetherby aside. "Where is she?" he demanded as he entered the bedroom.

"I don't know," Valentina said miserably. "After they locked us in here, I went to the en suite. When I came back, she was gone."

Alec raced toward the partially opened window. Fear gripped his chest even while his mind reasoned that she had made it to the ground safely. Otherwise they would have found her. Alec held back the wave of nausea that suddenly rose in his throat at the thought. He turned around and gripped Valentina by the shoulders. "Where did she go? Tell me everything she said to you."

The girl hung her head. "She told me *nothing*, Professor. I swear! She was so unhappy. So scared. And now you have come for her, and she is lost!"

Alec pulled the sobbing girl's head against his shoulder. "There now. Don't cry. I'll find her."

"You *never* should have sent her away," she scolded through her tears.

"Yes," Alec said softly. "You're right." Then he leveled a glare at Mr. Wetherby. "Where is Sir Alfred?"

As Alec stalked down the hallway to Sir Alfred's room, Wetherby was hot on his heels. "Stop! You can't go in there. He's not to have any visitors."

Alec paused by the door. "Oh, I'm no visitor," he said over his shoulder before entering the darkened sick room. There he found an older woman standing by the bedside helping an elderly man use a spoon to feed himself.

It was a moment before Alec recognized Sir Alfred.

His hair, always a healthy mix of salt and pepper, was now mostly white. Yet he looked almost childlike in a billowing nightshirt with a napkin tucked into his collar.

The sight brought Alec to an abrupt halt. The pair turned at his entrance and seemed just as surprised to see him.

Alec had come here to exact his revenge on a formidable opponent. To utter every word he had ever swallowed, express every emotion he had ever tamped down, every opinion he had ever been forced to doubt. But now . . .

Sir Alfred recovered from his shock first. He threw down the spoon and tore the napkin from his collar. "Get this out of here," he growled to the woman, who bobbed her head and immediately whisked the tray away. He then tried to sit up straighter, pushing against the mattress with one hand while the other hung limply by his side. Sir Alfred let out a low curse and glared down at his body, already exhausted from the movement. Scores of people had quivered under the weight of his glare, but it held no power here.

Before Alec could think better of it, he was at the bedside with his hand on Sir Alfred's shoulder, hoisting him up with uncomfortable ease. The man seemed to weigh no more than a doll. Sir Alfred wouldn't meet his gaze as he grumbled a word of thanks and resettled himself. Alec stepped back and gave a short nod, then detected movement out the corner of his eye. Rafe and Wetherby had entered the room.

"Sir, I'm so sorry for the interruption," Wetherby began. "I will have them dismissed at once—"

But Sir Alfred merely held up a hand to silence his secretary, and faced Alec. "So, then. You came after all." He spoke more slowly than Alec remembered, as if he was taking great care to pronounce every word. But with his spine straight and shoulders back, any trace of vulnerability had vanished. His brown eyes looked nearly black in the dim light, as familiar to Alec as his own. As Lottie's.

Alec's heart wrenched anew as his anger came rushing back. This man had betrayed Crown secrets, endangered Alec's life, and tried to marry Lottie off. "Of course I came."

Sir Alfred gave a dismissive sniff and turned away. "Well, you are too late. Everything is already arranged."

Alec couldn't stop the incredulous laugh from bursting out. "I'm sorry, are you referring to the bit where you tried to *force your niece into marriage*?"

"I'm not forcing her," Sir Alfred stubbornly insisted. "Lottie knows I only want what's best for her. For her future. She needs some time to come round. But she will." Then he faced Alec again, those brown eyes glinting. "She always does."

"Not this time." Alec shook his head. "She's climbed out of the blasted window."

"What?" Sir Alfred appeared genuinely perplexed by this development. "Why on earth would she do a silly thing like that?"

Alec practically quivered from the strain of holding back. How could the man not see how very *medieval* this all was? But then, perhaps he simply couldn't. Had the apoplexy affected his mind as well? Rafe must have sensed that his self-control was quickly fraying because he immediately came beside him.

"Sorry to hear your lovely niece has escaped your clutches," Rafe began, droll as ever, "but I'd like to say that it is a *pleasure*, Sir Alfred. One doesn't often get to meet a legend in the flesh."

Alec exhaled. Thank God for Rafe and his ability to defuse any situation.

Sir Alfred narrowed his eyes in suspicion, but insipid flattery had always been his weakness. "And you are?"

"Rafe Davies," he said with a grand bow. "Intelligence officer."

Sir Alfred grunted. "You're the Earl of Fairfield's bastard?"

"No sir," Rafe replied with staggering politeness. "I'm the legitimate offspring from his second marriage."

"Ah. He *married* that actress, didn't he?" Sir Alfred cast him a dubious look.

"Yes, to the great regret of nearly everyone in his life." Rafe smiled broadly. "But I'm here on Crown business. Someone has been selling valuable information to our enemies, and the leak has been traced to you." He leveled the charge so plainly that it took a moment for the words to sink in.

Sir Alfred's frown deepened to confusion. "I haven't a damned idea what you're talking about."

"Yes, well, be that as it may, the charge still stands. I've also taken the liberty of alerting the police. They should be here shortly." Rafe raised an eyebrow at Alec's surprise. "What? Surely holding one's niece against her will is breaking *some* sort of law."

Sir Alfred huffed. "Wetherby, what do you know about this leak business?" Alec had nearly forgotten about the secretary. He was still standing near the doorway but had gone even paler than before. Sir Alfred gestured to him. "He has been handling all of my correspondence for months now."

"*Months?*" Alec and Rafe both said in unison. If that included intelligence dispatches, it was a huge breach in protocol. The protocol Sir Alfred had always insisted upon.

"I couldn't manage it the way I had been," he now blustered. "But Wetherby said he developed a system to keep the information secure."

Alec inhaled sharply. *Lottie.* "No, he didn't, sir. He used Lottie to decode the dispatches for himself. Then sold the information." Alec turned sharply to face him. "*Didn't* you?"

Wetherby held up his hands. "You can't prove a thing. Not without implicating her."

"What?" Sir Alfred roared from the bed. "You—you duplicitous rat! Treasonous *coward*!" As he spoke, he turned so red that Alec worried he would have another apoplexy.

Wetherby looked at each of them, then he turned and ran from the room. Alec moved to chase him, but Rafe pressed a hand to his chest. "Don't bother. He won't get far," he said lazily and strolled from the room.

"My God. I had no idea," Sir Alfred croaked and slumped down against the pillows. His color had returned to normal but the fight had gone out of him. He turned to Alec. "You must find Lottie. She can't be dragged into this."

"Of course," Alec said. "But I won't bring her back here. Not unless she wants it."

Sir Alfred let out a sigh. "You think I've gone too far, but you don't understand—"

"Try me," Alec said through gritted teeth. He had never spoken so harshly to Sir Alfred, and the man noticed.

He shook his head. "After her parents died, I was supposed to protect her. I failed her mother, the poor girl. I couldn't fail Lottie, too. If things had carried on between you, it would have been a disaster for her. And then all of it—*all of it*—would have been for nothing."

Alec knew that Sir Alfred was still haunted by the death of his younger sister, but Lottie had paid the price for far too long. They both had.

"That wasn't your choice to make. And I never should have agreed to your terms. I should have gone to Lottie. Instead I—" his throat tightened at the realization "—I was no better than you, was I?"

The barest hint of remorse crossed Sir Alfred's face before

the anger returned. "I made your career that day. Gave you a future."

"No. You made me a killer. A liar. And I hurt the person I cared about most. Because I thought I was nothing. That I could give her nothing—"

"I'll hear no more of this rubbish," Sir Alfred grumbled as he reached toward the bell pull, but Alec snatched it away.

"Ah, but you *will*. And I've only gotten started." He moved closer until he loomed over the man, but Sir Alfred merely tilted his head up, refusing to be intimidated. Even now. Even in this state. Alec couldn't help but admire his pluck, but he wouldn't back down. Not until he knew everything once and for all.

"Tell me what my mother was doing for you."

The old man said nothing. Just stared back at him in silence. Alec swallowed a frustrated sigh. What he would give to have Rafe's interrogation abilities...

"You owe me the truth, Sir Alfred," he began again, taking care to hold back any note of the desperation currently flooding through him. "After all I sacrificed for you. For Turkey."

Sir Alfred's expression faltered at that. Perhaps he had a heart after all. "Her husband was a duplicitous scoundrel," he said reluctantly. "But I needed information to prove it, and she agreed to spy on him. After she took up with your father, she still returned to the count on occasion to stay in his good graces. He refused to give her up completely, and he was a powerful man. They needed his approval."

Alec inhaled. It wasn't anything he didn't already know, but it was still difficult to hear Sir Alfred confirm it.

"Somehow the count found out," Sir Alfred continued. "He demanded Maria leave Edward or else he would have him thrown in prison. Edward was already regarded as a troublemaker because of his irritating habit of championing the cause of the common man. One word from the count was all it would take. There was no way he would have survived the filthy place, so Maria left." Then Sir Alfred looked away. "It... it was not an easy decision for her to make.

"But if your father was imprisoned, she would have been forced to go back to the count anyway. And she would have lost you. Appeasing him to keep you with one parent seemed like the better option. And the count was an old man. He could have died at any time."

Alec squeezed his eyes shut. The count had ended up out-living his mother by two years.

"But neither of us could have predicted your father's reaction," Sir Alfred said softly. "I couldn't tell him why she had really left, of course, but I did try to make him see reason. How all he needed was to *wait*, that she would return someday, but he was weaker than I realized. God rest his soul, wherever it is."

And now Alec had done much the same to Lottie—told her a despicable lie in the name of saving her. Alec let out a bitter huff and opened his eyes to see Sir Alfred actually looking remorseful. Alec never expected to feel pity for Sir Alfred until he was faced with an old man who had nothing but a long life full of manipulation to look back on. It was a dire warning of a future Alec wanted no part of.

"I cared about them both, you know. And you. It was an ugly business, what happened." Then he paused. "I suppose... I suppose I felt partly responsible," he admitted with great reluctance. "So I took you when she asked me to. But you should know that your mother did not want to leave you. She did the best she could given the confines of her marriage."

"And yet you would have forced your own niece into a similar arrangement."

Sir Alfred seemed startled by the comparison, but then nodded. "It appears so."

"All because the idea of her marrying me was so utterly *distasteful*." Alec couldn't keep the bitterness out of his words.

Sir Alfred gave him another long look. "You could have told me to go to hell five years ago, you know," he pointed out. "But you didn't. You saw the benefits of my offer."

Alec thought of that morning. Of how easily Sir Alfred preyed on his deepest fears. And of another morning only days before when he had performed a similar manipulation. "Only because I believed the things you said about me. I believed I would ruin her life. That I didn't deserve her."

Sir Alfred seemed to consider this. "And now?"

Alec let out a dark laugh. "Oh, I still most certainly don't deserve her. But I owe her an apology. One that is long overdue. And the truth."

"We both failed her, didn't we?" Sir Alfred sighed. "I know you love her, Alec. I've never doubted that. But I—I—" His voice broke as he collected his thoughts. "I've had to make a great many sacrifices in my life. Personal sacrifices. Some of which I have come to regret very much." His gaze grew hazy, and Alec had the distinct impression that he was thinking of a certain beguiling Irish housekeeper.

One who clearly wasn't in this town house...

Then Sir Alfred narrowed his eyes. "I suppose I didn't see why *you* should have been any different."

Alec had long assumed Sir Alfred's strict discipline stemmed from dislike, but the man had simply been holding him to the same impossible standards he'd set for himself. There was a time when Alec would have been bullied into agreeing with him; now he could only hear the resentment lacing those words.

"But I *am* different, sir," he said with absolute certainty. "If given the chance, I would have always chosen her. Over everything. Every time."

Alec knew where Lottie was. And there wasn't a moment to waste.

CHAPTER TWENTY-THREE

⌇

Though Lottie's childhood predilection of climbing out of windows had finally proved useful, she still hadn't mastered her fear of heights. Sheer panic had fueled her shaky descent down a conveniently placed lattice while she focused on the brick wall in front of her.

By some miracle she landed safely with only a few scratches and had taken enough money for a ticket to Surrey. It was poor form to leave Valentina behind, but Lottie knew she would only dissuade her. She would find a way to make it up to Valentina later, when the threat of marriage to Mr. Wetherby wasn't quite so imminent. After she arrived at the tiny village train station, Lottie took a shortcut through the forest. It was late afternoon by the time she reached Haverford, bedraggled, famished, and cold; but the sight of the sprawling Tudor mansion, home to six generations of her mother's family, warmed her with relief. Mr. Wetherby could not touch her here.

Lottie must have looked worse than she felt because Ailish, a housemaid, gasped at the sight of her while Ben, a footman, begged her to sit and immediately fetched Mrs. Houston. She had been working for the Lewis family for nearly three decades now, beginning as a scullery maid. There was no one Lottie trusted more on this earth than her.

"My goodness, Miss Carlisle!" she cried out, her large brown eyes as wide as a startled doe's. "Don't tell me you came all this way on *foot*?"

Lottie ran a sheepish hand over her hatless head and pulled away a twig. "Only from the train station."

Mrs. Houston tsked as she cast a worried gaze over her. "Come with me. Ailish, make us some tea, then."

Lottie followed Mrs. Houston to her sitting room where they could talk privately. She had always loved this cozy little space and whiled away many rainy afternoons by the hearth listening to Mrs. Houston's stories of her youth spent in Ireland's West Country. For a time Alec had joined them, until he grew too old for such things. Lottie's throat tightened at the rush of memories.

The events of the day suddenly pressed down upon her and Lottie slumped into an overstuffed armchair clothed in faded green velvet. Mrs. Houston took the one opposite, her brow puckered with worry. She still retained much of the striking beauty of her youth, though her dark brown hair was now heavily streaked with gray. There had never been a Mr. Houston, and not for the first time Lottie wondered what had kept her here all these years, when she could have had a husband, a family, and a home of her own.

Ailish promptly arrived with the tea tray. Once they were alone again, Mrs. Houston began to pour. "Now," she said as she handed Lottie a steaming cup and saucer, "am I right in supposing Alec found you?"

Lottie nearly dropped the china.

"No one else knows about Florence," Mrs. Houston added.

Lottie's eyes fell. "I know it was childish to leave the way I did, but I couldn't spend another minute with Mrs. Wetherby. And Uncle Alfred was putting so much pressure on me to marry."

Mrs. Houston gave her an understanding nod. "Where did you end up?"

Lottie let out a breath. "I went to the village my parents visited on their honeymoon."

"Oh, my dear. No wonder Alec found you." The sadness behind her words turned Lottie's heart inside out. "But, he did not return to England?"

Lottie fiddled with the edge of her saucer as her throat tightened. "He thought it for the best," she said hoarsely. "We . . . we quarreled before I left." She had to look away from Mrs. Houston's sympathetic gaze. "But that's not why I'm here. It's Uncle Alfred. He isn't well." Her voice cracked on the last word.

"I know," Mrs. Houston said. "But he's being taken care of. I hired Mrs. Ragmoore myself."

"But why did he send *you* away?"

A faint tremor of emotion passed over the housekeeper's face until she mastered it. Mrs. Houston swallowed hard. "I must respect his decision."

"His or Mr. Wetherby's?"

"You weren't here, Lottie," she frowned. "It was only natural for Mr. Wetherby to handle the arrangements. The doctors thought it best if your uncle had as much peace as possible until he regained his strength."

Lottie shook her head as her mind whirled. There was so much Mrs. Houston didn't know. "This morning Uncle Alfred told me I was to marry Mr. Wetherby. This afternoon."

Mrs. Houston's teacup clattered against the saucer. "*What?*"

Lottie explained her uncle's reasoning, along with Mr. Wetherby's role in the charade. "I think Uncle Alfred has been in decline for much longer than anyone realized," Lottie added, voicing the theory she had been piecing together since the previous night. It was the only thing that could explain his increasingly erratic behavior over the past year. "Mr. Wetherby likely knew from the start because they work so closely together. That meant he could manipulate the situation for his own gain."

Which explained why Mr. Wetherby's aunt, of all people, had been deemed a proper companion for her. And why they needed to be married while her uncle still had some control over her finances.

Mrs. Houston brought a hand to her mouth. "Oh, Lottie," she gasped. "I—I think you're right. I saw he was growing more short-tempered, more forgetful, but I thought it was just due to his age. And Mr. Wetherby always seemed so competent. I thought he was *good* for Sir Alfred."

Lottie furrowed her brow. "The only part that doesn't fit is sending Alec for me. That could have ruined Mr. Wetherby's plans."

"That was my idea," Mrs. Houston said sheepishly. "Your uncle was so worried. Mr. Wetherby offered to go, but he had never been to Italy and—and Alec was already *there*. It seemed like the best choice. He went searching for you immediately. Your uncle fell ill only a few days later."

Lottie recalled the torturous look that had briefly passed over Alec's face as he related all this to her only days before:

When I received Sir Alfred's telegram, I nearly—

Nearly *what*?

Now she would never know.

"What caused you two to quarrel?" The cautious hope in Mrs. Houston's eyes was even more wrenching.

"It doesn't matter," Lottie groused. "No one seems to care about what I want, or consider what *I* might think is best for *my* life."

Mrs. Houston listened patiently to her little outburst. "Your uncle has always believed he knows what's best for everybody," she gently explained. "But that also comes with a sense of responsibility when things go wrong."

Lottie sniffed at the idea. "He isn't God."

The hint of a smile touched Mrs. Houston's lips. "No, he most certainly is not. I think he has finally started to realize that." Then she hesitated. "Did you know your dear mother lingered for nearly a day after the accident?"

"I . . . I try not to think of that day very often."

Or ever.

Mrs. Houston gave a thoughtful nod. "As well you should. Your father died right away, bless him. But your mother was brought to your uncle's town house, as it was nearby. I'll never forget that night as long as I live. They had always been so close. And after your grandparents died, he was more of a father to her than a brother. Sir Alfred did not leave her side for more than a minute. He called in every last favor he ever had and brought in every doctor available." Her eyes lowered. "But you know how it ended."

To her utter embarrassment, Lottie found herself brushing a tear away. How silly to cry now over something so long ago. Something so utterly beyond her control.

"I believe he has always seen you as his one chance at redemption because he couldn't save her. He wants your life to be perfect in a way your mother's wasn't. That's why he didn't mind you being so choosy these last few years."

"I wasn't being *choosy*. They weren't—they weren't Alec," she said hoarsely. Voicing the admission nearly broke her heart all over again.

"I know my dear. I tried to tell him, many times, but he wouldn't—or *couldn't*—hear of it."

Lottie was astonished. "You talked about us?"

"On occasion. If he wished it. But we often disagreed, especially regarding Alec. He thought you two were too much together." The housekeeper hesitated, watching her carefully. "That it would give the both of you ideas."

"So he thought it better to separate us through *lies*?" Lottie fumed. "I know the truth about Alec, Mrs. Houston. About his parents."

If the housekeeper was surprised, she did not show it. "As I said, I did not agree with all of his decisions. But I know with all my heart he was only doing what he thought was best." Mrs. Houston's face warmed with affection as she defended her longtime employer.

It was as if Lottie had finally discovered the last piece of a long, unfinished puzzle. "You *love* him," she marveled.

"Yes," Mrs. Houston admitted, blushing like a schoolgirl. "For many years now."

"Does he know?"

Mrs. Houston laughed. "I should hope so, considering he's the one who said it first."

"I'm sorry. I...I had no idea." It seemed impossible to think of Sir Alfred saying such things to anyone, really.

"Well, of course not. That was the point."

"But you did not wish to marry?"

Mrs. Houston fixed her with a look. "Lottie, I've listened to you bang on about women's suffrage for the last year. Are you really going to turn your nose up on me now?"

"No!" Lottie was mortified to realize that Mrs. Houston was right.

"We've an arrangement that suits the both of us. Your uncle has his work, and I have mine," she said with characteristic firmness. "Besides, if we married it would only cause talk."

Lottie balked. "What does that matter if you love each other?"

Mrs. Houston gave her a kind smile. "Oh Lottie. You've no idea what it would be like for me. People would say I tricked him into marriage. That I was putting on airs. He would lose the respect of his peers and I of the staff. I would never be accepted as the mistress of a house I once worked in. And I don't want that. For either of us."

"But isn't it hard being here while he's in London?"

Mrs. Houston's smile slipped a little. "More than I could ever say. He doesn't want me to see him as anything less than the man he was."

Lottie grasped her hand. "I understand, but in this case I think you shouldn't heed his wishes."

"Thank God you came here. We'll need to contact your uncle's solicitor immediately."

Lottie nodded in agreement. Mr. Jenkins was her solicitor as well.

Mrs. Houston then leveled her eyes. "I'm also going to contact Alec."

"*Why?*" Lottie tore her hand away. "This isn't any of his concern."

"But if your uncle has been in decline for this long, and if Mr. Wetherby did know and said nothing, then his work may have been compromised," she pointed out.

Lottie's breath caught. She hadn't thought of that.

"And besides, even if you did quarrel, Alec would want to know if you were in danger. No matter what happened in Venice, he still cares for you."

Lottie stared at the unlit hearth. "Perhaps he did once, but he feels nothing more than a sense of obligation toward me now."

Mrs. Houston clucked her tongue. "I don't believe that for a minute—"

"He said those very *words*, Mrs. Houston. After I told him I loved him." Fresh anger and hurt flooded her veins with such force she vaulted from the chair. "That I had always loved him. That I didn't care about his parents or his past. But he wouldn't hear *any* of it!"

Mrs. Houston motioned for her to sit back down. "It's true I don't know the circumstances, but I think you need to understand how his past has shaped him. *You* may truly not care about the differences in your station, but I imagine Alec would find that difficult to accept."

"What differences?" Lottie spat. "We are both the children of gentlemen."

Mrs. Houston gave her an exasperated look. "Tell me you aren't that naive. He is *illegitimate*. His own family does not recognize him. That has always haunted him."

Lottie crossed her arms. "He hardly seemed 'haunted' while he was explaining that our friendship was based on nothing more than *convenience*," she muttered. She had gone over their exchange so many times that his look of mild irritation was burned into her brain. It was free of turmoil. Of devastation. She might as well have been a persistent fly, or an overzealous saleswoman.

"Is that what he told you? And I suppose the whippings he received were for fun as well?" She let out a laugh of disbelief. "No, Lottie. Nothing about your friendship was *ever* convenient. But he has always sought to protect you, above all else. Since you were both children. Your bond was extraordinary even then. We all saw it."

Lottie angrily shook her head. "It was nothing of the kind. Alec made that very clear."

"He's used to thinking of himself as a burden, especially to you." Then Mrs. Houston dipped her chin. "And believe me, I can understand why."

A fresh wave of misery broke over Lottie. She could not accept that Alec had turned her away out of selflessness. That so many of his choices had been made to preserve her standing in a world she had never cared for. Or that their parting had been one last attempt to save her reputation. Couldn't he see that in doing so he robbed them *both* of love? No. Even Alec would not be bullheaded enough to do such a thing.

"Inform him of Mr. Wetherby's actions, if you must," Lottie said as she turned toward the exit. "But please, I beg you, tell him nothing of me."

Mrs. Houston called after her as she hurried out of the sitting room. But Lottie could take no more revelations today. She bolted up the stairs, barely registering the grand portraits of so many dour-faced ancestors as she raced toward her room. Until she turned a corner and her mother's familiar green-eyed gaze brought her to a halt. The formal portrait had been commissioned shortly after her mother's eighteenth birthday, in accordance with Lewis family custom.

Lottie stepped closer and closer until she could reach out and brush the heavy gilded frame with her finger. Ada Lewis would meet John Carlisle less than a year after this was painted. It seemed unthinkable that Lottie was nearly the age her mother was when she died. She had possessed a tranquil wisdom that made her seem ageless. But Ada had been a young wife and mother, with a life very different from her daughter's.

And what would she say now?

Lottie abruptly turned away from the portrait. Her room no longer seemed like a welcome refuge. It was full of reminders of the parents she had lost, of the life she had never gotten to have. But one place remained where she could truly be alone.

The fairy cottage was only a short distance from the main house, but it was tucked away in a hidden glen few knew about. Dusk was approaching as Lottie picked her way along the path overgrown with weeds and wildflowers. The cottage itself was covered in thick tangles of ivy, all but forgotten over the years.

Lottie's grandfather had erected the tiny cottage as a playhouse for his youngest daughter and was partially inspired by Marie Antoinette's model village in Versailles. Ada had christened it the "fairy cottage" when she was a child, and the name stuck. It was not a grand building by any means. Nothing more than two small rooms. But it had been sturdily built from area stone, and the thatched roof still appeared intact. Lottie found the cottage key in its usual spot under a large stone planter by the entrance and brushed away the accumulated dirt.

She couldn't remember the last time she visited. Had it really stood empty all these years? The door would not budge until Lottie applied her shoulder with some vigor, and when it abruptly swung open she nearly toppled onto the floor. She shook out her skirts and took in the space. It smelled of damp and moss, but otherwise was just as she remembered. The larger of the two rooms contained a little wooden table, two chairs, and a lantern, while the other housed a camp stove and narrow cot.

The cottage's lone diamond-paned picture window was partially covered in ivy, letting in only a bit of fast-fading daylight. Lottie found a remarkably dry pack of matches in the table's drawer and set to lighting the lantern. Once the room was cast in a comforting glow, she curled up on the window seat, tucked her skirts around her legs, and rested her head against the glass.

Her heavy sigh filled the room. Mr. Wetherby had been thwarted, and she had every faith that Mrs. Houston would inform the suitable parties, but instead of planning her future and reveling in the independence she had sought for so long, here she was hiding away again in another cottage. But the loneliness that had once been so constant she'd barely noticed now chafed against her skin, rubbing her bruised heart raw. And there would never be any relief. She wanted something that was beyond money, beyond machinations and subterfuge. She, wanted to be needed by a finite heart, even if it meant enduring pain when it ceased to beat. She wanted to give love and be loved in return, even if it meant giving up possibilities. She no longer wanted to live for herself alone, guided only by her own desires, but to be deeply known, like she had once been.

And she could not have it.

Eventually Lottie dozed off, but her dreams provided no respite. Alec was here in the cottage, wrapping her in his strong arms, murmuring her name against her ear. Lottie's heart ached so badly for it to be real that she was wrenched awake. But, strangely, the dream did not end.

She blinked up sleepily into Alec's face. "You ... you can't be *here*," she whispered in confusion. He was a thousand miles away.

Alec's eyes filled with hurt and he gave a brief nod. "I'm sorry. I needed to know you were safe. I'll go." He began to pull away but Lottie's fingers dug into his arm, her body already recognizing what her mind could not.

"This is real?" She feared uttering the very words would make him vanish.

A relieved smile broke across his face. "I'm afraid so," he said. When she pressed her face against his shoulder, she could have sworn he whispered *Thank God*.

"How," she gasped. "How did you get here so quickly? Mrs. Houston only just contacted you."

"I'm not here because of her." Alec clasped the nape of her neck and she wanted to cry from the tenderness of his touch.

"I left Venice the day after you did. I came here for *you*." He crushed her even closer. "But when I got to London, I discovered what Mr. Wetherby had planned. Rafe and I came just as the vicar was arriving. I nearly lost my mind when I realized you went through the window." Alec gently tipped up her chin. "I thought you were afraid of heights."

"I am," she said. "But I really didn't want to marry that man."

Alec smiled. "I can understand that."

"But... you knew to come here?"

"I had a hunch." He shrugged, as if his ability to find her across continents was perfectly normal.

She pressed against him once again as hot joy fanned out from her heart through every limb. "Mr. Wetherby must have been very angry," she said after a moment.

Alec drew her away from him, his expression grave. "He's been arrested. Those codes you were deciphering didn't come from your uncle. Wetherby was selling sensitive information. Rafe wants to charge him with kidnapping in addition to conspiring with foreign agents. He will likely hang."

A shudder rented through her as she recalled the man's words: *Being poor is a tedious business. I intend to avoid it at all costs*

And now he would pay with his life.

"My God. Did my uncle know?"

"It doesn't appear so. He has had a rather large number of lapses in judgment lately. Most likely he has been in decline for much longer than anyone realized."

"Yes, I thought the same." Lottie glanced down and ran a finger along the lapels of his jacket. "You saw him, then?"

"We talked for a long while."

Lottie hesitated, but Alec needed to know the truth. "Did he tell you about your mother, and the work she did for him?"

"He did."

Lottie pulled back and stared into his eyes. The coldness that had always accompanied any mention of his parents was entirely gone. Now he looked broken. "I'm sorry," she said. "I learned everything from him yesterday. That must have been so upsetting for you."

Alec dipped his chin, as if her words embarrassed him. "It was something of a comfort to know the truth behind why she left, but I've realized I let her absence dictate far too much for too long."

"Alec, you didn't—"

He held up a finger to her lips. "Please, just listen before you say anything. I know I don't deserve such an indulgence, but I've had a long time to think on everything these last few days.

"It would be so easy to blame all my troubles on Sir Alfred, but I don't want to spend the rest of my life feeling angry or bitter over the mistakes of others." He paused as his eyes lingered on her face. "Or continue letting those mistakes dictate my life. Like I did five years ago."

Lottie had to take a long breath before she could speak, and even then her voice still trembled. "What do you mean?"

Alec tilted her chin once more, and the tenderness in his gaze was as intoxicating as it was terrifying. "What you said in Venice. You were right about everything. About me. I spent all these years trying to make myself forget you. Trying to force everything I ever felt for you into nothingness." Lottie tried to glance away, but Alec stopped her. "But it didn't work. Lottie, it *never* worked." He began to gently stroke her cheek and she remembered to breathe. "The morning after your ball, I came to Sir Alfred and asked to court you properly. I said that though I had always loved you, at some point I had fallen *in* love with you. Irrevocably." His words were strangely humbling. How long she had ached to hear them. Lottie reached up and covered his hand with her own. Alec cleared his throat and looked away. "But then I walked away at the first sign of trouble."

Lottie couldn't stand the guilt that now seemed to consume him. "You were *deceived*."

"It doesn't matter," he insisted. "Sir Alfred said I could have told him to go to hell that day, and he was right. I could have told you the truth about my parents as soon as I found out, but I ran instead. I chose to put my life in danger rather than reveal any weakness to you. I told myself I was doing what was best for you. That it was a sacrifice. But I didn't trust you to accept me. Because I was a coward. And I didn't deserve you for that reason alone. Never mind the hundred other ones." He raked a desperate hand through his hair, further rumpling the already disheveled waves. It looked as if he had barely slept in days. Just like her.

"I've spent all these years thinking—*knowing*—I wasn't good enough for you. I always blamed it on things beyond my control—my circumstances, your uncle, my parents. But it was my fault all along." He let out a weary sigh. "I let other people's opinions determine our future when I should have fought for you. For us. Instead, I diminished your feelings and ignored my own. And I will always consider that the greatest mistake of my life."

"Oh, Alec," Lottie whispered thickly. She could not let him shoulder this burden alone. "I should have made more of an effort to understand your silence about your past instead of taking it so personally. I don't blame you for keeping the truth about your parents to yourself. You were in an impossible position."

"It's no excuse," he burst out, turning away in anger. "I destroyed *everything* between us that morning in your uncle's study. Then again in Venice. And I wish to God I could take it all back. To start over with you, but I can't—"

"You're being much too hard on yourself."

He stubbornly shook his head, still refusing to look at her. "But *you* would never have done that."

Impossible man.

"Only because I never had the chance to!" Lottie let out a frustrated cry as she reached for him. "I'd like to believe that I would have accepted you without worry five years ago. That I wouldn't have cared about your parents or my reputation. That I would have taken Uncle Alfred's disappointment in stride and run off with you. But I was a different girl then. And more concerned with what people thought of me than I'd like to admit."

She gripped his shoulders and forced him to meet her eyes. He was no longer the boyish young gentleman who had wooed her one evening. The careworn man that stared back had a few more wrinkles and had likely seen things she could never imagine. But he was also the man who had bounded up a mountain to find her, who made sure she saw Venice, who brought tears to her eyes both in pleasure and pain—and been prepared to die for her.

In so many ways, they were still the same people who had slept side by side in this very room years and years ago. But they had grown so much since then. Perhaps more than they ever would have if they hadn't been forced to part.

She brought a hand to his jaw and stroked the rough bristle. "I think we both needed time to become who we are today. And I'm grateful for it. I only wish that you hadn't had to endure so much pain."

Alec stared for a long while, as if he was seeing her for the first time. Then the corner of his mouth lifted. "Very well. If you insist on being less than perfect, I'll try to accept it."

"Perfection is not what I aim for, Alec," she said gently. "And it is not what I expect from you, either."

"No, but there is something you should expect from me: an apology. For everything I said in Venice. I was so cruel to you, but believe me, I never meant a word of it. I was angry and ashamed, but more than anything, I was scared. But it's still no excuse. I should have treated you better."

Lottie bowed her head at his admission. "I forgive you."

Alec gave her a pained look. "Give me the chance to *earn* such a gift, will you?" he said hoarsely. "I came here with no expectations. I only wanted to apologize. To make sure you were safe. And to say that being able to call you a friend has been the greatest honor of my life, Lottie Carlisle."

Lottie's gaze grew watery as her heart burned for him. She didn't want some other Alec who hadn't made those mistakes, or even the man she had known five years ago. She wanted only this man. This Alec. As he was now.

As the tears began to spill down her cheeks, Alec reached out and brushed them away with his thumbs. His touch lingered there before he cupped her face in his hands. "And I will spend the rest of my days trying to deserve it. But I want you to be happy more than anything, in whatever shape that may take. Just know that I am here. I will always be here for you. As whatever you wish."

She frowned slightly through her tears. "Are you making me a proposal of...friendship?"

Alec brought her hands to his lips. "I don't dare ask for more," he said with a kiss. "But my feelings are unchanged from five years ago." As their eyes met, he suddenly shook his head. "No. No, that's not true at all. I love you so much more, Lottie. I didn't think it possible, but I do. You're so brave, and kind, and strong—" He paused and shook his head again. "I'm sorry. I didn't want to burden you with this," he added. "It isn't fair to—"

Lottie pressed a finger to his mouth. She was consumed with a fierce tenderness for this man who still, even now, placed her own desires above his. "Consider this my acceptance," she said as she pulled his head down to hers. "Of all that you are. And everything you will be," she murmured before pressing her lips to his.

Lottie had intended the kiss to communicate the sweetness in her heart.

I love you. I want you. Forever.

But it soon turned heavy with need.

Their bodies writhed and twisted together on the small window seat, each angling for the most pleasurable position until Alec managed to press Lottie's back against the window frame. Then he tore his mouth from hers.

"I shouldn't let you forgive me so easily, Lottie," he panted, "but dammit, I'm such a fool when it comes to you."

Lottie raised an eyebrow. "Respecting my ability to make decisions doesn't make you a fool, Alec. It makes you my *partner*."

He groaned as he sank heavily between her thighs. "I can happily live with that." He caught her lips in another deep kiss. Waves of aching need rolled through her until it felt as if her entire body was made of fire. She began to hike her skirts up in rough, jerky movements, determined to sate this impossible hunger. But the movement seemed to wrench Alec from their cloud of lust. He pulled back, his eyes as hot as coals. "No. We can't do this now," he gasped. "Mrs. Houston is waiting back at the house."

Lottie could hear the slight note of hesitation in his voice. She ran her fingers through the front of his hair and Alec stretched into her palm, like a cat begging to be scratched.

"But then we might not have another chance to be alone together."

Then he arched a brow. His gaze was so sharp, so intense, that Lottie felt it in her bones. "Now that you've accepted me, you think I have *any* intention of not marrying you as soon as possible?" His incredulousness sent a delightful shiver through her. "I've wanted this too much for too long."

Lottie grinned. "Yes, my thoughts exactly."

Alec let out a chuckle and threw up his hands in resignation. "Fine, I'll respect your decision. But may I suggest we move to the camp bed at least?"

"I defer to your excellent judgment in such matters, seeing as your knowledge supersedes my own."

Alec gave her an amused look as he pulled her to her feet. "Perhaps." Then he wrapped a hand around her waist and drew her close. "But I suspect it will always feel like the first time with you," he whispered against her ear, his voice both rough and warm.

"I'm beginning to think your father might not have been the only poet in the family," she said as she moved them toward the ancient camp bed.

Alec smiled softly as he kneaded the nape of her neck with his warm fingers, weakening her knees even more. "I just needed to find my muse."

Her eyes prickled at the potent mix of burning desire and endearing fondness swelling within her. "And I'm so happy you did." She sat down and pulled Alec's mouth toward hers once again.

And this time he offered no resistance.

EPILOGUE

❧

Three months later
A village near Pistoia, Italy

Alec looked up from his book and shielded his eyes against the bright Tuscan sunshine. The better to see his wife as she stepped out onto the terrace, having just bid good-bye to Signore Ernesto for the day.

After their lengthy reconciliation in the fairy cottage, Mrs. Houston had insisted that they all travel to London immediately. "I know you're both angry with Sir Alfred, and rightfully so, but give him the chance to make amends," she urged. "You won't regret it."

The old man had been quite overwhelmed by their appearance the next morning, but his eyes had taken on an unexpected shimmer at the sight of Mrs. Houston. Even Alec found himself moved watching as Sir Alfred reached for his lover's hand in their presence, then whispered private words that brought tears to the formidable woman's eyes.

Then she straightened and gestured to Alec and Lottie. "The children have something to tell you."

Sir Alfred turned to them, a knowing little smile on his face. "And I'd like to hear it."

Lottie, who had been as still as stone the moment they entered the room, suddenly burst out in a surprised laugh and went to him. Sir Alfred hugged her close for many minutes, murmuring words of regret. Then he shook Alec's hand and simply said, "Take care of our girl."

A few days later they were married in the back garden of the South Kensington town house in front of Sir Alfred, Mrs. Houston, and Rafe. Alec formally resigned from Crown service, and he spent the following month mostly in Sir Alfred's company, where together they worked to heal from the pain of their shared past until he suffered another, more debilitating apoplexy. Lottie, Alec, and Mrs. Houston were by his bedside when he took his last breaths, and the tears they spilled for their former guardian were genuine.

But the enigmatic man still had one more surprise left. Though most of his fortune was left to Lottie, he provided a generous settlement to Mrs. Houston, and also to Alec. His will had been updated only once—when Alec had first become his ward. Neither could fully make sense of his motives. Sir Alfred remained a puzzle until the very end. But they already had plans for his money, beginning with the founding of a Venetian orphanage and a large donation to a London-based charity that provided aid to women and children.

After the last paper was signed and filed, they headed back to Venice. Signore Cardinelli had finally crossed the wrong official and was promptly arrested, so Alec felt comfortable resuming his teaching post in the fall. But first came a lengthy stop in the village. For where else would Lottie learn to paint her sunset?

"Will you tell Marta to make custard tarts for tea?" Alec asked as Lottie approached. "I've another craving."

"*Again?* That will be the third batch in as many weeks." Her lips curved as she came beside his chair. "You're in danger of becoming predictable, Professor."

"I might as well, now that I'm a properly married man."

He grinned and reached for her hand. Alec still felt that spark every time they touched. He would never take it for granted.

"Well, I'm afraid it will have to wait for tomorrow," Lottie said. "She's left for the day."

Alec raised an eyebrow. "So soon?" It was barely the afternoon. Marta usually stayed to make the evening meal.

"I thought we could fend for ourselves tonight."

"Are you sure that was all?" Alec murmured seductively, as his mind filled with the image of having Lottie for dinner instead.

A most becoming blush stained her cheeks. "I confess I may have ulterior motives."

"Ah, you shouldn't have admitted that so easily. I would have quite enjoyed extracting the truth from you. I've a few tactics in mind."

"I don't doubt it. Perhaps I could still convince you to use them?" Lottie let out a shriek of delight as Alec pulled her down on his lap. Then she gasped and immediately sprung up, rubbing her backside.

He had forgotten all about his book. "Sorry darling." Alec pulled the book off his lap and drew her back down.

She plucked the tome from his hands. Her eyes skimmed the cover. "Are you enjoying it?"

Alec brushed his fingers against the nape of her neck. "I'm not sure 'enjoying' is the right word, but it has been surprisingly comforting," he said. "I hadn't realized how much I still remembered of his work."

After the announcement of their nuptials had been printed in all the London papers, Alec received a letter from his cousin, the Honorable Nigel Gresham, who now held his grandfather's viscountcy. Apparently it had been the late viscount's dying wish for his brother's son to be welcomed back into the family. Alec initially balked at the suggestion—

he had gotten on perfectly well without the Greshams all these years—until Lottie's gentle suggestion that perhaps this could be a way to further make peace with his past.

Alec responded to the letter merely to please her, but much to his surprise Cousin Nigel turned out to be a delightfully witty epistoler—not at all the tweedy lout he was expecting. A warm correspondence quickly developed between the cousins, and there was even talk of Alec and Lottie visiting the family seat in Norfolk over the Christmas holiday. Several weeks ago Cousin Nigel had forwarded him a letter from a Cambridge professor eager to write his father's biography. After mulling it over, Alec had finally agreed to answer his questions and figured he should brush up on his father's catalogue in preparation. But seeing Italy, his mother, as well as himself through his father's words helped him to understand Edward Gresham a little more, and to remember the man he had once been.

Lottie turned to him and smiled tenderly. "I'm so glad to hear that. I know it's not anything like having him here, and it can't make up for the pain of losing him, but it's better than trying to forget it all."

She was right. Like always.

His heart ached with love for this woman who knew him so well. Who had always been able to see him so much better than he could ever see himself. And love him for it. Alec was growing more used to the idea that he really was the man she thought he was. And even if he wasn't, he had every intention of becoming so.

The intense, gnawing regret he used to feel for all the time they lost had begun to fade, replaced by happier memories. These days it was easier to look toward the future. *Their* future. The past, and the pain it contained, would always be there, but it could only hurt them still if they allowed it.

Alec paid his penance a dozen times over. Now that he had Lottie, and they had a life of their own, he would not waste any of it.

He stilled his fingers and opened his palm to cradle the back of her neck. "Don't you ever grow tired of being right about me?"

She smirked and sank against his chest. "No. Do you ever wish you could go back to being the mysterious, globe-trotting agent of intrigue, instead of just another boring old husband?"

The thought of being anywhere else with anyone other than her held absolutely no appeal.

He placed a finger under her chin and gently tilted her face up to his. "As long as I'm *your* boring old husband," he began and watched her eyes glaze over as he drew her mouth closer. "Never, my dear," he whispered against her lips. "Never."

Look for Rafe's tale
in the next thrilling
League of Scoundrels story
Available Fall 2021

About the Author

Emily Sullivan has been an avid reader and writer since child-hood and in 2019 won RWA's Golden Heart award for Best Historical Romance. A lifelong New Englander, she shares her home with her husband, shelves of books, and a piano she should really use more.

You can learn more at:

Website: https://www.emilysullivanbooks.com

Twitter: @paperbacklady

Instagram: Paperbacklady

Looking for more historical romances?
Get swept away by handsome rogues and clever
ladies from Forever!

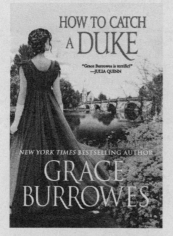

HOW TO CATCH A DUKE
by Grace Burrowes

Miss Abigail Abbott needs to disappear—permanently—and the only person she trusts to help is Lord Stephen Wentworth, heir to the Duke of Walden. Stephen is brilliant, charming, and absolutely ruthless. So ruthless that he proposes marriage to keep Abigail safe. But when she accepts his courtship of convenience, they discover intimate moments that they don't want to end. But can Stephen convince Abigail that their arrangement is more than a sham and that his love is real?

THE TRUTH ABOUT DUKES
by Grace Burrowes

Lady Constance Wentworth never has a daring thought (that she admits aloud) and never comes close to courting scandal...as far as anybody knows. Robert Rothmere is a scandal poised to explode. Unless he wants to end up locked away in a madhouse (again) by his enemies, he needs to marry a perfectly proper, deadly-dull duchess, immediately—but little does he know that the delightful lady he has in mind is hiding scandalous secrets of her own.

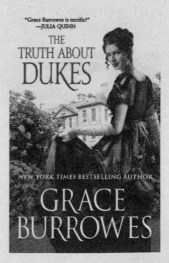

SOMEDAY MY DUKE WILL COME
by Christina Britton

Quincy Nesbitt reluctantly accepted the dukedom after his brother's death, but he'll be damned if he accepts his brother's fiancée as well. The only polite way to decline is to become engaged to someone else—quickly. Lady Clara has the right connections and happens to need him as much as he needs her. But he soon discovers she's also witty and selfless—and if he's not careful, he just might lose his heart.

A GOOD DUKE IS HARD TO FIND
by Christina Britton

Next in line for a dukedom he doesn't want to inherit, Peter Ashford is on the Isle of Synne only to exact revenge on the man responsible for his mother's death. But when he meets the beautiful and kind Miss Lenora Hartley, he can't help but be drawn to her. Can Peter put aside his plans for vengeance for the woman who has come to mean everything to him?

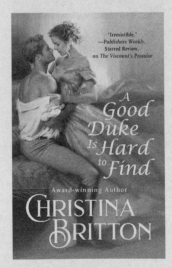

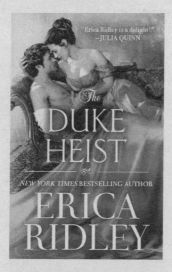

THE DUKE HEIST
by Erica Ridley

When the only father Chloe Wynchester's ever known makes a dying wish for his adopted family to recover a missing painting, she's the one her siblings turn to for stealing it back. No one expects that in doing so, she'll also abduct a handsome duke. Lawrence Gosling, the Duke of Faircliffe, is shocked to find himself in a runaway carriage driven by a beautiful woman. But if handing over the painting means sacrificing his family's legacy, will he follow his plan—or true love?

A ROGUE TO REMEMBER
by Emily Sullivan

After five Seasons of turning down every marriage proposal, Lottie Carlisle's uncle has declared she must choose a husband, or he'll find one for her. Only Lottie has her own agenda—namely ruining herself and then posing as a widow in the countryside. But when Alec Gresham, the seasoned spy who broke Lottie's heart, appears at her doorstep to escort her home, it seems her best-laid plans appear to have been for naught…And it soon becomes clear that the feelings between them are far from buried.

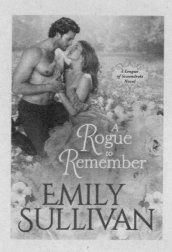

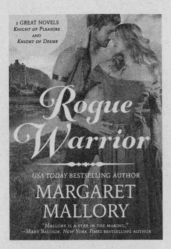

ROGUE WARRIOR (2-IN-1-EDITION)
by Margaret Mallory

Enjoy the first two books in the steamy medieval romance series All the King's Men! In *Knight of Desire*, warrior William FitzAlan and Lady Catherine Rayburn must learn to trust each other to save their lives and the love growing between them. In *Knight of Pleasure*, the charming Sir Stephen Carleton captures the heart of expert swordswoman Lady Isobel Hume, but he must prove his love when a threat leads Isobel into mortal danger.

ANY ROGUE WILL DO
by Bethany Bennett

For exactly one Season, Lady Charlotte Wentworth played the biddable female the *ton* expected—and all it got her was Society's mockery and derision. Now she's determined to take charge of her own future. So when an unwanted suitor tries to manipulate her into an engagement, she has a plan. He can't claim to be her fiancé if she's engaged to someone else. Even if it means asking for help from the last man she would ever marry.